The EAGLE and the WIND

BY

HERBERT E. STOVER

CATAMOUNT
PRESS

an imprint of Sunbury Press, Inc.
Mechanicsburg, PA USA

CATAMOUNT
PRESS
an imprint of Sunbury Press, Inc.
Mechanicsburg, PA USA

For information about special discounts for bulk purchases, please contact Sunbury Press Orders Dept. at (855) 338-8359 or orders@sunburypress.com.

To request one of our authors for speaking engagements or book signings, please contact Sunbury Press Publicity Dept. at publicity@sunburypress.com.

FIRST CATAMOUNT PRESS EDITION: March 2023

Set in Adobe Garamond | Interior design by Crystal Devine | Cover by Lawrence Knorr | Edited by Abigail Henson.

Publisher's Cataloging-in-Publication Data
Names: Stover, Herbert E., author.
Title: The eagle and the wind / Herbert E. Stover.
Description: First trade paperback edition. | Mechanicsburg, PA : Catamount Press, 2023.
Summary: During the American Revolution, an indentured servant is forced to work on weapons for the British. Ultimately, he seeks his freedom and helps the patriots at great risk.
Identifiers: ISBN : 979-8-88819-052-4 (softcover) | ISBN : 979-8-88819-053-1 (ePub).
Subjects: FICTION / Historical / Colonial America & Revolution | FICTION / Small Town & Rural.

Product of the United States of America
0 1 1 2 3 5 8 13 21 34 55

Continue the Enlightenment!

To
ROBERT PAULING
who introduced me to Migun

Also by
HERBERT E. STOVER

Song of the Susquehanna
Men in Buckskin
Powder Mission
Copperhead Moon
By Night the Strangers

FOREWORD

THE GREAT FLASH FLOOD of the Tiadaghton in the early fifties finished the demotion of the stone chimney of the old smithy and gunshop by undercutting the bank until the great chisel-shaped stones fell in a tumbled mass. After the passing of the gunsmith who had worked here beside the great creek for many years, a fire had gutted the shop completely. Then the flood performed a great service for the man who was gone; evidently, he had kept a small iron box in a niche in the stone chimney, and this was now found. It contained information that served to round out the history of the smith who, in a bold hand, signed his name, Jeffry Claus.

The box contained three tools carefully wrapped in several sheets of foolscap paper. First was a small intricate device fitted with tiny wedges. To this, the old smith had often referred, explaining that, in the long ago, it was used to "freshen" the grooves of a rifle barrel. Then it had been his most cherished possession. There were also with the cutter a tiny pair of pincers and a short, round file. On being unfolded, the paper proved to be covered with fine writing, the ink brown with age, and to the surprise and delight of those who found the box, it had appeared that here Jeffry Claus had set down a record of his early life; events heretofore unknown to his descendants. Unfortunately, the paper was badly wrinkled and stained by oil from the tools, but the following was carefully transcribed by the finders of the box.

"Whereas it has been said that I fled the old country, a criminal, I, Jeffry Claus, of the Fair Play country. Lately claimed by the County of Northumberland, do set down the following:

"Born in the south of England to a German father, John Claus, an armorer from Alsace, and an English mother named Mary Candice, who schooled me rather thoroughly in Reading, Arithmetic, and Writing. I was early apprenticed to my father and learned his trade, though never quite his skill. He operated a small shop . . . a seaport town . . ."

(Whether by accident or design, many names were destroyed; some erased, some obliterated by the oil. Note that he did not give the date of his birth.)

"With the death of both my parents of a fever and, later, the loss of my home, I lived in a small Inn kept by Barnabas Holt and kept up my father's business and was coming along well, having saved a little money and being well fitted with tools, my inheritance from my father.

"You who will read these lines know little of the hardships of persons in the older days who knew nothing of the liberty you enjoy. Young Englishmen, if not of wealthy or prominent families, had scant security from the clutching hands of the military or the press gangs of the warships which entered towns and snatched young men from their homes.

"Late on a fair spring evening, I, Jeffry Claus, now a rising young artisan, sat in the common room of the Inn and worked at a gun problem, drawing figures with a sharpened bit of lead on a piece of smoothly planed board. Other young men of my age had been in and out of the place, some of them lingered out front, and abruptly there was . . . squad of sailors in varnished hats with cutlasses at their sides. A huge, pudgy lieutenant, younger than I, clutched young Barnaby Felter by his shirt and jacket. Barnaby was an only child who lived with his mother up the street and was always a quiet, almost timid boy. Now he screamed in fright and jerked away from the man holding him. The officer, enjoying this as much as a cat cornering a mouse, leaped after the boy. All of us in the room had risen. . . . The place was shortly a shambles of broken chairs, bottles, and tables. Barnaby passed me as he stumbled up the stairway, and his eyes implored my help.

"The lieutenant had a drawn cutlass in one hand and now snatched at my coat as I blocked the stairs. His touch roused me greatly, and I brought the board, which I had not dropped, down on his head with all the force I could summon. His eyes went glassy, and he tumbled back, upsetting two of his sailors as he fell . . ."

(Here a long break.)

". . . a brig, the Seagull, lay in the anchorage, and it carried emigrants from the German country to America. They . . . told me the officer I had struck was badly hurt, that he was a member of an important family, and a search for me was going on most thoroughly. Barnaby Felter had escaped, for which I was thankful, his mother needed him . . . the Captain saw I was in no position to bargain since I had nothing but my soaked shirt and breeches in which I had been swimming. So I signed papers and was directed to work with the crew. Also, I was warned that there were two first-class passengers who were English barristers, to whom I would be turned over if I was not completely obedient to the Captain's wishes.

"The voyage was a nightmare, the Captain having a fiendish pleasure in the torments he visited upon me from time to time, and these I have schooled myself to forget.

"We landed in Philadelphia . . . herded with others, was exposed for sale. The price put on me was high since I was young and a smith by trade. This prevented several from buying my indenture. So I was kept in the public jail of the city of Philadelphia . . . until Mark Fultz saw me. . . .

(Here followed a long break.)

"So, I did not flee as does the robber or the murderer as has been hinted by those who were jealous of my craftsmanship or the small prosperity which has come my way. I was simply trying to defend scared Barnaby Felter and, afterward, myself. I . . ."

The manuscript finally broke off in the midst of a sentence. Likely Jeffry Claus had been interrupted in his writing by a customer, but he had set down enough, if one would read between the lines, to explain why and how he had come to be a worker on the pack train of Mark Fultz, trader into the Indian country.

CHAPTER 1

ONE BY ONE, each of the seven small, laden horses of Uncle Mark Fultz's pack string stepped over the lowered pole bars and took its place in the line winding up the narrow tree-shaded lane from Thread Hollow Farm to the road. From where he stood by the bar post, his sun- and wind-tanned face dark as an Indian's and now almost expressionless, Jeffry Claus, who had been Uncle Mark's bondsman, touched each horse lightly as it passed.

It used to be that the old trader who loved horses would whistle, and the trained animals would step into their proper places to be loaded. But the old man was over there beneath the big walnut tree under the freshly piled earth mound, and his pack string was moving out of the home place for the last time. The little horses would no more return to their familiar pasturage, and the old trader would never whistle to them again.

After he had pushed the bars aside, Jeff walked toward the cabin, before which stood two huge carts laden with a miscellany of furniture and other goods. Brendy, a hugely fat man who owned them, came forward. His limp waistcoat dropped straight down from its arm holes and hung on either side of the man's stomach. Above the taut line of his trouser band, the soiled shirt gaped, showing a small expanse of bare skin.

"Now we go," the stout man was saying. "Be back for the rest this evening or come morning."

His thick fingers fumbled in the pocket of the sweated waistcoat and came out holding a paper which, in spite of the fact that it was wilted, still looked official. Tilting back his head and holding the paper at arm's length, he read ponderously.

"Whereas Abner Fultz, nephew, is the sole heir of the late Mark Fultz, Trader, lately deceased intestate, Thomas Brendy, Court Bailiff, is, directed to seize and transport all furnishings, goods, and other chattels lately belonging to the said Mark Fultz."

"Yes," Jeff interrupted, a frown about his cold eyes, "you read all that once before. It finishes: 'The said Abner Fultz will then expose these goods, chattels, et cetera for public sale.'"

Brendy was nodding half-admiringly at Jeff's rendition, but now he broke in with a correction.

"The word was 'vendue,' 'public vendue,' it said."

He frowned heavily and lifted a dirty forefinger with which he scratched the stubbles on his unshaven jaw.

"You, Jeffry, are a bondsman. Should maybe you go with the stuff?"

Jeff grinned, though there was no mirth in his eyes. He was watching the bare spot on the fat official's belly.

"No, Brendy, there was a year and a half of my time to go, but Uncle Mark set down that I was to be free if he died. You'll find that paper in the big leather wallet among his things."

The bailiff shook his head.

"I wouldn't see that, a thing with papers in it. Abner Fultz would have all such stuff."

Jeff's eyes had gone completely cold as he stepped a little closer to this man from the sheriff's office.

"Besides, Thomas, my friend, I'd be damned before I stood up to be sold like a horse."

The bailiff retreated a pace while Jeff fought back his unreasonable urge to poke the bare spot on the man's stomach with his thumb.

"No, Jeffry," he agreed, "you wouldn't."

His heavy round face relaxed into a conciliatory grin.

"Anyways, you're thin like a rail. And with that black hair of yours, if it wasn't for them light eyes, folks would take you easy for an Indian, and who wants to buy an Indian when there's plenty in the woods."

Moving ponderously, Brendy went to his cart and clambered into the driver's seat, from which he nodded to his helper, who started his load. Then he clucked to his own team and, as they moved off, called down to Jeff.

"Don't worry about the old man's horses. I will see, personally, that them animals get good places."

Jeff watched the creaking, heavily laden carts disappear before he walked back toward the barn. When he passed the fresh grave, he paused a moment and muttered half-aloud.

"Scarce two months gone, Uncle Mark, and they've nigh cleaned the place out."

Half an hour later, he was at work in the brush- and tree-enclosed north field. He had planted that crop at Uncle Mark's direction. While the farm would likely be sold, he, Jeff Claus, meant to keep everything in order since the place had been his home for two and a half years.

He moved slowly along the crooked rows of knee-high corn, occasionally striking viciously at the bind weed. His strokes with the hoe sent little puffs of dust over his broken moccasins. Halfway across the field and less than a dozen steps from the near-by brush, he paused to wipe sweat from his forehead. It was very quiet. Alert to the nature of this still wild country, he noticed there was no chirping of crickets, no bird twitters or stirring of leaves. So, the click of a gunlock, when he heard it, was startlingly loud.

Jeff pitched forward between the corn rows and started crawling rapidly toward the end of the field where his ax lay. He had made a good rod of distance before the musket thumped, and powder smoke bloomed above the near-by thicket. He did not pause but managed a backward look and stopped abruptly. The powder smoke was thinning, and a black hat with a small hawk feather in its band was emerging from the brush from which the shot had come. Jeff came to his feet with a bound and shout.

"Migun!" he yelled. "Up to your old tricks making me think a scalp hunter was after me!"

The small, trim man who stepped into the field carrying a musket over his arm was an Indian who wore a grin that matched Jeff's. In sharp contrast to the white man's soiled shirt, nondescript leather breeches, and broken footgear, the newcomer was dressed neatly in a linen shirt, cloth breeches, and even good thread stockings. The feather in his hat was the only concession to his race's love of the bizarre in costume. But then, Migun, the young Delaware who had worked with Uncle Mark and Jeff on the pack train, thought and talked like a white man, excepting on the rather rare occasions when he chose to drop behind an Indian mask of stolidity and became as uncommunicative as any savage dressed in a blanket and bear-claw necklace.

"My brother is pretty quick," he commented dryly, "and likely he will keep his hair if he remembers his lessons."

Jeff slapped his friend between the shoulders, and as the two young men looked into each other's faces, Jeff's cold blue eyes appeared to darken. He tapped the musket with a forefinger.

"But, Migun, I am sad for my brother who will not keep his hair, although he does wear a hat. He had forgotten that Uncle Mark taught us always to reload."

Migun said nothing for a moment but reloaded his piece with swift, accurate fingers. After he had primed the pan, he chuckled deeply in delight at the way his own joke had backfired. In a moment, however, he sobered.

"Squire Fell wants you to come up to Burnet Hall."

"When?" Jeff demanded, and Migun produced a clipped shilling.

"Right away, he sent this for the ferry."

Jeff took the coin and grinned.

"Squire's sure in a hurry if he sent money."

The friends walked to the end of the field, and there talked for a while. Jeff explained what had happened at the farm.

"The bailiff was here this morning, cleaned out the place: tools, furniture, horses, even took my bag with all my clothes in it. He also talked about bringing me along so Abner Fultz could sell me along with the rest of the livestock."

The young Delaware frowned thoughtfully.

"But," he said after a moment, "you're free. Uncle Mark wrote it that way on the back of the indenture paper, and I signed it as a witness. If he died, you would go free with a hundred pounds and your gunsmith tools."

Jeff nodded.

"I know all that, and I mentioned to the bailiff the big leather wallet where Uncle Mark kept his papers, and he told me this Abner Fultz had it and all the papers."

He touched his friend's shoulder gingerly.

"I'm uneasy, my brother, more so since Squire wants me in a hurry. Did he tell you why?"

Migun shrugged his shoulders in a gesture that was almost French. His face became stolid, typical of an Indian who had finished talking.

"He said come and sent the shilling. You go."

Half an hour later, the friends parted. Migun went down country on an errand of his own. Jeff, having returned his hoe to the cabin, headed north along the river in the direction of Burnet Hall to keep the appointment with Squire Christian Fell, who had been one of Uncle Mark Fultz's best friends.

He traveled fast, feeling it was better to use his energies that way rather than in futile speculation on what lay ahead. Occasionally he touched the mutilated shilling in his pocket. The Squire was close with money, and the fact that he had sent ferry fare indicated the urgency of the summons.

But when he made the turn where a point of Peter's Mountain came down almost to the river, he stopped, his attention arrested by a dead pine that stood on the bluff. Stripped by the weather of its bark and all but two branches, the old tree, silhouetted against the sun-silvered river, looked like the naked mast of a tall ship, reminding Jeff sharply of the bitter voyage which had brought him to this country, of the captain's abuses, of the jail in Philadelphia where he had waited so long for someone to take up his indenture. Then Uncle Mark had come, and good years had followed.

Jeff started on slowly. He was thinking now of how the old trader, one evening in camp, had taken out his copy of the legal document which made Jeff his property for four years. It was an official form which began in ornate capitals: "This Indenture Witnesseth." Uncle Mark had written on the back: "In the event of my death, Jeffry Claus's indenture is hereby canceled, and he shall receive from my estate, in addition to his tools, one hundred pounds specie as his freedom dues."

The young man moved faster at a half-run, half-walk. He didn't care too much about the money or the tools; the thing which interested him was that he was again a free man.

Bower Samuels had already cast off the mooring ropes of the crowded ferry and was hooking the guard chains in place when Jeff came up and vaulted the yard of muddy water to land lightly on the plank floor of the flat boat. Big, heavy-shouldered Samuels, his red hair now shot with gray until it was the color of a roan horse, grinned and shook his head at his new passenger.

"Almost he misses the boat, and he jumps like a grasshopper. Big business held him up, business like watching a crow in a tree or teasing a black snake. Then our Jeff must run himself out of breath to make up time."

Jeff proffered the mutilated shilling, but the ferryman shook his head.

"Save the money till it gives something you want worse than a ferry ride. Today you should help with the boat like you did when the pack train came over."

Moving to opposite sides of the unwieldy craft, each man took down a heavy iron-shod pike pole, thrust the end into the mud, and pushed the boat slowly,

"That Migun," Samuels grunted, putting his heavy shoulder into his thrust with the pole, "offered me the same crippled silver piece this morning. But he would not work, sat on a keg like the lord of the manor, and even borrowed tobacco from me."

The big man straightened and finished his comment on the young Delaware.

"He did have his own flint and steel though."

Jeff chuckled. That sounded exactly like Migun. He bent again to the pike pole.

His badly clothed body was thin and looked almost emaciated, but effortlessly, he matched Bower Samuels in the hard poling work until the current began to take hold. The ferryboat was fastened to a big pulley which ran on a cable stretched from shore to shore so that the current would move the great flat- boat almost as the wind does a ship when it tacks. The big sheave creaked as the weight came upon it, and Jeff glanced upward, then commented:

"That pulley ought to be greased, Bower."

The old man nodded in agreement.

"Yes, but I grow too old and stiff to climb up to the cable moorings to reach it. Jeff, after I heard Uncle Mark was killed by a bad horse, I thought maybe you'd come with me. I'd build a shop on the west bank. You could work at gunsmithing and help me on the boat when the rheumatism is bad. Bower Samuels would be fair with you like Uncle Mark was when he said you'd be free if he died."

Jeff, really moved by the offer, looked into the steady brown eyes of the older man, then impulsively dropped his big hand on the broad but bowed shoulders.

"Bower, I'd like that, and I'm mighty grateful, but just now, I don't know where I stand. Nobody has said anything to me about freedom. Abner Fultz has all of Uncle Mark's papers. Migun came down to tell me Squire Fell wanted me to come up. Do you know Abner Fultz?"

Samuels shook his head.

"No, but Uncle Mark didn't either like or trust him. That much he said to me often."

The big ferryboat was crowded on this trip. Teams hitched to linen-topped carts stood quietly with their drivers at their heads.

Pack horses were tied to the rail, and a small flock of about a dozen sheep huddled together near one of the carts. Up front, close to where some saddle horses were tied, Jeff noticed a small group of people, two women and a big man who talked and gestured across the water to his companions as if explaining something. He was as tall as Jeff but much heavier. Neatly dressed, his black hair was drawn tightly back from a high-boned face, and occasionally he smiled down into the face of the slim, brown-haired woman who stood near him. Jeff saw now that the second woman was just a girl. With an impatient gesture, she pulled off her shading bonnet, and her bright hair gleamed like cornsilk just before it ripens. The girl was laughing as the man reached past the woman, caught the bonnet, and replaced it. At that moment, behind Jeff, Samuels swore.

"The damn fool mounts up."

Near the middle of the boat, close to the tethered pack horses, was a spirited-looking mare. The man who had evidently just mounted was foppishly dressed for this back country, showing lace at his throat and wrists. In spite of the fact that his face had reddened from the effort at mounting, it looked pasty.

The mare swung her body half about and jammed her flank into the corner of the box load on the nearest one of the pack string. Promptly she squealed in either anger or fright and lashed out viciously with her hoofs. Before either Jeff or Samuels could move up, the center of the big flatboat was a scene of confusion; the mare plunging, pack horses straining at their tie straps, men trying to keep their own mounts out of the squealing, kicking tangle.

Jeff had moved faster than Samuels and, used to pack animals, he came among them, speaking quietly and pushing them toward the rail. Then he turned, laid his hand on the nervous mare's shoulder, and spoke softly again while he patted the horse.

"You'll have to get down, sir," he addressed the rider. "Nobody stays mounted on a ferry."

Samuels was approaching, pushing his way through the carts and animals. From the corner of his eye, Jeff saw the black-haired man he had observed up front approaching, followed by the two women. The rider of the mare looked down contemptuously, taking in Jeff's disreputable clothing.

"Let go of my mare, you, don't tell me—"

Jeff stopped patting the horse, and his hand clamped down on the man's knee.

"Get down, sir, before there's trouble."

The red face above him lost its pastiness in a rush of more angered color, and up came the riding whip, ready to lash down. At the sight of the whip, rage swept through Jeff. Without hesitating, he shifted his hold, grabbed the rider by coat and leg, and jerked him neatly from his saddle. Before the man could recover himself, the whip had been snatched from his hand and thrown into the river.

"Don't raise that damned whip on a man again," Jeff snarled. Before he or the discomfited horseman could do or say more, the big man with the black hair had pushed between them.

"Sir," he said, and there was a savage edge to his voice, "that's my pack train horses your mare was roughing up. This young man's right. He prevented real trouble."

The horseman interrupted roughly.

"I'll not have a filthy lout putting his hands on me or my horse, and I'll have him and you up before a magistrate—"

He was interrupted by a powerful hand dropped on the shoulder of his brown coat.

"I'm Peter Grube, sir. Stop your threats or I'll make you swallow them. There's a young lady with me to whom you offered advances as we came aboard, and it's my notion you mounted your mare so you could resume your ogling. Say another damned word, and I'll soil the river with you."

The name, Grube, meant nothing to Jeff, but it evidently did to the red-faced man who, with no further words, led his mare up between two of the big carts. Grube clapped Jeff on his shoulders.

"You did me a real service, young man. Those packs are not fastened to stand a scrimmage, and the horses are touchy. If you had not been so quick, there would have been real trouble. May I have your name?"

Jeff grinned.

"Jeffry Claus, sir, and it wasn't much. I used to be with Mark Claus's pack train."

Grube's companions had come up and the big man partly turned.

"Mistress Grube, Susan Keiner," he introduced. "This is Jeffry Claus who has saved us trouble with the horses and he's a pack train man as well."

Jeff was suddenly tremendously conscious of his attire as the woman and girl looked at him. His shirt was not only soiled but torn. His leather breeches were stained and greasy, his shanks stockingless and his moccasins both cracked and dusty, but Mistress Grube helped him by extending her hand and smiling.

"Thank you, Jeffry. So my Peter has found another pack train man. You did help us, I saw it all."

The girl was smiling but she did not offer her hand; instead she dropped a little curtsy and Jeff found it hard to pull his eyes away from her face with its red lips and the tiny wrinkles at the corners of her eyes when she smiled. He tried to say something polite but Grube's big voice was booming again.

"Jeffry, come up to the Fair Play country some time. We need good men with horses."

The ferry was moving into its slip. Grube turned and with his companions walked back to where their riding horses were tied. Samuels nodded when Jeff joined him at the back of the big craft and took up a pike pole.

"That Grube's a big man up country even if he is a Fair Play man. But that fat fool took a chance if he sidled up to that girl. She's Susan Keiner and a bound girl. Only to the Grubes she's like a daughter."

Jeff went to work with his pike pole to cover his interest but his friend chuckled.

"Was I a young fellow again, even one with a black tan on my face and clothes fit for the ragman. I'd be thinking of that little lady with her hair like ripe wheat and a walk graceful as a wild thing."

Jeff's low snort of derision deceived neither the ferryman nor himself as to his interest in the girl with her wide blue eyes and the square tips of her small shoes showing as she drew back her skirt for the curtsy.

The road from the ferryslip followed a bend of the river toward Burnet Hall but Jeff took a short cut through the timber which he knew would save him a full mile's travel. He came out on the road less than a hunderd yards from the long squared timbered house on the bluff before which hung a sign board bearing the words: "Burnet Hall."

Two saddled horses were tethered to a hitching rack on the shady side of the building but there were no people in sight. Jeff's quick eye for horses gave him a start. One of the animals was the mare with whose owner the trouble on the ferry had occurred.

Thinking hard now, he mounted the steps slowly and stood in front of the wide door a full minute before rapping. He remembered the meagerness of Migun's message and wondered how much his friend had held back. Certainly the young Indian knew more than he had disclosed. A murmur of voices reached Jeff as he waited. Probably inside was one man who would cordially hate him; the rider of that bay mare.

"In the event of my death, Jeffry Claus's indenture is hereby canceled . . ."

The words came to him as vividly as though they had been whispered in his ear and he felt stronger. Lifting a hand, he rapped smartly, then raised the latch and opened the door.

After the bright sun outside, the long narrow room lighted only by a small high, western window, seemed dim. Two men sat in the shadow. Between two doors that opened back into the interior of the building was a table littered with books, papers, quills and a huge ink horn. There could be no mistaking the slight figure seated back of this array. There was the small round face that made one think of a very old and wise child. The faded green of the man's coat collar pushed up to a point in the back making the head look even smaller. It was Squire Christian Fell all right and he was smiling.

"You're late, Jeffry." The dry voice had the asthmatic quality of speech that comes with considerable effort.

"Yes sir," Jeff agreed promptly remembering the squire well enough not to argue with him about things of little consequence. Uncle Mark used to yield to the jurist often when they argued. Fell tapped the table with a blunted quill.

"Nice of you to agree with me, Jeffry. But since no time was set, you couldn't be late. We were just impatient."

Jeff laid the clipped shilling on the table and Fell's long fingers turned it over. Then he snapped.

"Did that lummox of a Samuels say 'twas no good, that he would not take it?"

"No, sir," Jeff hastened to explain, "I worked for my passage."

One of the seated men said something angrily to his companion and partly rose. From the corner of his eye, Jeff recognized the red-faced man he had encountered on the ferryboat. But Fell was speaking.

"Gentlemen, this is Jeffry Claus about whom we talked . . ."

The angry man was on his feet, pointing his finger at Jeff.

"That's the rascal, I demand . . ."

"Sit down!" Fell snapped. "Peter Grube stopped here and told me what happened. Jeffry, our irate friend is Abner Fultz, Uncle Mark's nephew and heir."

Jeff's throat was suddenly dry. He had never seen the nephew. He had simply been a name up until now. This was the man who took over the papers in the big leather wallet of the old trader, the man who had sent the bailiff for the Thread Hollow things. There was nothing reassuring about the loose mouth and the face red with anger. Fell went on.

"And this is Henry Ribner, down from the Mahantango."

The second man was much taller than his companion and was dressed well, though not as foppishly as Fultz. Instead of the commonly worn moccasins he wore riding boots and in the hand which rested on the chair arm was a pair of gloves. A bar of sunlight touched the man's face momentarily under his tricorn hat, and Jeff noted the lines about eyes and mouth. They were not deep; it was as though something back of the skin had drained away, leaving the face as flabby and emotionless as a wax cast.

"Jeffry," Fell continued, "Mr. Ribner rented and took over Mark Fultz's property on the Mahantango several years ago. It is situated where the creek comes down along the old McKee Path."

Jeff bowed slightly in the direction of the squire to indicate that he understood the location of the place. However he knew little of his dead master's property outside the Thread Hollow farm and the pack-train business. He did remember that once high water had compelled them to come out of the wilderness with the train well north of the Juniata along the Mahantango and Uncle Mark had mentioned he owned land there.

Fell cleared his throat. Talking became easier for him as he went along. After he had consulted a legal paper briefly he looked straight at the shabby figure confronting him.

"You were properly and legally indentured two and a half years ago on the first of this current month of June to Mark Fultz, Trader, for a period of four years?"

Jeff nodded his answer to the question, and the squire turned so he faced the others.

"This young man, gentlemen, the son of a deceased German gunsmith and an English woman, was bom and reared in England where he learned his father's trade and had some education."

He leaned back in his creaky chair and, with elbows set against his sides, made a tent of his fingers.

"It is a sad story. The father died and the mother desired to come to these colonies to make a home for herself and her son. Since there was money enough for only the one passage, the faithful and loving son, thinking of his mother's comfort and wellbeing, allotted the passage to her and, so he would not be tom from her side, he agreed to indenture himself to pay his own passage. Gentlemen, the mother died at sea, the son landed a stranger in a strange land, no money and no friends."

Fell paused dramatically, waved a hand toward Ribner and shot a sharp look followed by a question at Jeff.

"That's right, Jeffry, isn't it?"

The story was trae only as far as his parents' nationality and his father's trade were concerned but Jeff's steady eyes looked straight into those of the jurist. Squire Fell knew exactly how this tall, thin, dark-visaged young man had made his escape from England only a few jumps ahead of a press gang whose officer Jeff had struck senseless with a board. He knew, further, that Jeff's parents had died years before the escape. The whole yarn was a straight fabrication. As the young man's cold blue eyes read direction and warning in the old man's rheumy ones, he bowed.

"Yes, sir," he answered humbly and Fell was off again.

"Mark Fultz knew men and so valued his indentured servant, who is an excellent smith, that he wrote on the back of the indenture paper a holograph will which stipulated at his death this Jeffry Claus was set free with a hundred pounds in money and his , tools. This in lieu of the usual freedom dues. The bequest was pretty well-known though not recorded. Jeffry knew of it, Migun witnessed it and Bower Samuels saw it . . ."

Fell allowed his voice to trail away without finishing his sentence. In the silence that followed Fultz shifted in his chair and Ribner sat impassively drawing his gloves through the fingers of one hand. Jeff watched the squire but the drumming in his ears was louder, more insistent.

"Mark Fultz is dead, killed by a wild horse. Jeffry and Migun brought him back to Thread Hollow where they buried him. But . . ."

In the tense moment following, Jeff found himself leaning forward, the sharp lines of features seeming even sharper.

"The indenture paper we mentioned earlier has not been found among the old man's effects, so Abner Fultz has taken oath. In so far as we have record now, Mark Fultz died intestate!"

Jeff's big hands knotted as he fought back the tremor which passed through his back and shoulders. The drumming in his ears became loud and msistent, the dryness in his mouth, acute.

"Therefore I, Christian Fell, Justice of the Peace, declare that one year and a half of the indentured time of Jeffry Claus belongs to Abner Fultz, sole heir of his uncle, to dispose of as he sees fit. He has this day for the sum of fifteen pounds sold this same indenture to Henry Ribner of the county of Northumberland, to whose premises the said Jeffry Claus will now repair."

Jeff scarcely recognized his own fury-choked voice.

"Squire, you treat me like a horse. That fat pup who has just sold me has no more right to do it than I have to sell you. Uncle Mark set me free. We know that. He was getting old and he despised this . . ."

Fell nodded in quiet interruption. His words cut now.

"I, too, have my opinion of Abner Fultz who sits before me as a client, but the law is the law. Unless the lost indenture paper is produced nothing else can be done."

Jeff swung, took two paces toward Fultz who plunged out of, his chair and moved back.

"No violence!" Fell shouted. "It would only increase your time."

Ribner had risen and was putting on his gloves. Paying no attention to Fultz, he studied his new servant, noting the tightly drawn black hair, the dark face livid with anger. He looked at the dirty shirt, the worn breeches, the bare shanks and broken footgear. Jeff wore only two things of any value, even to a poor Indian. One was a wide leather belt; the other a short-bladed, stag-handled sheath knife which the belt supported.

The gloves were in place and properly smoothed; the trader's voice smooth, arrogant and assured.

"Report to me tomorrow on the Mahantango, Claus. Give me that knife."

Jeff had heard and seen enough of the tone and gesture in England to hate them. It was a master-to-dog command, perfectly certain of obedience. With a quick movement the young man drew out the wide flat blade and slapped a hard palm with the steel. This knife was a tool, not a weapon. With another gesture, this one decisive, he sheathed it and, with all the insolence he could summon crowded into his voice, he answered his new master.

"I keep the knife."

For as much as a minute owner and servant stared at each other, Jeff's face was clouded with anger; Ribner's was cool and appraising, as if he had noted a new phenomenon about which he was not much disturbed. The room remained quiet as Jeff turned and walked out.

Fell assembled his papers in a small bundle.

"Ribner," he advised gravely, "you have an excellent piece of property, properly handled. He is an excellent smith, pretty well educated, and Mark Fultz trained him to be a very good woodsman."

He held up a quill with a damaged point and inspected it. "But I would not try to drive the boy. Angered, he is as dangerous as a rattlesnake."

Ribner's faint smile vanished, for the squire's tone had changed radically. The room was charged with the little jurist's anger and he spoke savagely.

"Something in this whole business stinks to high heaven and I did my legal duty reluctantly. If I ever find anything amiss in this deal I promise to make it hot, damned hot for the guilty one. I have this day just sold a young white man like a horse and I have no stomach for such business."

Fultz and Ribner were almost out the door when Fell made his final statement in a voice as dry as the rustling of reeds.

"My fee is fifteen shillings. Fultz pays."

CHAPTER II

FURIOUS WITH anger and desperation, Jeff went down river fast. Since it was dark when he reached the ferry, he crossed the river in one of Bower Samuels' canoes. When, late that night, he reached Thread Hollow he realized, even in the dark, that the bailiff had come again to the farm, for the blanket and straw mattress from Jeff's bed were gone. However he found some hay in the barn and curled up there to sleep.

Tired as he was from his long walk he could not drop off at once as he usually did, for what had happened crowded into his mind. Uncle Mark, realizing he was growing old, had tried to insure Jeff's freedom in case he died suddenly. The old man had often spoken scornfully of his only relative, Abner Fultz. Now that man had everything: the pack horses, the farm, and the money he had made through selling Jeff's indenture for more than his uncle had paid for the four year term. Jeff squirmed; if he were free, opportunity was waiting. Bower Samuels had made a good offer and Peter Grube had been interested.

Turning about on the rustling hay, Jeff kept thinking about the old trader; his philosophy, his kindness, and how he would talk to Jeff and Migun as they sat about a camp fire. One day the three of them had watched a soaring eagle, and the old man had spoken of it that evening.

"Neither the eagle nor the wind will ever wear a yoke, boys. Trap either and it dies."

Finally Jeff slept and in the morning found that the bailiff had returned to make a clean sweep of the place. Even the food chest had been carted away so that Jeff had to make a breakfast of some small potatoes he dug in the little garden patch, eating them raw.

After his meager meal was finished he walked down to the place where they watered the horses at the river. A light breeze was drawing down the great water lane across which were the dark piled masses of timbered hills. Over there a man could lose himself for a lifetime if he kept out of touch with other white men, but Jeff in his travels with the pack train had seen what running away had done to others. There was always the standing reward. The longer the fugitive was away and the farther he had gone, the greater the reward. This was paid in money to whomever made the capture and for every penny paid the indenture period was lengthened. Jeff shook his head as though arguing; he wanted to mingle with people, to work openly at his trade. The freedom of the fox did not appeal to him.

Between the barn and cabin spring water came out of a little hill and was led through a wooden trough to a tub sunken in the ground. Jeff returned to this place, drank deeply from the water as it ran along the spout, then took off his clothing and ducked himself thoroughly in the cold water in the tub. There was no soap but some fine white sand helped. Invigorated Jeff walked about the buildings and found the bailiff had missed a small buckskin sack containing Jeff's razor, a tinderbox and pipe and a little tobacco. With these belongings he felt almost rich. He was going toward the cabin when he thought of something else. One day Uncle Mark had announced an opinion and made two gifts. "Young men should always have a little hard money."

That was the opinion and the gifts were two sovereigns, one to each of the young men. Migun had promptly, and Indian-like, spent his money, but Jeff had hidden his, saving it until he would have enough to buy a rifle barrel cutter of his own like the one in Uncle Mark's tool collection. The coin was in the cabin. He pushed through the door and climbed to the loft. He had learned in the dark that his blanket and mattress were gone but now he saw the bed frame remained even if some of the rawhide lacings had been stripped away. Lifting the one post of the structure his face broke into a delighted grin. They had not moved the bed, and there was his money.

For a while he polished the coin with his thumb. Here was enough to purchase decent clothing. He remembered his chagrin on the ferry when Peter Grube had presented him to his wife and the girl with the corn-color hair and direct blue eyes. In nice clothes he could stand before her with some ease. It would be possible to get a little ribbon and club his hair with it instead of an eelskin. Abruptly he remembered. With Uncle Mark things were different but a bondsman could not walk into a store and spend a gold piece without inviting suspicion. The new master could claim this money as he had Jeff's knife. He, Jeffry Claus, was a bought chattel with the same status as a horse.

Jaw set, he wedged the bright coin into his tinderbox and covered it with a bit of charred linen. Then he left the cabin. Coming up the lane he was overjoyed to meet Migun who had food, tobacco, and information. He already knew in some way what had happened at the Hall, and Jeff suspected him of following him rather than going down river. However, Migun listened gravely to Jeff's account. With it finished the Indian touched Jeff's knee and blew out a wreath of smoke.

"Before long the British armies will be in this state. East of Harris Ferry they try to get new soldiers for General Washington. They'll need gunsmiths. Ribner could not take you out of the army."

Migun left within the hour making no further hints about the army. In Squire Fell's presence Ribner who now owned him had told Jeff to report to his home this day. Jeff could do it by walking northward through the daylight hours. Instead, he acted on the young Delaware's suggestion and, rather than north, went south along the narrow road that led to Harris Ferry.

Pride's Mill to which he was directed in the Ferry proved to be a small collection of cabins clustered about a huge stone flour mill. One of these cabins boasted a short flag pole from which a discouraged-looking ensign hung limp in the sunshine. As Jeff approached he saw three men in the faded remnants of buff and blue uniforms lounging about. One of these gestured toward the cabin with a shrugged shoulder when asked about enlistments.

Two uniformed men occupied the room. One looked out the window, the other lounged back of a littered table reminiscent of Squire Fell's. Jeff faced him,

"I've come to join up, sir."

The man raised a florid face, belched lightly and glanced toward his companion at the window who turned and came over. Jeff saw some insignia on his shoulder. Evidently he was an officer, for the first man relinquished his seat at the table. When he looked up at the visitor, the officer's eyes were tired and there were deep lines about his mouth and across his forehead. Drawing a printed form toward him, he picked up a pen.

"Name."

Jeff answered questions as to his age, residence, health, and the branch of service which interested him. When finally gunsmith work was mentioned the officer looked up and stopped writing.

"Good Lord," he ejaculated, "you're a smith, where did you learn the trade?"

"In England, sir, from my father who was an armorer," Jeff answered.

"How long have you been in this country?"

"Close to three years, sir."

"The officer looked down at the paper before him and picked up his pen again. Finally he looked up directly into Jeff's eyes.

"Claus, my name's Strader, Lieutenant Strader. We need gunsmiths like a thirsty man needs water. Men like that are working in the gunshops getting rich and they dodge the army religiously where they've got to learn to do without most everything including wages. But, even so, Claus, I've got to ask you a question. You are an indentured servant, are you not?"

Jeff nodded; with an oath the Lieutenant crumpled up the paper on which he had been writing and tossed it to the floor.

"That settles it, this double damned Congress says the army may not enlist Indians, Negroes or bondsmen. It's no use, Claus, I can't take you. Go back and help some damned slave driver make money."

Jeff looked down at the table top, Strader rose, came round and placed a hand on his shoulder.

"You're in trouble, Claus. Just bear this in mind: all they have of you is time. Swallow anything, keep the peace. Time passes. You'll likely be a free man long before this cursed war ends. Come back then. Maybe this damned Congress will let you fight for freedom."

Jeff took the proffered friendly hand, wrung it, and went out without further word. He felt as limp and discouraged as the flag which hung above the house, showing neither its color nor design.

So it was the morning of the fourth day since he had left in anger that Jeff arrived at Burnet Hall. He had slept in barns and missed a number of meals; consequently he looked more disreputable than usual when he entered the place and encountered the landlord. Squire Fell frequently used the big common room of this inn as an office to care for people in the southern part of his county, but his regular seat was up river where the old McKee trading post had been. No table or paraphernalia showed today as Jeff faced a lubberly fat man whose small eyes were all but lost in folds of flesh. He glanced at his visitor, noted his clothing, and then growled.

"Get out, you. It gives no free meals here."

Jeff scowled, he had endured too much in this big room to be overly civil and he stepped toward the tavern keeper.

"Tell Squire Fell, Jeffry Claus is here."

The stout man was still hesitating when a rear door opened, and Fell stood there making an absurd figure in his too long coat. But there was nothing amusing or absurd about his tone when he spoke.

"Burnet, when my friends come here don't keep them standing. Also I think I heard you say something most unkind."

His sharp eyes were studying Jeff, but he snapped again at the now embarrassed innkeeper.

"Have a good meal laid out, landlord, our friend looks hungry." Burnet was moving away after an obsequious bow when he was halted.

"And none of that soup, Bumet. God knows what's in it and He'd be ashamed to tell."

Minutes later, served by a bowing and anxious host, Jeff was eating almost ravenously while Fell, smoking a laurel wood pipe, looked on approvingly.

"Eat hearty, boy," he directed, "I charged Fultz a steep price the other day so he's feeding you."

Jeff finished finally, pushed back his chair and thanked the squire.

"They cleaned out Thread Hollow. I've been on mighty short commons."

Fell blew out a small cloud of smoke.

"So they took everything?"

"Yes, horses, furniture, feed, clothing, food, guns and tools." Fell shook his head a little and spoke softly.

"Uncle Mark'd turn in his grave if he knew. You're half-naked, but Ribner will have to clothe you. If he doesn't, report to me." He rose stiffly and led the way to his bedroom upstairs, closing the door carefully, then commenting:

"Burnet's ears are nigh as big and busy as his mouth and I want to talk. Uncle Mark always said you had a close mouth. Somehow I can't get straight why Abner Fultz was in such a tearing hurry to turn everything into cash. I believe he and Ribner are partners of a sort."

When they were seated, the squire's first question was sharp.

"Where have you been, Jeffry? You shouldn't begin by rubbing Ribner wrong."

Jeff spoke frankly of his trip to Pride's Mill and his attempt to enter the army. The old jurist's eyes did not leave him.

"I could have told you that before. After Uncle Mark died and no papers were brought to me—no will I mean—I made it my business to see if the army would take you as a smith, but got nowhere. Our righteous penny-pinching Quaker government doesn't want a man who owns servants to lose money. A free man may die in battle but a servant is an investment. Listen, Jeff, did you make any trouble down there?"

He held up his hand protesting when Jeff started to sputter angrily.

"All right, all right, I shouldn't have asked but that gunpowder temper of yours is the thing that worries me. If I can get you to sit on your own lid to keep it from blowing off, I'm sure you'll be all right with Ribner. After all you have only a year and a half. Now look, was your indenture like this?"

He passed over a paper, a printed form beginning: "This Indenture Witnesseth" in big letters followed by others much smaller and blank spaces to be filled in by pen. He passed it back.

"Yes, sir, it was like that. Two of them were filled in at Philadelphia, one was kept there and Uncle Mark had the other in his big leather wallet. I don't remember seeing it but once or twice but he wrote on it about my freedom, the money and the tools."

Fell was frowning, he tossed the paper to the table.

"The whole thing's queer. Abner Fultz stepped in and gobbled everything he could touch. He might have found the indenture and destroyed it. That would save him a hundred pounds: the value of the tools and what he got out of selling you. But I'll watch things. Just now your personal freedom isn't as important as some other matters."

Jeff frowned but the old man paid no attention. Instead he sketched rapidly on a piece of paper and held up a rude map for his visitor's inspection.

"Here, Jeffry, is what is important and you should lend a hand even if you're bitter at the army and other things. The war's coming to Pennsylvania, fast. Now, here's the river and there's the Ribner post on the Mahantango right where the old McKee Path from the Juniata river comes out. My place is just across the river. Back in the hills the McKee Path crosses a mess of Indian trails running north and south. We call them warrior paths. Above us less than a dozen miles is Fort Augusta, the only real fort on the river. Out on the Juniata is where Mason's Tories are drilling and making plans, hissed on by British agents, we suspect. They want to come east and destroy Lancaster grain and gunshops."

Moving impatiently in his chair he touched the spot marked as Ribner's post with the pen nib.

"Jeff, I don't trust that man. They say his wife is a friend of our cause, which may be true. She has given some money. But her husband is doubtful and that post is an open door. Tories could come through it from the west. Indians could boil down from the north. Two weeks ago I tried to tell the Committee of Public Safety there would be an invasion of Pennsylvania through the back doors somewhere but they laughed at me. Danger does threaten. It will come, if not in months, then in years. But it will come, don't doubt it."

Jeff had kept his face expressionless and the squire was studying him with little satisfaction.

"Young man, you've only been half-listening." The old voice was grim. "A man's entitled to just as much freedom as he deserves. If you'd forget your own plight, you could serve well by letting me know what goes on at Ribner's. But you're bitter and self-centered and dead asleep to any troubles except your own."

He snorted derisively.

"Ribner's smooth. His wife is a clever woman, very clever. Why did they come up here into the wilderness? You could find out but you go to them with a temper like the hair triggers you make on guns. Uncle Mark loved you, Jeff. You could be of real service to his friends if you chose. Now I'll get you some food to carry with you. The way is long."

Jeff sat thinking while the squire was out. What he had been told both hurt and challenged him but his own dilemma was so new he could only think of solving that. The squire returned with a packet of food and Jeff had a question for him.

"What's the Fair Play country, sir?"

The squire handed over the packet and then explained. "Roughly it's the land north of the West Branch of the Susquehanna and west of Lycoming Creek. It's Indian land and anybody settling there, under the Penn laws, was subject to a fine of five hundred pounds and a year in prison. But the land is superb and men have settled there caring little for the threat over them. Ordinarily the Northumberland county officials don't bother them and they have their own code of laws. 'Fair Play,' they call it. Peter Grube is one of their big men."

"How about indentured people up there, Squire?" Jeff queried, and the old man pursed his lips.

"The Grubes have an indentured girl but she's like one of the family. It wouldn't help you to go there, for if you ever stepped out, the law would grab you. Or it might be the Fair Play men would turn you over. Remember, a runaway pays five days for each day's absence from his master."

Jeff walked toward the door but turned.

"Squire Fell, I'm just too mixed up to think straight. Maybe I'll come to see you up there. You're just across the river."

Fell snorted.

"In the long run, my young friend, you'll probably come out in first-rate shape, only it's likely to be a very long run indeed." When he left Burnet Hall, Jeff followed the road which in its turn followed the river. He had a general idea of the country and knew this rough cart path would take him past the location of the Ribner post and on up to where it was possible to ferry across to Fort Augusta. Occasionally points of the mountains came down close to the water and, from time to time, the river was broken by great ledges of flat-topped, gray rocks where a man could cross the wide stream dry shod.

Late afternoon the road led him to the top of a low hill which afforded him an excellent view. From his memory of passing the place with the pack train probably two years ago, he realized his journey's end was down below. There had been vast changes. Where a single huge cabin once stood, a half dozen buildings clustered together.

Here was a huge mountain cove containing several hundred acres of level land pushing back into the arc of the mountains through which, on the north, a large creek broke. This divided the level land, and the road disappeared beyond in brush country. To the north of this creek was the trading post, flaunting a sign on a high pole. To the south, closer to the road, stood the big house and back of it were smaller buildings and a huge barn. Jeff's attention was caught most sharply by the fact that here was a big farm with most of the land well cultivated.

There was no use delaying his arrival. A half hour later he turned in the lane from the highway and walked back toward the barn. The house was a big, two-story building with gabled windows set on the roof. It could be built of either wood or stone but it was neatly plastered all over. Directly behind it, across the flower and vegetable gardens, were three small log cabins. Near the stream was a long story-and-a-half building; evidently the shop for an anvil was set outside the door on a stump. From this a narrow bridge spanned the creek, and Jeff could now read the sign, RIBNER POST, neatly lettered on a plank set high on a strong pole. A big colored man back of one of the cabins worked slowly with a scythe. Jeff approached with his question.

"Where can I find Ribner?"

The big man wiped his forehead with an arm almost as big as an ordinary man's leg.

"Yes, sir, Mister, He would be in there. Rap at the back door."

Jeff nodded his thanks. Crossing the gardens and the smoothly mown lawn he approached the back door of the house. Before he had time to rap a colored girl dressed in a bright print dress emerged. She was lighter in color than Migun and she stared boldly at Jeff, the tip of a red tongue showing between her white teeth. He spoke to her.

"Please tell Mr. Ribner, Jeffry Claus is here."

She stared for a moment longer, then tossed her head and reentered the house. After five minutes or so she reappeared, passed close to Jeff, and Ribner stood in the opened doorway, his face impassive.

"You're late, Claus," he said coldly. "Of course we can take care of that."

He came out and walked slowly about his new servant as one will about a horse. Then he spoke again.

"Now, young man, you struck me the other day as an impudent fellow. Remember, I bought you because I need a good mechanic. Do your work well and you'll be all right and will be treated fairly. Keep your place, that's all, and remember that no one leaves this post without a pass."

Jeff made no reply and Ribner half-smiled.

"I'll put you to work in the morning. You sleep over the shop and eat with the colored people. Becky, their cook, is every whit as good as ours at the house."

That was dismissal. Jeff walked slowly toward the long building before which he had noted the anvil. It was a shop and through the wide door he saw there was plenty of equipment thrown hit-and-miss about the place. When he went inside he saw a heavy-runged, short ladder leading to the second story and up that he found his room. Other than a stool and a wide slatted bed there was no furniture. A small high window let in only a faint light. Jeff's lip curled. This was to be his home for a year and a half.

When he went downstairs the black man he had met first was standing at the shop door, smiling.

"I'm Eli," he explained, "and supper's jest about ready."

In the largest of the three log cabins was a long plank table set for a meal. The other people had gathered about it when Jeff and his mentor entered.

"They's seven of us," Eli explained. "Clara, my wife, cooks and eats at the big house where Melody waits on table. The lady with the big spoon at the fireplace is Becky."

The big woman who was serving the supper of corn-meal mush and pork smiled at the mention of her name, showing her teeth.

"The big man's John, Becky's husband, and the little feller's Fred,
Folks, this is Mister Jeff come to be with us."

"Just Jeff," the newcomer counseled with a smile which all the others,
with the exception of Fred, a small ashen colored man, answered.

"We's all married folks but Fred and Melody. John and me works the
fields, Fred's the store boy, and you, Jeff, has the shop. Now I'm mighty
hungry, let's be eatin'."

Becky knew her cooking, and the food was plentiful. After the meal,
Eli escorted Jeff to the barn where he furnished him with a good blanket
and a big bag filled with chopped wheat straw for a mattress which he
helped carry to the shop.

"Breakfast's at daylight," the big man said in parting. "I hope you
likes us here, Mister Jeff, I means jest Jeff."

Ribner, brusque and businesslike, appeared at the shop shortly after
breakfast. Jeff was looking over things.

"Now, Claus," he directed, "the first job will be for you to put this
place in working order. All the tools from Thread Hollow are on the floor.
Check them carefully. Movers are careless and I hope none is missing."

Jeff repressed an exclamation of pleasure at the sight of his tools
which he had thought would be sold out of his reach. The feel of them
in his mechanic's hands would be like the handclasp of friends. Ribner
opened a closet back of the forge and motioned to Jeff to come near.

"The front of this building is a storehouse for the post. Look here."

Jeff's eyes widened, and Ribner rubbed his palms together, "Muskets,"
he announced triumphantly. "I bought that job lot a year past. When
you have things in shape in the shop your job will be to recondition the
lot of them. There's a real profit in sight if you can fix them."

The guns were piled up like cordwood. Some of them had bits of
the original wrappings clinging to them. Others had broken locks and
were rust covered. Jeff marveled. The continental army was desperate for
weapons and here in this small frontier post were enough pieces to equip
a company. Having made himself clear to his new servant, Ribner closed
the closet door and left.

In three days, Jeff, assisted by a reluctant and sullen Fred who had
been sent to help, had the place in good order. The bellows and forge

were working, and the tools had been arranged neatly in wooden racks. With those things ready, Jeff had Fred bring out the muskets. After a quick inspection, he ordered him to place them in piles depending on what repairs were necessary. Broken stocks went on one pile, rusty pieces in another. He had grown so engrossed in his work that he had not noticed Ribner's presence late one afternoon until he spoke.

"Why get out all the guns at once?" he demanded, and Jeff explained. In this way he could concentrate on one type of repair at a time and have all the necessary tools ready for it. Ribner listened and frowned a little but finally nodded his approval.

"Looks like a good idea, Claus, but lock this shop when you go out and don't let any visitors in. Those guns are valuable."

At the end of a full month Jeff was proud of the neatly stacked weapons he had repaired, and Ribner, in his cold way, was evidently much pleased. Then one afternoon, he had a question. "Claus, can you make a new gun?"

Jeff wiped his greasy hands on a piece of cloth before answering. "Yes, I could, but the rifling cutter we have is just about good enough to freshen old rifling in worn bores. It would be hard and take a lot of time to make a new rifle."

The trader agreed and explained a bit further.

"What I had in mind was a pistol for Mistress Ribner. Think about it after all the musket work's finished."

In another day, however, he had a new task for his new servant.

"Claus, you worked for a good trader several years. Likely you've been in a lot of posts. Look over my stock, for trade'll open soon. See if we've any great lack."

The post proved very well stocked. There were bales of blankets, watch coats, and woolen strouding which were the important backbone of Indian trade. Powder and lead were surprisingly plentiful, considering the much discussed shortages of these munitions in the patriot army, and Jeff found a bag of the black Ticonderoga flints so much in demand among riflemen. The ordinary flint might serve well enough for a score of shots but one of these hard black ones would spark twice as long. In addition there were beads and small trinkets by the quarts. Jeff grinned when he located a box of jew's-harps and remembered the eagerness of savages to buy such instruments from Uncle Mark.

"Your stock's fine," he told Ribner, "only those black flints are too good for muskets. Riflemen would jump at them."

Ribner had gone out, Fred was down along the creek somewhere, and Jeff was having a last look around when he noted at the edge of a pile of blanket bales, a ring on the floor. Acting on impulse, he shoved the bales to one side, thrust a finger through the ring and pulled. A neatly fitted trap door lifted up, and in the small cellar thus exposed were kegs, bottles and straw-wrapped demijohns. No labels were necessary to identify this store. Here was enough liquor to make a small army drunk. The moment Ribner sold this stuff to savages he was outside the law.

Jeff had just closed the trap and replaced the blankets when Fred appeared. Jeff had the feeling that the little ashen-faced man had been watching from some vantage point and noting the whole performance. He thought suddenly of Squire Fell. There was enough here to invite suspicion: muskets, too much powder for a small trading post, liquor, outlawed in Indian trade, and a colored man whose business it might be to spy.

CHAPTER III

FROM THE first night Jeff got on well with all the black people except Fred who never worked in the fields but spent his time in the post store or in the shop where he made a sullen, uncooperative helper. From the first, too, he had not even tried to hide his dislike for the white man thrown among them as a servant. Whatever may have occasioned his first dislike, certainly Melody added to it, for the ashen-faced man was obviously jealous of the girl. Occasionally she would come into the dining cabin, perch herself on the corner of the table and hold forth on the doings in the big house: who the visitors were, how her mistress dressed, what was eaten at table. As she talked, she would roll her eyes at Jeff. She also found occasion to walk past the shop every day or so, swinging her supple hips and doing more talking with her eyes than with her voice.

Fred missed none of these performances. He was back in the shop at the bellows one day when Melody stopped. She was wearing the print dress Jeff had seen on the night of his arrival. It was obviously her only garment. He was working near the door and she leaned against the lintel, setting the sole of one foot against the top of the other and twisting her body as she talked.

"What do you do for fun, Jeff?" she asked. "You're always working."

He looked up at her sharply, then dropped his head and grunted.

"Work, Melody. It passes the time faster, that's all I want."

She looked at him provocatively, her eyes half-veiled by long lashes, "Is that all, just all, Jeff? Ain't you human?"

Abruptly, he grinned at the girl.

"No, Melody, I'm just like a horse, bought and sold to work. Whoever asks a horse if he has fun?"

She put her tongue in her cheek for a moment and glanced into the shop.

"Some horses do," she said so softly that it was almost a whisper. Then she puckered her full lips and went off whistling, her hips swinging.

A moment later, Fred, his face still contorted with anger, tried to walk out of the shop, but Jeff stepped in front of him. For a long instant they looked at each other, then Jeff's big hand came up, knotted into a fist. He looked at it gravely then back into the colored man's face. Neither spoke until Jeff stepped aside, allowing the other to pass.

He was still debating what he should do about his knowledge of the guns and the liquor when, several days after Melody had stopped at the shop, the trouble with Fred came to a quick and sharp head. Jeff had walked out into the brush along the creek to find some young hickory sprouts which, peeled and dried, made excellent musket ramrods. In the nature of his work, he made little noise. Suddenly a commotion in a big thicket arrested his attention. Migun taught Jeff how to slip through the brush quietly and so he came upon the unsuspecting Fred in a small clearing in the heart of the thicket. Tied securely with a cloth wrapped about its muzzle was a small dog that usually hung about the dining cabin for scraps. One evening, trying to get out of the way, the animal had tripped Fred. Now the little Negro was literally cutting the animal's hide off with lumber birch switches. Blood and thick weals showed along the dog's back and sides.

Before he was discovered, Jeff caught the upraised arm of the Negro and twisted it hard. With a scream of pain, Fred twisted loose. When he saw who his attacker was, he jerked a wickedly gleaming knife from his shirt and took two backward steps, poising himself to throw the weapon. Feinting a forward dive, Jeff pitched himself aside and the flung blade missed. Then he was upon the gray man hurling him to the hard ground. Grabbing the switches used on the dog, Jeff thrashed his cringing victim until he screamed for mercy. After cutting the dog loose with Fred's knife, Jeff booted the cringing Negro to his feet.

"Now you little devil, hurt another animal and I'll cut your sneaking heart out."

Fred screamed when the knife was thrust toward him to give point to the threat. Then he took to his heels, and Jeff tossed the weapon into the creek. He knew Fred was dangerous, a man who treasured his grudges, loving cruelty. Two days later a grimfaced Ribner accosted Jeff.

"Claus, you forget you're as much a servant here as the colored people. When punishment is due, I mete it out. Keep to your place."

Jeff's cold eyes met those of his master's without flinching. The two men stared at each other like fencers trying for an opening. On Ribner's part it was as though he was curious about the reactions of this young man he had bought; on Jeff's it was pure hatred.

The moment passed. Before he left, Ribner added some directions.

"Remember, no leaving these premises without a pass. Fred helps me watch about here. Tomorrow, get to the fields. We'll see what hard work will do for you."

Jeff suddenly had the thought that his master was goading him with pointed threats and the statement that Fred would watch. It would have been a satisfaction to snarl back, but he remembered Squire Fell's injunction about a gunpowder temper which might lead to a longer term of servitude. Ribner just might be trying to excite this temper and lengthen his hold on the new servant.

Thinking of Fell and his warning reminded Jeff sharply of the squire's desire that he report any strange happening at the post. But there was nothing too unusual here. After all Ribner, like all traders, was out for profit and a lot of liquor went back into the wilderness with traders to moisten dry Indian throats. The guns might have been a lucky purchase made before war gripped the colonies. Jeff dismissed the idea of trying to see the squire; there was no use in further antagonizing the trader whose arrogance would make him doubly angry at any infraction of his orders.

He liked the heavy work in the field with the big men and the horses. There were acres of sowed corn which had to be mown with scythes, tied into bundles like big wheat sheaves and then carted to the barn for the cattle. There were potatoes to dig, wood to cut for fireplaces and pigs to be butchered. The daylight hours were scarcely long enough to do the work of the big farm.

The old McKee trading path entered the big cove from the southwest, crossed the creek and went down past the trading post. At midafternoon on an unseasonable warm day, Jeff and the two men were getting in corn bundles when John stopped working and grumbled deep in his throat. Eli and Jeff glanced up to see what had excited their companion's attention. Beyond the fringe of brush along the stream a long single file of Indians was passing toward the post. They moved silently, with bright feathers showing in their scalp locks and blankets slung across their bare shoulders.

"Dirty red hellions," John muttered. "Hope he don't give 'em lots of licker again."

Jeff's question came too quickly, startling both colored men.

"That's against the law. Does Ribner sell booze to savages?"

Eli looked sharply at John. These men were close-mouthed about important things, especially those which, if discussed, might lead to trouble. Finally Eli nodded.

"Ef one of them red devils has money or silver or the likes of that, he might trade licker for it but it's mighty seldom and they gotta take the stuff away to guzzle it. He don't want any drunk Indians on the place. Once they did git some, and me and John had to stand guard with axes."

Jeff offered no comment. Too much of that or too many questions would make these men hesitant to say anything to him. The three watched until all the Indians had disappeared, probably into the post. As the loaded wagon came on in toward the barn Eli seemed to have forgotten all about savages. Something else had come into his mind and he leaned over toward Jeff.

"That Melody, she's jest plain poison."

Jeff stretched his wire-hard body back over the fragrant sheaves and laughed lazily. Eli rolled his eyes and repeated his observation emphatically:

"Jest poison."

His listener took lightly what was obviously a warning. He didn't give a damn for Ribner, Melody, or Fred; this morning he remembered that he had already served two months of his term. The wagon rolled on. The farm, the gardens, the trim buildings and the flashing of the stream were beautiful, for two months were gone, a full ninth of his sentence of servitude.

"Eli," he announced gravely, "it's a nice day."

The big man showed his agreement with a smile, displaying his fine white teeth.

The corn was all safely stowed in the barn mows by late the following afternoon. Eli wanted a log chain welded so Jeff took it to the shop. He walked directly to the forge to start a fire when a chuckle made him turn. Seated on a workbench, his face wreathed in a delighted grin, was Migun.

"Our Jeff grows even more ragged. He walks like a man asleep forgetting these are war times. He should be alert."

The friends shook hands eagerly.

"It's been a long time, Migun, my friend, since Thread Hollow. Likely you know all that happened."

"Yes, the squire told me about things when he sent me over here. Now he wants to know how things go here; what you know and how you get along. He says Fultz comes here."

Jeff shrugged his shoulders. He had not seen Abner Fultz. As far as he was concerned the big house and its guests might as well have been across the river. Ribner's servants worked. The house was out of bounds for all but those whose duties lay there.

"Migun, I know nothing. Like the other livestock, I work, eat, and sleep. My room is over the shop. I eat with the slaves and I don't give a damn what they do in the big house. I seldom cross the bridge to the trading post."

The Delaware's lifted hand was a strong, expressive gesture. "We both miss Uncle Mark. With him, things were different." Jeff felt a tightness in his throat and nodded.

"Yes, he was our friend. I forgot I was his bondsman. It was like being his son."

Migun slipped from the bench with a warning.

"Someone comes. When the moon is up tonight we will talk under the oak in the back field."

He was gone through the small side door near the forge in his usual silent manner, and Fred entered.

"Eli sent me for the bellows," he announced sullenly while Jeff busied himself getting a fire under way. When the first coal was glowing he set his tinderbox on a bench so he could cup the tiny fire with his palms until it was stronger. When the broken link was welded Jeff carried it over to the vise and filed away some roughness.

"That's all," he snapped at Fred who promptly sidled out of the shop. Jeff stopped work to look after him. Always furtive and sullen, he was even more so today.

Migun was waiting at the rendezvous under the big oak. He had brought with him a small linen bag from which he produced big pieces of white bread into which were wedged thick pieces of venison roasted as only an Indian can do. Jeff wolfed his share, recalling how often he, Migun, and Uncle Mark had enjoyed such a feast before evening camp fires. The meat finished, Migun took out laurel wood pipes and presently two friends were seated, backs to the tree bole, savoring good tobacco.

Jeff had told Migun of his experience with Fultz, Ribner, and the squire down near Thread Hollow. Now he brought his friend up to date with all that happened at the post.

"Ribner hates me, Migun, and I can't figure why. All I want is to keep the peace until I'm free. Like Squire Fell told me, I try to keep from blowing up."

The Delaware was silent for a long moment after his friend had concluded. When he spoke it was in a thoughtful vein.

"It may be you cannot finish, my brother, for the war comes closer and closer and there will be hatchets in this river valley before long. There is a story of Tories coming down the Allegheny from Lake Erie and a prophecy that they will come east over the Kittanning Path gathering help as they march. They want to wreck the lower counties where they make war things. Ribner's post would be a grand doorway for them and they'd have no trouble taking both Fort Augusta and Harris Ferry.

"Squire Fell is worried about this place and you. He figured that you may not be able to get away. He'll send men here who pretend to trade at the post and they will talk with you. This post is strange; there is little trading done but it is prosperous. Ribner's an Englishman . . ."

Jeff interrupted his friend by laying a hand on his knee.

"The squire's worried about how good a spy I am, and I'm only concerned about getting free, counting the days carefully. They won't let me fight in their army. Why should I worry myself about a war? They won't enlist you, Migun, because you're an Indian. If they are so fussy about who shoots let them fight their own battles."

Migun's grunt was expressive and derisive.

"Don't be a damned fool, Jeff. We'll be fighting to keep hatchets from our heads soon enough whether we're Indian or bondsman. Now, listen, Jeff. You've told me of the muskets, the whisky, and Ribner's hatred. What can you tell me about Mistress Ribner?"

"Women!" Jeff exploded. "What would a bondsman in a dirty shirt know of the lady of the manor. Hell, she lives in a different world. I'm a bought man, what do I know about women?" His friend chuckled gleefully.

"My brother forgets the Shawnee girl out near Burnt Ordinary and the straw-haired one at Well's tavern, she of the greasy apron. It always seems to me that a man who scorns women is just about to make a fool of himself and likely about women."

Both men rose, and the Indian tapped Jeff's chest.

"I go now and I'll tell the squire everything. Maybe he can find a reason for Ribner's hating you. Watch the trade here, look out for Senecas appearing."

He dropped his hand and then spoke slyly.

"Two weeks ago I talked with Peter Grube. The little maid with the bright face listened."

Jeff was astonished to find his heartbeat had quickened.

"Did she say anything, Migun?" The Delaware was silent for a moment as if trying to remember.

"No, not to me. But she did say to Grube about you when we talked, 'he must have patience' and that is one thing, my brother, of which you are very short."

A moment later the Indian was gone, but he had left behind the small linen sack in which were tobacco and a single shilling piece. Jeff handled the money recalling how Uncle Mark had insisted that young men should always have some money. He wondered if Migun had that in mind in leaving the coin.

Jeff walked slowly back to the shop and climbed to his room. He felt restless and hungry for the long trails over the timbered mountains and the free sweep of the wind on high places. He had been free too long and now felt trapped. He also thought of Susan Keiner and her graceful curtsy on the ferryboat that day.

Next morning, he needed his tinderbox and recalled leaving it close to the forge in the shop. It was there all right, but when he opened the lid and raised the charred linen he saw that his gold coin was gone!

Wild with rage, he was still standing there holding the box when Fred shambled through the door just in time to meet the full force of Jeff's fury. He caught the little man and pinned him against the wall.

"Where's my money, you rat?" he demanded, but the colored man merely gibbered in his fright.

"Get your clothes off!" Jeff commanded.

There was nothing in Fred's pockets but a broken clasp knife and some tobacco. He was half-dressed again and still declaring he had not touched the tinderbox when Ribner entered the shop, his eyes taking in the scene.

"What's the meaning of this?"

Jeff's angry gaze met that of his master directly.

"Some day, Ribner, I'll just ruin this little gray man of yours. Ask him your questions."

The trader's features tightened but he did nothing except tap at his riding boot with the switch he carried. Jeff had the sudden notion that there had been a time when this man would have met such insolence with a blow, but that now something in him would not answer such a mental summons. Fred hitched into his clothes; Ribner pointed to the chain.

"Eli needs that, take it over and work with him today, Claus."

Bitterly enraged though he was, Jeff could still feel a slight stir at the way Ribner had carried the incident off. He had met open anger and insolence with complete control. Jeff concluded that Ribner had almost welcomed the situation so he could test his own reaction: whether it would be the violent one of former years or the calmer one he had just shown.

Before the day was out Jeff temporarily forgot about the coin, for Becky, John's wife, came to the field to summon him,

"He wants Jeff," she announced. "A man is here with some work. You are to hurry."

Two men, one of them Ribner, and a horse waited at the open shop door. As Jeff came up, the newcomer turned and there was no mistaking the tall strong figure and face of Peter Grube.

"Claus," Ribner spoke casually, "we have a nervous horse here that has thrown a shoe. See what you can do."

Grube showed no sign of recognition as Jeff stepped up to the gelding and laid a hand on its twitching shoulder. It was a powerful, Roman-nosed brute, with the light-colored glaze over one eye which has given the name "wall eye" to such animals. When Jeff took the bridle rein to lead the horse to the shop, it promptly went up on its hind legs, striking viciously with its forefeet. He tied the animal near the shoeing post and calmed it down talking softly. When he had noosed the unshod foot, he drew it up to the post. He worked swiftly now, paring down the hoof, fitting the shoe cold and finally tacking it on.

"You have a good smith here, Ribner," Grube commented when the horse was resaddled. "I hated to bother but my wife and our girl are impatient to get to Harris Ferry, and I didn't want that horse's hoof spoiled."

Excitement stirred in Jeff at the mention of "our girl" which must mean Susan. Ribner and Grube walked ahead with the former insisting he was glad to be of service.

"You have a beautiful place here, Ribner," Grube said. "Trade must be good."

"It was," Ribner assured him. "Now it's pretty spotty but I get buckskin, a little ginseng, and something else I'll show you in a minute."

Grube paused and half-turned while he gestured with one hand. "That's the McKee Path?" he questioned. "Takes off from the Kittanning, doesn't it?"

Ribner smiled.

"I believe so but the fact is I have never been a dozen miles into those hills. When trade comes to me I take it but I do not go after it. Fortunately this farm does well, very well, and Mistress Ribner and I are so placed we need not worry too much about trade."

"Any Senacas come in?"

Grube's tone was almost harsh, but Ribner did not seem to notice.

"There never have been many of them. We're a little far south for that tribe. Most of my customers are Delawares and occasionally some Shawnees. Excuse me a moment."

Ribner hurried over the bridge, and for a brief moment, Jeff and Grube were alone. The big man winked and his forefinger crossed his lips in the Indian gesture demanding silence.

Ribner carried a soiled-looking lump of metal when he returned and he laid it in Grube's palm.

"That's silver," he explained. "Some of that stuff comes in occasionally. Don't ask me where they get it. I'm sure they won't tell me. Notice the lump's worn. Likely it's laid around in a wigwam for generations. But, it's better than buckskin for a trade. Claus!"

Jeff came up and took the metal proffered him.

"Try to melt that down sometime, Claus. Be careful, it's all but pure silver."

The two men and the horse went on up the road. Jeff watched them while he balanced the absurdly heavy lump in his hand and wondered at the purpose back of Grube's visit. He had noted that the nails in the horse's shoe had been pulled with a pincers. That job had merely been an excuse!

On an impulse, Jeff tossed the silver and his hammer down beside a bush and moved with long silent strides into the garden from which he could look out on the front lawn without being observed. Two women were out there, both brown haired. The taller was Mistress Grube, and the other probably was Ribner's wife. There was no sign of the girl. He turned back and then, at a turn in the garden path, he all but collided with her.

She was smaller than he remembered, a slim, rounded figure dressed in a sprigged gown which showed at the throat of her dust coat. Silver buckles shone on her small square-toed shoes.

"Oh," she said as though breathless. "So I've found you, Jeffry Claus. There has been talk of how they sold you and I just wanted to tell you to be patient and that there's something queer about this place. Peter Grube claims so and he should know."

She turned. Jeff had forgotten the women on the lawn, and the girl raised a small forefinger in the same gesture Grube had used a few minutes before, motioning her small head toward the lawn. Then, impulsively she reached out and patted Jeff's big fingers with hers before darting away to join the others.

He stood staring stupidly at his hand where her light fingers had rested. She had come and gone, and he had not managed a word. He was again conscious of his ragged, dirty clothing and his poorly tended hair. Minutes later, he saw Ribner and his wife escort their guests to the road. He saw Grube hand up his wife to her saddle and lift Susan bodily into hers after which the big man mounted the "wall eye" in one swift motion. The little cavalcade disappeared down the tree-lined road where the gum tree leaves already showed red, announcing the approach of autumn.

CHAPTER IV

MELTING THE silver proved to be a task beyond accomplishment and when Jeff showed Ribner his poor results, the trader agreed they did not have the necessary equipment. However, he directed that the big lumps should be broken up and pounded into more or less regular blocks.

"After the war I'll take these to the city, and silversmiths will snap them up."

Ribner smiled in satisfaction.

"Buying silver from Indians is a real trade. Now, Claus, I want you to start work on Mistress Ribner's pistol. She will show you what she wants."

Half an hour later she appeared at the shop door. Jeff had seen the mistress of the place often enough but always at some distance. This was the first time he had been close to her. Not a tall woman she was dressed today in a simple linsey-woolsey gown such as a servant might wear, but there was a grace in her wearing of it that made it seem very different. Short sleeves showed her smoothly rounded arms, and the neckline was low toward the swelling of her ample bosom.

She moved to the gunrack, after she had smiled a greeting, and took down a heavy pistol which she examined closely. Jeff, watching her and waiting for directions, had time to note the softness of her piled hair and the shadowy depth of her eyes. Still half-smiling, her wide, red-lipped mouth was pursed a little in concentration.

"Make my pistol like this, Jeffry, only much smaller."

When she moved to place the weapon in his hand, Jeff caught a hint of perfume. He picked up a smooth board and with a bit of lead began to sketch the outline of a smaller pistol. He was exasperated to find that his fingers were not quite steady. Abruptly she moved closer and took the board from his hand, dropping it on the work bench.

"See," she said, "it must be small to fit my grasp."

She laid her hand palm upward in Jeff's and slowly closed her fingers while she smiled into his eyes.

"Just a small pistol then, Jeffry. You will remember how small my hand is."

Jeffry found himself trembling as she stepped back, and he felt a little out of breath.

"Your clothes," she exclaimed, "they're just rags. I fear my husband does not notice things. I must look about the place more."

She left then, and he watched her going up the garden pathway with her light, graceful walk. That afternoon Fred came with two decent linen shirts, a pair of good cloth breeches and new moccasins.

"He says, wear these," Fred said. "He's tired of that old shirt." Jeff handled the clothing, knowing that under the law a master was compelled to clothe his bond servants properly; but he had been determined not to ask for anything. Fred's manner irritated him and he laid the garments on the worktable.

"Freddie, my lad, you always get under my skin. Tomorrow though. I'm going to work a little of the hell out of you. We're shoeing all the horses and you'll be busy—mighty busy."

He wondered as the man shuffled off just how much he knew about the post and how far he was in his master's confidence since he worked in the store and must witness all transactions with the Indians. Surely, for one thing, that lump of silver had been purchased with liquor. After Migun's visit, Jeff had checked; thirty of the muskets were gone although there had not been half that many Indians about the place at any one time to his knowledge. Besides, Ribner would not have sold thirty muskets for one lump of silver. His conclusion was that Squire Fell could well be right in his suspicions of this man who prospered so much on what looked like meager business.

The horseshoeing did not materialize as Jeff and Eli had planned. There was a field of buckwheat and Ribner directed that it be cut and put on shocks. That work took three full days of John's, Eli's and Jeff's time. After supper on the day when the shoeing was finally done, Eli came to Jeff as he was seated in the door of the shop.

"Jeff," he said softly, "they's two men back of the corn field as wants to see you. Guess they knows he don't like folks bothering the help."

"Who are they?" Jeff asked, and Eli shook his head.

"Don't know but both has been at the post before. One's a old man that wears a fancy powder horn."

Having delivered his message, the kindly colored man was about to leave when he seemed to have an afterthought.

"She went away couple of days past; Fred's off on a errand to Smiley's, take him couple of hours; and he's sitting in his dining room. Been drinking since four o'clock, Clara says."

This was the first time Eli had commented so freely on the situation in the big house and he had meant his comments to indicate that no one would spy on Jeff's interview with the two strangers. So Eli understood that Fred was watching; also he had suggested that Ribner was trying to drown something in liquor. He got up, thanked Eli, then walked back through gathering shadows past the com field. Close to the tree where he and Migun had visited were two buckskin-clad men. He recognized the older one who carried the ornate powder horn at once.

"Ben," he said, "Ben Haider, so it's you spooking about."

The old woodsman was another of Uncle Mark's best friends. He was dressed in worn buckskin, and even in this poor light Jeff could see the ornate powder horn which Eli had mentioned. He remembered Uncle Mark speaking to Haider one time about it. "Some red will take your hair for that horn, Ben."

And Haider had replied: "He'd have to get me good and dead first, Mark. I fancy that old cow's hooker."

"That's Peter Pentz," the woodsman introduced his companion. "He can't help it that he's a hard character but I have to travel with him now and then."

Pentz was a big smoothly shaven man with a grip in his fingers that matched Jeff's.

"Ben's hard on me, friend, and it's his errand partly that brought us here. Speak up, Ben. This Ribner's touchy about his help, and we won't keep Jeff too long."

"It's silver," Haider said. "Don't ask me how it got there but I found it high up on the west branch of this here Susquehanna. It was in the water and I got out more'n a man could well carry. Well I left it in the hollow back of Round Island on the Sinnamahoning with an old Indian friend. When I went back a week or so past, the old fellow was dead. Looked as though he fell off one of them big rocks. He was pretty doddery. Anyway, after I buried him, I found my silver was gone, and Peter Grube tells me your boss Ribner's buying such stuff from Indians. What do you know, Jeff?"

"Yes," he answered. "Ribner showed a lump of silver to Peter Grube the other day. I broke it up in smaller pieces. Ribner says he expects to trade for more."

Old Ben whistled softly through his teeth, and Pentz cleared his throat.

"You know if this Ribner's a Tory or not? Squire Fell would like real well to know."

Jeff hesitated for a moment.

"I don't know. You see I'm kept in the fields or about the shop and don't know as much of what's going on as if I lived in Harris Ferry. But tell Fell more than thirty of those muskets I repaired are gone."

Haider cut into the conversation bluntly,

"In a day or so I'm going to have a talk with this kingpin himself. Thet silver means a lot to me. They say the Congress'll pay any price fer it now. Gin I get it mebbe I'll buy out your papers, Jeff. Always did want to have a smart boy to load my gun for me." Pentz now spoke quietly and seriously to Jeff as they prepared to leave.

"Just hold the fort, friend. There's nothing that a little time won't fix, and I'll pass your word about the guns along to Fell. Let him worry about such things."

Jeff liked the big man better after his remark, for there was under-standing and kindness in his tones.

The moon climbed high, but he remained there thinking. Ben Haid-er had been a soldier in the old Indian wars. Jeff wondered about him and the silver. Surely if there was any question about the stuff Ribner would not have volunteered to show it to Grube the day of his visit. So it was late when he went down the path to the shop where he was puzzled to find the door a bit ajar. He always pushed it shut when he left. He felt tired now but there was enough moonlight showing through the shop windows for him to pull off his shirt and wash his head and shoulders in a huge wooden bucket which he kept filled with water for this purpose. Then he climbed the ladder to the loft.

Jeff liked his bed. It started out by being a big box of whip-sawed boards with a bottom made of springy poles. On these he had placed two bags of freshly chopped straw and over them a stretched blanket forming a wide, soft and restful place to sleep. At the side he had a low bench to use as a step.

Moonlight filtered through the small high window and he stood for a moment, thinking he heard a light stirring. After that he fancied he caught a trace of perfume, the same Mistress Abigail Ridner used. He wondered if it could still linger from the time she had been in the shop. Finally he stepped over the high side board and was asleep in another five minutes.

Some time in the night, his first sleep gone, he began to roll about and dream. Migun was there arguing that Haider should not try to find silver; Susan Keiner was making a hole in the dust with the square toe of her small shoe and telling Jeflf to be patient. Probably he dropped off to a sounder sleep but this time he woke to something more definite than a dream. Someone was stirring beside him in the wide bed, and the odor of perfume was strong in his nostrils.

Turning, his outflung hands gripped soft, warm, yielding flesh. He shifted them and knew he held a pair of naked shoulders.

"Who's here?" he demanded thickly. "What?"

"It's Melody, Jeff. Melody and you're hurting me."

He jerked to a sitting position and, in the dim light, looked down at the tumbled mass of the girl's hair and saw the shine of her eyes.

"Listen," he said grimly. "Get out of here, quick."

The girl half-turned her supple body, and her hands touched his face.

"Don't, Jeffy. I'm scared. I hung around all night till I was cold and crawled in with you. Now you chase me out, and that Fred'll get me."

He had released her shoulders. Now he took hold of her again and shook her until she started whimpering and rubbing her eyes with her fists as a child will do.

"I couldn't help it," she mumbled. "She went away, and he got after me again till I told him I was going to have his baby. He went clear wild and shook me worser as you did and swore he'd turn me over to Fred. I'm awful scared of him. So I hid me in the shop. I was cold and scared."

"Quit your crying," Jeff commanded. "So he was going to give you to Fred?"

She was leaning against him now, and the dim moonlight was full on her face as she pushed her hair back.

"I jest lied to him about the baby and I'm fixin' to run off today. Plenty'll take me in. A man tried to buy me the other day, I heard him. Jest hide me, Jeff, till I can slip in and git my things."

She was very close now. Her arms slipped about his neck, and her breath was warm against his face.

"You won't send me off, Jeffy," she whispered. "I ain't cold no more nor so scared."

His arms were tight about her rounded body now. Her lips met his eagerly, and a little later, she moaned softly.

"Jeffy, oh, Jeffy."

What seemed like hours later, he woke to her shaking him as the first gray of daylight entered the little room. There was a stir below, then steps on the ladder. Yellow light flashed into the faces of the couple in the bed.

Fred was standing there holding the light. Ribner, a pistol in one hand, looked past the Black man's shoulder.

"So," he said, his voice rich with sarcasm, "our smith has strange visitors who seek news. Now we find him in bed with a colored wench. Get up, Claus, and dress. Likely you don't know what happens to a white servant when he meddles with a colored girl."

He chuckled softly, and the sound made Jeff think of a snake crawling over dead leaves. When he chuckled again, Jeff swung over the bed side board and pulled on his clothes. Melody had drawn the blanket up about her body. Fred had not once taken his eyes off her nakedness even to watch Jeff.

There was no talking later in the morning when the three of them, Jeff, Ribner, and Fred, went down the old path and crossed the river in a canoe. They proceeded only a few hundred yards to the little town and the house where Squire Fell had his permanent headquarters. Ribner stalked ahead.

Fell was already in the littered room he used as an office, and there was the usual table on which were piled lawbooks, paper, quills, ink-horns, and a sand dish. He looked up sharply, searching Jeff's face first, then turning to his companions. Ribner spoke.

"I arrested this man, Squire, and brought him to you."

The trader only partially concealed his satisfaction, enjoying the dis-comfiture on the old squire's face and the stunned look on Jeff's. Fell tried to clear his throat and spoke with his usual difficulty.

"What is it? Did this man run away?"

"No," Ribner answered, "it might have been better for him if he had. I've just caught him in bed with a colored slave girl."

In the long, pregnant silence that followed, a rear door opened. Without turning his head, Fell snapped, "Get out and stay out!"

The door slammed, and Fell's eyes searched Jeff's face again. Sheer anger thickened his speech even more than usual when he spoke.

"You damned young fool," he all but screamed. "Is this true?" Jeff's back stiffened, and he took two steps toward Ribner, his hands opening and closing. Then he thought better of it and stopped, facing his in-quisitor once more. He pinched his lips shut as a feeling of desperation flooded through him. He nodded slowly, and Fell, seeming to shrink back a little more into his coat, drew a brown law book toward him.

"The law is," he announced reluctantly, "that the cohabiting of a white servant with a colored woman is punishable by lengthening the term of servitude of the said white servant by seven years. A justice has no choice but to sentence the offender or offenders. You, Jeffry Claus, were caught by your master with a colored slave girl. Nothing can be done about it. I sentence you to four more years of indentured labor under your present master, Henry Ribner."

Jeff drew a long shuddering breath, and the strength seemed to flow out of his body. There was no speech in him. He recognized the shocking finality of Fell's sentence that ended all his hopes. Ribner stepped forward.

"Squire," he protested angrily, "you have no right to cut the sentence. Seven years it should be—"

Fell came out of his chair with the sudden fury of a wild cat, his eyes blazing, his finger shaking under the nose of the trader.

"Ribner, there's something hellish rotten about this, as rotten as I feel you are personally. You've trapped and tricked this young man for some purpose of your own. I warned you and Fultz before that God help you if I ever learn why or how. Men like you don't belong on our clean river. Now get out of here, and I'll send you the necessary papers in due time."

Ribner turned to the door, but before he reached it, Fell yelled at him.

"Come back and pay your fee, ten shillings!"

The trader hesitated, his eyes narrowing. The look Jeff had seen before when the trouble about Fred had occurred, came across his face. But it passed. He took the money from his pocket, laid it on the table, and, followed by Fred, walked out. As Jeff went by the table, Fell muttered:

"You poor young fool, I warned you."

When he had finally returned to the shop, Jeff sat motionless for a long time. The whole place, the shop, the farm, seemed to have closed about him like stone walls, shutting out the world bright with freedom. After three years, he was further from his goal than he had been when taken from the jail in Philadelphia. There would be other tricks, other stratagems. He was still in his place when Eli slipped in. He was carrying a small reed basket.

"Becky sent you some eating," he whispered.

Jeff stared vacantly at the big Negro. Then, rather than hurt him, he took the basket and munched at the food it contained, but the good things were dry and tasteless.

"Eh," he said, "I was a fool."

"She poison," the big man said gravely, after which remark he went to the door and reconnoitered.

"Jeff, Melody sleeps in my cabin tonight, and mebbe you can make she talk."

His thinking still in confusion; Jeff thought some other trick was coming, for Eli showed he believed Jeff had been duped.

"You mean . . ."

"Make Melody talk," Eli said emphatically and walked away.

The long day dragged, and Jeff ate the evening meal with the others. Melody was at the big table, but she kept her head bowed. Fred, however, was cheerful until John looked at him soberly. After that, he relapsed into his usual sullen manner.

An hour after supper, when it was fully dark, Jeff returned to the dining cabin where Eli and his wife, Clara, sat on the porch. At his approach, they rose to leave, Eli gesturing with a heavy shoulder toward the cabin.

There was no one in the dining room when Jeff entered, but light showed under the door of another room. Moving quietly, he dropped the bar of the outer room door into place to make sure there would be no interruptions. Then he crossed the room again and pushed open the panels from which the light came. Melody, fully dressed, stood staring at him with eyes wide with fright.

"What'cha want?" she demanded as he approached, and she stepped backward until she was against the wall.

"Four more years, I got, Melody. Did you know that? Come on. I'm taking you back to the shop so Fred won't get you."

The girl was moistening her lips with her tongue.

"What's the matter, Melody?" he continued. "You ought to be glad; now you look scared."

Her mouth dropped open, and he forstalled the scream by pressing a hard palm across her lips.

"Now," he gritted at her, "out with it, the whole dirty story. He sent you over last night, wanted to tie me up longer."

In a fury, he grabbed her shoulders and shook her until her hair loosened and the small knitted bag she had been holding in one hand dropped to the floor and opened.

"Don't be rough to me, Jeff," she pleaded. "He made me. He'd hev whipped the hide off me like he did once before."

Jeff swung her around and pulled the back of her loose dress down from her neck.

"No scars, Melody. You're lying. Now talk."

His eyes were blazing. She cowered, but he was not sure whether she was really frightened or just acting. He did see her glance down at the bag she had just dropped, and her slippered foot went out and covered something. She was a bit too late. He saw the thing, a gold piece, a worn sovereign!

There was a roaring in Jeff's ears as he picked up and recognized his own lost coin, the one Uncle Mark had given him, the one that had vanished from the little tinderbox in the shop. Two men had a chance to take it, Ribner and Fred. This time his fingers sank deeply into the girl's soft shoulders until she writhed in real pain.

"Where did you get it—from Fred?"

Through dry lips, she muttered: "He."

There could be no doubt she meant Ribner. That was what all the Black people called him. Jeff was sure that she was finally telling him the truth. He had been tricked, and this girl was paid for her part in the scheme with money stolen from him by the man who set the trap. Squire Fell had said there was something rotten, and here it was. The trick had been clever. The girl had been in his bed. The facts could not be undone or erased.

Melody had dropped to her knees, twisting herself clear of his hands, "Jeff," she begged, "don' hurt me no more, he jes uses me . . ."

"Bait," he spat at her. "Just bait. No, I won't hurt you."

For a moment or so, he fumbled the worn coin in his fingers, touching the dent where someone had started to punch a hole through it. Probably Fred had stolen the coin for his master, and Ribner had used it in a very refinement of cruelty. His was the responsibility.

Knife in hand, Jeff was halfway through the vegetable garden, advancing toward the lighted windows of the big house, when two dark figures leaped from the shrubbery. Strong arms clutched at him, flung him to the ground, and swathed him in a blanket in spite of his frantic struggling. Then a rope went about his arms and ankles, and he was lifted and carried.

Minutes later, fumbling fingers pulled away the blanket, and he found that he had been dumped into his own bed. In the light of a candle stub, he saw Eli and John, their eyes rolling. When he tried to sit up, their big hands pressed him back. Eli did the talking.

"You was fixin' fer real trouble, Jeff. Gin you touch him, they'd hang you, so me and John fetched you here. We jest hed to be rough and tie you like we did."

He reached forward and untied the ropes.

"Don't you let he see how bad you is hurt. Thet man likes to see things squirm, like Fred does."

John leaned forward and spoke slowly in his heavy voice.

"The Book sez, 'Better a live dog than a dead lion.' You lays hands on him, and you'll be a mighty dead-looking lion."

By and by, these friends snuffed the candle, but they remained at the bedside until the drowsiness of complete mental exhaustion claimed Jeff. When the gray morning came, and he awoke, he was alone.

CHAPTER V

RIBNER'S TRICK had shocked Jeff profoundly, so much so that even now, in the morning, his hands trembled like those of an old man. Melody had played her part very well indeed, and Jeff was willing to agree with Squire Fell that he had been a fool. But in the semidarkness, the girl had first invited his sympathy, and then her nearness had stirred him until he had lost his judgment.

Back in England after the fight with the press gang and through the miseries of that seemingly interminable voyage, he had looked forward to a new world which he had indeed found with Uncle Mark Fultz and the pack train. Now there was no challenge ahead to soften the weight of the dragging years, no possible freedom but that of the runaway and the hunted. It took conscious effort for him to swing his long legs out of bed to the floor. He stood there for a minute by the candle shelf, absently picking at the hardened grease with a thumbnail.

The two big, friendly men had been right. He had meant to kill Ribner, and they, understanding what such an act would mean, had taken the only way to prevent his acting when he was still wild with rage. He sat down on the three-legged stool and pulled on his moccasins. Eli had said, "He likes to see things squirm."

Jeff's jaw closed until he felt the strain on the muscles of his neck and face. A wisdom born and bred in slavery was in the Black man. He possessed a deep well of the spirit into which nothing like ridicule, threats, dangers, nor scorn could reach. It was this spirit which helped men like Eli and John to labor cheerfully, laughing, and singing at times. No master could ever hope to gloat over their condition.

"None of the woods folks worries about something when it's past."

That was Migun's often repeated philosophy. The young Indian, in spite of his years, knew a lot about the futility of worry.

Jeff crawled down the ladder and washed his face, hands, and shoulders in the tub of cold water, after which he joined the others at breakfast. No one mentioned what had happened, and Jeff even managed a smile when Becky accidentally spilled some milk on John's neck. When they got up and went out to work, Eli looked at Jeff and made an almost imperceptible nod of his head, a gesture of approval.

Ribner did not appear during the day, and Jeff did little work, but he did walk back over the farm and into the edge of the forest. Here was the Indian path, already old generations ago. It would go on through the hills, down to the Juniata River, and there join the Kittannmg Path, which ran westward. Temptation stirred Jeff. He could keep on moving. Somewhere, he could obtain an outfit for the old coin used in his betrayal. Beyond Kittanning would be Fort Pitt and down the great rivers was Spanish land. Abruptly he remembered Ribner's face as it was when he sought to reprove Squire Fell and when earlier, he had shown Jeff his hatred for the first time. Migun always claimed that hatred came from fear. If the trader was afraid of something, it might be better to stay close to him. Squire Fell had told the man there was something rotten in the affair. If that came out, it might be Jeff's opportunity to square his account with Ribner. He turned and walked back to the shop.

Ribner appeared with an announcement in the morning while breakfast was being eaten.

"Visitors this afternoon. I want all of you to work at cleaning things up. Everything must be in apple pie shape, and I don't want any slips."

He did not look directly at Jeff, but when all had finished eating, he gave more directions and later worked with them. First, a peeled pole twenty feet in height and bearing on its end, Becky's version of a Liberty cap, was set up after it had been rubbed with earth to make it look weathered. All floors were swept, lawns and lanes were well raked, and the trading-post goods were nicely arranged. The women worked in the preparation of huge joints of beef and pork and set up long tables in front of the dining cabin.

About an hour after noon, the visitors appeared, a troop of a dozen motley-dressed men tramping down the road and across the bridge in something like military order. All but three carried guns ranging from good rifles to muskets in poor condition. Ribner walked forward over the smoothly mown lawn to the log fence while the servants stood in a knot near the house. One of the approaching men did wear a uniform of buff and blue; directly back of him were two buckskin-clad men carrying rifles.

"Major Whitkin, Continental Army," the officer introduced himself as he took Ribner's extended hand.

"And mine is Ribner, Henry Ribner," the trader said. "I'm glad to see you gentlemen. These are troubled times, and it's nice to know our friends have weapons in their hands. Now you've marched a long way and may be both hungry and thirsty."

"Local Committee of Public Safety sent us," Whitkin explained. "No offense, we hope."

Ribner made a deprecating gesture. He listened politely while several introductions were made and then led the way across the lawn to where the laden tables waited. The militiamen stacked their weapons against the cabin and, much too eagerly for good manners, took their places on the benches. To Jeff's surprise, among them were Pentz and Ben Haider, but neither gave him any sign of recognition. Jeff, John, and Eli served as waiters transporting bowls and platters of food to the table.

When all the visitors had eaten to obvious repletion, a huge pitcher of rum went the rounds. Ribner, presiding at the end of one table, leaned forward when each guest's cup was filled with the heady liquor.

"It's a relief to have you here, men. There has been talk, and now that your committee has sent you here, I can show you Ribner Post and settle all gossip. The fact is I even suggested such a visit to my good friend, Colonel Hunter, commandant at Fort Augusta."

"It's just a matter of form," Whitkin announced, "and we're most grateful for your hospitality."

Immediately he buried his face in his big mug, and his companions did not need his example to do the same with theirs.

"Come on, Fred and Jeff," Ribner commanded when he rose from the table. "I'll need you."

Trailed by his visitors, he led them first through the main house, where they were obviously impressed by the big rooms and the fine furnishing. Ribner explained these with a wave of his hand.

"My wife's dowry, she will be grieved at not being here today for your visit."

Even if they had been embarrassed in the house, most of the men were perfectly at home in the trading post itself and surveyed with approval the neatly piled shelves. Pentz, near the end of a counter, picked up a jew's-harp and twanged it softly while Haider looked about grimly. Major Whitkin, in familiar surroundings, developed a sudden sense of importance.

"Powder, Mr. Ribner, I see a small keg of it here. Do you sell it to the savages?"

"Yes, Major, the usual gill to a man provided he does other trading. That's regulation, I believe."

Ribner had answered quickly, even carelessly, and now picked up a gill measure to dust some powder grains from it while the major nodded and put his next question.

"Liquor and muskets now, I ask only because it is an order." Ribner set down the measure and smiled disarmingly.

"Of course, no liquor. We can't risk having drunken savages about a place like this, even if it was legal to furnish them with drink. We do repair broken guns when they are brought to us. My man, Jeff, here, is a gunsmith."

Ribner was carrying things off beautifully. The visitors were treating him with the greatest respect and nodding at his every word. Jeff's dark face flushed a little as the men looked at him. However, it was not from embarrassment. It was Ribner's "'my man" that stirred him, and his bitterness was so close to the surface that the least thing could make it break out. Ribner's lying was so smooth it was all but artistic. One of the visitors who had the hands of a mechanic turned to Jeff.

"Can you 'freshen' a rifle, young man?"

He nodded and explained.

"Yes, we have a good cutter. We're not set up yet to make a long barrel, but we can cut rifle grooves deeper and freshen the lands, and I can use a cherry on old bullet molds."

Ribner had been quiet. He had picked up the gill measure again, and Jeff saw it spring out of shape as the long fingers gripped it.

"Of course," Jeff added, "so far, my work's been on old muskets, repair jobs. No rifles have come in."

Whitkin pushed forward and interrupted the conversation with his question.

"About powder, young man, could you make it?"

Jeff smiled, but his eyes narrowed a little as he glanced at the trader.

"Yes, sir, anybody who has saltpeter, sulfur, and charcoal can make powder, but it takes a power of grinding and drying, sir. That is, to make it in any quantity."

Eli entered the post at that moment carrying a huge bucket which he placed on the counter. Ribner waved toward it.

"Talk's dry work, men. Drink hearty. Guess you can all use one ladle. It's fair rum, good for digestion."

None of the visitors had any reluctance about helping himself, passing the big iron ladle around and around. Three or four of them remained by the bucket when the tour passed over the bridge to the shop. There, the man who had questioned Jeff before was most interested in handling the tools and setting them back in place with care.

"Where did you learn your trade?" he queried, and Jeff answered him rather shortly. However, it did not dampen the man's interest. He inspected the rifling cutter again and, when the others had turned away, spoke in a low voice.

"Son, my name's Evander Krebs, and Squire Fell spoke to me of you. My place's over there at the sign of the anvil just south of the old McKee post."

With no further word, Krebs cleared his throat and followed the others. Evidently, there was more to this visit than appeared on the surface, with Whitkin merely a figurehead. Krebs, Haider, and Pentz probably were really looking into things.

Most of the visitors were now interested in more food and drink. Ribner led them back to the tables, where they gave themselves over to really serious drinking. Major Whitkin's red face became even more florid, and occasionally he patted his host on the back. Finally, he heaved his heavy bulk upward from his seat, belched heavily, and delivered his opinion.

"Mr. Ribner, this has been a happy visit, and we commend the way you do business with the savages. Now, we have a long march before us back to Sunbury and we must be going."

He frowned, looked puzzled, and then turned to a tall, quiet man near him.

"Evans, there is something I am forgetting; what is it? Come, man, tell me."

There was a sardonic expression on Evans' thin features. He had been drinking as much as the others, but he could still think clearly.

"Just this, Mr. Ribner, we are at war with a great power. The counties below us are the arsenal and granary of the Continental forces. The Indians have sided with England, therefore . . .

The force of the liquor he had consumed hit Evans suddenly.

"Therefore," he repeated, but his mouth hung open, and his eyes turned glassy. Whitkin, however, had received his breathing space and took over.

"Therefore, the Committee wishes to be sure no danger to the colonies can come in through the back door, which is the river and the trading posts on it."

Ribner bowed gravely. He had been drinking with the others but showed no effect from what he had consumed.

"Believe me, gentlemen, I understand, and this post is a closed door to our enemies. By the way, I have a little money for the cause. Perhaps you, Major Whitkin, would take it back to the Committee for me. It isn't much, but it is freely given."

He tossed a small, chinking bag on the table before the major while his companions looked on approvingly.

"One more thing, gentlemen, to report when you get home. Now that I have a good smith, we'll be glad to repair, free of charge, any guns and pistols belonging to our defenders. Our fighters must have good weapons."

After much handshaking and more loud talk, the visitors departed more or less unsteadily. Pentz passed close to Jeff, at whom he winked broadly before striding away.

Jeff had to concede that Ribner had handled a visit which might have been disastrous with the utmost cleverness. Whitkin's party had seen exactly what they were shown, nothing more unless Pentz, Haider, or Krebs had looked further. Profit from Ribner's whisky trade with the Indians had paid for the liquor and food consumed. Gossip would be stilled. It looked as though Ribner had checkmated Squire Fell's suspicions.

Late the night of the visitation, Jeff was awakened by a sound that brought him from his bed to the open window. It was the tramp of a horse's hoofs, and before he could get down the ladder, there was tapping and fumbling at the shop door. When Jeff opened it, there was enough light from the waning moon to see the late visitor wore a long horseman's coat and that his horse from which he had dismounted stood with hanging head, evidently nearly spent.

"Ribner's post?" the query came in an arrogant, high-pitched voice.

"Yes," Jeff answered, "the big house up front."

The horseman grunted irritably.

"Twice tonight, I've missed that double damned path, and it'll take a half hour to rout them out at the house. Here, take this damned thing. I want to get back through that beastly dark hollow behind your fields before the moon wanes entirely."

To get at what he wanted, the visitor pushed back his cloak, and in that moment, Jeff saw he wore a British uniform. He had seen too many of them in England to be mistaken.

In another moment, the man had swung into the saddle, turned his horse, and was on his way toward the dark line of hills. He had left in Jeff's hands a small, heavy package which he felt sure contained coin. He had no notion of giving it to Ribner. Instead, he routed a grumbling Fred out of bed.

"Here," he directed, "take this to him and tell him that a horseman who was in a hurry just dumped it into my hands."

The small African hesitated until Jeff shoved the article into his mid-riff so hard he had to grasp it. Evidently, he gave it to his master, for Ribner appeared at the shop before breakfast while Jeff was washing, with his shirt flung across a bench.

"Who brought that packet last night?" Ribner demanded roughly, and Jeff shrugged his bare shoulders.

"I've no idea. The man was in a hurry and grumbling about losing the path. He dumped the package in my hands and then rode for it."

Ribner stood quietly, his lips set in a straight line. Jeff began to wipe his face with a badly torn towel. He stopped and looked directly into his master's eyes.

"The man was a soldier. A drink of that liquor you claim you don't sell would have done him a lot of good."

The trader's face became a mask of fury. Calmly, Jeff pulled on his shirt and walked out in the direction of the dining cabin.

So it was probably a bad day for Ben Haider to visit the post. In the afternoon, Jeff was back in one of the fields starting a kiln to make charcoal for his forge when the old woodsman appeared. He was chewing tobacco and spitting copiously, but he grinned at Jeff.

"Well, son," he said ruefully, "I braced your lord and master on the silver stuff. He wasn't so friendly today."

Jeff met the woodsman's eyes and remonstrated.

"You didn't talk silver with him, Ben?"

Haider spat copiously at a small sumac bush and nodded his gray head.

"That I did, Jeff. I jest told him plain he was getting silver that be-longed to me. At first, he denied having any, after which he called me a woods rat and told me to get the hell out."

He pushed back the battered hat he usually wore and scratched his head meditatively.

"Was going to argue with the man about where he figgered hell could be jest now, then I called to mind that he'd fooled that fat major good the other day and the folks with him. So, it didn't seem the right time to spoil him none, and I come away."

For a moment, there had been a wild light in the woodsman's eyes. It was entirely likely that his method of argument would not have been a vocal one. A knife and hatchet hung at his belt, and the butt of his rifle would make an excellent club.

Jeff grinned.

"There's enough silver on that powder horn of yours, Ben. Why not forget it till more peaceful times?"

Haider hitched up his belt and shook his head.

"No, sirree. I'll agree there's hatchets and redcoats on the river, Jeffy. Them boys is getting closer and closer. But I found me this silver, and I figger old Sento, the warrior that watched it fer me, was kilt. Now I'm bound up river; gonta hunt me a redskin that calls himself Ktemque. Claims he's a Delaware, but I'm told he's a Seneca."

Ready to move away, Haider was still not satisfied. He took several steps, then returned.

"Jeffy, I jest seen your boss man with his hair down, and it makes me itch fer a little leeway fer you. The man's bad, Jeffy, worse'n mebbe you think. Somethin's eatin' at him inside, I figger. He's the kind of feller that would hire his murders done and then cheat the fool that did his killin'. Look you out, Jeffy, don't take no chances with this Henry Ribner man. Squire Fell is kind of sore at you jest now, but could he find that paper Uncle Mark writ, then you was a free man when you hed your big night with the colored help, and the new paper Ribner holds wouldn't tie you no more."

Jeff continued to work at the preliminaries of starting his charcoal kiln, and since that merely meant digging out the ground a foot or more in depth, he could think as he plied his spade. It seemed odd that Ben Haider had been so disturbed. Certainly, Ribner had not frightened the old man, but he had made a very definite impression. When a man who had lived on the danger fringe of the wilderness for a long life said a man was dangerous, it paid to watch. And the statement about the indenture was intriguing. If that could be found, it would cancel the entire indenture at once. Abner Fultz must have seen that paper if it was in Uncle Mark's effects. But even if Jeff confronted the nephew, it would amount to nothing since a bondsman had no status in the courts.

For several days Jeff divided his time between the shop and the charcoal kiln. Trade in the store just across the bridge was brisker now; the stock of muskets had almost disappeared. One day Jeff carried an armful of firewood into the store building. Fred was back of the counter, and an Indian stood before him studying the merchandise on the shelves. In one red hand, resting on the counter, Jeff saw the gleam of a gold piece, but almost at once, Fred carelessly tossed a piece of woolen strouding over the palm.

There were few peltries in the storeroom and not more than a dozen bales of deer hides. Ribner was doing business for money which could only mean British coin, and he was selling the two things most valued by Indian customers: guns and liquor. Fred's little gesture today indicated he was party to the secret. Word about the visit of the British horseman and the gold transaction must be taken to Squire Fell. But before he could plan getting away from the post, another development occurred, which claimed all his attention.

The little charcoal kiln had burned down to the point where it shed a warm glow for a radius of several yards, and there was enough bite in the air this day to make the heat welcome. Jeff, busy covering holes in the kiln where too much fire showed, did not notice the Indian until he grunted.

He was a big, burly brute swathed in a dirty blanket drawn up so it partially covered his face but not enough to hide the pale scar running from the corner of his thin mouth to the tip of his ear. Two dejected turkey feathers drooped from his scalp lock.

"Cold," he muttered, stepping close to the kiln and spreading his hands to the heat. Jeff, irritated at the surprise, said nothing while the unwelcome visitor warmed himself thoroughly, then rubbed his protruding stomach.

"Fire much good," he mumbled. "Ktemque get rum, keep warm long time."

Jeff scarcely listened but kept tossing earth on the kiln with his spade. His visitor turned and started toward the trail, which was only a matter of fifty yards away. As the savage moved, a branch caught and pulled aside the corner of the dirty blanket. In that moment, Jeff saw and recognized a silver ornamented powder horn. There could be no doubt. This was Ben Haider's horn, the one of which he was so proud. The savage's name meant something now.

"Ktemque."

When his work was finished, he walked slowly back toward the shop, thinking hard. Ben Haider would not have parted with that horn except for a mighty high price, more than an Indian could have paid unless he had silver. Ben had encountered Ribner, and the trader had denied having silver. Abruptly, Jeff made up his mind to follow the Indian and talk with him, at least.

He moved swiftly at the fast forest pace Migun and Uncle Mark had taught him, eager to come up with the Indian before darkness set in. Probably Ktemque, as he called himself, would have a good explanation for the powder horn, but whatever he had to say, Jeff was determined to hear it. As he hurried, he felt sure the Indian would not go too far before he camped to enjoy the liquor he had boasted of having.

The narrow trail looped over the top of a long ridge, dipped into a valley, and climbed again. This was the McKee Path. Presently it would be joined by the Warrior's Trace coming down from the north, and that junction would be nearly a dozen miles from the post.

Well down over the crest of the second ridge, Jeff stopped in a clump of trees. His nostrils had caught the tang of woodsmoke. From then on, he proceeded cautiously. The early fall darkness was coming on, and he was entering thicker timber. Presently, dead ahead in an open place, he saw what he had been searching for: the glow of a fire half-hidden by a bulky figure. Jeff moved on, but he was watching the Indian, not his footing. He stumbled, and half fell. His floundering probably saved his life, for the warrior, at the first sound, had swung up his musket and fired, the flash of the discharge half-blinding Jeff.

It was a poor place from which to make a safe retreat; before he could go far, the Indian could recharge his musket, and Jeff had no weapon but his short-bladed sheath knife. The only thing to be done was to rush forward and overpower the savage, who was probably drunk already.

Ktemque had been sitting when he fired, but he tried to stand up as Jeff pitched forward through the brush at him. The Indian's big hand flashed back to snatch out his tomahawk. The firelight was bright. Jeff saw hanging from the same thong belt which supported the ax and ornate powder horn, a scalp with long gray hairs on it.

Savagely he drove at his antagonist, pushing the Indian away from the fire into the brush. The warrior had rolled a bit to one side, avoiding the full power of Jeff's impact. Then brush entangled the feet of both men, and they came down together with a sickening thump. When the greasy red arms went about his body, Jeff had the frightening knowledge that this Indian was stronger than he was. They wrestled back and forth, trying to hold each other's wrists. Ktemque's foul breath almost choked his antagonist. The warrior, crazed by liquor, had the strength of desperation. Slowly the hand that held the war ax twisted from Jeff's grasp, and Ktemque leaped to his feet with the small bright blade lifted high.

The shot made little more noise than the clapping together of a man's palms. Jeff's desperate eyes saw the small blue hole in the shaven head just before his opponent sprawled forward upon him.

When Jeff had scrambled out from under the body of the dead savage, Pentz was standing in the firelight reloading his rifle.

"No gun?" the woodsman asked. When Jeff shook his head, Pentz thumped his ramrod down hard on the charge in his rifle, pulled it clear, and thrust the hickory into the rifle thimbles.

"You damned fool," he said with full conviction, "to tackle a warrior like that."

Jeff rolled Ktemque over and took the powder horn and pitiful scalp.

"I was after him about the horn," Jeff explained. "When I saw the scalp, I knew he'd killed Ben, and I saw red. He was full of Ribner's whisky."

The big rifleman nodded.

"I knowed. He got Ben from a sumac thicket a little south of Great Island. Then he streaked it down here to get his pay, and I was following him. He slipped me three times. I was hanging around the post waiting fer him and then followed you. I was damned near too late."

Pentz took the scalp and the horn.

"I'll bury these where Ben figured his home was. He was kinda foolish about that silver business. Guess because he knew he was gettin' old, he wanted it."

Jeff was thinking hard. "Peter, do you figure Ribner sicked this savage after Ben?"

Pentz examined his rifle with some care. "Could be, son, but we ain't got too much to go on. Anyway, this is my business, not yours, you damned young rooster. You stick to blacksmithing. I'll kill the snakes as needs it."

His malevolent grin showed his meaning clearly. Then he gave his attention to the dead Indian.

"Ground's too hard to bury this red devil, but dead Injuns has a way of starting trouble."

He passed his rifle to Jeff, then swiftly built up the fire until it was burning furiously. Forcing the liquor bottle into the dead man's hand, Pentz thrust the head and shoulders of his victim into the flames.

"Poor Ktemque," he mocked, "got to drinkin' and fell in his fire."

He wasn't satisfied. Pulling the stopper from the silver horn that had belonged to his friend, he shook the black grains on the Indian's blanket and parts of his body not in the fire.

"Gon'ta give him a chariot ride to hell with Ben's powder. Now let's get ourselves out of here, Jeffy. I never did get me used to the smell of cookin' Injun."

Pentz parted with him a mile from the post. Jeff had missed his supper, but he was not hungry. The big house blazed with light. There was a cart outside on the road, and Jeff saw Ribner walking toward the front door. He was accompanied by a woman. Evidently, Mistress Ribner had returned from wherever she had been.

Jeff climbed to his bed thinking of Ben Haider, the dead Indian, and the possibility that Ribner had engineered a murder.

CHAPTER VI

IT WAS TWO DAYS BEFORE THE STORM broke or, rather, that long before Jeff was aware of anything unusual. On the way home that evening, following the death of Ktemque, Pentz had promised to tell Squire Fell about the British soldier's visit and the Indian making purchases with gold coin. What really concerned Jeff was whether Ribner had been concerned with Ben Haider's death. The fact that the trader had shown the silver to Peter Grube quite casually was in the man's favor, but the sight of the half-dried scalp with the straggly gray hair had shocked the young man even more than he realized. In spite of Pentz's warning, he would have had no choice but to do something drastic had he been convinced of Ribner's guilt.

Everyone had been silent at mealtime, and even Fred was more subdued than usual. In the forenoon of the second day after the Ktemque episode, Jeff had seen Ribner drive away northward in the cart. There was a woman with him, her identity was hidden by something wound about her head, and the cart had been going at a fast clip. However, the matter did not interest Jeff. He knew Mistress Ribner was often absent, that she went down country frequently, probably to Lancaster or Philadelphia. Even though she had just returned, she might be leaving again.

Fred finished his supper quickly that evening and slid out of the cabin. He walked slowly toward the storeroom over which he slept. Becky and Eli had not quite finished their meal when Clara, Eli's wife, appeared. She resembled Becky, John's wife, who did the cooking for the servants, only she was older, and this evening she was excited, shaking her head ruefully and clicking her tongue.

"'Twas no place fer me the other night," she announced. "Mistress Abigail sure did clean house."

She looked at the expectant faces, evidently waiting for one of them to question her, and Eli spoke.

"Go ahead, Clara; our tongues is jest hangin' out waitin' as you knows."

Divesting herself of a shawl-sized kerchief which she tossed on the table, the big woman seated herself carefully.

"Well, she'd come home from one of them visitin' trips of hers. All was jest sweetness and light with him all dressed up in one of them lacy shirts and Melody waitin' on the table like she always does. Thet girl is somethin', walking with a swing to her hips even when she totes a tray. I'd noticed when she come in the kitchen she had on some of that skeerce perfume the Mistress uses."

Jeff's mind flashed back to that night in the loft and the scent he had noted before he went to bed.

"Mistress Abigail, in her blue dress, sat at the foot of the table and he at the head. Once when I peeps in, I saw her sort of sniff, and then Melody brushes against he when she passed."

Clara paused. This was the dramatic point, and she wanted to savor the full measure of attention she had arrested. She drew a long breath, and her ample bosom heaved.

"Then she jest opens up. It was ladylike but what she said'd jest about take your hair off. 'Henry Ribner,' she says, 'tomorrow take this little swamp doxie up river and sell her.' Then she really does blister him. Says it's no matter to her how he fools around women when she's away, but she won't stand one of them in the house stealin' her perfume and then rubbin' about a man's legs when she's sittin' there. She says there's lots of things fer which she's sorry and that she's so tired of he. There was more stuff I ain't even tellin' Eh. Thet woman knows things a nice woman jest guesses at."

Jeff walked slowly over to the shop after Clara had finished her story. So that was the end of Melody at Ribner post. There was no doubt that the girl was a wanton, but he kept thinking of what Clara had said about Mrs. Ribner. He recalled vividly her visit to the shop and the sudden, alarming intimacy he had experienced when she had placed her hand in his so that he might judge how large to make the stock of her pistol. She had about her a mighty power to disturb a man, and there had been almost a challenge in her eyes that day.

Suddenly an impulse seized him, a prompting he knew to be wild, utterly foolish, and tremendously dangerous. Entering the shop, he set fire to some shaving in the forge. By this light, he found and took down the small walnut box he had fashioned and opened the lid with his thumbnail. While his light lasted, he admired the small pistol he had built in odd hours. Modeled after the big weapon which hung on the wall, its weight and balance were just about right for a woman's hand. Closing the lid and refusing to allow himself to think any longer, he tucked the box under his arm and went out.

There were lights in the big house. Ribner, he knew, had not returned; perhaps he had encountered some difficulty in disposing of Melody. Jeff rapped for the third time before he heard a light tapping of heels inside, and the door swung open. Framed against candlelight, which made a brown nimbus of her partially loosened hair, stood Mrs. Ribner. She smiled when she saw him and gestured with her hand. He stepped inside. To his surprise, she pushed the door shut behind him and shot the bolt into its socket. He bowed and offered her the small walnut case.

"Madam, I have brought your pistol."

She took the proffered box, opened it, and, a moment later, settled the stock of the pistol in her hand and drew back the hammer.

"It's loaded," he explained quickly. "It shoots a buckshot for a bullet."

He had thrust out his hand involuntarily to prevent her from discharging the weapon and touched her shoulder.

Her sultry eyes half-closed at his touch. Suddenly she tossed the cocked pistol to an upholstered settee and snatched something Jeff had not seen from the chair. It was a coiled whip made of braided rawhide, its tip like the tongue of a snake. She tossed out the lash full length on the floor. Her eyes were wide open again, but they seemed to have darkened, and her parted lips showed the white line of her teeth.

"So," she snapped, "you paw me when you come. You, the second white man on this place to be brought to heel by that wench. She had a taste of this before she was taken away."

Her lip curled.

"He grows old and stale, this husband of mine. Perhaps he has needs that cannot be met otherwise, but you—you poor young fool—let yourself be trapped."

Her arm swept back, lifting the whiplash slowly, and Jeff stepped closer.

"Madam, I've been a fool and am paying for it. I am a bondsman and should not have come here this night, but I will not be whipped."

Her arm raised just a little, and her purpose showed itself in her eyes. Jeff took another step. One arm went around her slim shoulders, holding her fast. The other snatched away the whip and threw it into a corner of the room while the woman twisted her supple body, straining toward the settee where the cocked pistol lay.

Jeff shook her roughly until her already loosened hair tumbled about her shoulders. The tormenting fragrance of perfume was in his nostrils, and tiny drums were beating in his temples. Suddenly, all her resistance ceased, and she lay back limp in his arms. After a moment, one of her hands lifted and rested on his shoulder; she was looking into his face, half-smiling.

"Why not?" she asked softly. "He took my slave; why should not I take one of his and have the revenge which would hurt him most?"

The sleeve fell back from her rounded arm as she locked it about his neck drawing his head down. Then her lips were on his. All sense and reasoning went from Jeff as he lifted her from the floor and carried her. She was laughing deep in her throat.

"He would have the savages burn you for this, Jeffry," she murmured. Then there was no speech from her. She was fire and hope and despair and hope again.

In the gray of the morning, she went with him to the door and stood there shivering a little. She spoke mockingly.

"When I tell him, Jeffry, do you think the savages' fire will be too awful?"

He caught her to him roughly and shook her a little.

"You will not tell him," he declared triumphantly. "I will come to you again, and you will come to me."

She did not answer him, but she did not stir until he released her and stepped out into the chill of the early morning.

Walking slowly to his quarters in the gathering light, Jeff's mind was racing about the unbelievable incident which had happened. He had gone to the house on a whim he had refused to analyze. There was no doubt how far the wrath of Ribner would lead him once he knew, and there was no trusting this woman of impulse and fire. She was entirely capable of boasting about her revenge. Squire Fell had called Jeff a fool. Probably that was what he was again, but he felt a change in himself. In the past few months, he had passed from crisis to crisis, each of which had dragged him down. There had been the loss of Uncle Mark's will, the trickery worked with Melody, and the death of Ktemque. Each time he had met what came to him with savage, hopeless anger. Now he was fully alive. Stirring in him was a rise of recklessness that he felt would mount higher and higher, and he was glad for it. He recalled the days of his boyhood in England and the drabness of young manhood there. Then had come the press gang and escape. It was likely depression would follow what had happened to him during the night, but now he felt release.

At the wide shop doors, he stopped. To the east, there was color in the sky, cold color but full of the freshness of a new day. His arms came up and extended like those of a sun worshiper. This was a new land. Some day, perhaps presently, he would be free.

Ribner returned that afternoon evidently in an evil humor, judging by the way he began to drive his people almost at once, setting new and harder tasks through the week. The Negro men were put to cutting and splitting cords of wood for the fireplaces, which would burn through the winter with scarcely any letup. Jeff was directed curtly to work in the smithy on farm equipment which needed attention. During the day, small groups of Indians came to the post and departed, blankets drawn about their shoulders.

On the second day after her husband's return, Mistress Ribner came to the shop carrying the small pistol in its case.

"You must now teach me to shoot this well," she told Jeff. There was a mocking look in her eyes as he took the weapon from her with fingers that he could not keep steady. However, he started drawing the charge and had finished reloading when Ribner appeared. The woman was now standing close to Jeff; her lips parted a little in concentration. To be sure she would understand, he repeated the operation. Then she took the loaded pistol from him, brushing his hand with warm fingertips as she did so.

"So, Henry," she said to her husband, and Jeff thought there was hidden meaning behind her words, "I am learning to shoot." She tapped the little weapon.

"'Tis a great leveler and makes even a weak woman as strong as the strongest."

Ribner said nothing, but his eyes searched Jeff's face momentarily. Mistress Ribner drew back the hammer with a skill that argued former practice with such a weapon. Bright powder grains showed in the pan. Jeff pointed through the doorway to a stump where a piece of bark made a target. The pistol came up and steadied. The hammer fell. There was a flash of fire and a report which was deafening in the narrow confines of the shop. The bit of bark flew to pieces.

"Good," Ribner cried. "I hope it wasn't a lucky shot."

"I'm always lucky," she rejoined and began to reload the pistol herself. She fired five shots in all, most of them good. Then Jeff ventured that the barrel should be wiped out. She gave him the weapon.

"I'll be out again, Jeffry," she promised. "Perhaps tomorrow." She walked away in the direction of the house, a cloth bonnet swinging from one finger, her hair bright in the sharp fall sunlight. Ribner picked up the pistol and turned it over several times in his fingers.

"Has she practiced shooting before, Claus?"

Jeff looked back at him sharply. It was possible that at any time, Abigail Ribner might betray him under the pretext that this servant had attacked her, and it looked now as though the trader was vaguely suspicious about something. Jeff picked up the small cleaning rod he had placed on the bench and kept his voice steady and noncommittal.

"That I wouldn't know."

A slight flush appeared on Ribner's face, but he asked no further question. In ten minutes or so, he left, and Jeff, after cleaning the pistol, went back to mending a broken plow.

Winter settled in with occasional snows that did not lie long, for there were still some days of bright sun. The monotonous work of the place went on. Wood was cut, split, and then hauled to the buildings on sleds. There was corn to be shucked and ground, beans to be shelled out of their dried pods, and the care of livestock. Jeff was busy all the time. When there was no shop work, he liked to be outdoors with the Black men. Occasionally there was a little news of the outside world, usually supplied by Fred. The war, after the first Boston successes, was going badly. Washington had been beaten on Long Island and was in full retreat toward Pennsylvania. There was another disquieting item, and Fred looked toward Jeff several times in telling it. John Weston was organizing the Tories about Kittanning town and would bring them eastward to destroy the Lancaster gunshops.

Jeff thought of Squire Fell's conjecture. The old Delaware Indian town of Kittanning was at the western end of the great trail, which ran eastward to Philadelphia. The McKee Path, which emerged here at the Ribner post, took off from it. Uncle Mark's train had come over the Kittanning Path a number of times. It was a familiar way to Jeff, and he knew the name of Weston. He was a man of some wealth living close to the old path, near Sinking Valley, where the colonists were already mining lead and erecting a fort to be called Roberdeau.

A strong restlessness seemed to be upon Ribner these days, and he was away from the post often for a day, occasionally for a week. Jeff knew he should manage to see Squire Fell during these absences to tell him Fred's story and that all the muskets were now gone. It was possible that they had been received by Weston, who would be in need of arms. Meanwhile, the trader's absences were opportunities to meet Abigail Ribner. Sometimes she went to the shop quite openly with an excuse about the pistol or some household contrivance which needed mending. At each visit, her attitude was different. There were times when she came into his arms quite simply; at others, she held him away scornfully. Jeff's first elation had passed. He did not fancy too much slipping in and out of the big house. Much as he despised Ribner, he felt cowardly, and he was pretty sure the Black people knew what was going on though they said nothing. Yet, he could not keep away from her.

There were long evenings by the fireside when this woman visited with him as though her hunger for talking was stronger than any other she possessed and her frankness amazed Jeff. She hated her husband and debated about going to the Colonial authorities, for Henry Ribner was a Tory, and the post could be an open door to British and Indian raids. However, she insisted that no definite plan was under way.

"Black Senecas," she said of the Indians that patronized the post. "They come here with British money. He arms them and fills them with whiskey, hoping, with their help, to be master along this river some day. Even now, he wraps Colonel Hunter at Fort Augusta about his finger."

She leaned back in her chair and laughed until her robe slipped from one white shoulder.

"He would be king of the river, Jeffry. I would be his queen, and my lord would be old and dry and jealous."

On another evening, she shook his shoulders savagely.

"You do not love me," she whispered, and he looked down into her partly closed eyes and then at her full, pouting lips. "But," she continued, "I stir you so much you have forgotten how to think of anything else but me. Is it not true?"

Jeff nodded soberly, then tightened his arms about her body, but she twisted away a little. She had not finished.

"Some day, Jeffry, if you live, and that is doubtful, there will be a wife and children, a wife like that girl who came here with the Grubes and stole away to the garden so she could see you."

Jeff stared dumbfounded, and she laughed at his confusion.

"You will then be angry at yourself, for you will not be able to forget me. You will remember, great God, how you will remember. You will not be able to keep out the thoughts or the hunger even with her kisses on your lips."

Now she leaned so far back that she was partly clear of his arms and lifted her heavy, loosened hair with both hands.

"All this if you live, my eager black-haired friend with the strong hands and the too-cold eyes. Your chances are poor. He will learn some-day that you have had me these many times, and the manner of your dying will be bad, very bad. The savages will be glad to help him for some of his whiskey. Ribner says there is a dead Seneca back in the hills, and you were away that day. Also, in Philadelphia, a wise woman learns much, especially if she has friends in the mayor's office. British police may want you someday."

So Ribner's periodical absences continued. Abigail Ribner both attracted and repelled Jeff, but he could not shake off the spell she had meshed about him. When she had referred to Susan Keiner's visit that day, he resolved to keep away from the woman, but when night came, his resolution melted. Once more, he waited outside her door, eager to rap and find her waiting.

The winter was well along when Abigail Ribner made her final and startling challenge. She and Jeff had been together for a long evening, seated side by side before the big fire which blazed in her bedroom. Shadows danced in the corners, and the single lighted candle burning in a three-pointed silver holder on her dressing table added little to the light. Tonight she wore a soft black robe that accentuated the whiteness of her neck and arms. This was one of the evenings when she chose to talk.

"I will shock you tonight, my Jeffry. Once I was almost as poor as you and well on the way to being a bond girl. But I lived with my aunt, who was a wise woman, if not a good one. She did not crave the expense of bringing me up, so she taught me how a girl may advance herself through the weaknesses of men."

She rose, tossed a chip of wood on the fire, watched it flame up, and then sank down again beside Jeff while his arm tightened across her shoulders. Half smiling, she continued:

"Money came to me, and I always put some of it by. No, I shall not tell you where I began my life, but Ribner found me in Philadelphia. I will not tell you more about him nor how he wronged me until I hated him. Perhaps I was caught in my own trap. Anyway, I married him. The little money I let him think I had went into this trading venture. He, Abner Fultz, who is a greasy man who watches me, and I are equal partners. We made wills. If I die, Ribner will have this place between him and Fultz. If Ribner dies—as well he may—" She shook her head, interrupting herself. "Then I shall have his share though I already have enough. In his weakness for me, I have bled him of money and put it by."

She leaned back and laughed, testing her supple body until Jeff shook her lightly.

"I have been his wife," she whispered thickly, her voice half choked with laughter, "but, God, how he has paid for the favors you, you young black devil, have had for less than the asking." Springing to her feet, she whirled about the room in a mad dance until her robe loosened. The fire-light playing on her white skin revealed that she was all but naked. The brown cloud of her hair swung about her shoulders and face. Breathless at last, she dropped back into Jeff's hungry arms,

"Who knows?" she questioned hoarsely. "He might return tonight and find you here. You would have to kill him then with your knife or my small pistol. That, or he would cut you to pieces with a whip and turn what was left of you over to a Seneca fire." A warning coldness stirred at the back of Jeff's neck. Now she was stroking his face with soft, smooth fingers.

"If he dies, my Jeffry, I might want a tall young husband. Anyway, you would belong to me, and I would keep my bondsman near."

A sudden eagerness to be out of this room, with its cloying fragrance of mingled perfumes, seized him. He wanted to be in the clean cold wind which could blow the fog from his brain. The wine he had drunk earlier in the evening had not affected him. This woman in his arms, with her warmth, her closeness, and her beauty, was more intoxicating than liquor. But the veiled challenge to murder had sobered him.

Later that night, he slept little in his bed over the shop. There was too much to think about, and there was fear in him, fear that if she summoned him again, she could lead him down the road to murder. Much as he hated Ribner, he could not in cold blood kill the man merely to gratify this woman. He might have done it the night Melody had admitted how the trap had been set for him, but this was different. Before sleep came, another idea occurred to him. It could be that he was being led into another trap. All Abigail Ribner's yielding and her wantonness might be intended to make him a slave to her bidding, even to the killing of her husband and Fultz.

Eli gave him a message the next morning after breakfast.

"Squire crossed the river wants to see you, Jeff. There's a canoe in the willows, and there ain't much ice."

Reckless of Ribner's definite orders not to leave the place, Jeff set out from the shop shortly after dark to obey Squire Fell's summons. He was going up through the vegetable garden in the direction of the house when the sound of a horse's walk stopped him. The animal came down the path from the wilderness side, crossed the small bridge at the trading post, and then went up the path toward the house. Keeping in the shadow, Jeff saw the rider swing out of the saddle just as Ribner opened the back door and stood framed in yellow candlelight. As the visitor walked past him to enter the house, he pulled off his long horseman's cloak. The man wore the uniform of a British army officer.

Jeff waited long minutes and then walked through the yard. Once on the path, here as wide as a cart track, he trotted toward the river. He did not wonder that Eli should have the message; these Africans knew all that transpired in their small world.

The river showed black with small flecks of white where there was floating ice. Jeff found the canoe easily, but he stood irresolute for a few minutes, telling himself he had better return to the post. There was too much ice for safe passage, and it might pay him to observe the visitor back there. But after these minutes passed, he shoved the prow of the birchbark into the water. He knew well enough that it was not fear of the water that restrained him but his hesitation about facing the squire again.

It was a rough crossing. Several times chunks of ice all but tore the paddle from his grasp. Once, he debated turning the prow down stream, allowing him to drift out of this locality which had brought him so much misery of mind.

The dark line of the shore loomed before him sooner than he had expected. When the canoe bumped into soft mud, he held it in place so he could get out without wetting his moccasins. Then he drew his frail craft from the water, turned it over, and pushed his paddle under it.

There wasn't much of a village left about the place where, before the old war, McKee had had his trading post. Tonight Jeffry counted twelve houses, only one of which was lighted. He started toward it, believing this must be Squire Fell's headquarters. The old man traveled about his district like a circuit-riding minister, but this was his home. Jeff walked slowly up the hill, mounted the house steps, and stood before the door, ready to rap. The coming of the British officer would be real news. Pentz must have turned in information about Ktemque's death and Ben Haider's passing. But the squire would probe more deeply than that. He would ask questions Jeff might not wish to answer.

CHAPTER VII

WHETHER HE planned to have it that way or not, Squire Christian Fell always appeared to be the same. He would be seated back of the inevitable table littered with the tools of writing and perhaps a leather-bound book or two. His small head would be cocked like that of an inquisitive bird, his young-old face alert. Everything was this way when Jeff finally knocked on the door and was bidden to enter. Fell showed no surprise or concern. As usual, his voice was slow in getting under way.

"This time," he began caustically, "you are months late, my friend, months. Of course, Pentz and Haider kept me well supplied with news, but you brought none yourself except the record of your foolishness."

"Ben is dead," Jeff explained shortly in interruption, and Fell nodded impatiently before he asked his question:

"I know all about that and the death of the Indian who scalped him. What I want to know is whether Ribner sent him to his death because Ben was getting at Tory secrets or whether it was a private feud between two money-loving men?"

Jeff frowned. If either he or Pentz had been as entirely convinced of Ribner's part in the affair as Fell seemed to be, it was not likely the trader would still be alive.

"I'm not sure. Squire, nor is Pentz. Ribner was open about his lump of silver the day Peter Grube visited the post. But you seem sure—"

Fell interrupted with a raised hand. "Now, don't you get your back up. I've had a hard enough time getting that bloody-minded Pentz away from finishing Ribner. Ben's dead. Now I want to know how much of a Tory this Ribner is and how much he's involved in this Tory plotting out about Kittanning. Further, I want to know how it comes he trades for British gold and what these midnight visitors of his mean."

Jeff stared at the old man. Some of his resentment at the tone in which he had been addressed vanished as he wondered at the information the jurist had gathered. He thought, too, of the packet given him by the impatient messenger that night and Ribner's irritation. Even now, a British officer in uniform was at the post.

"There is gold, sir. I've seen it, and you know about the packet brought at night. And, as I left, a British officer went into the Ribner house."

Fell half rose, then settled back into his chair and, for a long moment, paid no attention to his visitor. When he spoke, it was as though he thought aloud.

"No, I can't get Pentz, and what in hell would I do with the man? Ribner has Colonel Hunter wound tight about his fingers. If I could only learn what passes—"

Fell's meaning was so strongly implied that Jeff spoke: "I've no chance of learning things. All I get is fragments. I work all day in the shop or fields with the slaves, and one of them watches me. I walk back and forth from the shop to the dining cabin—"

"And up to the big house at night when you're summoned," Fell shouted. He slapped the table with his palm.

"Here we are. Enough muskets went out of that post to arm a full company. Likely they went to the Tories just waiting to come through Ribner's place upon the soft side of our colonies. British gold is coming in. We know Ribner is a bought man of some kind. I work with a piddling bunch of Public Safety men who can't see the woods for the trees. When I get a man inside the Ribner post, a man with two eyes, two ears, all he sees and hears are women. He has stolen a man's wife but does not seem eager to steal the same man's secrets."

Jeflf's first resentment of the evening, which had passed, now flared up again. His eyes narrowed, and he took an involuntary step closer to the table. Fell roared at him to take a chair. To his own surprise, Jeff obeyed, and Fell leveled a quill at him.

"You're trapped again, Jeffry Claus, and this time far beyond any help, for Abigail Ribner is a clever and dangerous woman. It's not the charm of your dark and homely face that appeals to her; it's the possibility of using you. She has destroyed other men. Her god is money, and she will have it. One bond servant more or less will not trouble her nor will a husband if she is ready to be quit of him."

Fell paused. There was nothing in his eyes to indicate he cared for Jeff's anger. Instead, he seemed to be studying. Finally, he leaned forward, pressing his thin chest against the table edge.

"We have taken some pains to find out about this lovely lady who has such a way with men. We do know that she hates the English and that she, in spite of her love of money, gives liberally to our cause through her agent in Philadelphia. It is my notion that she is playing Abner Fultz and her husband against each other. Some of the British gold that comes to Ribner as payment for the schemes he puts through about here gets into her fingers. What the woman wants of you, Jeffry, in God's name, I do not know unless it is—"

His narrowed eyes met Jeff's with the force of a blow when he spoke his next word: "Murder!"

Jeff came out of his seat, remembering what had happened last night with the woman. Her talk about the pistol and knife bore out the Squire's conjecture. Far better than this old man could guess, Jeff realized Abigail Ribner's hold on him. But Squire Fell ran on, ignoring his visitor's wrath.

"I used to think you quite a boy when you were with Uncle Mark, but you let that snake-blooded Ribner trap you. Now his wife has you wound round her finger, ready to do whatever bidding she has—"

Jeff's angry roar finally stopped the old jurist's harangue.

"Squire, a while ago, you said you got me inside the Ribner post. Great God of the Mountains, have you a finger in this pie? I had my freedom coming, and you know it. Now I'm cheated out of four years of my life by your sentence. Why should I spy for you or a damned Committee of Safety that sings songs about liberty while I'm a slave bought and sold like a hundredweight of beef on the hoof? Hell, I'm just an animal, a horse that takes his mares where he finds them when he's out of harness."

Jeff stopped, breathless. His face and eyes still showed his wrath, but Fell had leaned way back in his chair and now waved a thin hand.

"Good, Jeffry, good. I had begun to think all the sap was out of you, that they'd finished something inside you. Your shoulders are squarer.

There's a difference even in your voice. Go ahead, take your women when and where you find them. Let the recklessness in you ride; it will either lead you to fight that nest of Tories over there at the post or to your own hanging."

That was the final word between them before Jeff walked out and down to his canoe. The thing which bothered him most was that he had been pretty certain Fell had been smiling when he stalked out. The Squire was long-headed. He knew a lot, and maybe his bitter tongue was used for a purpose. It might be a stimulus to action.

The big house was still bright with lights when he came up from the river and crossed the edge of the lawn. On impulse, he turned and approached the house. Damn, Squire Fell. He had said that he, Jeff Claus, was not eager to steal Ribner's secrets. Anyway, he wasn't serving the squire now, he just wanted to have a look, and that was easy. By standing on tiptoe, he could look in the dining-room window.

The table was still spread with a linen cloth from which the table service had been removed. It now bore an array of bottles and glasses placed before the four people seated about the board. Ribner was at the head with a man in full-dress red uniform of the British army at his right. Across from this man, his heavy face flushed from eating and drinking, was Abner Fultz. With pasty-looking fingers, he was slowly turning a wineglass round and round. Abigail Ribner, in a gown that left white shoulders and arms bare, sat at the foot of the table. Her lips were moving, and both the officer and Fultz were looking at her intently. Of course, Jeff could not hear what she was saying, but in the brightness of the candles, he could see the hunger on their faces. Ribner wore a half-sardonic smile.

Jeff turned away. Fell had thought of arresting the British officer but had dismissed the idea. Halfway to the shop, he came upon the man's tethered horse. On impulse, Jeff stripped off the saddle and bridle, tossing them into the creek. The released animal moved slowly away toward one of the small haystacks close to the barn.

A big pile of dry leaves, brush, and other trash had accumulated in the vegetable garden. The winds had dried this pretty thoroughly. Jeff was moved by a sense of his own futility. In the big house, Ribner entertained an enemy of this valley. Fultz was in there, guzzling liquor. The three men felt secure, and there was one way to break down that feeling; to make Ribner feel he was being watched. Jeff knelt by the stack and worked busily with his tinderbox until small bright flames started to lick up among the leaves.

When the cry of fire rang out a good quarter of an hour later, Jeff emerged from the shop door scantily clad in breeches and moccasins. He had done better than he had hoped. The rubbish pile had become a great, roaring beacon that lit the whole premises. A nearby haystack was beginning to burn, and the blacks were working desperately because the hay fire threatened the barn. As Jeff joined them, Ribner, his wife, and guests stood outside the back door of the house. After a minute, the officer, clutching his cloak to him, ran toward the tree where he had tethered his horse.

In a shed, Jeff found a pile of buckets used for watering the garden and got a bucket brigade started with the black women and men. As he worked at the end of the line pouring the water on the hay, he saw Fultz enter the house and reappear with a cloak which he placed over Abigail Ribner's shoulders, taking his time for the task. Ribner now darted across the lawn toward the fire.

Gradually the flames died down, and shadows crowded back. The bucket line had done its work well. Presently the rubbish pile was a mass of lighted coals which the soft breeze stirred. Then the officer reappeared, strode up to the angry Ribner, and spoke sharply to him. The trader stared at his guest, then swore savagely.

"Fred!" he yelled, "get a saddle and bridle for the horse there in the barnyard."

When the horseman had finally galloped out of the farmstead, Ribner herded all the servants into the light of the nearly dead fires and demanded to know if any of them knew how the fire started. Blank faces stared back into his angry one, and heads shook in negation.

"Ain't seen nobody, sir, we wuz all sleepin'," Eli declared, and even Fred had nothing to add to that. Ribner strode up to Jeff.

"You," he snapped, "did you see anybody about?"

"No," Jeff answered truthfully, "none but us after the fire started."

After Ribner had followed his wife and Fultz indoors, Jeff, John, and Eli carried a little more water to make safety doubly sure. Then they stacked the buckets in the shed. Jeff had started to the cabin when Eli came up and shoved a small object into his hand. Jeff identified his tinderbox.

"Powerful careless, Jeff," the man commented. "Found it lost to the fire. 'Deed it's possible you could git them big fingers burnt. It's really mighty possible."

Before noon of the next day, the prowling Fred found the officer's saddle lodged against a drift in the creek, and Jeff watched the small gray man carry it into the house, a look of triumph on his face. Within another twenty-four hours. Mistress Ribner, with Clara beside her on the seat of the cart, drove off, taking the road down river. Jeff had not talked with her, and she had sent him no word.

The night of her departure, Jeff was tired from a long day at the forge pointing plowshares and reshaping horseshoes, so after supper, he went almost immediately to his little room over the shop. Until sleep claimed him, he thought of Squire Fell's harangue. The old jurist was disturbed, very much so. If he, with his knowledge of what was going on, was disturbed, there must be good reason. There had been close to a hundred muskets. All of them now were gone, and the Indian trade would not have been great enough to have taken them all. He thought, too, of the dead Ktemque who had killed Ben Haider far up the West Branch of the great river and then must have come almost directly to the Ribner post.

At first, he was dreaming. Once more, he was wrestling with the big savage whose bullet had just missed him, and again, the arms pinioning his were too strong for his own. But he had not been dreaming, for he woke to find himself pressed down to the bed by the strong arms of both Eli and John. The narrow room was flooded with candlelight from a lanthorn held high by Fred. Back of him was Ribner, a pistol ready in his hand.

"Hold him!" the trader snarled in a choked voice, "hold him or—"

Jeff twisted, brought up his knee into John's stomach, and hurled him against the wall with a force that made the building quiver. Then he was over the side of the bed, diving for Fred. Too late to avoid it, he saw

Ribner swing up the barrel of the heavy pistol. It crashed down, and Jeff felt himself falling into blackness.

When he was conscious again, he found they had worked fast and thoroughly. The tattered shirt in which he slept had been ripped away, and his naked body was tied to the center post of the smithy. A loop of rawhide pulled his arms up over his head until the tips of his fingers brushed the ceiling beam to which the thongs were fastened. His body ached. Probably they had thrown him down the steps. Again there was candlelight, so much it made his eyes ache.

Slowly he turned his head. Ribner and Fred were over at the forge. The trader held a whip which Jeff recognized. It was made of neatly braided rawhide, which tapered from the wooden stock to a tip no thicker than a knitting needle. Ribner, seeing his victim conscious, slowly stepped closer. The man's face twisted spasmodically. His lips were drawn back from clenched teeth, and his fingers jerked at the whip they chutched. He came closer until his face was only a foot from Jeff's, and his speech was that of a man who had been running.

"You filthy Dutch swine . . . I knew you'd been spying . . . Fred watched. Then, you, you got after her. He saw you go in the house . . . She told me she pitied you, how she fought you . . . drove you away with this whip. You laid hands on her. Now I'm going to—finish you."

Ribner paused from sheer lack of breath and twisted his head as though his stock was too tight. Then he brandished the whip.

"Each night, we'll use this until you're dead. Then we'll bury your filthy body in the barnyard. Hell, why did I keep you alive this long? I should have—"

Jeff stared steadily into the man's face while a cold hand seemed to grip his vitals. Ribner's words did not mean anything, but the bloodshot, narrowed eyes and the tiny flecks of moisture at the corners of his lips showed Jeff there was now no sanity in the man.

"So," Ribner snarled, "after I'm through with you—you dared to touch her. You filthy, filthy—"

His voice mounted into a high wordless shriek. The whip licked back and forth with all the force the trader could summon. The lash cut, and Jeff choked back a scream at the fiery stripe that wound about him and would not let go. After that, he pressed his face against the post and gnawed at the wood as the whip rose, fell, cut, and pulled out of the gashes it had opened. He could not keep back his groans. His stretched hands and arms tried to contract as if to pull his body up from the stinging fire that wrapped it again and again. Finally, his senses reeled. There was no thought in him, nothing left but this monstrous agony. Merciful unconsciousness came to him as the breathless Ribner reeled back against a workbench, dropping the bloody whip and then kicking it across to Fred.

Minutes passed while Ribner recovered his breath, and Jeff came back to consciousness. Fred stood before him, holding the whip. Suddenly he spat full into the tortured man's face.

"I shows you whippin' as is whippin'."

Again the lash whistled and fell. It was harder to bear now, for one stroke would cut the shoulders, then next the buttocks.

"Don't mark his face," Ribner shouted as Fred continued.

Jeff's mouth was full of blood from bitten lips, and his fingernails had broken against the rafter. After a deep, retching groan, he slipped once more into blackness.

He thought they had destroyed his eyes when he became conscious. It was dark about him. He lay at the foot of the post, his whole body an aching mass of tortured flesh. Perhaps a half hour passed until the outer door opened, someone carrying a lanthorn entered and crossed to him.

"It's Eli, Jeffy."

The cold water from the cup pressed to his lips was unbelievable in its goodness. When it was empty, it was filled again.

"Jeffy," the big Negro sobbed, "he made us hold you, held his pistol in my ribs. Effen was I to cut you clear, he'd kill me and Clara by inches."

He brought back circulation to Jeff's hands by rubbing the wrists and laid a big water-saturated cloth over the back of the man on the floor. That done, he tried to get Jeff to eat a bit of meat, but he retched against it.

"Jeffy," the big man's lips were close to Jeff's ear. "We can't help you, but I sent John fer them as kin. They'll be here come mornin'."

Another cup of water and the big man was gone into the darkness; his light snuffed out.

Jeff had little idea of the hour. Probably the beating had come some-time before midnight. Occasionally he dozed a little when the waves of pain brought in their wake a coma of exhaustion. But he was wide awake in the cold sunlight of the morning when his torturers reappeared. Fred looked particularly pleased. He had brought softened tallow in a dish, and with this, he anointed Jeff's back, then used the remainder to soften the blood-stiffened whip.

Ribner's face had the drawn and puffy look of a man who had slept little and who had been drinking heavily. Dark pouches showed under his eyes, and his face twitched. Jeff watched the men, numbly aware that the whipping was to begin again. A feeling of nausea surged through him when they drew him up to the post. He vomited and then laid his face against the pillar. Eli had failed to bring the help he had promised. Jeff had in him no more will to resist or to show bravado. When the whip began its devilish work, he whimpered like a child.

The lashing did not last long, for Ribner and Fred must have real-ized their victim could no longer react to pain. Ribner cut the thongs that held his victim's arms to the beam, and the tortured man slumped to the floor. A second knife slash freed his feet. Rolling instinctively to get his weight off his tortured back, Jeff jerked up his legs. The gloating Fred had stopped too close. With one desperate, almost reflex effort, the lifted legs lashed out, catching the small Negro full on the chest, hurling him back against the anvil where his head struck, and he slumped to the floor.

Jeff only half realized the collapse of one of his enemies when Ribner was upon him swinging an inch-thick stick of dried hickory used to make gun ramrods. He struck savagely. Jeff screamed when the club struck his side, and his legs jerked. Ribner struck at them and then kicked the prostrate man in the side.

Their victim left unconscious, Ribner and the groggy Fred left the shop. The hickory stick lay beside the bloody whip as the two men walked slowly across the little bridge to the store.

A quarter of an hour later, three Indians came through the fields instead of along the path. When they passed the shop door, they stopped and looked in curiously at the huddled figure on the floor. Their faces expressionless, after a keenly observant moment, they trotted across the little bridge to the post store. In ten minutes a second such group repeated the performance, but the bloody victim made no movement to indicate that he was alive.

When Jeff's eyes finally did open, his head was whirling. He tried to move, sensing that someone crouched near him, but he could not see who it was.

"No," he begged. "No more."

"It's Migun, Jeff." The voice was soft with pity, and a piece of water-soaked cloth was placed between the suffering man's lips. Careful hands straightened his body, but Jeff screamed when his leg was touched.

From somewhere close, a flat, heavy voice said tonelessly: "Broke below the knee there,"

The voice shifted, seemed to come from higher up.

"Jest pounded the living hell out of him."

There was the sound of receding steps, and Jeff was alone again. Henry Ribner stood behind the counter on which was a folded blanket and a roll of strouding cloth. The knot of Indians before him had fingered both with filthy hands. Fred was busy with beads and pots of vermilion at the end of the same counter. The scene was all business. One Indian reached inside his blanket and was withdrawing a buckskin sack when the door opened. Peter Pentz, followed by two Indians dressed in white man's clothing, entered. All three carried rifles,

Pentz leaned his weapon against the door jamb and pushed roughly through the knot of Indians until he faced Ribner. His bearded face showed little expression.

"You murdering son-of-a-bitch," he said softly. His arm shot across, and his powerful fingers seized the trader's hair. In spite of his weight and struggling, Ribner came over the counter like a bale of goods. Pentz moved toward the door dragging his prisoner.

"Git the other, Migun."

Fred screamed as the young Delaware repeated Pentz's performance. When Fred tried to bite, Migun released him and then savagely struck the Negro on the side of the head. After that, he dragged his man to the door by the ear and some hair clutched with it in merciless, iron fingers.

The Indian customers had looked on passively. The other Indian who had entered with Pentz stood with rifle ready until they turned back to the counter and once more began examining the goods.

Jeff had revived sufficiently to raise his head a little when Pentz and Migun entered with their prisoners. The big woodsman shoved Ribner against the benches with a force that made some tools drop from their racks.

"You," he growled at the cowering Fred, "get a horse and saddle."

The Indian who had guarded the door of the store had appeared. Now he followed Fred.

"Ribner," Pentz's voice was lethal, almost flat. "I ain't much fer law. You might have come clear with this whip business, but that boy's leg's a different thing. There's a fine fer that, and even this damned Quaker government would say you was spoiling property."

Ribner cautiously stepped forward one pace. There was more confidence in his bearing. He had mustered the courage of anger at having been manhandled.

"Get off my property!" he yelled suddenly. "You—"

He had jerked the little pistol Jeff had made for his wife from inside his coat. Migun, crouched beside his stricken friend, snatched the hickory club and threw it lancelike. His aim was true, for it struck the weapon from the trader's hand. There was a roar as it discharged, then Pentz struck hard with the flat of his hand.

Ribner staggered. Slowly, methodically, the woodsman slashed with his fists until the trader's eyes ran with tears of pain. A heavier blow dropped him to his knees, and Pentz jerked him up.

"Now, my stinking Tory friend. I got no time today to fix you proper fer what you did to Ben Haider and this boy, but I'll be back." His heavy voice lifted suddenly to a shout of sheer, savage anger. "You stinkin' yellow belly. Jest touch a dog on this place, and I'll cut you to pieces with your damned whip and hang what's left with its lash!"

With a swift movement, he snatched the whip from the floor. Ribner's hands went up to guard his face as the lash licked out, bringing bright blood from the man's ears and wrists. A second blow brought a scream of mingled fear and agony. Pentz shook his heavy shoulders, bunched the whip, lash and stock into his huge hand and then hurled it into Ribner's chest with a force that knocked him down.

Fred had arrived with a saddle horse, and after wrapping him in blankets, Jeff's friends lifted him into the saddle. The Indian customers had emerged from the store to watch what was going on. Pentz had taken the horse by its bridle when he paused.

"Clean forgot," he grunted.

Fred squalled, but the big hands lifted him into the air like a sack of grain. A few yards away was the creek, covered now with a thin film of ice. Pentz strode forward, bearing his struggling captive high, and then hurled him, so his falling body broke through the ice into the black water underneath.

The watching Indians looked at each other and rubbed the heels of their hands into the palms with complete enjoyment. Pentz and his two friends, walking beside their reeling friend in the saddle, moved slowly away over the fields.

CHAPTER VIII

MILES BACK in the forest and not far from where Ktemque had met his end, the little cavalcade turned into a hemlock-honed hollow where a small stream clattered its way through mossy rocks. Pentz and Migun worked swiftly and skillfully. In minutes a good fire was burning, and a deep browse bed was prepared. Afterward, the three men eased the suffering man from the saddle and stretched him on the fragrant hemlock. Migun felt his friend's forehead gently.

"Jeff," he said, presenting the other Indian, "this is Gokhotit, who is good with medicines. He will set your leg. It's broken, you know."

Gokhotit looked down and smiled, showing white teeth in his broad mouth. There was gentleness on his face, already lined, though he did not seem to be an old man.

"I have a little opium," he explained. "It will help some. You have already had much pain."

Kneeling, he pressed a tiny pellet between Jeff's lips and then gave him a stiff drink from Pentz's flask. His big, square fingers slowly stroked the patient's forehead, then came down along his neck and back of it to the base of the spine. It was as though those fingers smoothed away a great deal of pain and discomfort. Minutes passed. Jeff had become too drowsy to see the Indian doctor nod. Pentz stepped astride Jeff's body and kneeled so his knees would come into the armpits.

"Only a minute," Gokhotit spoke almost under his breath. He turned the leg carefully but firmly, and perspiration came out on Jeff's face. The turning stopped, and there was a tremendous pull. The sensation was so real the suffering man thought he heard a snap, and immediately the pain lessened. Ten minutes later, he was given more liquor and helped to a sitting position so he could look down at his leg. The break was midway between ankle and knee. There was a moss-padded splint in place along his bony shin. Gokhotit was grinning.

"One moon and a half, Jeff's leg good as new. Now we'll warm balsam salve for the back,"

The red man seemed to have everything he needed in his buckskin bag. He took out a wooden peg which he held close to the fire for a moment until an aromatic odor lifted from its contents.

"Balsam bud salve," he explained. "We take only the buds, bruise them well, being careful to lose no juice. After that, we fry them in grease until we have a salve. Goose grease is best for the frying, but I had none, so I used bear fat."

All the time he was chattering, his light and careful fingers were anointing Jeff's cuts with the ointment. After the first smarting sensation, there was definite relief.

"And now a dose of hemlock tea, my friend," Gokhotit continued. "A rib may be broken. In the summer, it would heal with no danger, but now you might get lung fever. The tea is to drive away that danger."

Pentz had already prepared the medicine in his small kettle, and Jeff choked down a full pint of the bitter brew. Afterward, he was eased down on the bed and covered with a blanket.

The big ranger left in the morning, but before he took his leave, he talked to Jeff.

"There's things I have to watch. The Senecas might come down. Peter, I'm off for Great Island. Mebbe I'll go clear to the Sinnamahoning. The Delaware boys will take good care of you."

They remained in the camp through the day, but the next morning, they were on their way with Jeff mounted. Migun led the group over the hills, across wooded valleys, and through ravines where cold streams brawled. Jeff was stiff and sore. It took all his energy to keep his seat in the saddle. He noted that Migun carried a pistol thrust through his belt in addition to his rifle. Gokhotit had no arms, but his knife and a short bow carried unstrung across his shoulders.

They toiled up another mountain, and Jeff became so weary that he began to weave in the saddle. Gokhotit supported him, and Migun stepped back.

"Half an hour more, my brother," he promised, "and we'll be home."

A small natural meadow stretched up from a stream to the edge of the timber. There stood a small cabin under the now leafless chestnut trees. Unlike conventional white men's cabins, the logs stood upright. The chimney was a mud and stick affair but the roof showed excellent clapboards.

Migun was proud of his place. He showed the two pole beds, the stools, and the table, after which he started a fire on the broad stone hearth. Then he helped Jeff into one of the beds.

"This is my hideaway, Jeff. I come here when I'm tired of people, particularly white ones who weary me with their doings and their harsh voices."

Jeff tried to grin.

"I'm pretty tired of them myself, my brother."

Gokhotit entered presently, having tethered the horse where it could crop the long dry grass of the meadow, which was entirely clear of snow. Jeff rested on the bearskin which covered his bed while the Indians roasted dried venison and made ash cakes. Then, drawing stools close to the bed, the three of them ate together, and the injured man had the better appetite for the company.

The little cabin was a pleasant place with its bright fire going and the comfort of the crude but well-designed furniture; Jeff tried to pronounce the name of the healer a number of times before he mastered it.

"It means Little Owl," Gokhotit explained with a grin. "When I was a small boy, there was a little owl, one with a big voice, close above me on a limb. I shot three arrows at him. Each time he would jump a little and chirp, for my arrows merely brushed his feathers. Then my father stopped the shooting, and I have been Gokhotit ever since."

"The medicines," Jeff queried. "How did you learn?"

The Indian had his pipe going and blew a cloud of acrid smoke. "Many men taught me, my father most of all. A white doctor down in Lancaster county employed me many years, and I learned from him. He was overfond of a bottle, and I did many things he directed me to when his hands were shaky."

He grinned and blew more smoke.

"So now I go up and down with my medicine bag. White folks who have no money and do not trust the powwow doctors call me in, and there are many sick among my own people. It's blackberry root for the little fellow with the stomachache and lose bowels, ladyslipper root for the woman whose nerves are bad, and I rub sore joints with rattlesnake oil."

Gokhotit stayed two days. Then he left to return the horse and to visit sick people east of the Susquehanna. The touchy matter of returning the horse seemed no problem to him. He gave full directions for the care of his patient to both Migun and Jeff.

"People, mostly white folks, get the habit of dying in bed, so move around as much as you can. Move, then rest a little. After eight days, put a little of your weight on the bad leg."

After he had ridden away, Jeff remembered that he had not even thanked the man, and, of course, he had nothing with which to pay him. Likely Fred had his tinderbox with both the gold coin and the shilling Migun had given him in it.

"Migun," he said bitterly to his friend, "how can I pay?"

"Who and what for?" the Delaware asked in some surprise, and Jeff pointed to him.

"You, Migun, you and Gokhotit, Pentz, Eli and others."

The Indian stopped cleaning his musket and laid down the ramrod.

"The Great Spirit has given gifts to some of us, white or red. It may be that we are allowed to give food and shelter; it may be healing or any sort of kindness. If we do not divide and serve, we lose our chance to use the Great Spirit's kindness. If we use these good gifts, we become like Him who is the giver of all."

Jeff lay back upon his bed, thinking hard. He had plenty to be bitter about, but there had been so many who were kind. Eli and John had been compelled to tie him up for Ribner's torture, but Eli had risked sending for help to save him from being crippled or killed.

For three days after the departure of Gokhotit, Jeff's condition improved rapidly. The balsam salve worked wonders with the cuts on his back and sides, and he learned to swing out of bed, put one knee on a stool and so get about the cabin fairly well. Migun had shot a small doe, solving the food problem. For hours, especially in the evening, the friends would sit before the fire, talking or sitting without speaking while the sparks leaped upward. Then came a cold rain, sheathing everything outside with a film of ice.

Migun could sit in the cabin well enough when he was not compelled to do so, but this confinement due to the ice irked him. So at dawn of the second morning following the freeze, he dressed Jeff's back carefully and prepared food for the day. Then he took his gun and went out into the icy wilderness.

Time dragged, and finally, Jeff eased himself out of the bunk. He could manage the injured leg pretty well. His main trouble was with a sharp stab of pain in his side when he twisted his body even a very little. Gokhotit thought a rib had been broken by Ribner's clubbing. This morning things went pretty well, and Jeff was suddenly hungry for a look out-of-doors as Migun had been. He persuaded himself that he should get some fresh water from the little spring at the edge of the porch.

From the open cabin door, he looked upon a world made into a fairyland of ice crystals. The evergreens bowed under winter burdens and sparkled m the thin sunlight. All twigs had trebled in size, and rocks and stumps had their outlines neatly rounded with ice film. Jeff, carrying the small wooden bucket, hobbled out on the porch. He had not put on extra clothing as the spring was only a few steps away.

Holding with one hand to the cabin log and to the wooden pail with the other, he took two hops toward the end of the porch. Then he slipped on the thin film of ice which covered the floor and came down full length, his injured side striking the pail.

His body must have slid off the end of the porch, for when he became conscious, he was lying in the shallow water of the spring. Each time he tried to move, savage pain brought a return of blackness until finally, he lay still, water freezing on his clothing.

Migun, returning, found him entirely helpless. Making no comment other than a clicking of his tongue, he dragged Jeff inside, stripped off his clothing, and wrapped him in a blanket. It was something of a job to boost a man as big as Jeff into the bed, but the Indian accomplished it, paying no attention to the patient when he yelled with pain. Afterward, he built up the fire until the cabin was as hot as the interior of an Indian medicine hut.

A well man might have exercised and conquered the effect of the exposure which he had undergone, but Jeff was too badly weakened from the brutal handling he had received. At nightfall, he had a rising fever; in the morning, he was delirious at times.

Migun worked to keep down recurring chills when the fever momentarily let up. In the afternoon, the Indian talked soberly.

"This is what Gokhotit feared, Jeff. You have lung fever, and we must get help. Tonight I go over the hills for Peter Grube."

He helped Jeff from the bed to a pile of skins by the fireplace, where he placed wood, food, and water in his friend's reach. With that all finished and dressed for his trip, Migun kneeled at his sick friend's side,

"My brother has suffered much in mind and body. But it comes to Migun, whose mother was a reader of dreams, that his friend with the big hands is needed by people. So he cannot die until his work is finished."

He left as quietly as he had spoken, leaving Jeff to wonder about the odd prophecy. At the moment, he, Jeff Claus, was tormented by fever, sore of body and mind, but the Indian's voice had been sure.

The night passed in a succession of chills, fever, and wild fancies. He saw Abigail Ribner coming toward him smiling. From her hand trailed a long whip which she lifted slowly. Jeff screamed.

The fire burned down to coals and tiny wisps of flame. He lay on his well side. There was another ache, a heavy, dull throbbing between his shoulder blades. No wind stirred the trees outside, It was very still, and it did not seem worthwhile to put more wood on the fire. He tried to think of Migun's last words but could not remember exactly what they had been.

He may have slept. At any rate, a gust of wind and snow driving into his face roused him. The cabin door was open, and Jeff had a vague notion that he should crawl over and close it. Then there were voices, one of them surely a woman's. Migun's cold hands were on his shoulders now, and he was calling:

"Jeff, Jeff."

The sick man tried to shape his lips into a smile while strong hands slid under him and lifted him back on the bed. Liquor was trickled through chill, clenched teeth by a huge man who stood over him, shutting away the lanthorn light.

"Coming round," a heavy voice boomed. "Get the broth heated, Faith."

In another half hour, strengthened by liquor and broth, the patient was sitting up, recognizing the big man as Peter Grube and the slim, smiling woman as his wife, Faith.

"She would come," Grube explained. "Said men are too clumsy with sick folks."

Her voice answering his gibe was low and vibrant.

"He ought to say that, Jeffry. I brought him through the lung fever, big and stubborn as he is when he's sick."

In spite of a foot of loose snow that carpeted the woodland in the morning, they left Migun's cabin. Mistress Grube had bandaged Jeff's side with a long strip of linen cloth, and they had rolled him into a veritable cocoon of blankets.

There were horses. Faith rode beside the sick man, Migun led the way, and Grube brought up the rear. The animals were surefooted beasts like those of Uncle Mark's pack train, and it was good they were because the going was rough. Jeff was almost exhausted when they crossed the river on the ice. Ahead, beyond a long brushy slope, a "U"-shaped cove pushed back into the timbered northern hills. To the east, beyond the mountain which bounded the open land, a great creek could occasionally be seen through openings in the timber which lined it.

The cavalcade came to a halt before a huge sprawling house built of stone and squared timbers. Back of this was a barn and many outbuildings. Grube dismounted and lifted Jeff's blanket-swathed form from the saddle.

"Welcome to Travelome," he boomed. "I'll carry you over the threshold like a new bride."

Pushing open the door with his shoulder, he called:

"Susan, got that room ready?"

A girl's voice answered. Grube carried his burden along a hallway and then into a sunny room, where he deposited Jeff on a rawhide-laced cot.

"Now, son," he promised. "The women and I will get to work on you."

In the next few days, Jeff mended rapidly under the good care he received. Faith Grube was the nurse, easing his side with bandages, anointing the sore back with salves, and seeing that there was always a pillow under the broken leg. Like Gokhotit, on the first sign of recovery, she had her patient sitting up and moving as much as he could.

"People die in bed," she insisted, and Jeffry grinned, remembering that was almost exactly what the Indian doctor had claimed.

The second day of his arrival was the big one for Jeff. A girl's figure passed the door, and Faith called:

"Come, see our patient, Susan."

She entered shyly, seeming quite different from the girl on the ferry and the one who had visited Ribner post that day. She gave her hand to Jeff a little diffidently and smiled. Her arms, with the sleeves rolled high upon them, were softly rounded, and her bosom swelled under the white kerchief she wore, Quaker fashion. But, sick as he was, Jeff's eyes were mainly for her hair, the rich color of late corn silk before the frost blackens it. Today she had the mass of it braided, and the braids were wound about her small head. Her eyes were deeply blue and looked frankly into Jeff's cold ones. She curtsied lightly.

"I'm glad to see you," he said inanely, and then for no reason excepting that he was embarrassed, he muttered a German expression, and she replied quickly:

"There's no need for the tongue, sir. I speak good English even if Peter does laugh at me sometimes."

She smiled understandingly at Faith as though the two understood each other very well and indicated that she knew that the young, unshaven man on the bed was embarrassed. From that moment on, she ran in often for a few minutes at a time, and Jeff would watch for her visits. All the other members of the Grube household came in, as well, including Harriet, the colored cook who reminded Jeff of Clara, and her husband, Charley, a tall, thin black man.

One day after Jeff was getting about on crutches, Grube came in and sat down to talk a while.

"You're a good man with horses, Jeff. I saw that on Bower Samuels' ferry and that day when you shod the 'wall eye' at Ribner's."

"That shoe had been pulled off," Jeff said with a grin, and the big man laughed.

"I thought you saw the pincer marks when you got to work. I wanted an excuse to look about the place, and Susan said she wanted to give you a little warning, something we had talked about here at home. Susan's a kind girl, even if she has half the boys about her dangling from her apron strings with no mercy for any."

He frowned and pretended not to notice the disturbance on Jeff's countenance at this talk of Susan and her friends.

"Well, Jeff, your hurts will be mended come time to travel. Now I do a little trading. Maybe I could hire you when you can work."

Since his beating, Jeff had lived in a world dominated by pain, and it was enough to try to get well. Now he looked directly at this man to whom he already owed so much, then down at the floor. Here was an opportunity, just like Bower Samuels had offered. But he was a bond-servant with years of labor ahead before he could make a free choice. At this moment, his was the status of a runaway. He answered Grube bitterly:

"I'd like that fine, sir, nothing better. But, in time, they'll take me back to Ribner."

Grube frowned again and took time to light his pipe. When it was going well, he leaned back in his chair.

"Jeffry, suppose you tell me your full story. I'm a good listener. Start with your home in Germany."

"England it was, sir, I—"

Grube interrupted with a wave of his big hand.

"No 'sirs,' if you please. Here at Travelome, we are Faith, Susan, and Peter. To these, we now add Jeffry."

Jeff smiled. There was that about this man which invited confidence, and presently he was talking freely. Grube's pipe went out because he followed the tale so closely, and he interrupted just once with a question.

"If Squire Fell was so sure Ribner was a Tory, why didn't he arrest him?"

Jeff shook his head.

"I don't know, but the squire has to have everything legal before he acts."

Grube gestured with his cold pipe.

"I'll not say Ribner's crooked, but he's a friend of the 'higher-ups' which takes in Colonel Hunter, commandant of all this region. Fell would need to have real evidence. Now that musket business puzzles me. Where did he get them? Of course, the Indians are great travelers. They could have brought them down from British Niagara. Could be the Wyoming folks who do not love us about here could have sold them. There are more rotten things on the frontier than the buzzards find."

Jeff studied. He had thought a lot about those muskets. By now, he believed they had gone to Tories somewhere rather than to Indians, though they would have received some of them. At Grube's signal, he continued his story and finished it. The listener rose and walked to the window. Then he turned back to the door and pulled it shut.

"You've left a lot out, Jeff. Remember, news travels fast in a sparsely settled country. You couldn't have a peacock in Fort Augusta and keep it secret for a week. All the woods runners would have come down for a look. Would Henry Ribner beat a valuable servant nigh to death without a strong reason? When a lovely lady with fine dresses and a wandering eye comes to our backcountry, it's real news."

He worked a moment with his tinderbox, relighting his pipe.

"Yes, Jeff, the woman had something to do with it, and I'm agreed with Squire Fell that you've made something of a fool of yourself. I'll take your word the colored girl came to your bed; she was just bait. But when a cold-blooded fish like Ribner goes on the warpath with a whip, then I remember Abigail Ribner and the light in her eyes."

Jeff's face colored, and Grube shook his shaggy head.

"I'm thinking you had some of that beating coming to you. But young men are young men. I remember an Indian girl long, long ago who had midnight in her hair, warmth in her hands, and eyes that had me dizzy for a time. Also, there was a tavern woman—"

He frowned, broke off his reminiscence, and struck his hands together in emphasis.

"Never mind the women. I'm sure if you went back, Ribner would kill you—by inches if he could. He couldn't forgive what he either knows or suspects. But you could fit in on this river, for there'll be Seneca raids come spring. Colonel Hunter wants us all out of here. He says he cannot defend us, though so far, he hasn't tried. We'll need every man, and you're a smith and a godsend."

Jeff frowned but nodded. Grube went on:

"We have to put our rifles in shape. You could do that. As to their coming after you, this is Fair Play country, and they won't take too big risks. It might be possible to buy your indenture, though I doubt that. Also, there is a law about brutal treatment of indentured persons. However, we of this country would have a hard time in Northumberland courts. Under the law, we cannot settle here. It's Indian country, and every man of us who built a cabin north of the Susquehanna and west of the Lycoming is subject to a five hundred pound fine and one year in prison. So far, they haven't meddled with us, that is, the regular colony courts and the new state is too busy with the war to bother. Fair Play Men we call ourselves. There is no law up here but from our Committee."

He rose swiftly.

"I've talked too much. Just think things over and don't worry. Faith says you're bothered about your keep here. God almighty, son, you're a godsend, something to think about. There'll be no going back to Ribner. That is one fact we understand."

Susan brought Jeff some broth a while later, and he smiled as he took the bowl from her small, firm hands.

"Did you ever see a lazier man than I am?" he queried. "One that just sits around and eats."

"Oh, yes, I have," she declared with enthusiasm. "My mother's Uncle Daniel was like that, and he lived so long everybody was tired but him, I guess."

They both laughed, for there had been no sting in her remark. He liked the tiny wrinkles that formed about her eyes, and, today, her hair was dressed more loosely about her face, making her look less prim.

Grube returned when Susan, carrying the emptied bowl, had left. "I forgot. The thing that really bothers me is the Ben Haider and Ktemque mess. A white man is dead. Maybe he wasn't where he belonged. But there's an Indian dead, and the Senecas would be glad for a blood feud now that there's a market for scalps in British forts. And they know we're weak in the valley. All the young men are off to war excepting a dozen or so."

He scowled.

"Migun buried what was left of Pentz's roast Indian, but the fire didn't hide the hole in the redskin's head. Some other Indian may have seen the dead man. Pentz is just too damned careless. He can kill all the Senecas he wants, but he ought to bury his dead and hide the graves so even a hungry wolf can't find them."

CHAPTER IX

JEFF WAS getting about well with the aid of a crude crutch when the ever-restless Migun returned from one of his trips downriver. He brought with him a printed placard which he boasted he had stolen from the common room of an inn close to Fort Augusta. The entire Grube household gathered about Peter as he read it aloud:

> Run away from the subscriber, Henry Ribner, of the county of Northumberland on January twenty-eighth, 1776, a bondservant named Jeffry Claus. Born of German parentage in England, he speaks the mother tongue with no accent and is, by trade, a gunsmith. He is six feet high, black-haired, and complected but has blue eyes.
>
> He had on when he ran away a brown woolen shirt, leather breeches, woolen stockings, and moccasins. The described bondsman is a saucy fellow and has a scarred back. In addition to the reward fixed by law in such instances, whoever secures the described runaway shall have five pounds sterling. The said Jeffry Claus can be dangerous with his hands though he has no weapon. The reward will be paid on delivery of the runaway either to the subscriber or the nearest magistrate.

When Grube finished, Jeff sat quietly in his chair, poking at the puncheon floor with the tip of his crutch. "Five pounds . . . dangerous fellow . . . So Ribner would pay hard money for a further chance to rip the life out of him with a whip. His eyes narrowed and turned cold as he got to his feet, propping himself with his crutch.

"No need for him to waste his money," he said slowly as if the words were forced out. "When I can walk, I'll go back to him—" His throat tightened so he could not speak, and his hands knotted. He was thinking of the trader's triumphant face in Fell's office when the Melody trap was sprung and of the same face twisted satanically in the candle-lighted shop before the whip began to flay. Nothing mattered but getting back there and taking that wrinkled throat in his hands. Still holding the placard, Grube placed his arm across the younger man's shoulders.

"No, not the way you mean. Don't throw your life away by killing the man. Fell thinks there is more to the whole affair than meets the eye, but he's helpless. Now you know too much about the post: Indians spending gold, British officers at night, the liquor, and the muskets. Your life wouldn't be worth a musket ball. It would be easy to represent killing you as a defense against a vicious servant. No, stay here. Let Fell look into things and find out why you were bought in the first place."

Faith stepped over to Jeff's other side and put her slim fingers on his crutch while her husband continued:

"Up here, you can be of real use, as I told you. One of these days, the Senecas will swoop down with hatchets and fire. You can put our guns in shape, and you'll be another rifle."

While Jeff had been sick, Grube had put the workshop, built against the side of the barn, in good order. It was well supplied with tools, and there was a small forge. After his talk following the reading of Ribner's advertisement, he took Jeff out there. On successive days the young man puttered about putting the tools in place. That done, he had Grube bring in every firearm and all other weapons for an overhauling. He sharpened knives and axes, made ramrods for the guns, installed new flints, and cleaned the bores. Peter's pet rifle, a short big-bored weapon, had a broken stock. Jeff found a piece of old walnut and restocked the rifle. Grube whistled softly when he handled the weapon.

"You're a real workman, son. That gun comes up like my arm. This is a country of riflemen, and we can surely use every minute you can give us."

Jeff turned to the bench and then looked back to ask his question.

"Peter, do the women know about—"

Grube's face crinkled about his eyes, and he passed his big hand over the smooth wood of the new stock.

"About the women, you mean, Jeff? Both of them know about the black girl in your room; mind you, it was your room. Faith knows you must have tangled with the Ribner woman, and I'm never sure how much she tells Susan. But, Jeff, there's a kind of fascination to a good woman about a man that's kind of got himself singed by the devil."

He tucked the gun under his arm, picked up a drawshave, and tested its edge with his thumb.

"Faith's a grown woman and wiser than you or I would ever guess. Likely she understands a lot of things. Now, this Susan girl—well, she might get the notion you were a bit too fond of bait."

That afternoon, Jeff made a butter mold for the prints Faith made. It would stamp a star on them. For Susan, he fashioned a big mixing spoon from dry maple. Both pieces were smoothed with a bit of sandstone. Faith was very pleased, but Susan took her spoon with perfunctory thanks.

Winter relaxed its grip with occasional snowstorms that turned to freezing rain. The more open weather brought to Travelome settlers who had learned of the presence of a smith. Each had some piece of broken equipment, from log chains to rifles. One bearded man who lived down the creek close to the river wanted stocks made for his pistol. Then he sheepishly pulled a small buckskin-wrapped packet from his pocket. It contained a cameo pin split through the middle.

"My woman sets store by that picture thing," he explained. "She ain't much for crying, but she broke down when it fell on the door stone and cracked. Could you figger to fix it?"

Jeff turned the little thing about in his big fingers. The crack left the face of the ornament intact. It was split diagonally from the edge of the face across the back. He knew such stones were carved with a spade and that the material was fairly soft. He had among his tools an Indian woman's drill for making wampum from shells. Grube had picked it up somewhere. Now, for a drill point, he fitted a piece of sewing needle with the point filed flat.

"You ought to have a squaw drill this," he told the watching man whose eyes followed the little bow as it whirled the drill point. Jeff worked carefully, trying to bore a smooth, even hole. When he had each piece ready, he fitted a tiny dowel of wire and smeared a thin film of glue on the broken edges, pressing them together. When he had carefully wiped off bits of glue, he split a small piece of dry hickory part way through and inserted the cameo to pinch it fast.

"There," he said, "just let that wood on till the glue sets."

"Well, I'll be damned," the settler said softly. "My woman'll be mightily pleased."

Susan appeared just then to call Jeff to dinner, and the bearded man stepped toward her, holding the cameo on his broad palm.

"Lookya here, miss, at what your young man fixed."

He dropped the stone and its splint into her palm just as she started to say with spirit:

"He's not my—"

Looking down at the jewel, the girl pursed her lips, and there was a suspicious gleam in her eyes.

"It's real pretty," she told the man, "and your wife will be glad to wear it again though I do think our smith does better mending horseshoes."

Jeff followed her through the passageway to the house. When her thumb was on the kitchen door latch, she turned swiftly and put out the tip of her red tongue at him. Then she whispered: "He said 'your young man.' You're not my anything."

She was going through the door and probably did not hear Jeff's rejoinder:

"Not yet."

So long as he had been sick and needing care, Susan had shared with Faith every duty their kindness and patience suggested. But after he could get about, she had been sharp with him as she had been just now. He liked to watch her at work. She was usually humming softly some old German song, the words of which were vaguely familiar to him. Also, he liked to see her walk, her small shoulders held squarely and her rounded hips twitching as though she wished to break into a run. Once, at the table, when Peter was indulging in a long grace, Jeff raised his head a little so he could watch the crown of bright hair on the girl's head. Suddenly she lifted her head and caught his look. He knew that when she looked down again at her plate, she was laughing at him, and he could not keep his ears from turning scarlet.

This year spring came almost suddenly in the great valley of the West Branch of the Susquehanna. First, the maples were scarlet torches against the drabness of the woodland. Then came the tufted buds of the willows breaking as if glad to be free of the restraint of winter. Jeff's leg was sound enough again to permit him to go up the little stream which watered the cove to try his luck with the speckled trout. He brought back a good string of them together with a huge bunch of fragrant arbutus and some frail anemones. These spring gifts he took into the kitchen where Susan was at work. She was delighted, turning over the brightly colored fish with a small forefinger and then sinking her face into the flagrant bouquet. When she looked up again, Jeff saw a tear in the corner of her eye.

"Susan," he said clumsily, "you are crying, and you should be glad."

She nodded and wiped her eyes vigorously with the corner of her apron. She sniffed loudly and ungracefully.

"That's why," she said illogically. "It's because things are so good here, not like they were in the old country. Here I am not a servant but just like a daughter."

Jeff frowned.

"Yes, Susan, you were lucky to find a home like this, and you fit into it as well as their daughter would if they had one."

When her features relaxed, she seemed to realize Jeff's position in contrast to her own, and there was pity in her eyes.

"But you," she started, and he interrupted her bitterly:

"Yes, I'm just property. Any man that takes me back to my owner would have five pounds for his trouble. That's as much as a laboring man earns in a year. You saw my back when I was sick and know what will happen when Ribner gets his hands on me again."

Impulsively, she put her small hand on his big, work-hardened fingers.

"But Jeffry, you will not go back. You will stay with these good folks. They are kind."

"Noboby knows that better than I do," he countered, "but you saw the paper Migun brought back; I am a runaway. Every day of freedom means five more of bondage. I see no light; there is no answer."

His voice went higher as he talked, and she drew away her fingers.

"I see no answer either. But I know it does no good to fight too much. If you go back and that man is killed, with blood on your hands, you will never be free."

Impatiently, Jeff turned to the door and walked out. Faith, entering the kitchen minutes later, found Susan crying. The older woman slipped her arm about the girl's shoulders.

"I heard the last of what you said, Susan, and it's right. He must not go back. This Jeffry is so much like my Peter was when he was younger. He would kill if the lash touched him again, just as Peter would do in the same fix. We must keep the boy here with us."

She turned up the girl's face and looked into her eyes.

"Susan," she said softly, "do you—"

The girl drew away so she could reach her small handkerchief in her apron pocket.

"I don't know," she answered the unfinished query. "If only he was not so—"

She interrupted herself, reluctant to speak her mind, and suddenly found a way to change the subject.

"The bread. Faith," she cried. "It must go into the oven right away."

Grube entered the shop late that afternoon when Jeff was working at a gun. Seeing the big man, the smith spoke impatiently:

"Peter, what this damn gun needs is to have the rifling freshened and a new bullet mold. I wish I had the tools Uncle Mark wanted me to have. There was a little cutter old Ely down at Shatway gave me; with that, a man could deepen rifling by hand if he was careful."

"You're a mechanic," Grube said. "Couldn't you make one?"

Jeff shook his head emphatically.

"No, I'm not fixed to work steel that hard even if I had some. That cutter is down there in Ribner's shop in a box with some other little tools. If I had it, I could improve every rifle in these parts."

Grube picked up the offending gun, squinted through the sights, and laid it down.

"No doubt you could, Jeff, no doubt, and I know what's in the back of your mind. Stick your nose down there, and there'll be real grief. I can't help thinking there's more back of your troubles than any of us sees, and the reward troubles me. There are a lot of poor men to whom five pounds in hard money would be a fortune. They might be sorry for you, but money talks. Listen, Jeff, I start for the Sinnamahoning country tomorrow, and I want you along. I have goods for some traders up that way: Beniel Sherrod at Young Woman's Creek. Cathcart on the Sinnamahoning and for Brady above Quinn's Run. These men will have fall-dug ginseng for me and maybe a few skins."

The prospect of going out with a pack train delighted Jeff and made him think of the good days with Uncle Mark Fultz. He helped pack the bundles of strouding cloth, the beads, the paint, powder in gill packages, and the inevitable handful of jews'-harps. There was also a small clock and a tiny music box.

"A man can make a real deal for those toys," Grube claimed. "Never saw an Indian that could resist either of them. One time a fellow on the Tiadaghton tried to trade his squaw for a music box."

When they were all ready to start at daybreak, Peter went into the house for a last word with Faith while Jeff paced up and down, flexing his leg, which seemed as good as it had ever been. When he turned, Susan stood in the kitchen doorway, a loose robe wrapped about her small body, her heavy hair in long braids hanging down before her shoulders. In three strides, Jeff was beside her.

"Where is Peter?" she asked lamely. Then his long arms were about her, and her eyes widened. There was no reason in him, only hunger as he swept her close. His impatient lips found her mouth. For a moment, she was stiff and cold. Then her bare arms emerged from the robe, linked themselves about his neck, and her lips answered. For a long moment, they clung together. Finally, she freed herself and pushed back her loosened hair. Her sudden anger was just as complete as her momentary yielding had been.

"I am glad you go away. You are a bad man, Jeffry Claus, you and the women downriver. It gives nothing—"

Her small fists drummed against his chest in angry emphasis.

"It gives nothing between us, ever."

Heavy braids swinging, the robe flapping about her bare ankles, she fled indoors, and Jeff stood as breathless as though he had been running.

His temples throbbed. He knew, with full force, that he would give everything he would ever own, including his freedom, to have this girl with her warm lips, her sudden tempers, and her loyalties.

The pack train moved out along the well-trodden pack trail up the broad valley of the West Branch. Peter, riding a roan mare, led with three stocky pack animals tied head to tail behind him. Jeff, on a rangy black gelding, brought up the rear. They moved easily, letting the pack animals have their time. The outfit was very like Uncle Mark's, only smaller, and his horses had worn little bells.

As they moved a little to the north of west, the valley narrowed where the big river crowded a line of high hills. Occasionally from their path, they could see the smoke from chimneys of widely scattered cabins. At midafternoon they passed the Great Island, where the creek Grube called Bald Eagle entered the river. Peter stopped the train and pointed out landmarks while they lounged in their saddles.

"The main Shamokin Path goes up the Bald Eagle and hits the river again at the Indian village of Chickalamoose where it forks. The south branch goes to Kittanning, the other straight west."

Jeff told Peter he had been in the village of Kittanning and grinned as the big man waved his arm in an expansive gesture.

"That's white man's country, Jeff. Look at the level acres on the island, and it's only an Indian hangout. Good land's wasted on the savages."

He shrugged his heavy shoulders.

"It's away beyond the purchase line. This is all Indian country beyond the Lycoming to hell and gone. Remember, Jeff, we farmers up here in the Fair Play country are really outlaws. The Penn people would have been glad to burn us out like they did to the folks down Bedford way."

He chuckled deep in his throat.

"Only the Penn sheriffs were slow to come up and run us out. Oh yes, Northumberland officers come up sometimes to round up a criminal, and we're glad to get rid of people like that. But when it comes to chasing us out, they sing low and small."

The trail presently wound around the base of high cliffs, and they could look across to a cluster of cabins which Grube called "Fort Reed." They camped for the night in a great natural meadow the trader called "Muncy Flats."

It was very comfortable that night with the horse string grazing close by and a soft breeze drifting dovm river. Peter did most of the talking. Jeff sat, listening and watching the sparks from the fire lift into the air then vanish against the curtain of darkness. It was all very like traveling with Uncle Mark. He suddenly missed Migun.

"You know, Jeff," Grube explained, "it isn't the value of the trade that brings me up here. I like to keep in touch with things up river. The Indians use the trail across the river. They usually camp at Young Woman's Creek, and there's always a half dozen lodges on the first fork of the Sinnamahoning. I keep thinking they'll strike down through here one of these days. If I was the British commandant at Niagara, I'd figure where to hit. They could come down over the hills and hit the Sinnamahoning. From there, it would be straight canoe travel. Or they could come southeast across the Iroquois country along the Gohocton River, then the Chemung, and down the North Branch of this river. The Wyoming country over there would be richer in scalps for the red devils."

Jeff felt only a mild interest in Peter's concern, but he tried to be polite about it.

"You're sure they'll strike somewhere sometime?"

Peter rose and tapped the ashes from his pipe.

"Yes, Jeff, I'm as sure of that as I am that old Beniel Sherrod'll try to chisel a little when we trade tomorrow or the day after." After he had checked the horses carefully, Jeff rolled into his blanket and lay down beside Peter, who was soon snoring. He did not sleep for a long time, thinking of Susan. He had held her close, had found the sweetness in her, but she had drawn away.

"Women down river," she had said scornfully, and there had been finality in her voice. Jeff remembered Abigail Ribner suddenly, her tempting mouth, the perfume, and the warmth of her lips and body. She had said he could never forget her. It irked him to find that true even now when he wanted to think only of Susan.

After an hour, he sat up and listened to the little tearing noises made by the horses as they pulled at the grass. Occasionally they stamped their hoofs. But there seemed to be something else out there in the darkness, a shifting of shadowy masses as if some presence moved there.

The animals, however, showed no uneasiness. He lay down again and, this time, slept.

In the morning, they climbed the hills into the pine woods and rode for hours in the seemingly endless, shaded stillness of the forest. The footfalls of the iron-shod horses made no sound on the deep, century-old accumulation of pine needles. The country finally got on Jeff's nerves, and Peter noticed it.

"This shadow country does get you, Jeff, but we'll be out of it in honest sunlight before long. This is mighty good country to get lost in. Even the redskins stick to the streams when they travel. Mebbe the shadows get on their nerves if the damned hellions have nerves."

They emerged finally on the wide, deep-running creek Peter called "Young Woman's" and turned southward after they had forded it. From a low rise and across a clearing a quarter of a mile ahead, they caught a glimpse of the river into which the big creek emptied.

The two men were now riding side by side. The pack horses followed and made considerable noise, crowding through the bushes. Suddenly, Peter reined back his horse and caught Jeff's bridle rein.

"Smoke," he whispered. Jeff caught the odor, the slight acrid taint of burned logs.

"Beniel's cabin," Peter whispered. "That's logs, not a campfire."

Without further talk, they slid from their mounts and tied them. Then with rifles ready, they moved forward cautiously. Presently they reached the edge of a natural clearing, perhaps an acre in extent. Near the woods where a spring broke out of the bank was a pile of charred logs with wisps of smoke lifting from some of them.

Ten minutes of careful scouting through the brush fringe of the opening assured both men there was nothing alive in the vicinity. Yet Peter directed Jeff to cover him with his rifle when he stepped into the open and walked to where the cabin had stood.

"Beniel Sherrod's place, all right," he said. "Burned maybe early yesterday morning."

The charred embers yielded no further information. Jeff left his companion and scouted down to the river. Beyond it, a huge mountain loomed, so high its shadow reached a quarter of the way across the moving water. He looked at it for a while and was about to return to his companion when his quick eye caught sight of a stave broken from a keg. The odor of rum still lingered on it.

"Yes," Peter said when Jeff gave him his find. "That was a rum keg. Beniel always had some of it. Likely the savages learned of the liquor and came down like flies for molasses. When he wouldn't give them any, they wiped him out."

He rubbed his chin carefully and passed the stave from one big hand to the other.

"I can't see, though, how they trapped Beniel. I warned him, but he always figured he could take care of himself. Now, likely, his hair is marching north to Little Beard's town on the Genesee. An Indian won't waste a scalp, war or no war."

Before dark, they scoured the area of the clearing again without result. They camped for the night up the creek, where an opening permitted the horses to graze on the creek bottom grass.

The night reminded Jeff of the one at Muncy Flat. Peter did not seem uneasy. He fell asleep shortly after he had wrapped himself in his blanket and lain down. But, again, Jeff was restless. So it was that he awoke later than he had planned. Peter was stretched on his back, snoring lustily when Jeff sat up in his blanket. High on a ridge top to the east, a thin sliver of morning light showed, and there was movement close by.

He threw back the blanket and stood up quietly. He could hear their horses walking steadily as they might on the trail rather than just tramping about as they grazed. Jeff stooped and touched Peter's shoulder, awakening the big man at once.

"Our horses," he whispered, "moving."

It was still too dark for rifles. As the two white men buckled on their belts, they could hear the steady tramping of the herd moving up along the creek. Once, Indians had attempted to steal Uncle Mark's pack string, so Jeff understood what was going on. One savage would be riding the lead horse, and his companions would be driving the others from the rear. Peter had shipped his limber-hafted war ax from its loop on his belt. Jeff snatched up a heavy oaken cudgel which he had been whittling the previous evening.

"Circle them," Peter directed. "Take their lead man. I'll manage the rest."

Whatever noise Peter and Jeff made in following was probably drowned out by the sound of the horses. Morning light was breaking fast. When he sighted the dark-moving mass, which would be the thieves and their booty, Jeff swung to the left and circled, coming out close to the creek. The horses approached at a smart walk, and he could see the dark bulk of the leading rider. Standing in the heavy shadow of a tree, he waited. As the first animal passed him, he leaped out and struck. The rider toppled from his seat as though poleaxed. At the same moment, from the rear of the herd came a startled yell of pain. When Jeff got there, Peter had another Indian down on his back and was throttling him.

"Jeff?" Peter hissed. When he was answered, the big man stood up.

"Only two of 'em. I got this one choked. Let's get these red boys and our horses back to the clearing."

It was fairly light by the time they had thrown the two Indians across horses and had moved back to the clearing where Beniel's cabin had stood. Their captives, now coming back to consciousness, were a hard-faced savage who reminded Jeff of Ktemque and a boy probably in his late teens. Peter tied them up swiftly.

Grube's methods were undoubtedly rough. When he had finished knotting the thongs on his prisoners, he dragged them both against the base of a tree.

"Now," he said to Jeff, "let's eat breakfast. We can kill these woods lice later."

Jeff built the fire, and the two white men took their time making ash cakes and toasting meat over the coals. Both ate heartily, sitting where their captives could observe every movement. When they finished, they saddled the horses, put the packs in place, and were ready for the trail.

Peter strode over to the prisoners and stood looking down at them. With slow movements, he slipped his ax back into its loop and drew his knife, a long broad-bladed weapon. He tested the edge carefully with his thumb. At his gesture, Jeff approached and drew the younger savage aside.

"My brother has an evil spirit in him," Grube said. The savage's eyes showed he understood English. "He steals horses. With this knife, I will open his belly and let the spirit out."

He bent over and pricked the Indian's naked belly with the point of the bright weapon, drawing a scream of fright and pain.

"Ah," Peter said, "it is a strong devil. Did it lead my Indian brother to burn this little house?"

The captive's eyes followed the gesture toward the charred logs, and he shook his head vigorously. Peter kneeled beside him and used the knife again. But all he could get from the man were yells of fear. There was none of the vaunted Indian stoicism about the captive. Between cries, he babbled something earnestly. Grube stood up and turned to Jeff.

"Can't understand the damned cuss. Let's cut them loose." The moment their bonds were off, both men ran for it, disappearing in the brush. Grube gathered up their weapons and pitched them into the creek. Then he swore savagely.

"I'd like to have put a bullet through that old bird. He looks bad to me. But a dead Indian on the river would almost be as bad as pulling a trigger on the home folks."

Jeff spoke of his feelings the night they spent on Muncy Flat, and Grube resorted to the familiar gesture of scratching his chin.

"Could be these boys followed us. They'd make as good time on foot as we with the horses. Anyway, I don't think they had aught to do with Beniel or his cabin. They were just horse hungry, and they'd have made a big splash in their home place if they'd rid' in on our stock. Next to guns and rum, these red hellions like horses."

Jeff made no comment. He was thinking of the sudden ferocity exhibited by this usually kind man. There had been no doubt in his mind that Peter would have used his knife. No wonder the Indian had been convinced.

CHAPTER X

A GRIM and unusually taciturn Peter Grube led the pack train through the morning and part of the afternoon. The route followed was like that below the Young Woman's Creek before they had taken to the pine lands. In spite of the fact that he had recovered his horses, Grube apparently was chagrined that the savages had come so close to getting his livestock and trade goods. Now he took no chances and neglected no precaution. Close to another creek, they found old dead campfire ashes. When they crossed the stream, Peter went first, directing Jeff to cover him with a rifle. As Jeff crossed with the other horses, Grube stood with ready weapon.

The two men rode side by side now for a while, and Peter talked, "Likely they had their eyes on us all the way from Great Island. What I want to know is whether they're after horses or scalps. We won't know 'till we've found what became of Beniel. He knew all the hiding places and was as wary as an old tom turkey."

Jeff offered a suggestion.

"Maybe he was up at Cathcart's, and his place was burned when he was away."

Peter nodded in partial agreement.

"That could be. Ed's cabin's not too far ahead. But Ed's touchy about the current squaw with whom he's living, and he wouldn't welcome Beniel too much. Ed has a whetstone quarry that he keeps a secret. Once a year, he brings a canoe load downriver. The rest of the time, he sells to Indians. Still and all, Beniel might have gone up just to bedevil Ed. He's like that at times."

Another half hour's travel brought them to where the mountains swung back from the river in a great arc. Peter pointed.

"Cathcart's place is up there, back from the river on the bluff. There's a good spring—"

A sound from up ahead, like the slapping of two boards together, stopped Grube before he could finish his sentence. Both men reined in their mounts.

"Musket," Jeff muttered. Then the sound came a second and a third time. The fourth report was different, more like the breaking of a dry stick.

"That's a rifle," Peter said grimly. "There's a fight on. Let's get rid of the horses."

Grube evidently knew the country well, for he located a hemlock-shaded hollow where they tied the animals securely and, at Jeff's suggestion, fed them their grain ration.

"Keep them from fussing around," he told Peter, who agreed.

Each man looked carefully to his weapons. Then they moved forward in the direction where Peter had indicated the cabin stood. The timber thinned, and in a minute or so, they looked out over a clearing perhaps three acres in area. Here was a small strip of tilled land, and beyond it, standing out in the open, a cabin of peeled logs. Earth had been banked along its sides almost up to the bases of the small slotlike windows. As they came in sight of it, the rifle cracked again, and smoke showed at one of these window openings.

Jeff and Peter had dropped prone. A good hundred yards from them was a log, probably abandoned in the building operations, and there was movement back of it. Jeff watched. He saw the tip of a bright feather and pointed it out to Grube.

"Drive him out," Peter directed. "I'll get him in the open."

Jeff steadied his rifle and held the copper sight he had fashioned from a penny at the top of the log. When his gun cracked, the bullet tore splinters. An Indian leaped up and sprinted for the shelter of the woods. Grube swung the barrel of his rifle as if leading a running deer. When the weapon cracked, the runner pitched forward in a half somersault and lay still. Both men reloaded rapidly.

Minutes passed while they watched. Nothing more showed in the clearing. There was no sound.

"Well," Grube said, "let's go on in."

Jeff had drawn his pistol where they had lain. As they walked forward into the open, he carried his rifle in one hand and the pistol in the other preparatory to thrusting it back into his belt. He was a little to the side and partly behind Peter when he saw the movement in the brush. With one frantic bound, he knocked Grube aside with his shoulder a split second before the musket roared. Then Jeff's pistol flared.

The Indian who had stolen up behind them still stood erect with his hands pressed against his chest as Jeff lifted his rifle. Then, as though very tired, the savage's knees buckled, and he fell in a crumpled heap. Grube stared for a long moment before speaking solemnly.

"I'm getting old, Jeff. First the horses, now this."

The cabin door had opened, and a tall, buckskin-clad figure, straight as an arrow, walked toward them. The man wore a broad grin on his smoothly-shaven face.

"Beniel," Peter cried. "What goes on here? Jeff, this is Beniel Sherrod. So they burnt you out day before yesterday?"

Sherrod shook his head while his eyes searched around the clearing.

"No, that was close to four days past. If you saw smoke, it's them oak logs'll smolder a week or more."

There was relief on the man's thin, sharp features, but his eyes were still searching as he continued:

"There was three of 'em. I got one early this morning when they first hit. They kilt Ed close to a week back. His woman came down to tell me, and I come up, found Ed, and buried him. After that, I hung around while she fixed to pull out. They hit just after daybreak this morning."

Peter looked at the man thoughtfully and then led the way to the dead Indians. Again, two of them were little more than half-grown boys. The one Jeff had shot was a mature warrior who wore a fox skin fastened to his belt. Beniel pointed to him.

"He's been down to my place. That's just a little fox skin. Wanted to trade me English shillings for some rum."

"Yes," Peter growled, "it's you and your damned rum to blame. You know better." The woodsman only grinned.

"I had that rum for a purpose. Some of the river Indians have a lump of silver now and then, and I was saving a little keg to buy if any showed up. The fellow I wanted was called Ktemque, but he ain't been about lately."

Neither Peter nor Jeff volunteered any information as to how the Seneca had died. Beniel jerked his shoulder toward the cabin.

"She says this aint a reg'lar war party. Ktemque and this foxtailed bird jest had some boys with them when they was prowling about looking for deviltry. They burnt my place for rum and jumped Ed for God knows what. He wasn't scalped."

They were still talking but had moved a little closer to the cabin when the Indian woman, carrying a bundle on her back, emerged. She stopped when Peter called to her.

"I go," she said sullenly when they asked her what she was about to do. Peter gestured toward the dead savage at the edge of the woods.

"War party?"

She shook her head emphatically.

"No, hunt scalp, hunt women, mebbe silver."

Peter made her wait in Jeff's custody until he could go back and bring up the pack train.

"After all, she's practically Ed's widow," he declared. "We can't send her away empty-handed."

The woman stood stoically while he loosened a pack and made a small pile of strouding, needles, and linen thread which he placed in her hands. Then he frowned, turned back to the pack horse, and took out the little music box. He showed the squaw how to wind it and how to start it playing.

All the woman's impassiveness vanished. Her eyes shone, and she smiled. When the tune had tinkled out, she took the little machine to her breast as one would a child. Then as if she was afraid her new riches would be taken from her, she ran for the nearby woods.

The three white men made short work of burying the dead Indians in a shallow ravine, tossing into the grave all that had belonged to the

savages. Jeff picked up one of the muskets, examined it, and then spoke
to Peter:

"I repaired that lock down at Ribner's. How did the gun get way up
here?"

Beniel snorted.

"That's easy. All these hellions has to do is travel. I'll bet this gang
ranged as far down as Harris Ferry."

Peter looked sharply at the woodsman.

"You ever see British officers up here, Beniel?"

Beniel grunted and spat in the direction of a lichen-covered stone.

"Peter, what would one of them pipsqueaks want here in the big
woods?"

"There's a war on, Beniel," Peter said dryly. "The Senecas love the
Great White Father—"

Sherrod interrupted.

"Thet war jest ain't worked its way this far up yet. What happened up
here was about rum or mebbe a woman. Thet squaw of Ed's was pretty
loose. She told the truth. The fellows we put back there in the ravine was
jest private outlaws, hunting horses, women, and such. No, the war's
not here yet, but it could break any minute and sweep all the white folks
out of this country clear to Harris Ferry. Our fight here at the cabin
ain't going to help none. A dead Indian can start more trouble than a
live one." They spent the night in the cabin. Getting an early start, they
reached Young Woman's Creek by noon. There, standing by the ashes of
his cabin, Beniel made what, to Jeff, was a startling announcement.

"Well, Peter, let's get our trading done. I got a lot of ginseng and
some prime fur. Let's look it over."

Grube nodded, showing no surprise. Sherrod took the bridle of the
leading pack horse and led the way up the creek and beyond where Jeff
and Peter had discomfited the Indian horse thieves. He left them in a
small clearing, directing them to wait.

Jeff was thinking hard. The whole situation, even the death of one of
their friends up river was being taken pretty casually by these men. One
of the killers had used a Ribner musket. Beniel had been burned out
but still expected to trade. Grube was standing at the creek watching for

trout. It was all very confusing. In fifteen minutes, Sherrod staggered out of the woods bearing a huge bundle on his back which he flung to the ground between Peter and Jeff. Opened, the furs lifted their guard hairs softly until Jeff's lips shaped into a soundless whistle at their fineness. Beniel saw him and grinned.

"It's all prime stuff; I can't bother with less."

He made two more trips to his hiding places, returning with a second bundle of fur and a heavy bag of ginseng roots. Peter frowned when he looked at the piles.

"Have to put a pack on my mare," he commented. "It'll be a load getting the furs and Ed's goods out."

Beniel spat into the stream.

"Them furs and roots'll cost you a full pack load and a half. You know I kin hide that stuff, so no red stick kin ever find it. I'm staying up here a spell, no matter what happened with Ed; you leave me his goods on tick. Hell, I don't want to go down like you birds and die in bed. Now, let's trade, and don't be so damned tight when you've got only one customer."

Jeff and Peter waited until Sherrod had transported all the goods to what he considered safe hiding places. As an afterthought before they left, Peter presented the woodsman with the little clock. "Here, Beniel, use this in place of rum; it's safer."

As the now lightly loaded pack train filed away with Jeff in the rear, he looked back. Beniel was watching, a grin on his straight lips, and the clock cradled under his arm. Dressed as he was in a dirty linen shirt, buckskin breeches, and battered black hat pulled well down over his eyes, the man looked capable, alert, and confident of his ability to take care of himself.

"God knows what that old reprobate has up his sleeve," Peter commented a little later. "Don't know why I call him old, either. He's probably not five years older than I am. And he's got some scheme. He's hot after money, and he made a real profit today. I'm not too satisfied about that squaw business. Why did she come down to him instead of trotting off to her people? But Beniel likes a chance, likes to match himself against the woods and its people. I saw him kill a bear one day with a six-inch knife. Claimed he was short of powder."

"Will the Indians get him?" Jeff queried. "He must have had a close shave this time."

Grube shrugged his wide shoulders.

"There's always a chance they will, but God help the warrior that gets careless about tackling him."

In the evening, by the firelight, Jeff spoke of the musket.

"It's kinda hard, Peter, to know a man way up here in these mountains was killed by a gun I fixed. How many white men will die because I repaired Ribner's guns?"

Peter nodded.

"I've thought about that gun, too. We should have brought it out. Maybe we could have pinned something on Ribner. But how could we prove who had it or even that Ribner sold it directly to the savage?"

He was quiet for a while. When he spoke again, it was on a different subject.

"After we get home, I'll take the furs and the roots on to Harris Ferry, where I can get a good stock of powder, lead, and other stuff."

"Flints," Jeff suggested. "This yellow stuff's no good. Ribner has a good stock of the black Ticonderoga flints. A careful man can get forty, fifty shots with one of them, and he can't get twenty with the ordinary kind."

The fire was pretty well burned out when Peter spoke again, musingly.

"Now Ben Haider and Ed Cathcart are gone. It's too bad, but after all, they were taking chances at a venture into dangerous country. I'm not concerned too much with this silver stuff. Woodsmen have been chasing that phantom ever since I remember. What does bother me is the dead Indian business. The Senecas are always spoiling for a chance to fight. A shot or a careless word might set them off. Our Fair Play Committee will have to get together."

Jeff half smiled, and there was light enough for Peter to see his expression.

"Don't forget, son, we're beyond the Lycoming, and so we're squatters on Indian lands. There wouldn't be too many tears shed downriver for us. The same goes for the Wyoming people on the North Branch. No, they don't love us much from the Northumberland line south. We're on our own. Only they have to figure the Senecas will have to get past our rifles to get at them. Yessir, for us, the Fair Play Committee is the law and the prophets."

When they finally rode into the farmyard at Travelome, Faith ran out, and Peter swung her up in the saddle in front of him. Jeff looked for Susan. He did not see her, however, until supper time when she gave him a brief smile and turned her attention to Peter, who was detailing all the events of the trip up river.

"So," he concluded, "I've a good load that has to go downriver to Harris Ferry. You women will ride along. Jeff will run the place while we're gone."

He did not start until a week later because it was necessary to go up Lycoming Creek to the post of the white man's friend, Job Chilloway, to get more furs and some medicinal roots like golden thread, ladyslipper root, and the hot spicy tuber called kiimmel. So it was that, when Peter did start, he had four laden pack animals and three riding horses for himself and the two women who were dressed in woolen jackets and buckskin breeches. Each carried a bag of clothing fastened to her saddle.

"Dresses," Faith had commented to Jeff as she touched her bag. "We'll want to dress up a bit at the Ferry."

Since his return, Jeff had had no opportunity to talk with Susan, and he remembered her words in their German idiom; "It gives nothing between us, ever." But she had given him her lips the morning of his departure. He seized his opportunity. First, he swung Faith into her saddle.

"Lordy," she cried, "Jeff is strong this morning."

Susan had been fumbling with a small square-toed slipper at her stirrup. Her horse was tall, and she was a short girl. Jeff seized her and swung her so high her slim legs came astride the saddle.

"You're very welcome to the help, Susan," he said mockingly.

Her eyes snapped, and in a voice as low as his had been, she countered: "I was not going to say thanks."

Jeff grinned at the way her speech thickened when she was angry. The cavalcade filed away, and at the first bend, surprisingly, Susan turned in her saddle and waved. Warmth flooded through Jeff. The girl was unpredictable, but it was good to know she thought of him as she was leaving.

Charley did most of the farm chores, so Jeff worked in his shop. Being alone, he had plenty of time to think. The nagging awareness that he was a fugitive never left him. Jeff had often talked with Migun about the indentured servant situation and knew only too well that each day's freedom he now enjoyed meant five days added to his indentured time. But he was also sure, as were his friends, that a return to his master meant death. Jeff had looked into the man's jealousy-crazed eyes before the whip began to fall.

One afternoon, Jeff was working out some of his indignation and feeling of frustration by shaping horseshoes at the forge. He was beating the hot iron with powerful strokes and thought himself alone and unobserved. The shop door stood open as usual. A discreet cough startled him. Then a voice spoke softly:

"My brother strikes the iron overhard."

Jeff, still holding his hammer, turned slowly and looked directly into the face of an Indian dressed in a buckskin shirt and leggings. His smile showed a wide mouth and strong teeth.

"Perhaps," the man continued gravely, "my brother beats an evil spirit out of the metal so it may keep a horse safe on the rocks." Jeff was puzzled and a bit helpless at the gentle, derisive talk coupled with that disarming smile. It seemed this Indian read his mind.

"No," he answered the savage, "the iron is good. It may be the evil spirit is the anger of the smith. I'm Jeffry Claus."

The big man put out his hand in white man fashion, and his fingers were strong and warm about Jeff's.

"Migun has spoken to me of you. I trade with Peter Grube, and my name is Job Chilloway."

Jeff nodded, acknowledging that the name was familiar. He had often heard it mentioned by men who came to the shop. This Indian was a staunch friend of the white men. Now he stepped back to the door, where he picked up a rifle propped against the post.

"They tell me you are a good smith," he said. "I want my old gun bored out. It has grown tired from shooting many deer. It must be freshened."

Jeff liked the balance of the piece the moment he handled it. Testing the lock spring first, he finally tapped the silver-ornamented maple stock and shook his head.

"It is too bad," he commented shortly. "I could rig a boring machine which would make this gun new, but I have no small cutter to follow and deepen the rifle grooves."

The Indian's eyes studied him soberly. He did not interrupt but waited for the younger man to continue. It seemed as if he knew Jeff's mind was back in the Ribner shop, where there was a small box marked "cutter" on a shelf near the forge.

"But," Jeff continued, "if my brother is not in a hurry, I will clean his gun from the breech and fix the lock so the hammer falls stronger."

Chilloway smiled again.

"Only the white men are in a hurry. I can wait, but I will tell my wife."

The woman who answered his call was handsome, almost beautiful. She was dressed well. Brooches showed at the throat of her soft deerskin shirt, and bangles clinked on her rounded arms. But there was too much of an appraising look in her bold eyes.

"This man," Chilloway spoke gently, "is Jeffry Claus, who will fix the gun. Her name," he added to the already busy Jeff, "is Betsy."

With swift, sure fingers, the smith removed the pins which held the barrel to the stock. He fastened the heavy octagonal barrel in a vise and removed the breech plug. The Indian watched every movement with keen interest.

Harriet later fed the three of them at the big table on the back porch, the Indians eating with deliberation and appetite. But Jeff was uneasy at the sly glances the woman kept throwing his way. Afterward, in the shop, when Betsy was walking about the barn, Chilloway put his big hand on Jeff's shoulder.

"My young brother must not mind Betsy, who has wandering eyes and thinks all men are tempted by women. When one becomes weak before her, she boasts to me of her conquest. It is a game she likes as trapping foxes is to me."

Jeff looked directly into the man's eyes. Then he turned back to his bench while Chilloway, lounging close by, continued to talk.

"My young friend with the wise fingers must not burn them in the fire. Perhaps he has already burned them a little and so is wiser."

Jeff, suddenly angry, wheeled. This Indian was presuming far too much, talking too much. But the face turned toward him wore the serenity and innocence of a child. He was chewing placidly at the birch twig he had used to clean his teeth.

Chilloway was pleased when Jeff put the finished weapon back into his hands. The bore had been cleaned thoroughly, and a new spring had gone into the lock. All moving parts had been oiled. As the man tested the cocking of the piece, Jeff offered a suggestion.

"If my brother, who is good with foxes, will use heavier patches for his bullets, the gun will shoot harder."

Chilloway fumbled in his pouch and took out some silver, but Jeff shook his head emphatically.

"Migun's friend owes me nothing. I owe him much, even my life."

The big Indian grunted, then beckoned Jeff to follow and led him down under an oak out of earshot of the house.

"Job did not come alone about the gun. He wanted to see Peter. Since he is gone, you will hold the word for him."

Kneeling, he made a rough map on the ground and pointed to spots as he talked. "The Senecas watch here on the Sheshequin Path, and some Delawares are with them; Peter will know that is Mohawk country and wonder, as Job does. There are more of the same totem clan on the Tiadaghton and a small party above the Great Island. But the big camps on the Sinnamahoning are empty, and Job does not know why."

He paused, and Jeff almost asked a question, but it was not necessary. Chilloway answered it as directly as though it had been voiced.

"They have found dead men at the Cathcart cabin, one a white man. Ktemque is dead on the Mahantango, so is a bearded man who sought silver. Too many men are dead; the warriors watch. Some day they will strike when they think the white men are weak."

Jeff stared at the calm face wondering about the news he had heard, news of a vast forest area. Again Chilloway seemed to read his thoughts.

"It is Job's business to know many things. Since he loves both red men and white, he hopes the killing may not come."

He laid his big hand on Jeff's shoulder quite suddenly.

"There is much change at the trading post on the Mahantango. All the slaves but the small gray one have been sold, and two men who watch each other live in the big house. The woman is there. She looks at one then the other, and hands knot under the table. She is evil, turning men to water, so they run where she wishes."

When Job Chilloway and Betsy departed early that evening, they left an even more puzzled and uneasy Jeff behind. There were no closed books or secrets on the frontier. Job Chilloway, Migun, Squire Fell; they knew everything.

CHAPTER XI

THE GRUBES and Susan returned to Travelome late on the after-noon of the tenth day after their departure with the pack train. All of them were in excellent spirits. Even Susan had a warm smile for Jeff, and Faith, leaning forward in her saddle, kissed him lightly on the forehead before he helped her down.

"'It's nice that you help me, Jeff. My Peter so often forgets."

To counter his wife's words, Peter dismounted, swung Susan from her saddle, and held her high in the air while her small feet kicked fran-tically. Then the women went on into the house while Jeff, Charley, and Peter unloaded the horses. Peter thumped one of the bundles.

"I've brought plenty of good imported powder, Jeff. Then I have a lot of good woolen cloth and blankets. Such stuff is getting hard to get. But I turned most of the loads into cash money—specie. We may need—"

"Flints?" Jeff questioned, and Peter frowned, motioning to a small bag.

"Just the common yellow sort. We came up past the Ribner post, and that man, Fultz, was in the store. He claimed they had no Ticonderoga stuff, hadn't been able to get any for the past year. The Negro, Fred, about whom we've talked, was there, but he just kept in the background."

Charley took the horses to the bam. Jeff and Peter worked at piling the articles on shelves in the small storehouse. Grube was smiling when they finished.

"The women had another visit with Abigail Ribner."

Jeff felt his face beginning to redden and turned to make an unnecessary arrangement of some goods. He wouldn't have to question Peter.
The big man was primed to tell all that had happened.

"I stopped about the flints, and the women dismounted to wait.
Trust our Faith to maneuver, she saw a beautiful bush on the lawn and
was looking at it when Mistress Ribner appeared. She was the soul of
courtesy and hospitality, asking the girls in for a dish of tea which they
declined. Our Susan put on an act. She was the humble servant girl with
her 'Yes ma'am and No ma'am.' Somebody ought to jolt that way out
of her."

He frowned.

"I got nothing for my pains, not even a glimpse of Ribner, and the
women found nothing but courtesy, graciously given."

It was Jeff's turn to feel like frowning. If Peter Grube just blundered
into the Ribner post thinking to learn something, he was plainly foolish,
for Ribner was too smooth a man to leave things in the open. He had
completely set at rest the minds of the local Committee of Public Safety and made friends of the most influential men of the area, including
Commandant Hunter at Fort Augusta. Jeff thought of the hundreds of
black flints in that bag. He had handled them. Then there was his little
cutter to freshen rifle bores. It would be wrapped in its oiled rag with the
small pliers and the round file.

"The flints are there," he said bluntly. "The damned Indians couldn't
have taken them all. Ribner would have taken a fox skin for one of them,
and I'll bet he hasn't a dozen fox pelts in the place."

Peter looked a little puzzled but made no comment. After supper, he
and Faith walked back over the fields. For once, it took no strategy on
Jeff's part to keep Susan on the porch, and she seemed eager to talk.

"You had a nice time," he offered, and she was enthusiastic at once.

"Very, very nice. We stayed at the John Harris tavern and dressed up
real ladylike. There was always dancing in the evening. Peter dances well,
though because he is so big, you'd think him clumsy."

Jeff, seized with sudden jealousy, tried to keep his voice casual. In a
moment after he had voiced his question, he knew he had left Susan an
opening to torment him. He asked: "Officers there?"

"Oh yes, Jeffry, two of them. They were lieutenants in those lovely blue coats with buff facings. I liked the way they held their cocked hats under their elbows when they bowed as they asked for a dance. Then there were traders and fur buyers from Lancaster."

She leaned forward, seemingly intent for the moment on the land sloping down toward the river from the porch on which they were seated.

"Some day," she said musingly, "I would like to see the cities again. It seems so long ago. I was just a child when the ship brought me to Philadelphia, and I was bound out for housework. It was pretty hard to do all that was expected of me, but I did find some time to look out the windows and see the fine people walk by. I liked the silver buckles the men wore in their shoes, not moccasins, and the lovely gowns of the women with their big panniers."

She was a strange girl, this Susan. Jeff knew the talk about the dancing had been to tease him, but almost at once, she had turned thoughtful.

"Peter saw me when he visited at that house and brought me to Faith. A girl child is bound until she's twenty. In two years, I'll be free."

"Susan," he said sharply, "aren't you happy here?"

"Oh yes, of course," she cried, "and so lucky. My girl friend, Elspeth, was sold to a family where the man was bad. I saw her before I came away, and she told me things. I know how good things worked out for me."

Her small hands, spread upon her lap a moment before, were now clenched. She turned her face toward him in the mounting shadows.

"But it's like you said, Jeffry; we bound people are property like horses, cats, and dogs. You can love a dog, but he is not free. Look at you. Every day of freedom means five of serving if they catch you."

He interrupted her in mild irritation.

"Well, Susan, it won't be long till you're as free as you wish. What then?"

She shook her head vigorously.

"Only the wind is free, and it doesn't care. When a person thinks he's free, he doesn't stay so."

They had both risen and were staring at the shadows under the tree when Faith's light laughter, followed by Peter's heavier tones, sounded.

Susan whirled as if some new energy had flooded through her. She said sharply: "Anyway, she is not beautiful. Maybe she is just a little fat."

Jeff stood stock-still in amazement at her last words while she darted into the house. There was no doubt in his mind that she had been talking about Abigail Ribner.

"Damn," he muttered savagely. "Damn the woman."

Vaulting the porch rail, he walked down to the river and stood looking over the dark flood. It made no noise out where it was deep, but near the shore, the little eddies chuckled among the stones. After that, he walked until he was tired before coming in and going to bed.

After breakfast in the morning, Jeff told Peter of Job Chilloway's visit and the news he brought. He emphasized the finding of the bodies at the Cathcart cabin.

"Of course," Peter commented, "they'd find the bodies, and as for watching, let them watch. There wouldn't be too much we could do about it. Colonel Henry Antes is starting a new fort just across from Long Island. The Horn stockade is the other side of the river here, and they're going to stockade the Reed place. Of course, all the defenses are across the river, where you can settle legally. Over here, we're not much concern to the powers that be. Hunter is already claiming he cannot defend us. If he hears too many scare yarns, he might ask all settlers to vacate the valley." Jeff made no comment, and Peter's serious mood broke with a wide grin as he asked a question,

"Did Job have his Betsy with him?"

Jeff swore softly and commented, "She's a loose piece—"

Peter's chuckle interrupted him.

"Job ought to give her what Indians hand to wandering women, a ceremony of lopping off her nose. She earns that treatment once a month. Once, we had a young fellow here cultivating corn. Betsy fancied him and went swimming in the creek near where he worked. Faith helped her get dressed with a horsewhip, but Job never knew."

On Wednesday of the week the Grubes returned, the man for whom Jeff had repaired the cameo delivered a message at Travelome.

"Fair Play Committee meets Friday, mouth of the Tiadaghton at the big elm."

"It'll be a man meeting," Peter said at the dinner table. "There'll be too much whiskey loose to have women folks about."

Faith looked at him with a half smile and spoke casually: "There are usually some women at Staier's tavern down there who don't mind whiskey. Anyway, Susan and I are behind with our work. We'll be happier staying at home."

On the appointed day, Peter and Jeff stabled their horses at Staier's tavern. They walked the remainder of the distance to the meeting place, a field level as a floor in the angle made by the Tiadaghton and the Susquehanna. Here a huge elm offered shade for a good-sized company. Three men who currently served on the Committee sat on three-legged stools back of a rude table made from a split log. Other men sat or lolled on the grass, and a few stood, leaning on their rifles.

Jeff was not much interested in the deliberations of the body, but he did hear a man reporting that the British were now buying scalps at eight dollars apiece. He wandered about the field, talking occasionally to men for whom he had done work. Like himself, most of these were young fellows who laughed, talked, and indulged in rough horseplay. Back along the road to the big tree was a bench on which a small black boy had an open keg of whiskey. In one hand, he held a number of tin pannikins. When a man stopped near him, he would fill a cup of the amber liquor and offer it.

"Compliments of Squire Rude, sir," he would chant, then grin, showing his beautiful teeth. Peter and Jeff had stopped there, coming in just to note how much the boy was enjoying his task. There was a throng about the bench now.

"Squire's poorly," the boy declared. "Sent the liquor real friendly. One cup to a man. Squire says."

Laughter greeted these remarks. Then a heavily set, bearded man swaggered up to the bench. His eyes were already bloodshot from drinking when he stopped. The Negro served him. He downed the liquor and slammed the cup on the bench.

"Fill 'er up again, darky."

The boy shook his head and looked scared.

"Squire says, one cup to a man, you is—"

The man's huge hand lifted. Jeff was close enough to see the black hair growing down to the knuckles as he struck the boy on the side of his head, sending him spinning to the ground. The circle of men drew back, but none interfered.

"You black pup," the fellow roared while he fumbled in his belt through which the short handle of a whip was thrust.

"I'm getting out of here," a man near Jeff mumbled. "That's Tom Dilson, and I don't want to see the Squire's boy manhandled by that ape."

Others pulled back while the colored boy pleaded with his attacker.

" 'Deed, Mister Dilson, sir. Squire said—"

The savage slash of the whip ended the slave's words in a shriek of pain. Jeff moved closer, impelled by something stronger than his own will. When the whip lifted again, he leaped, caught the handle, and tore it from the bully's grasp. A groan ran through the watching crowd.

"Younker," an old man near Jeff muttered to him, "let the brute alone. He'll gouge you."

Dilson, roaring curses, charged Jeff, who stepped aside. Jeff had seen a lot of this brutal type of fighting in England and some about frontier posts. Dropping the whip he had snatched, he drove two sharp blows home to Dilson's head and felled him to his knees.

The bully, shaking his head to clear it, worked around in a circle, still on his knees. He saw the whip, grabbed it, and leaped up.

The lash missed Jeff's face, but it licked over his shoulder, touching him where the old scars were. An awful fury raced through him. Paying no attention to Dilson's swinging blows, he crowded in, chopping with iron-hard fists at the throat, mouth, and stomach of his adversary. Jeff looked slight compared to the burly man he was fighting, but his body was all lean, hard muscle. His savage pounding was sickening his opponent.

Dilson, reeling, swung up his arm, his fingers clawing at Jeff's face. Next instant, that wrist was caught. Jeff swung the arm over his shoulder and heaved. Dilson screamed in agony when something snapped. The arm had either been broken or disjointed, but there was no mercy in the younger man. Jeff's knuckles cut Dilson's face again and again until it was covered with blood. Finally, the big man dropped prone, crowding his face to the ground,

Jeff did not know it, but there was a whining snarl in his throat as he leaped astride the prostrate victim. He jerked the bloody head up and down, pounding the earth with it until men pulled him away. When he saw the whip again, he snatched it and lashed Dilson's back, each blow cutting through the shirt and leaving a bloody track.

"Jeff." Peter's cry finally broke through the killing fog in which the younger man moved. "You'll kill him."

Jeff looked at his friend, at first seeing his face as though he stood a long way off. Then slowly, his eyes cleared, and the pounding in his temples stopped. Twisting the whipstock in his hands, he broke it and threw the pieces at the battered head of the man on the ground. The little Negro had decamped with his jug, and Peter led his friend slowly up toward the tavern stables. Finally, Jeff turned.

"I'm all right now, Peter. You go on back. It was the whip. Don't let that man ever come close to me again; I'll kill him. Now I'll go home."

At Travelome, Jeff put his horse away quietly and walked back into the hills until he could settle down to normal. The touch of the whiplash had roused him so terribly that he was utterly weary, as though the internal fire had burned something out of him. He knew now that a fury could be roused in him that would lead to murder. He had no control over that rage. When he was sure Peter would have returned from the meeting, he went down to the house. He was about to enter when he heard his name mentioned. Peter was talking to Faith and Susan.

"Yes, he nearly killed Tom Dilson, the biggest, worst bully this valley's seen. He did it because Tom abused a little colored boy, Squire Rude's Tad."

There was a murmur of questioning by the women. Jeff wanted to move away but could not resist listening to Peter's final words.

"Dilson just couldn't seem to stop him. Jeff isn't hurt. God help the man who ever tackles him with his hands. I'm big, but I'd want a ten-foot club in my hands before I tried it. The only thing is that Dilson keeps running down the river. He'll report Jeff's being up here, sure's sin."

The Committee's deliberations had come to little, Peter explained at the supper table.

"All wind and no fire," he concluded. "They wanted to put a price on Indian scalps to counter the British offer, but nobody had any money. Besides, who wants a lousy Seneca scalp hanging around."

Word had gone around at the meeting that Colonel Antes was ready to start work on his stockade, and all settlers were asked to help. Since Peter was busy at the farm, Jeff volunteered to take his place. Every fort added to the security of the region.

Starting from Travelome well before daylight, Jeff was set over the river in a canoe by a man who said he worked for Colonel Antes. Already forty or fifty men were at work on the bluff. Among them moved a quiet man who wore a neatly pointed, short beard.

"Yes," he answered Jeff's query and explanation that he came in Peter Grube's place, "I'm Colonel Antes, and while I'd liked to have Grube with us, I'm sure you will do very well in his place. Start to work anywhere."

A stout house and grist mill had been erected at this place more than a year before. The fort itself was being erected on the bluff above the river. Here a four-foot trench was dug, following the lines laid down by Colonel Antes. Into this were set the ends of heavy logs, which formed the palisade. Each log was roughly pointed at the upper end and notched to carry the firing platform, which would be set in place when the whole palisade was finished. Jeff worked on the stockade for a week when the Colonel took him aside.

"Jeffry, they tell me you are a gunsmith, and I have more important work for you than with hammer and ax. I have muskets that must be put into better condition."

Jeff brought down Peter Grube's meager stock of tools and set to work in one of the newcomer blockhouses where the light was good. He reconditioned the muskets, after which workmen brought him their own rifles.

"You should have better tools," Antes said. "They could be had in Lancaster county."

"No," Jeff told the officer. "Peter Grube tried, but they're so busy with army work they won't sell a rifling cutter."

He smiled and added, "Besides, I have no money."

Antes appeared to be thinking through some problems before he spoke.

"I have made some inquiries concerning you, Jeffry. I know that you are a runaway indentured servant, one who had been savagely treated. I am a magistrate; probably, it is my duty to arrest you."

His smile checked Jeff's flare-up of anger, and he continued: "But I would be foolish to do that when I want those swivel guns set up. Selfishness makes me a poor magistrate. Besides, I am sure you are a greater good to the peace of this valley than you could be as a servant of any one man."

Abruptly he broke off and tendered a small hand with pointed fingers in a gesture of friendship. Jeff grasped it, and the two men looked steadily into each other's eyes.

"I do not like slavery, either white or black," the officer declared with conviction. "We cannot fight England with a clear conscience when we hold anyone, white or black, in slavery."

Jeff worked with a will on the four swivels, each having three times the bore of a musket. Finally, he got them securely mounted on the four comers of the fort and so placed that two of the pieces could pitch their shots across the river or rake canoes afloat upon it. The others covered the cleared ground to the fort's back, and it was planned to load them with buckshot. All four pieces were fired as a salute when Colonel Antes announced that the post was completed.

On this day, when Jeff was ferried to the north bank of the river, a man younger but closely resembling Squire Fell was waiting. He walked rapidly but used a cane.

"Sir," he greeted when Jeff had landed, "I am David Rude, and you will be Jeffry Claus in whose debt I am."

Jeff waited. For the moment, the name meant nothing to him. The man was continuing.

"I have been slow, because of illness, in thanking you for saving my colored boy, Tad, from a severe handling. I am deeply grateful and offer my thanks."

Jeff took the proffered hand and smiled.

"That day, I lost my temper, sir, when the man tried to use his whip first on the boy, then on me."

Rude nodded.

"If you did, young man, it was at the right time and in the right place. You have rid our valley of a notorious bully."

Jeff walked with Rude to where the horses were tied. There Rude offered his hand.

"I understand this Dilson has reported your presence here to Northumberland authorities. Sometimes they send their officers into this Fair Play country, and sometimes our Committee allows them to take a man from here. But Colonel Antes speaks well of you, as does Peter Grube. If you need legal advice or help, I am at your service. Dilson will not be with us longer. He returned a few days ago, and I assured him that I would shoot him on sight if I caught him again this side of the Lycoming."

He gripped Jeff's hand and, with unexpected nimbleness, mounted his tall horse.

Peter was in the barn when Jeff arrived and stabled his horse. The big man was in high good humor.

"Squire Rude was here, Jeff. You made a good friend in him. He wants to thank you. He's one of the original Fair Play men, and his word travels a long way in this country."

"He saw me," Jeff told his friend, "just after I crossed the river. But after all, Peter, I didn't do it all for the boy. It was the whip." His hands knotted involuntarily as he stepped closer to his friend.

"Someday, I might kill a man who used a lash."

Peter busied himself tossing hay into the manger and made no comment. A moment later, he had news.

"Migun's about somewhere; came in just after noon."

Jeff found his friend on his way to the barn. The two pumped each other's hands, and Jeff slapped the Indian between his shoulders until he protested.

"My brother should not be too glad. It is hard on both Migun's fingers and his back."

CHAPTER XII

THE YOUNG Delaware was always a welcome guest in the Grube household. He was doubly so this evening as he sat relaying the news he had gathered in his travels up and down the Susquehanna. He was not very enthusiastic about the progress of the war in which the Continental armies had so often gotten the worst of things. But he was almost excited about the work going on in the lower counties, the storehouse, the granary, and the workshop of the Revolution.

"Everybody works," he declared. "Even the children fill powder cartridges using kitchen spoons. It's guns, wagons, and clothes turned out steadily in all the houses and towns from Philadelphia to Harris Ferry. So long as we can make enough war goods, we can't lose. So long as our militia fires a few shots and runs, that long the British cannot destroy it or end the war."

Peter snorted in some derision.

"Militia's scared of its shadow."

Migun frowned.

"No, my friend, the militia is not cowardly, having learned a lesson from my people, that of attack and retreat. The British in red coats and tall hats stand in solid ranks, and they fight a shadow. Today they seem to face an army of five thousand, and tomorrow it will be only a few hundred. Someday the shadow will be great enough to swallow up the king's armies."

Grube did not argue the militia situation longer. Concerned with the threat of a possible Indian foray down his own valley to strike the lower county, he asked a question:

"What will we do, Migun, if the Senecas come down and run over us so they can destroy this lower county work?"

Migun frowned and answered gravely:

"The answer to that is in the smoke of the council fires up there in the lake country beyond the Forbidden Way. There is much talk in council. The warriors of the Seneca nation will strike, but when and where depends on these same council talks. If they come, the men along the river will fight. They will fall back but keep on fighting. The bad thing would be not to know when or where the blow will come."

He stopped talking with an apology.

"Migun has talked too much and very like a prophet. He must stop. Yet, he has said nothing, only what he hears and what the wind whispers to him."

Much as the young Indian liked to sit at table and talk, he seldom slept in a house other than his own place in the hills. Jeff accompanied him outdoors tonight, and the two spread their blankets under a big oak. Before he lay down, he gave Jeff a sad bit of news.

"I did not want to sadden them in the house, but Gokhotit is dead. A dozen warriors had rum, and our friend's camp was close. In a drunken frenzy, one man was slashed badly. They brought Gokhotit to look at the hurt man's wounds, but he died. Then one of the warriors killed Gokhotit with a hatchet."

"Ribner's rum," Jeff spat, and Migun agreed.

"Migun, we should go down there and kill that man. There should be two bullets, one for him and one for Fred."

"No," the Delaware disagreed, "if you tie a string to a puppy by-and-by he gets himself so tangled he cannot move."

Jeff grunted disdainfully, but Migun elaborated.

"The woman, Abigail Ribner, is the string. You forget Abner Fultz. She has her string about him already and a fever for her burns in his brain. Her husband watches, and she will lead them both to death. No, my brother, soil your hands at the forge, not with blood."

They lay for quite a while longer, with neither man saying anything. Both looked up into the star-studded sky. A light breeze passed, rustling the leaves for a moment. Down in the barn, a horse stamped on the floor of his stall, and far across the river, a dog barked his question of the night.

Abruptly Jeff sat up, full of a sudden and exhilarating release which he could not understand or explain. Beaten close to death, he had lain while his broken bones and skin healed. After that, he had gone about humbly under the shadow of the years of servitude that hovered over him, lengthening as the days passed. Now, he was suddenly alive, eager. He reached out and shook his reluctant friend into full wakefulness.

"Migun, in the morning, we start for the Ribner post. I want my tools, and I'll steal them or take them boldly, whichever is the handier."

"Lordy, Lordy," the Indian said mockingly, "how tall our Jeffry talks. But tomorrow is tomorrow. Now is the time for sleep, not boasting."

They did not go down to the house in the morning. Jeff had no mind to offer any explanation or to enter into any argument as to the wisdom of what he proposed doing. Migun accompanied his friend because the project amused him. Sunset of the following day, which was spent in hard travel, found them on the hills where they could look down on the Ribner post. From this vantage point, the fields of the big farm appeared slovenly, but the post and all the buildings seemed as trimly kept as ever. Jeff's mind was a confusion of remembered things. First, he thought of the candlelight and the colored girl, Melody, beside him in the bed while Ribner looked on triumphantly. That was the closing of the trap. Four years of his life had been snatched from him there.

Something of the exhilaration Jeff had felt a few nights before left him as he watched the post. So far, in spite of his suffering, he had not admitted to himself that Abigail Ribner had been to blame for her part in the torture her frenzied husband had meted out that night. Fred's spying had forced her to say something which would clear her. "She pitied you," Ribner had snarled. Jeff thought of her now, remembering the soft cloud of loosened hair, the mocking light in her eyes, and the demanding warmth of lips which broke a man's will and judgment. Under the warmth of her was a coldly calculating mind. She had told Ribner she had driven Jeff away with the whip as a sop to the man's vanity, confirming his hope that his servant had done no more than touch his wife.

Two men, whom he assumed to be Ribner and the Negro, Fred, emerged from the house and crossed through the garden toward the shop. Jeff snatched Migun's rifle, which lay close to his big hand. It came up to his shoulder with the sights on the taller of the men below. Before he could thumb back the hammer, the Delaware snatched the weapon from him roughly with a snarl of sheer irritation.

"My brother has already made enough of a damned fool of himself," he growled and dusted the priming from the gun lock.

"Anyway," he concluded dryly, "two hundred yards are too far for this gun. Also, the man may not have been Ribner. I could not see."

Neither mentioned the incident again. Jeff was ashamed of his impulsiveness. Over their campfire back in the timber, it was agreed that it might be wise to talk to Squire Fell before raiding the toolboxes for the cutter. When it was finally quite dark, they went down to the river, found a canoe with paddles placed under it, and crossed to the eastern shore.

The Squire was in his usual position back of a table, writing busily. The two young men rapped and were bidden to enter, which they did without formality. The quill scratched on for another full minute before the old jurist looked up to see who his visitors were.

Shocked surprise held the old man's head rigid as he stared at the figures before him. His mouth dropped open, and his eyes widened.

"You," he gasped, pointing a finger at Jeff. "You here now, good God, now!"

Jeff tried to smile to cover his embarrassment at the greeting. "Surely, sir, you don't seem to find us very welcome, and we've come a long way."

"Welcome!" the Squire shouted. "They're hunting you like a fox, and you walk into my place. I am a magistrate."

Jeff, angry, stopped all pretense of smiling. There had been no compelling reason for coming here except that the Squire would like to know that the tools Jeff wanted really belonged to him as a gift from Uncle Mark. Further, he did not like Fell's expression.

"Come, Migun," he said roughly to his companion. "We'll leave before this man who claimed to be my friend chokes at the sheer joy of seeing me."

Fell was thumping the table with his fist, for in his excitement, it was difficult for him to speak coherently. Jeff continued talking:

"Of course, I know they hunt me and that I'm worth five pounds, as the advertisement says. They can hunt and be damned. Ribner's whip will never touch me again, nor will I stick my neck into any more of his filthy traps."

"Jeff!" Fell found his voice at last, explosively. "Ribner's dead. Fultz found his body in the shop with your knife in his throat. They want you for murder!"

He was almost screaming as he uttered his final words, and it was Jeff's turn to be speechless with surprise.

A moment later, he managed one horrified word: "Murder!"

"A week past!" Fell explained. "Fultz found the dead man in the shop. He had been bludgeoned, and then the knife, which you would not hand over that day at Burnet Hall, was driven into his throat. They have been scouring the country for you, Jeff, and Fultz offers fifty pounds to any man who drags you before the Sheriff in Sunbury town."

The first shock a little deadened, Jeff stood quietly, thinking. There was no dismay in him and no elation at the death of the man who had tricked him. He found his mind cold, calculating. There had been several times when he could have killed the trader. A few hours ago, the impulse had almost mastered him. Facing the squire, he could hear Abigail Ribner whispering, "He might be back tonight . . . you would have to kill him . . . your knife." The short heavy blade had been in his belt as she talked. Fultz had found the body, Fultz, with his bloated face hungry for this woman.

Jeff shook his head to rid his mind's eye of the picture of the woman with the rounded white shoulders and temptation on her tongue. Migun broke the silence.

"Squire, a week past Jeff worked on Colonel Antes' stockade on the West Branch of the Susquehanna,"

The Justice swung his attention to the Indian, and he nodded slightly as he listened.

"Jeff's knife was on the tool bench the day Pentz, Gokhotit, and I carried him away. There was nothing in his clothes which I took from his room and brought away, nothing, not even a tinder box. He was naked when they used the whip. No, Jeff did not have the short knife with the wide blade he used to carry."

"Jeff is no murderer." Fell's voice was calm again. "He would kill in anger and might at one time have strangled Ribner with his hands. No, Migun, this blank-faced young man who stares at us did not murder Henry Ribner. He is trapped, though, like the fox which steps in the beds where traps are hidden under the lye chaff. First, he catches one foot, then the other. So he is held until they come and club the life from him."

Jeff's body and face relaxed. He liked the look on Fell's face because, in addition to anger and dismay, he read pity there.

"Fultz," Fell said shortly, and his features seemed smaller than they actually were as his head fell deeper into the coat collar. "The woman is in this somewhere. Fultz is wild about her. He cannot keep his eyes from following her, so they say. Ribner, in his cold way, as Jeff knows, was all but insane about her and could not bring himself to send her away even though she tortured him with jealousy."

He picked up a quill and made a shaky-looking "I" on paper. "First, I was never satisfied as to why Ribner bought Jeff and kept holding on to him through tricks. There are other smiths." Jeff shifted his feet a little, and the squire continued his summation.

"Second, there is Uncle Mark's property. Ribner rented the post from him. Right after the death of the old trader, Ribner registered a deed of sale to the place in Sunbury. Fultz seems to be a partner of sorts. Ribner always has money."

Migun crossed to the door, and Jeff interrupted the squire.

"Sir, let's quit wondering about Ribner and Fultz. I'm going to Sunbury and demand a trial."

Fell slapped the table with his palm until the inkhorn toppled, and he had to retrieve it.

"You, Jeffry Claus, will then be demanding six feet of rope. There are more traps in the fox bed. Listen, a jury called by the sheriff after the murder found that the trader had come to his death by the hand of a runaway bond servant, Jeffry Claus. There would be no other trial. Ribner was a friend of the commandant and of the sheriff. They would hang you, my foolish young friend, and there'd be a holiday on the date they did it. It's the woods for you, and give me time to work through this whole mess."

Jeff's lips tightened as he turned to Migun at the doorway.

"Tonight I'm going into that shop and take the tools Uncle Mark wanted me to have. The men upriver must have good rifles if the savages come down."

The old squire offered no word of protest but sat, huddled down in his coat. His mind seemed busy with the ideas he had mentioned earlier as Jeff and Migun left the room.

The post was quiet. Not even a dog barked as the friends opened the unlocked shop door. Jeff did not need the little light which filtered in from outside to find the box he sought and to take from it the small tools he wanted, including the rifling cutter. EH down Lancaster way had made the little instrument of hard steel with tiny wedges, which permitted it to be used in different bores. A skillful smith could "freshen" rifling with it so a weapon would shoot like new.

Jeff dropped the things he had taken and returned the box to its place on the shelf. Minutes later, in the closet where the muskets had been kept, he found the still heavy bag of black Ticonderoga flints and gave it to Migun.

"Flints," he whispered as his friend's fingers closed about the neck of the sack.

For a moment more, he stood there close to the workbench where he had labored so many hours. He was glad that his familiarity with every inch of the shop had made a light unnecessary. The whole place still seemed to be filled with the emanation of hate from the man who had tortured him here. Now he had died close to where he had meted out that suffering, struck down and then stabbed by the very knife he had demanded from Jeff at their first meeting.

When they were outside again, they stood listening to the little sounds of the night. Nothing stirred but a few insects. No lights showed excepting in the big house. Jeff touched Migun's hand.

He was off, moving rapidly to prevent any protest from the cautious Indian. Walking lightly, he passed through the garden, then crossed the lawn and gained his vantage point used on the night the British officer had visited Ribner.

Again it was a dinner scene. Branched candlesticks stood on the table littered with dishes and the remains of a heavy meal. Over near the kitchen door, a wooden-faced white woman sat bolt upright in a straight chair, and at the table were Abigail Ribner and Abner Fultz. A third place was set. The chair before it was empty, and beside the plate lay an overturned wineglass.

The woman wore the sort of dress to which she was partial, one that revealed her white bosom and bare arms. She was leaning forward, twirling a wineglass stem between thumb and fingers. A mocking smile played about her full lips.

Fultz sat at the side of the table, his heavy face flushed with overeating and drinking. His eyes were on the woman, following the movement of her hands and arms. Occasionally he moistened his lips with the tip of his tongue. When he raised his glass, his hand trembled perceptibly.

As Jeff watched, the whole meaning of the scene was apparent to him. Abigail Ribner was playing with Fultz as only she knew how to do with a man. Hunger for her was in every move and look of the half-drunken man. Slowly she rose from her seat. Fultz pushed back his chair so quickly that it toppled over when he stood up.

She remained standing close to the table while Fultz approached her. His hand went out and caught her smoothly rounded arm. She was still smiling when his other arm went about her bare shoulders. Then she twisted her supple body and came clear of his embrace. Fultz's mouth stood open. Turning to the table, she picked up a filled glass, and when he raised his hand again, she placed it in his fingers. Fultz was still staring at his hand and the wine when Abigail Ribner walked about the end of the table.

She smiled at the stony-faced woman, evidently a servant, and left the room with that smooth, tantalizing walk of hers.

Jeff slid down from his position. Abigail Ribner had been entirely mistress of the situation, and it was obvious that she had created it. Fultz's naked hunger for her must have grown from some concession or promise she had made. Ribner was dead, murdered, and in his house, this gross man sought the favors of the widow.

Migun was thoroughly impatient with Jeff when he joined him.

"This is a mighty poor place to fool around. Think what would happen if you were just seen about here, much less caught. People sleep in those cabins. Fred may be prowling about."

All the long way back to Travelome, Migun set a hard pace, probably to prevent much talking or speculation on the situation. So long as Jeff had to extend himself to keep up, he would be too busy to worry. Peter

Grube met them near the barn and showed only mild interest in the tools and the flints. As they walked toward the house, Jeff turned to the big man.

"Things are worse now, Peter. Henry Ribner is dead, my old knife in his throat. Abner Fultz has placed fifty pounds on my head."

Peter stopped dead in his tracks and drew a long breath.

"Fifty pounds. Good God, man, that's three or four years' wages for a good man."

He started on toward the house before he finished.

"Anyway, we heard about the murder but not the reward. Come on in."

Faith and Susan, seated beside a table, were sewing. Both their faces were solemn, and there was a suspicious redness about Susan's eyes. Faith put down her work and tried to be cordial with her greeting. Then, to it, she added:

"It's bad news again, Jeffry."

He nodded, and she continued:

"A man was here today from the Fair Play Committee and says the sheriff of Northumberland is coming up to arrest you for the murder of Henry Ribner. Tom Dilson, whom Squire Rude ran out of the valley, informed down there as to where you were. Peter should have told you. You are to be tried day after tomorrow for murder."

She drew a long, quivering breath as she finished. Peter frowned and cleared his throat.

"You're supposed to be in my custody till the trial, Jeff. I rode down, and Squire Rude will defend you."

Jeff stared down at the floor. The pent-up emotions of these friends disturbed him greatly. He sensed that the murder charge had shocked them profoundly. Only the top of Susan's head showed, for she kept her eyes busy with the bit of sewing on which she was engaged. Migun spoke abruptly, his voice strong with conviction.

"The day Ribner was killed, Jeff was working for Colonel Antes."

Peter nodded.

"Squire Rude knows that, and Colonel Antes will testify to it. But here's the rub; Northumberland officers don't often come into this Fair

Play country and then only on our sufferance. We can't run the risk of sheltering criminals. They might come up then in force. What I fear is that they'll come asking for the return of a runaway so they can try Jeff in Sunbury. The reward's the thing that makes them eager. It's big enough to tempt a man like me."

Although he laughed at his last sally, there wasn't much mirth in his laughter. Peter Grube was troubled.

In the evening, when the Grubes were taking their usual walk, and Migun slept under his oak tree in the pasture lot, Jeff found Susan alone on the front porch and approached her.

"Susan," he said, taking her hand and drawing her to her feet.

He could not restrain himself. His long arms swept round her. He bent and tasted the coolness of her lips. After a moment, her arms lifted as though to go about his neck, but they dropped, and she drew away.

"Yes, you kiss me, Jeffry Claus. I let you this time, for I'm sorry for a man who will hang because he was foolish about women." There was real scorn in her words, and he stepped back. She had hurt him deeply and she was continuing:

"Like I said before, you mean nothing—nothing at all. If it is like this again, we are not even friends."

Anger stirred in Jeff, anger which became stronger than his hunger for this girl who faced him in the dim light, her small face a blur. He wanted to say something sharp.

"Don't bother to be sorry, Susan. It's my neck. You—"

The words would not come. Turning his back, he stepped off the porch into the darkness.

CHAPTER XIII

MIGUN DID NOT come in for breakfast the next day. He did not reappear until the morning when Peter was scheduled to take Jeff down to Staier's tavern, where the Fair Play Committee was holding the trial. The two days of waiting passed without incident at Travelome. Jeff worked away grimly in the shop, using the cutter he had taken from Ribner, and fitted the new black flints on all the guns about the place.

Faith was on the porch when the three men mounted, but she offered no word either of hope or discouragement. Colored Charley and his wife appeared at the kitchen door with solemn faces. When they reached the final turn, Jeff reluctantly looked back and saw that Susan had joined Faith on the porch. He promptly turned and watched his horse's ears as it plodded forward. Susan had convinced him that he meant nothing to her. Let things go at that. Peter finally broke the silence.

"There's no jail up here, Jeff. That's why I promised to bring you down."

Jeff made no reply, but his lips twisted into a bitter grimace. He wanted to say something sharp, but he remembered the kindness of this big man. Before Uncle Mark had purchased his indenture, Jeff had become only too informed about the Philadelphia jail. Anyway, there was no reason for discussing anything.

A thing which always surprised Jeff in the colonies was the speed with which news traveled. Word of the trial had gone out fast, judging by the number of men who either appeared on the road or were gathered about the dirty inn on the lower Tiadaghton. Here men were talking, laughing, and skylarking. The trial was a holiday for them.

Through his work on their guns and his time spent at Antes Fort, Jeff had become pretty well acquainted in the valley. When he dismounted, a group promptly gathered about him offering rough chaffing. They clapped him on the back, pulled off his hat, and rumpled his hair. One big fellow who had notched logs at the fort put his fingers clear around Jeff's throat.

"It won't take much rope, Jeff, for the hanging. It's lucky you're kind of skinny."

Jeff thought he understood the raillery and took it in good part. None of these men could offer sympathy in a polite fashion. They were doing what they could to assure him of their faith in him.

David Rude, looking much like a well-dressed Squire Fell, had just arrived carrying a bundle of papers under one arm. Seeing Jeff and Peter, he came over and shook hands with them. Migun had faded back in the crowd. Their greeting had just been finished when three newcomers rode up and dismounted. One was a huge man dressed as smartly as any Philadelphia dandy with lace at his wrists and throat. The second was shorter in stature but heavily built and dressed like a farmer with two pistols thrust through his broad belt. The third man was evidently a servant and took charge of the horses.

The newcomers pushed importantly through the crowd approaching the group that now included Jeff, Peter, and Squire Rude.

"Just a minute," the big man boomed, partly facing the crowd. "I'm Phineas Baxter, prosecutor for the county of Northumberland, and my companion is Levi Safert, sheriff of the same county."

He pointed to Jeff.

"That man answers the description of Jeffry Claus, the murderer. Now it will save time, money, and possibly bad feeling, if we take him down to Sunbury and try him there. Sheriff, take the man into custody."

Ordinarily, Peter Grube was soft-spoken, patient, and guarded in action, but as the Northumberland sheriff stepped forward, Grube thrust out a huge hand and shoved the officer back,

"Like hell he will, Baxter. This young man is in my custody to appear before the Fair Play Committee. Shut your foghorn month and get inside. We've all heard you, beller before."

A mixed murmur of laughter and approbation passed through the crowd. Someone opened the tavern door, and the prisoner and the officials entered.

The big ordinary room of the Staier tavern was probably the largest roofed place in the valley. That was why it had been selected by the Committee. It was now filling rapidly with a tobacco-chewing, jostling crowd, A small log laid from a window sill to the end of the bar fenced off a comer in which the three men who formed the Committee sat back of a table. Jeff recognized two of them. The big, burly, red-whiskered one would be Andy Carson, who lived fairly close to the Grubes. The old man, dressed carefully in a threadbare coat and worn linen shirt, was Alexander Donaldson, whose place was directly across the river from the Horn plantation and fort. The third man, and the one who seemed to preside, was a stranger to Jeff. In spite of his civilian garb, he looked like a soldier. Peter whispered to Jeff: "We're in luck, Jeff. That's Captain James Parr. He's a militia officer."

Near the rail, his back turned, a tall man in buckskins stared out the dingy window, and when he finally turned, Jeff's heart leaped a little. It was Peter Pentz. Probably Migun had found him somewhere and persuaded him to come.

At Parr's gesture, Rude and Jeff seated themselves outside the railing log but facing the Committee. Baxter and the Northumberland sheriff took the two remaining stools. As Jeff seated himself, he was struck by an odd thing. In this country, a man was only partly dressed without his rifle. But no firearms showed in the room excepting the pistols in the sheriff's belt. Almost as though he had read the thought of the prisoner now before him, Parr frowned. His black eyes were level and hard.

"Sheriff, we have a rule. No one comes into this court armed. Hand over your pistols."

Safert half rose, his face a sudden thundercloud of wrath.

"I'm a court officer. I—"

"Not of this court. You're here on sufferance only. Pentz, take his weapons."

The woodsman's face wore a broad grin as he stepped forward, jerked the pistols from the officer's belt, tapped out the priming, and tossed them back of the bar. Parr thumped on the table with his fist quieting the murmur in the room.

"Gentlemen, we are here on a solemn duty and need guidance. Alexander will pray."

Donaldson rose slowly, removed his hat, and faced the assembly. His words came haltingly in the now completely quiet room where the spectators stood with bowed and uncovered heads. When the "amen" came, Parr tapped the table with his blunt fingers and then made his announcement.

"This special meeting of the Fair Play Committee is called because a newcomer in our midst has been accused of sundry crimes and misdemeanors. This locality does not condone crime, nor does it offer sanctuary to criminals. Yet any man is entitled here to have his case heard and passed upon. Officers from the court of a neighboring county—"

Baxter's ejaculation at the word "neighboring" brought a frown to Parr's face and a moment's pause before he continued.

". . . are here to present their case. The prisoner, Jeffry Claus, is before you. Prosecutor Baxter, state your case."

At Parr's gesture, Jeff moved his stool inside the enclosure. Baxter rose, smoothed his waistcoat over his too-ample stomach, and cleared his throat loudly and portentously.

"Gentlemen, it is my understanding that this is simply a hearing since no real trials can be held excepting in the village of Sunbury. Sheriff Safert and I have come to apprehend a runaway bondservant of the late Henry Ribner, who did, on the night of July seventeenth, murder his master. The weapon used, a knife, had been identified as belonging to Claus, and he was actually seen at the Ribner post by a witness, one Fred, a slave of the same Henry Ribner. I have here the sworn statements of the witnesses and the findings of the coroner's jury."

He tossed a small packet of papers on the table. Parr examined them briefly and passed them to his fellow Committee members. Baxter looked about the room, then at Jeff.

"It is a well-known fact that this same Jeffry Claus is a person of violent and criminal ways. It is supposed that he brought about the death of a peaceful Indian who had traded at the Ribner post, where Claus was

THE EAGLE AND THE WIND

a bondservant. He cohabited with a female colored slave, and Squire Christian Fell, therefore, lengthened his term of service according to law. On several occasions, he threatened his master and was duly punished for his misdeeds. Abner Fultz, partner to Henry Ribner, has offered a reward of fifty pounds for the return of this Jeffry Claus to Sunbury, where the jury mentioned before holds him guilty of murder."

Satisfaction on his heavy face, Baxter seated himself. Rude had been listening intently, his fingers propped together like a tent before him. Now he rose.

Jeff had stared straight ahead at the wall while the roaring voice of Baxter accused and shamed him before these men. Every word spoken would be whispered up and down the valley in a day or so. Here was the Melody story, the death of Ktemque, everything. Fred was in this. The weapon used had been taken from him the night of the whipping.

Rude's voice was low, but it carried well.

"Jeffry Claus, stand up."

Jeff rose. Donaldson made him place his hand on a Bible and take an oath to tell the truth.

"Give the Committee your name, place of birth, and condition in life."

The room was quiet but for the heavy breathing of the listeners. After his first word or so, Jeff spoke firmly.

"Jeffry Claus, sirs. I was born in England of German-English parents and came to this country on the brig Seagull and was indentured to a trader named Mark Fultz."

He stopped, but Rude gestured for him to continue.

"Go on. Your full history, please."

Jeff was about to go on when there was a shifting in the closely packed audience as a man pushed through. It was Colonel Henry Antes. Rude greeted him warmly, and the officer smiled at the Committee.

"I'm sorry to be late, gentlemen. Every boat and canoe had been taken, and I finally made shift with one that leaked."

He glanced down at his soaked breeches and stockings. Then he looked at Baxter and Safert. Parr spoke:

"I have the feeling that we may save time by letting the prisoner's story wait while we hear Colonel Antes. Donaldson, the oath."

The Colonel looked surprised but dutifully placed his hand on Donaldson's worn Bible and took the oath. Rude asked the questions.

"Do you recognize the prisoner, Colonel?"

Antes smiled pleasantly and nodded to Jeff.

"Of course. He worked on my stockade and my swivel guns. I hope you will all visit my place; so many of you helped to erect it."

"How long did you employ him? Was he at work for you on July seventeenth?"

Antes smiled again and glanced around the room. "I really did not employ the young man since I paid him no wage. He took the place of my friend, Peter Grube. As I said before, many helped at the post and charged no wages, thinking my place might provide safety as I trust it will."

There were pleased looks on many faces. Colonel Antes was a very much respected man here, even if his place was out of the real Fair Play country. He was continuing. "Jeffry worked for two weeks or thereabouts. When I found him a gunsmith, he furbished all my muskets. Yes, Captain Parr and members of the Court, I do remember the seventeenth, for it was the day before our work was finished. Jeffry worked all through that day on a swivel gun, and it was close to darkness when he had it ready to fire."

Rude nodded his thanks to Antes, who stepped back into the throng. Then the Squire directed his remarks to Baxter.

"Prosecutor, how far is it from here to Fort Augusta—I mean Sunbury?"

"Fifty miles, give or take one or two," was the answer. Rude followed quickly with his next question, which brought a quick flush to the cheeks of the Northumberland man.

"And from there to the Ribner post on the McKee Path?"

"Twelve to fifteen miles. But—"

He was lumbering to his feet, but Rude, ignoring him, turned to the Committee.

"You gentlemen have heard that this Jeffry Claus, before us accused of murder, was all of sixty-five miles from the scene of the crime when it was perpetrated. He was working on a local fort being erected through the generosity of Colonel Antes for our defense. Therefore, I ask, in the name of common sense and on the evidence, that Jeffry Claus be discharged from this evil and malicious accusation."

A growl of approval followed Rude's words when he finished. Parr turned to his fellow Committee members, who each placed a small object in the Captain's palm. He, in turn, added something from his own pocket. When he opened his palm in view of the bystanders, it held three white beans.

"We, the Committee of the Fair Play system, declare Jeffry Claus not guilty of the crime for which he was accused and direct his release from custody," Parr announced formally.

Baxter, still on his feet, was joined by Safert as the room shook with delighted clamor. The prosecutor was roaring.

"This is no trial. You are assembled outside the law. You are not even taxpayers of the county—"

The sudden blaze of tamper in Parr's face silenced the lawyer momentarily, and the Captain leaned forward.

"Baxter, I'm no Fair Play man, but they called me in so there would be an unprejudiced trial to have outside judgment. Now listen to me. These people are up in this country because they wanted homes and were willing to take the risks to make them. Maybe they were sick of the damned Penn laws. They had as good a right to settle on Indian land as most Northumberland ancestors of us had. Northumberland county never did a thing to help them. They let these Fair Play people sink or swim and didn't give a real damn when somebody was scalped."

Parr was really angry now, his voice a savage rumble.

"You build your soapbox forts on the south side of the river. Your lily-livered Commandant won't send a single soldier to help the Fair Play people. They've got along. They live decent, orderly lives outside the stink of Penn laws which cry at the evils of colored slaves and then sell white men like brood mares. Baxter, if I was one of these people and you and your sheriff came up here, I'd ride you ten miles down the Susquehanna on the sharpest rail I could find. You're here on their sufferance. Quit your hollering. Now I'll give you a chance for your last word. Make it short."

The room had become quiet during Parr's tirade, and Baxter stood in outraged astonishment. Probably he had never been beaten this way before. He hesitated a moment as if afraid to put his request.

"Just this, Mr. Parr. Jeffry Claus is a runaway. I ask that he be placed in the custody of Sheriff Safert to return him to his master."

Parr leaned back. The room stirred a little as Baxter seated himself. Then Rude signed Jeff to rise.

"You were a servant of Mark Fultz, trader; how long?"

"Two and a half years of a four-year indenture."

Rude gestured dramatically as if searching his mind for his next question.

"After these years, which I understand were pleasant, Mark Fultz died, and you believed he had set you free in his will. But your indenture was sold by Abner Fultz, Mark Fultz's nephew and alleged heir, to Henry Ribner?"

Jeff nodded, but Rude frowned.

"Speak up, young man, so all can hear."

"Yes, sir. That is correct, sir."

Rude started another question, then looked sharply at the Committee.

"If you please, gentlemen, I ask for a short recess and that the room be cleared for that time."

Parr glanced at his companions at the table, who nodded.

"Recess and get outside, men. The air will do you good."

Jeff was left back of the small enclosure. Rude took Pentz by the sleeve, and Migun stepped forward as they conferred.

When the session reconvened, the room was crowded, with the principals occupying the same places. Baxter and Safert were plainly angry. Colonel Antes had left. At Rude's direction, Jeff stood again, feeling impatient and confused. The throng of men crowded forward as if expecting something momentous.

"Now, Jeffry, the Committee is anxious to get at the truth, and you are under oath."

Jeff stared back at his inquisitor. He knew Rude was helping him and that he should be grateful, but he felt trapped. He had been freed of one crime. Now another was being presented.

"Was your service to Henry Ribner a happy one?"

Jeff tried to think of a proper answer. The feeling of being trapped was stronger now.

"I like to work with guns, sir. I repaired a hundred muskets—"

He thought of the liquor, Ktemque, and the dead savages on the upper river. Rude was frowning as he shot his question.

"You were accused of cohabiting with a colored slave. Is this true?"

Jeff's anger rose as smiles went around the room. He was being stripped of everything which could have given him self-respect. Squire Fell had accused him of being a fool. Now Rude was making a laughing-stock of him. But he had to answer.

"Squire Fell sentenced me to four more years for it. He must have believed Ribner's story."

Rude pointed a bony finger.

"Answer the question. Is it true?"

Jeff's whole body leaned forward, and his eyes went completely cold. His temper was almost as high as it had been when Dilson's lash had stung his shoulder. His throat seemed constricted. For the moment, there was no reason in him.

"Go to hell," he snarled, and Rude stepped back a little from the fury he had roused.

"Many of us will, Jeffry. I'll ask another question. Did you run away from Ribner?"

"No!"

Jeff had not meant to shout the word, but he had, and Rude waved him to his seat.

"Peter Pentz."

The big frontiersman walked forward. He placed his hand on Donaldson's Bible and took the oath, after which he hitched up his belt and took a position only a few feet from Baxter. When directed, he told his story bluntly.

"Jeff didn't run away. He was senseless on the shop floor. Migun, Gokhotit, and I carried him out to a horse after Ribner and the slave, Fred, had damned near killed him with a whip and club. He had a broken leg and some ribs. Jeff, get up."

In two strides, Pentz had reached and yanked Jeff to his feet. Then he pulled the accused man's shirt over his head so the crowd could see the horribly scarred back.

"Hell, the boy couldn't run away. It was a month before he could even walk."

His voice slipped into a snarl as he spoke again,

"Me, I should have killed Ribner that night. He and that trained ape of his was out to kill Jeff. Migun here and Peter Grube know how close they come to managing it—"

Rude motioned the furious backwoodsman aside. In rapid succession, he called Migun and Peter, who corroborated Pentz's testimony. The crowd was getting noisy and angry. Rude mounted a stool to be better heard.

"Men, I'll save time and tell you myself what I learned from witnesses and others. Abner Fultz and Ribner were partners in a trading place that sold liquor, powder, and other stuff to Senecas, who slipped in there over the back trails. Ribner had Jeff fix a full hundred guns that went to either savages or Tories when our armies are short of weapons. We believe Ribner was a Tory and know British officers visited him at night."

He swung his attention to Baxter and Safert.

"You men get back home and clean up that place, or we'll come down and burn it. Tell Fultz if he sells another gill of liquor or powder to a Seneca, we'll burn him in his post."

Rude stepped down, a bit breathless. Parr pounded on the table to get order after he had conferred with Donaldson and Carson.

"The Committee finds Jeffry Claus not guilty of either murder or of being a runaway. Any of you woods rats that wants his gun barrel freshened can find him at Grube's house. Court's adjourned."

Jeff tried to thank Rude and to apologize to him for his outburst of temper. The Squire grinned.

"Jeff, I didn't know how thin the ice was. So long as you're touchy about such things, there is—"

He did not finish, but he gripped Jeff's hand, and his grin became a wide smile. Then his client was seized by the crowd, hoisted to tall shoulders, and paraded about the room and outside, where they deposited him on a stump.

"Speech! Speech!"

Jeff stood uncertainly, trying to stuff his shirt back into his breeches. Something stung the corners of his eyes. Perhaps for the first time since leaving England, he had really seen America and the place he had wanted to find.

"Men," he started stumblingly, and the stinging became worse, "I guess I just can't say a damned thing except that I now have a cutter. Bring on your guns. And I've got some good flints, too. Outside of being obliged, that's all."

CHAPTER XIV

IN THE WEEKS following the trial, Jeff stuck to his shop work and avoided everyone he could. He was pleased with the verdict, but he knew that every detail, every word which had passed, was now the common property of everyone in the valley, particularly of the women. Those who attended the trial had been enthusiastic about the acquittal. Jeff suspected a large part of the satisfaction which had come out of that day was due to the way the Northumberland officials had been handled by Parr and Rude. He, Jeffry Claus, had been a symbol, that was all.

There had been a subtle change in the Grube household, hard to define, but still there. Outwardly, Peter and Faith appeared as they always had been. But to Jeff's notion, they sheltered Susan, who was growing more distant day by day, and he avoided her carefully. Since he slept over the shop and only went to the house for meals, this was easy. Sometimes she would have company, either girls or boys from the locality, and then he kept out of the house completely. The whole situation soured him, and his anger would flare up as he worked until he savagely beat the iron on which he labored. He indulged himself in long tramps in the hills, which left him weary enough to sleep like a log.

Three weeks after the trial, a horseman trotted up and delivered a letter to Peter when he was standing with Jeff in front of the barn. There was, of course, no postal service of any sort north of Fort Augusta. Letters were relayed from one man to another. The rider tapped the letter in Grube's hand.

"Nigh ten days on the road, Peter. Guess it laid some place for a spell."

Peter broke the seal, read the letter quickly, and passed it to Jeff.

"It's from Fell about you."

The letter was brief and to the point. On Baxter and Safert's return, the reward for Jeff's apprehension had been increased another pound sterling by Baxter himself. The trial had been considered a farce, and every effort would be taken to apprehend the runaway and murderer. The letter concluded:

"I trust you to warn Jeffry to keep north of the river and west of the Lycoming. The reward, now close to fifty-five pounds, is most tempting. If he is taken, he will be convicted and hanged since there is talk of a second witness who places him at the Ribner post the night of the murder."

"A second witness." Jeff's lips set in a straight line. That could mean anything, and it could mean Abigail Ribner herself. If it were she, the implication sickened him; she wanted him out of the way. He remembered how calmly she had discussed the possible death of her husband. She might now be working with Fultz, using the man. Sacrificing Jeff to him might mold him to her purposes.

After supper, Faith seemed herself once more as she referred to the letter.

"Anyway, Jeff, you're well out of their clutches and among friends. You're needed up here."

Across the table, Susan kept her eyes on her plate, and Jeff caught the quick glance that passed between husband and wife. He fought back the impulse to shout something. Having finished, he pushed back his plate and rose.

"People have been good to me up here after I came, trailing a lot of trouble behind me. Not many homes have taken in a runaway and murderer."

"Jeff," Faith said sharply, "sit down again and talk this thing over. You've been a little strange lately."

Jeff wanted to rail, to cry out against the things which had happened to him. He wanted to hurt this girl sitting over there with her head bent, pretending not to hear. The bright braid of her hair shone in the candle-light. He mastered the impulse a second time.

"I'm sorry, Faith, but Ezra Feaster's gun isn't finished, and I have to get at it. Ezra thinks that gun's more important than me. Shouldn't wonder," he finished with a grin, "if Ezra was right." During the night, Jeff fought through his problem and came to a decision. He had entered the Grube household and had brought nothing but trouble. Peter and Faith sensed his feelings for Susan. They knew how hopeless the future was for a man who was a fugitive and whose every day of freedom under the law would bring five of servitude. Whatever sympathy the Grubes had for him, their love of Susan would make them shelter her from him. Then Susan, herself, was thinking of the stories about him and the women of the Ribner post. The only way out was for him to leave quietly.

Beyond Harris Ferry to the west was a vast country through part of which Jeff had traveled in Uncle Mark's trains. He would go there where there was always the wilderness if pursuit or capture threatened. It would be possible to ply his trade occasionally, then move on when suspicions pointed his way.

In the morning, before anyone else was out of bed but Charley, who was starting the fires, Jeff entered the kitchen and, with the black man's help, packed some food into a pouch. Later, in the shop, he took down two pistols he had made for himself and his knife and hatchet. Now that his gear was all ready for the hunt on which he told Charley he was going, he counted out his money on the workbench.

It amounted to exactly three pounds; all earned repairing guns and doing other smithing jobs. He pocketed fifteen shillings and shoved the remainder over to the black man.

"That's Peter's money, Charley. Give it to him."

By full daylight, he had crossed the river using an old canoe. He looked back from the vantage point of a hill. Travelome looked like a toy house nestling at the front of the mountain cove with a lazy strip of smoke rising from one of the big chimneys. The outbuildings huddled about the barn suggested a small flock of chicks with the mother hen. Far back of the wide circle, the hills lifted a blue background to the whole setting. Eastward, beyond the mountain shoulder, the broad water of the Tiadaghton sparkled in the early sunlight.

Over there was the Fair Play country where for a time, he had been a free man like the others. The side of the river on which he was belonged to Baxter and Safert's county. Here he was a fugitive with a price on his head. West of the Lycoming, north of the Susquehanna, that was Fair Play land. Rough and rude though the people were, they had defended him.

A lump rose in Jeff's throat. He loved this land and its people, especially those of the Travelome household; Peter, with his blunt kindness, Faith, with her understanding. He could not deny to himself his love of Susan with her quick flashes of temper, her small hands always busy, and the shine of her hair. She would be free in a short time and would marry one of the young men who came shyly to the house on occasion. There was no reason for a girl with her promise to throw herself away on a runaway bondsman with a price on his head.

That night he broke his journey at Migun's cabin and was disappointed at not finding the Indian there. For a full three days, he loafed about the place, often sitting in the doorway where he could have the company of the stream's chatter among the stones. There was nothing to disturb him, and he let his thinking range back to the good days with Uncle Mark Fultz and the pack train.

The old man had ideas, good ones, about many things: the weather, horses, politics, and the proper conduct of full-blooded young men on the frontier. There had been, as a matter of course, hunger, cold, wet, and hard, dangerous traveling in the mountains, but it had been a satisfying life. Uncle Mark made it so with his kindness and understanding.

The quiet here did much to wipe away the depression that had ridden him since the trial. There were new hills and valleys ahead and new people who would not know him as the man whose every slip had been exposed at the trial. There were things to see: homes, stores, taverns, workshops. It would be like turning over the leaf of an unpleasant book. Ribner, his wife with the smoldering eyes, Melody with her warm body, Susan with her bright hair would all be shut from his view. He would see a new world, and he thought of Migun's philosophy.

"The fox does not worry when he misses. He hunts another dinner."

When he had taken the trail again and had come to the Warrior's Path, which ran eastward toward Sunbury, the temptation was strong in him to visit the Ribner post. If Fultz surprised him there, he had his pistols. He remembered the look on the man's face that evening at the table as he watched Abigail Ribner. Fultz would never really possess her. She would own him and shape him as one would a bit of soft clay.

He shook his head. That was a place of traps, and he had no sureness in himself about his ability to escape them. Twice they had closed in on him. The third time would likely mean his life. It was a place for a cautious man to avoid. He bore right and came out on the McKee Path instead.

The old trace followed the south bank of a big creek for a long way, then left it to climb ridges and find its way through darkly timbered valleys. Trodden deep into the forest floor, this path had been used for many generations before the trader, McKee, had used it. At evening of the third day out of Migun's cabin, he came to Fort Shirley. This little village was once known as Aughwick, the Indian town where George Croghan had built his stockade and where the great and understanding Conrad Weiser had so often counseled with deputations of chiefs.

Before entering the village, Jeff took some pains with his appearance. He drew his black hair back severely and fastened it with a short length of ribbon which had been a present from Faith. His shirt was of heavy brown linen, his breeches buckskin, and he wore his high moccasins over thread stockings.

"Better for snakes," Uncle Mark used to say of high footgear.

Jeff carried his few belongings, which included the rifling cutter and his pistols, in a bag which was, in turn, wrapped in his blanket to be slung over his shoulder, knapsack fashion.

Halfway down the village street was a wide, deep lot. Set back in this stood a big stone and log building and, behind it, a huge barn. Directly across the edge of the porch roof was a broad plank into which letters had been carved laboriously, judging from the workmanship.

TRADERS' INN-MAN AND BEAST FED
B, Mead, Prop

As Jeff surveyed the sign, a tremendously stout man with a soiled apron tied about his bulging stomach emerged from an outbuilding and stood beside the newcomer. Presently he pointed a thick forefinger at the sign and spoke.

"Them 'S's' ain't too much. The boy couldn't make the curves good. But, my young friend, people can read that sign and be told what we do. B. Mead, that's me, the little you see of him."

Jeff smiled. He liked this man with the wide mouth and the twinkle in his eye. The pleasant rumbling voice continued.

"Taverns has all sorts of pictures on signs; horses, hens, coaches, and their names don't mean a thing. A man can't step inside expecting to be served a blue hen, leastways not before they got her clothes off."

Jeff was nodding in perfunctory agreement with the landlord's philosophy when the big man turned to him directly, studying his clothing and the bundle under his arm,

"Well, stranger, you don't look like a Britisher. Can I do something for you?"

Jeff explained that he wanted food and lodging, that he had money but preferred to work for his keep, and that he was a smith. The stout man dropped a huge hand on his shoulder and propelled him up the porch steps then inside a wide, clean, well-lighted common room which had the usual bar across its corner.

"Abby!" Mead yelled, and a woman promptly appeared through a door back of the bar. She was small, neatly dressed, and her brown hair was piled high on her head. She was wiping her hands on a ruffled apron as she entered.

"Abby," Mead explained excitedly, "here's a man who says he's a smith. Wants to work for room and board. Here's your kitchen crane fixed and the copper kettle mended. Who knows, mayhap he can even shoe Polly. Son, what do we call you?"

Jeff gave his name, said he came from the Fair Play country, and that he had been indentured to a pack train trader. Mead nodded his head vigorously.

"Figgered you was something like that since most lively-looking young folks is in the army, but I know how damned touchy they are about an indentured man."

Jeff assured himself that he had made the first hurdle in disarming any suspicion and followed Mead about while the light held. There was a good-sized blacksmith shop well furnished with tools and a big tight barn that made Jeff think nostalgically of the one on the Thread Hollow farm.

"My smith, Ben Heiger, went over into Lancaster county," Mead explained. "Been with me five years, but I can't pay the fancy wages they do in them gun and wagon shops. Don't blame Ben; he was a good man."

The innkeeper proudly displayed his mare, Polly, when they looked through the barn. She was a big, smooth-coated animal with the wide nostrils that hinted nervousness. Jeff moved about her talking quietly even when she plunged and kept it up until she quieted down. Supper was ready when they came in.

"Looks like a good man with horses," Jeff heard Mead tell his wife. "He made friends with Polly."

"You and your Polly," his wife answered partly in fun, partly in derision. "Better get out front and wait on customers. I'll feed the young man."

Jeff ate heartily of the boiled dinner in which the meat had not been stinted among the vegetables. When he finished, he smiled at Mrs. Mead.

"You folks will have to get together a good bit of work, Mrs. Mead. With meals like that, I'll be eating you out of house and home in no time."

She smiled and stood by the table for a moment.

"I like to see people eat. Maybe that's why Belfort is getting a little stout."

She leaned forward confidentially.

"Don't tell him I said so, but he had to use the block this morning to mount Polly."

"Abby," Jeff thought. That was the name of the woman upriver, Abigail Ribner. He was moving out of the dining room when the woman who was clearing the table spoke again, gesturing toward the common room.

"Don't mind if he asks a lot of questions. Belfort's worried about Tories."

Jeff looked at her in some surprise.

"Around here?" he questioned, and she set down a dish.

"Yes, but let Belfort be telling you. Just listen to him carefully; he don't stretch things."

The customers who frequented the common room went home early. Jeff was left alone with Mead, who closed up his bar and joined his new smith at a table.

"Jeff," he began, "I asked if you was a Britisher. That may look funny, but you didn't look like one, and it was safe to ask."

He fished out his pipe, loaded it carefully, then held it unlighted in his palm while he talked.

"Since you're going to work here, you'd ought to know the things that goes on. You ever been at Kittanning?"

Jeff studied a moment before he replied.

"Yes, I've been as far as Pittsburgh with the train. I've followed the Path through here up past Standing Stone, then over the hills to Frankstown."

Mead nodded, his face showing satisfaction.

"Well, there's a big bunch of Tories about Kittanning whooped along by a man named Weston. When the war first cracked, he started getting busy. The British kept in touch with him by slipping down the Allegheny from the Lakes. Kittanning is on that river, like you know. The idea was to take a Tory and Indian army through here, come out on the Susquehanna, take Fort Augusta and Harris Ferry. After that, they'd hit the lower counties and wipe out the gun-making places."

The stout man fumbled for his tinder box but did not light the pipe.

"They say a trader on the McKee Path was in with them, that he furnished guns to Weston's army. Well, they marched all right, not a thousand as they'd figgered but clost to three hundred, and we knocked hell out of that bunch dost to Standing Stone. Then word came through that this trader got himself kilt. We figger things is better now, but we jest ain't too sure. Couple of things help. A man named McAlevy is building a stockade not far from Standing Stone. South and west, the Congress had men open the lead diggings in Sinking Valley. General Roberdeau's in there now with a fair garrison. That's the picture up till now." Mead rose and lighted his pipe.

"Kind of a longish story, Jeff, but you ought to know. Weston ain't dead, though. I figger a snake ain't settled with till its head's cut off. So we watch and wait."

Jeff had a lot to think about when he climbed to the little room assigned to him. The trader was Ribner; it was clear now that Squire Fell had known what he was talking about when he suspected the aid the trader was giving the British cause. Whoever had bludgeoned the man and stuck that knife in his throat had performed a service to the colonies. Mead had mentioned that the British had kept in touch down the Allegheny River. Some of their messengers had been the red-coated visitors at Ribner Post.

In his first forenoon's work, he repaired Abigail Mead's crane, mended her copper kettle, and fashioned two big iron trivets to support her frying pans above the fireplace coals. The afternoon went mostly to the task of shoeing Polly, which turned out to be a touchy job, with Mead more nervous than the horse. Customers called the innkeeper away, and while he was gone, Jeff had no trouble with the mare. Both the Meads were delighted.

Jeff sat on the porch after a generous supper. There had been a huge piece of dried apple pie and a pint cup of milk sweetened with maple sugar and then laced with ground nutmeg. That dessert on top of a big meal made him content just to sit and admire the beauty of the scene before him as the colors of the evening played on the mountains which lifted to the west beyond the flat lands.

"Beautiful," he muttered half under his breath. He had thought himself alone until Mead spoke back of him.

"It is that," the stout man agreed. "That big, curving mountain is called Jack's, after an old Indian killer. Up river to the east of us was Fort Granville, burned in the old wars. Never was much fighting right here. Guess the savages couldn't forget this was a council place once."

"How about Indians now?" Jeff asked, and Mead studied a moment before replying.

"Well, they'd lose a lot of hair if they was to come down the Allegheny and east along the Path. Of course, that way, an Indian raid would be like an arrow straight at the heart of what this state's doing to supply our army. No, we're pretty well set here to stop such things. If the Indians come, likely it will be down the Susquehanna's two branches. There's nothing to stop them up that way. Augusta's too old as a fort."

Alone again after a few minutes, Jeff thought of his own route coming to this place and how easy it would have been for Weston's Tories and Indians to have pushed through to the Ribner post. He thought of Ed Cathcart, dead on the Sinnamahoning, of the fight at the cabin up there and the Indian woman with her music box. He wondered if Squire Fell knew of the Tory defeat at Standing Stone.

News travels fast, and work came into the shop, almost enough of it for two smiths. Jeff sharpened plowshares, made froes to split shingles, dressed out axes with blades thickened from much grinding, and turned his hand to the difficult job of making several grass scythes, the temper and balance of which had to be exactly right. His heaviest work was horseshoeing, and he came to enjoy tacking on the small, irregularly shaped shoes worn by the oxen. The great beasts would stand placidly chewing their cuds while he worked at their feet.

Jeff was careful to avoid any mention or attempt at gunsmithing, keeping in mind the Ribner advertisement, "by trade, a gunsmith." The appearance in this town of a gunsmith would invite comment. Such tradesmen would properly belong in the Lancaster county area. One man did see his pistols and examined them with interest.

"The man that made these knew his business," he commented. "Who was it?"

Jeff thought fast while he laid down his hammer and picked up a pair of tongs.

"Guess the fellow was hard up. I got them in a sort of trade, and there was no maker's name on them." Jeff's answer seemed to satisfy the man. What he had said was the truth even if shaped in a misleading way.

After some days, Jeff began spending part of his evenings in the big common room, where he visited with the men who came and went. There was usually some discussion of the war, but noticeably, no comment on Tories. Once, Jeff allowed himself a direct comment on colonial militia, drawing his ideas from Migun's remarks on the same subject.

"It's all right for militia to shoot and run. That way, the British can't destroy them."

A bearded farmer hailing from over close to Jack's Mountain and for whom Jeff had sharpened an ax leaned forward.

"That's exactly what a smart young fellow told me not long past. He was an Indian, used to work on a pack train, name of Migun. Smart as a steel trap, he was."

Jeff made no further comment, the cold finger of warning touching him between the shoulders. He wondered what would happen if his Delaware friend did wander into this place while he was here.

The weather continued fair and pleasant, and customers multiplied. They ranged from mountain men who needed new trap springs to the quiet, bearded River Brethren with their fine, heavy horses. Jeff was enjoying the community to the extent that he attended several square dances and husking bees. On the second week in November, the soul-seller arrived.

He was a little man wearing a poorly combed wig under a greenish-black tricorn hat. He had a wide mouth and small, closely set eyes. The stock about his scrawny neck was as dirty as though it belonged to an Indian. He drove a two-wheeled cart with a faded linen top. In the back of this was an array of cheap tinware and other goods which afforded scant space to a frightened-looking girl. Beside the driver on the high seat rode a seedy-looking old man.

"Howdy, Mr. Mead," the new arrival called pleasantly from his seat. "Got room fer three people as ain't too perticular?"

Mead followed the new guests into the inn. Jeff unhitched the horse, took it to the stable, where he rubbed it down thoroughly and then fed it liberally. The little man was in the common room when he came in and stepped forward, extending a dirty hand.

"My name's Eitler, Frederick Eitler from down Chester way."

Jeff took the hand and received a limp shake.

"I'm Claus," he introduced himself bluntly. "I'm the smith here."

Eitler sidled closer and spoke almost in a whisper.

"If you're a tradesman like that, I can get you higher wages down country."

Jeff did not answer but turned his back and moved off. He did not like the new arrival and saw no reason to conceal his dislike.

Eitler talked steadily through the evening meal though he did not fail to stow away more food than even Mead consumed. He had definite opinions on many subjects, and it was his considered opinion that Congress should get rid of Washington in favor of a general like Gates.

The girl's name was Regina. She seemed to grow more frightened and retiring as the evening went along. Thin almost to emaciation, her light brown hair was pulled back so severely that her cheekbones appeared to be more prominent than they really were. At table, she fumbled with her spoon and knife. Occasionally, she would eat hungrily then stop in confusion. The old man was obviously ill and ate as one does out of duty rather than appetite.

A nipping breeze was coming in from the mountains when Jeff went out on the porch. Presently the old man, carrying a patched quilt, joined him.

"Is the barn all right for me?" he asked. There was a fearfulness of refusal in his voice that made Jeff's lips set in a straight line.

"Here," he said and took the quilt, leading the way back to the barn. There he pulled down hay and spread a clean horse blanket over that to make a comfortable bed. As an afterthought, he added a second blanket to the old man's quilt.

Jeff had heard of and seen soul-sellers when he worked for Uncle Mark. They were men who haunted the auctions and bought the servants that did not command a good price or who could not be sold. Such purchases were taken up country to find buyers. Once, a soul-seller's caravan had passed the pack train, and Jeff remembered the look on Migun's face. Eitler looked to be a good example of the meanest of such merchants in human souls.

About two hours after he had settled the old man in his bed, Jeff came into the common room where Eitler was indulging in a loud conversation with several farmers. The girl, Regina, sat unnoticed in a corner. No one was paying any attention to her, and Jeff thought of a dog that crawls away into a corner to escape brutality. Even Mead did not look her way. He frowned when Jeff turned and walked out again into the clean air.

Ten minutes passed. Eitler must have come through a side door, for the front one had not opened. He sidled up to Jeff, who noticed there was an odor about the man, like the dregs of stale beer.

"Claus," he spoke almost in a whisper, "I noticed you looking over our Regina. She's a fine clean young piece."

He took Jeff's arm familiarly.

"Happens that I'm a bit crowded for cash money, and you're a young blood, Claus. I can see it in your eye. Put ten shillings in my hand, and I'll put the girl in your bed for the night."

He dug a sharp elbow into his listener's ribs and cackled: "Just for company, of course. The girl ain't ever been touched, so she wouldn't know."

Anger sent such a tremor through Jeff's muscles that his hands clenched. His impulse was to take this foul, little beast and break his dirty neck. He thought of the time Ribner had trapped him with Melody. This wasn't a trap; it was simply a foul exploitation of human merchandise. The girl knew what was coming. That accounted for her fright. Jeff's mind raced. If he did not buy the girl for the night, Eitler would peddle his wares to someone else. On impulse, he pulled out the money and laid it in Eitler's palm. The clap of the soul-seller's hand between his shoulder blades made Jeff's flesh crawl.

"She'll be there, my boy. She'll be there."

Later, Jeff found Mead alone in the kitchen, his wife having retired.

"Belfort, that girl's in my room, and I'll sleep in the barn. I paid Eitler for her so she'd have a night's peace. Tell her she's safe."

Mead looked into the savage young face and nodded.

The old man in the barn was obviously pretty sick and moving restlessly on his pallet. There was enough moonlight to show his face was ghastly. As Jeff knelt by him, clawlike fingers caught his sleeve. The man's words came haltingly.

"Did he sell her tonight?"

"Tried to," Jeff told him. "I gave him the money so she'd be left alone."

He pulled his sleeve away. So this was Eitler's regular procedure. The old man moved restlessly, and his voice was very weak.

"Looks like I'll beat the bastard this night. If I had a little liquor, it would be easier."

Mead always kept a small bottle of whiskey on a beam back of Polly's stall. It was more than half full, and Jeff gave it to the sick man whose fingers closed round the flask eagerly. His hand trembled so much Jeff had to help him place the bottle to his lips. He was stronger immediately.

"Eitler bought us cheap. Liquor was my trouble, and I sold myself, so I ain't no kick coming. One pound he put up for me, three for her, Regina, I mean. She's a good sort that would like to be decent, but he sold her half a dozen times coming up country. He had to horse-whip her the first time. After that, she was too scared to put up a battle."

He was quiet for a little but could not seem to get the girl out of his mind.

"Poor Gina. What's to become of her?"

His voice turned sharper.

"Now, you big young devil, get along and sleep. You didn't miss much. The girl ain't but fifteen, sixteen years old. Let me alone with this liquor."

When Jeff slid down from his bed in the haymow in the morning, he found the old man's body wrapped in the quilt, a small, untidy mound looking as though empty clothes had been piled in a heap. It was easy to realize now what he had meant about cheating Eitler this night. The man was dead with the empty bottle beside him on the hay.

Jeff removed the flask. Through the night, it had given some comfort to the dying man. So this was the way a servant, old and useless, died. A horse would have received more attention. As he looked down into the wrinkled and cold features, Jeff realized that this way, freedom could be bought. He, Jeffry Claus, was young and strong, but the years of servitude stretched ahead, doubling, redoubling for each day he remained free.

He did not knock as he entered the kitchen, where Mrs. Mead was busy at the fireplace. When she saw him, her eyes blazed.

"You," she snapped. "I thought you had the making of a man, but you have turned my house into a foul place. You let that beast sell you that poor, half-starved girl, and she's still in your room where you left her. Get out of my house, I'll—"

Her voice had become almost a scream, and Mead pushed into the kitchen from the bar.

"Be still, Abby."

She stared at her husband, surprised at the command in his tone.

"Jeff paid for that girl and slept in the barn himself. He wanted the poor thing to have some peace one night without some damn fool after her."

Abby stared at the two men for an instant, then raised her apron to her eyes and began to sob. Jeff spoke to Mead.

"The old man's dead. Let's go in and talk to Eitler."

The soul-seller raged when told of the death of the old man. "The old sot," he cried. "I never made a cent out of him."

Jeff stepped up, his eyes cold with menace.

"Get out the girl's indenture papers, Eitler. I'll buy her and I'll pay to bury the old man."

Eitler's face straightened. He rolled his eyes knowingly.

"I knowed you'd like her. I'll get the papers. It will cost you eight pounds since she's only seventeen and you'll have four years. Quite enough, too."

Jeff had paid for his food and lodging and now had saved close to five pounds in addition to his original fund of shillings. He had compelled himself to listen to Eitler's insinuations. Now he turned to Mead.

"Let's rout out Squire Evans. Bring your papers, Eitler. You'll get four pounds for the girl, no more. That's a full pound profit." The seller started to protest until he read the faces of the two men. At that moment, Regina came down the stairway.

"You've been bought," he snapped. "Come on."

Fear deepened on the girl's face. Mrs. Mead entered the room with a shawl about her shoulders. She put her arm about the cowering Regina and accompanied the men to the squire's office, where the indenture papers were endorsed. Squire Evans finished, and Jeff paid over his four pounds and the squire's one shilling fee. Abruptly the official pulled back the papers and glanced up.

"Just a moment, young man. Where is your home to which you will take this young girl?"

Jeff looked at him stupidly and stammered.

"Why, I have no home. I guess I—"

Evans frowned severely and spoke in righteous tones.

"Well, we can't sell a young girl to tag along in this unholy fashion."

Jeff stared at him and finally understood.

"Hell, Squire, I don't want her to tag along. I want her set free."

The taut look vanished from Regina's face, and for the moment, she was almost beautiful. Jeff thought of Susan and her good fortune compared to this girl.

"And I aim to give her work," Mrs. Mead announced stoutly. "I been needing kitchen help, and maybe she can sew. Can you, Regina?"

Jeff scarcely heard the eager: "Oh yes, I can."

Back in the tavern, Eitler paid his own reckoning and gestured to Jeff.

"He'll pay for the girl's keep. Mead, and you won't likely be charging for the old man."

The tension in Jeff snapped. He took Eitler by the frayed neckcloth and the seat of his trousers, pitching him face downward on the floor.

"Now, you filthy pup, you'll get what you handed out. You whipped the girl, didn't you?"

Eitler cowered on his knees, and Mead looked shocked.

"Only a little, young sir, only—"

Jeff dragged his victim to the porch. He picked up a good-sized fence picket, and with the soul-seller over his knee, set to work.

Eitler's first yells of agony dropped to frantic moans and gasps, but the picket rose and fell until Mead caught Jeff's arm.

"Don't kill him. Let him go now."

The released Eitler stumbled and scrambled to his cart, where the horse was already hitched in the shafts. He climbed to his high seat with the agility of a monkey, but when he sat down, he jerked upright with a cry of pain. Shaking his whip, he howled at Jeff.

"I know you now, you black devil. Wait till I get to a Squire, you bloody-minded runaway that durst to strike a free man."

Jeff leaped forward, snatching up a stone as he did. Eitler's whip came down on his horse. The cart clattered away, but Jeff's thrown missile crashed into the tinware in the back of the vehicle.

"Yes," Jeff said bitterly to the watching Mead. "I'm a runaway all right and worth fifty pounds laid down in Sunbury. The pimp was right."

With a quick jerk, he pulled up his shirt and showed the innkeeper his scarred back. Mead nodded soberly.

"Tull your shirt down, Jeff. I knowed who you was when we read that sign together. So did lots of other folks. We'd have warned you if anybody got hungry for that reward. Anyway, it'll be some time before Eitler can sit down to tell his story."

CHAPTER XV

TO JEFF'S SURPRISE, Mead made no reference to what he had revealed. During the next two days, they gave the dead bondsman a decent burial and made preparations for a trip Mead said he must take. When he was ready to leave, he came out with Abby and Jeff to the mounting block where Polly waited. He kissed his wife resoundingly.

"Be gone three or four days, Jeff. Run the place like Abby tells you, son. I'll be depending on you."

Work had slackened considerably, and Jeff had too much time for thinking. It scarcely seemed possible that Belfort Mead, who had immediately recognized him as a runaway with a price on his head, would have taken him in as he did. It gave him a warm feeling for the innkeeper. But many people had been kind; there were the Grubes, Migun, Peter Pentz, Squire Rude. If he could ever get out from under the shadow which hovered over him, he knew this would be a good land, rich, kindly, and full of promise.

Regina gave her last name as Metz, and she and Mrs. Mead got on well from the first. Once she was decently dressed and unafraid she was almost pretty. Her presence about the inn kept turning Jeff's mind back to Susan. She had been so fortunate. The indenture system had passed its evils by her, and she had become not a servant but almost a daughter to the Grubes. Regina had been bandied about the country unmercifully by the soul-seller as a source of income with no thought of her as a human being.

Mead, looking a bit gaunt for him, returned at the end of a week.

"Nobody cooks so good as you, Abby," he assured his wife. "Either the meat is maybe too hard cooked or just seared a little, and the sweets and sours is all mixed up."

He had brought gifts for all of them, dress goods for the women, and a tiny steel tinder box with a spring lid for Jeff. Mead smiled as he presented it.

"I heard you lost one once."

Jeff stared for a moment. It could be that either Migun or Pentz had given the innkeeper the full story of what had happened at the Ribner Post. He recovered himself.

"I'm obliged to you, Belfort, for I really needed one." His big fingers caressed the smooth metal before he slipped it into his pocket.

After the common room had closed for the night, Mead and his wife came up to Jeff's room and sat on his bed while they talked.

"Son, I hoped to bring back better news. I've been all over on my business and partly on yours, Jeff. That Eitler spilled his news all right, went right from here to Sunbury. The Northumberland sheriff will be down here in a day or so. Squire Fell had that news."

Jeff nodded. Sheriff Safert would be glad to wipe away his experience at the hands of Squire Rude and the Fair Play Committee. Abby touched her eyes with her apron, and Mead, glancing toward her, explained her strong feeling.

"Abby and me had a boy who'd be about your age now, and we lost him. He had his troubles, so we kinda know what young people go through. Now that he's dead and gone, maybe we both see something of him in young men like you. Anyways, we'd have liked to keep you, but I guess it's over the hills for you come morning."

Jeff made no comment because nothing he could have said would have amounted to a great deal. Certainly, he did not want to leave this place. He liked it and the people in it. It seemed like home. Mead filled his pipe, looked at the tobacco, and left it unlighted.

"Christian Fell told me a lot about you and Ribner. He knows that you couldn't be much worked up about the war after they'd turned you down and also that you had not really had a chance to learn what Ribner was doing."

He waved the pipe in a wide gesture.

"But my guess was right. Ribner's Post was to be the gate through which Weston's Tories and savages would have poured. Now we licked that outfit once, and Ribner's dead. Hell, Jeff, you'd have done a real service to the country if you'd have killed him yourself. Well, this Fultz would like to have taken over, but he can't swing things. Besides, Fell says the man is woman crazy." He shrugged his big shoulders.

"Anyway, we figger the threat to the valley from this direction is much less. Now the danger will come from the north. Here's what I come up to say before I got on this war business. You go east over the Path. At Wheterville, a few miles north of Lancaster, is Jonas Cultsizer's gun shop, and he'll have a job for you. There'll be no questions asked."

Jeff left early in the morning. Mead, Abby, and Regina were in the kitchen, and he found his few belongings had increased measurably. Now he had an excellent light blanket, a full change of clothing, and a good woolen jacket. Mead tried to force money upon him, but Jeff was firm about that. They all stood by while he made a neat pack of his things, adding a bag filled with provisions. He had put one pistol in the blanket roll, the other he now presented to Mead.

"Remember me by this, Belfort," he said. "I made it."

There was finally a quick handshake with Mead, a shy one with Regina, and Mrs. Mead kissed him on the cheek.

"Go with God, Jeffry," she said. "Some day, things will be all right for you."

There was no difficulty following this oldest of the Indian paths to Kittanning Trail. There had been a little snow, but not enough to obscure such a deeply trodden way. By noon he had passed through the gap in Blacklog mountain and had climbed the zigzag route up the side of Tuscarora, the last of the ridgelike mountains. From here, looking back, he could see the great arc of Jack's Mountain, but the lower ridges between shut out a view of the little town he had left. Ahead rolled the tumbled low country toward the faint flashing of the Susquehanna.

He shrugged his shoulders, easing the pack he carried. This was to be the pattern of his days: new friends for some weeks, perhaps months, then more flights through the hills. Some day the end for him would be like that of the old man in the stable. The light wind from the east touched his face. He was still young. "Some day, things will be all right for you." Mrs. Mead had believed what she said. He, Jeffry Claus, could believe the same. He thought of Regina and her new freedom. Eitler, who had owned her and exploited her, had set the law after him again. The soul-seller would not yet have forgotten the feel of that picket well laid on. Suddenly he grinned, put his hand over his lips, and sounded the wolf call Migun had taught him.

Having given full vent to his feelings, he glanced about sheepishly. There was little likelihood of his having company here on this windy summit on a late November day.

"Hell of a thing to do," he mumbled as he started down the slope eastward. "Just gave tongue like a lost dog."

Hours later, he explained to the ferryman at Wright's Crossing that he was a smith coming east to find work.

"That's the right direction," the man told him. "I can't keep a man here on my boat because of the big wages in Lancaster."

Jeff stood at the bow of the big flatboat as it moved out over the dark river. He recalled that other day when he had crossed this same stream half a hundred miles farther north. Then he had expected to be free in a short time, and Bower Samuels had offered him a good job. That same day he was to learn that Abner Fultz still owned him as he did the pack horses of his uncle's string. Jeff swore under his breath. A nearby passenger, dressed like a farmer, turned toward him.

"Did you say something?"

Jeff started.

"No, I guess not. I was just thinking of this dark water."

"Well, give it a month, and it'll be ice. You can skate across then."

Jeff liked the familiar, heavy accent of the man, for it was much like Susan's. For the remainder of the crossing, they stood and talked together about this river, the ferry, and the weather. The man said his name was Bredholz and supplied the information that there was a good cheap tavern in the town where they would land.

The crooked road Jeff followed the next morning after spending the night in the recommended place wound through fields, copses of woodland, and broken ground. It finally came to a fork where the hardboard advised that it was six miles southward to Lancaster and a mile ahead to the village of Wheterville.

The Jonas Sultsizer shop wasn't hard to find, seeing that it occupied a good fourth of the town's area. It was a succession of rough board structures with a half dozen smoking chimneys. Before he went to it, Jeff stopped at an inn which displayed two neatly painted black horses on a white background together with the words:

BLACK HORSE TAVERN

Jeff thought of Belfort Mead's opinion of such signs and went in to make inquiry of a noncommittal bartender.

"Jonas you will find somewhere in his shop which you can't miss. You get inside and look for a wide man with a broad beard."

The first building reeked with the fumes from charcoal fires, and three men worked beside a huge forge. Jeff saw that they were tempering gun barrels. Close by was a narrow vat half filled with oily-looking water from which a light steam lifted. None of them looked up, but they were all clean-shaven, so Jeff moved on into the next building.

This was a woodworking shop with high benches above, which were well-filled tool racks in easy reach of the half dozen mechanics at work on stocks, ramrods, and lock work. Jeff watched, fascinated. In the small shops, one smith made the whole gun from butt plate to front sight. Here each man worked on a separate part. Near where Jeff watched a man thrust a finished ramrod into the thimbles of a gun. Made of hickory, it carried a light bend, so it would use the spring of the wood against the thimble metal to keep it from dropping out, just what it might be needed. A rumbling voice made Jeff wheel.

"I'm Cultsizer. Could I do something for you?"

The hotel man's description was entirely accurate. The leather apron he wore made the gunsmith look even wider, and his russet beard was cut squarely across. The eyes that looked directly into Jeff's face were blue and set deeply under the hedges of heavy brows.

"You're Jeffry Claus," the man rumbled. "I knowed you from what Mead told me. We was expecting you."

In less than a half hour, Jeff was at work. By evening, Cultsizer had found him room and board in the hotel where he had asked directions. In a week, he had worked all over the big shop with Cultsizer watching him occasionally. At the end of this time, the blunt shop owner assigned his new man to the final assembly shop. Jeff's careful training under his father stood him in good stead in this work, for most of the gunlocks were imported from Switzerland through France. He had been taught to be critical of a gun, especially the size of the touchhole. Cultsizer came through one day when Jeff was looking dubiously at an iron ramrod.

"You do not like them metal rods either?"

When he was answered by an emphatic shake of the head, the big man rubbed his beard with a massive forefinger.

"I do not like the way the iron thumps itself down on the charge. Could be loose powder grains in the barrel get rubbed and fire. Wood is kinder as we know, but this damned Congress—it asks the metal rods for the guns."

Jeff agreed. He had found that Cultsizer really knew his trade and had a genius for organizing work. All the finished guns were fire tested by a withered rifleman named Obed Hussey, to whose opinion the shop owner bowed. Hussey also checked trigger pulls.

"The pull must not be light for a soldier," he declared. "A man's got to be sure when his gun goes off, and a hard trigger pull answers that. I seen a man in battle load three charges on top of each other. Thought he was shooting all the time."

Cold winter days slipped by in a steady, engrossing monotony of work which Jeff thoroughly enjoyed. He did little thinking about personal problems. When he wasn't too tired in the evenings, he worked on drawings of gun parts. Quite often, he returned to the shop at night to complete some project which intrigued him. Cultsizer now seldom stopped at his bench except to pay his wages. By February, he was receiving ten shillings for each eleven-hour day. Since he lived frugally at the Black Horse Tavern, he was saving money rapidly. Occasionally he thought of Susan back at Travelome, where she would be sitting, either sewing or knitting, before the fire with Faith opposite her and Peter likely asleep in his big chair. But he shut those pictures away as quickly as possible.

As Jeff's money accumulated, he had another idea. It might be possible to buy out his indenture. Barring the reward offered for him as a murderer, at the close of March, he would have enough to pay what Fultz had received from Ribner, plus the runaway reward. Of course, there were many legal entanglements, but he felt sure Squire Fell could arrange them once the murder charge was settled. There was the fact, however, that whatever he was earning as a fugitive belonged to his master under the old colony law, which likely was not greatly changed with statehood.

Spring, down here in the lower counties, was in the air. Up in the state's northern hills, there would be snow in the dark, hemlock-shaded hollows. Here, fields were already green. The shadbush in the thickets waved its lacy flowers in the breeze, and little peepers set up their chant in every bog. Early in April, Cultsizer stopped at Jeff's bench.

"Fretz, Kinrad, and Turner wants to go to the city. They want to leave Friday afternoon and get back Sunday morning."

The shopman made his remarks sound casual, but Jeff felt he understood. The trio were some of the best mechanics in the shop. Cultsizer's heavy brows lifted.

"I was thinking you might go along. You'd get your Saturday's pay anyway."

The big man was squaring his heavy shoulders. He seemed embarrassed by what he had to propose.

"Them boys has lots of money, and they'll be in every rot gut saloons and hoorhouses in the town. I was thinking if you went along, mebbe you could get them back here Sunday mornings. Then they'd have time to sleep it off come Monday morning."

Jeff wanted to laugh. Cultsizer had given him an excellent job, had accepted him without question, and now seemed entirely unaware how much Jeff owed him. He picked up a piece of iron and slapped it down.

"Ord'nary, I'd jest let them boys go to hell anyway they had a mind to, but these is war times. There's guns to be made, and I can't spare one of the three."

Jeff assured Cultsizer he would be glad to go. Friday afternoon, with a good horse hitched in a carryall, he and the three smiths took their way over the pleasant country road in the direction of the nearby city. All of them were in high good humor. Fretz, the red-headed man, did most of the talking.

"Tist, Jeff, we'll sample the liquor, and then we'll head for the women. They got all kinds in them houses from squaws to the painted gypsies the army officers fancies."

Jeff was perfectly familiar with Lancaster from being there so often with Uncle Mark's pack train. His companions had no taste for the business part of town outside of a tavern where the four shared a big meal washed down with plenty of wine. After that, Jeff stabled the horse in a livery and accompanied his companions in and out of a number of barrooms. However, he had little taste for liquor and knew well enough that a man with a price on his head could not risk drunkenness. Fretz noticed his growing restlessness.

"Jeffry, you ain't liking this business overmuch. Besides, Cultsizer said you was to bring us back. If you wasn't a damned fool, you'd come along, but we'll let you go now and no hard feelings. Likely we'll end up at Mother Accord's sometime early Sunday morning."

After a good bit of chafing from the other two, Jeff went back to the tavern where they had eaten and hired a room. There were a number of errands he would have liked to do but was afraid of the risk. Lancaster was a great crossroads town. There would be many pack train men who would recognize him, and there could be men from Fort Augusta here, as well.

Next morning, Saturday, he walked downtown to the gun shops. One of them he knew was using barrels bored in lumber and grist mills in contrast to the older method of welding strips of iron about a metal core. He wanted to see how this was done. Luckily a gray-haired man stood at the door of a big shed building, and Jeff approached him with his problem. The man smiled.

"My name's Berkland, young man. I'm a partner here, and we use those bored barrels. Come on in. I'll show you."

The shop wasn't working that day, and there was a big stock of gun barrels that did not look very different from those made in the conventional manner.

"The only thing, barrels are tricky, no two alike," Berkland said. "We have to straighten all we get, even those the Widow Smith on White Deer creek turns out."

Jeff had an excellent visit. The two men talked guns all forenoon. Berkland had seen little cutters like the one Jeff described but agreed that making rifle barrels with it would be very slow.

"You get tired of where you're working," Berkland said as they were parting, "come here. I can use a man with ideas."

Late Saturday evening Jeff started on his search for his fellow workers, and he had a quite self-righteous feeling. Cultsizer had trusted him to bring these men back. While they were carousing, he, Jeff, had been improving his mind. Now he found his new task unpleasant and the places he visited unattractive. In each tavern, he saw men in all stages of drunkenness, barkeepers short of temper, and the women he encountered, foul-mouthed and sodden.

About one o'clock, he was getting discouraged. Places were closing, and he had learned nothing of the whereabouts of Cultsizer's mechanics. In desperation, he accosted a tall, thin man who had just entered the lighted street from a dark sideway.

"Sir," Jeff began respectfully, "will you tell me the way to Mrs. Accord's?"

The man snapped to full height, and then, surprisingly, he poked Jeff's chest with a forefinger.

"Young man, you besmirch me by thinking I would know a place of that kind. Listen, 'her feet take hold on Hell, and her steps lead down to perdition.' "

Jeff stared, aware that he should have been more circumspect in questioning people. He was mumbling a word of apology half under his breath when the finger poked again.

"Last house, left side, this street. Best keep away. Three young hellions have been there nigh all day."

With a chuckle at the discomfiture of his questioner, the man walked on.

The Accord house was larger than its fellows along the street, and a gaunt, stern-faced woman admitted Jeff. He explained his errand briefly, pressed a coin in her hand, and asked to be shown a place where he could wait for his friends. She took the coin, examined it carefully, and dropped it into a capacious pocket.

"They're pretty well lit up, friend. Maybe you'll have to wait a couple of hours."

She ushered him into a little room that carried the sour smell of spilled liquor. There he sat down wearily beside a small, round table. He was pretty sick of the job Cultsizer had wished on him and disgusted with the carousal of his fellow workers. Hitching his chair forward, he laid his arms on the table, dropped his head on them, and presently slept.

He had no way of telling how long he had been asleep. He was roused by a hand pressed alongside of his cheek; a fresh candle had been placed in the holder on the table. He needed one look to recognize his visitor. The partially dressed girl who bent over him and who had touched his face was Melody.

"Jeff," she murmured softly and pleadingly. "I jest been sittin' lookin'. I knowed you when you come in right off."

He stared at the girl. She was beautiful in a tawny way with her almost white skin and big, sleepy eyes. She sank down in a chair and leaned toward him over the table edge.

"Jeff, I ain't got but a couple of minutes. Won't you take me out of here? I'm tired of being mauled around, and you could find me a place where I could work. She—"

Her bare shoulder gestured to where the woman of the house probably was.

"She'd let me go for a pound or so."

Slipping from her chair, she kneeled beside his knee.

"I'd go with you to old Fell and tell him how Ribner trapped you and how I was jes' bait."

Jeff's mind considered her proposition while his eyes searched her face. Perhaps something like that could be done, but there was no way of being sure. He'd have to talk to Fell first. He rose, but she clung to him.

"I'll see, Melody."

He reached down to loosen her arms, but she leaped up and flung herself upon him. She locked her arms about his body in a frantic embrace while her heavy perfume almost choked him. Then, as suddenly as she seized him, she jerked back, her lips curling away from white teeth.

"No, you don't expect to, Jeff Claus. You was always high and mighty, and you was bought and sold just like us. No, you ain't got the heart to get a girl out of a place like this."

Her eyes were no longer sleepy. They blazed as she padded back and forth like a big cat. Her feet in felt slippers made no noise on the rough floor. She came closer, her eyes narrowing.

"So, Mister High and Mighty, I knows about you and Ribner's doxie. They's money up fer you in Sunbury town, a lot of it. There's folks I kin tell you was here, and I'll come to your hangin'."

Whirling, she dashed out of the room.

Sheer blind luck—he sat and cursed under his breath. This sleek girl had tricked him into four more years of servitude. She had been paid with the only money he had owned and which had been stolen from him. Indirectly she was back of every evil thing that had come to him. Her threats carried a lot of weight. There was no safety for him about here if she dropped the slightest word. The reward was too high. Even the smiths for whom he was looking might turn him in to the officers for fifty pounds.

The candle burned lower and lower as he sat looking at his big hands and wrists on the tabletop. Two things were before him; hiding or coming to trial. Suddenly an idea broke through the fog of his thinking. Melody had left the post before Ribner's murder, even before the affair with Abigail Ribner. She was gone at the time of the whipping and the escape. How could she know so much?

A half hour had passed since the girl had darted out of the room. He knew he must find the workmen and get them started for Wheterville. As he got up stiffly from the hard chair, the gaunt woman reappeared.

"Better get them boys out of here. All three's dead drunk now."

"All right," he promised. "I'll get the rig."

Something of the grimness left her face.

"Tell Jonas I sent 'em back because I didn't want to slow up his work more'n he does. One of the girls will help you."

In another half hour, Jeff had hurried to the livery stable and returned to the back of the house with horse and carryall. Light showed under a door. When it opened at the first twist of the knob, Melody, now dressed decently enough, stood in a candle-lighted hall. Her anger had evaporated, and her voice was dull when she spoke.

"She said to help you out with them."

Turner was the only one of the trio who could walk, but eventually, all of them were in the carryall, placidly snoring. Jeff went back to the house with the girl, stepped inside, and closed the door. Then he took Melody by her shoulders.

"Melody, who told you about this runaway and hanging stuff?" She hesitated. Perhaps she would not talk. He stirred her shoulders a little, and she looked up into his face. There were tears in her eyes.

"Fred," she mumbled. "He was always crazy about me."

Jeff wiped her eyes with his handkerchief and cradled her head with his arm while she talked.

"Old Ribner sold me to a tavern man in Sunbury. Fred had some gold money he likely stole. Well, he bought me and kept me in a shack for a spell. When Ribner was kilt, he was free and brought me down here and rented me out like a cow."

She was weeping again. Jeff pushed open the door of the room which the three mechanics had occupied. There he made the girl sit on the bed and continue her story. Fred had been either freed or had run away. He had joined the Indians. Now he traveled with the scouting and scalping parties that infested both branches of the Susquehanna. Whenever he was close, he would visit Melody and boast of his standing with the red men and what he had done to settlers.

"Jeff," she said eagerly, "there's thousands of them red devils waitin'. They ain't comin' through the Post like it was once planned. They is going to hit places like Sina—something or other, and Wy—"

"Sinnamahoning, Wyoming," Jeff prompted. She nodded though he wasn't sure she understood.

"When, Melody," he demanded, "when?"

"I don't know, but I kin git it out of him easy—"

"Think hard," Jeff ordered. "Did he say when?"

"No, jes' the time of year when grain's ripe and folks is busy." Jeff stood up, shocked by the girl's information. It fitted in with the fears of friends up and down the river, the fear about a possible great blow by the savages. Melody slid from the bed and caught his shoulders.

"I remembers. Fred was here a week past, said he'd been to a big lake, big like the ocean. There was an army of green drest soldiers and Indians, getting reddy to go down a river as sounds like you was sneezin'—Chemung."

Jeff held her close while he considered. She started murmuring again.

"Fred purely hates you, Jeff. Says he'll burn you some time, Indian fashion. He wants the Ribner woman too. Says he can trade her for lots of money in a British fort."

Jeff scarcely heard what she was saying. He was thinking of the Fair Play country with its bounding hills, the quiet sweep of the river, the sunlight on brushland, and the wheat fields of the settlers. For a long time, he had tried to keep from thinking about Susan, but now she came into his mind even as he held this tawny woman in his arms. There was a fragrance clean as the out-of-doors about the girl up at Travelome and a sweetness he could not deny. Melody stirred and wrapped an arm round his neck. 'Take me away, Jeff. Fred'll kill me some time."

"I couldn't, Melody. They're hunting me. But would money help you?"

Her eyes shone, and she nodded her tousled head as Jeff counted into her sweated palm two gold pieces.

"That's twice what you got for trapping me that night, Melody. Likely it's more than any share you'd get for telling about me." She slipped her arms about him once more, pulled down his head, and kissed him while she thrust her soft body against him. Once more, she was crying.

"Jeff, Jeff, it wasn't the money, any time. I jes' wanted to be with you."

CHAPTER XVI

ON THE SLOW drive back to Wheterville Jeff kept turning over in his mind the astonishing and disturbing story Melody had told him. Discounting plenty of it due to natural exaggeration on the part of the girl, it fitted in with things he knew. Grube, Fell, and lately, Mead had been sure an attack would come. Melody had place names: Sinnamahoning, Chemung, Wyoming. The first two were where Indian routes came down. The Wyoming Valley was better settled than was the Fair Play country. "When the grain's ripe" was typical of Indian raids. Settlers, engrossed with the pleasant labors of harvest, would be careless. Too many frontier farmers had died with sickles in their hands.

Unable to sleep after he had delivered his three charges to their rooms in the tavern, Jeff walked down to the shop. Since the day was Sunday, the big barnlike interiors of the sheds were empty, but the open door of Cultsizer's office showed the big man in there. Jeff, after rapping on the door jamb, walked in. Cultsizer waved him to one of the two chairs.

"The boys are in their room," Jeff announced, and the gunsmith nodded.

"Mebbe someday we can work without wet-nursing men."

Whatever his reason for being about at this early hour, Cultsizer did not look sleepy, for his eyes under their beetling brows were bright and alert. Jeff hunched his chair forward.

"Jonas, Belfort told you all about me, didn't he?"

The eyebrows lifted, drew down again, and the big man's voice rumbled low in his throat.

"Well, if he did, I ain't said aught, have I?"

"No," Jeff said emphatically. "You've treated me far better than I deserved, given me a good job, handled me just as if I was a free man. Now I want your judgment about something that happened last night."

Cultsizer was an excellent and patient listener. He scarcely moved as Jeff told of Melody and her tale. Then he went back and explained all that had happened to him since Uncle Mark's death, leaving out only his feelings for Susan. He emphasized the reward business and his fear of a big Indian raid. Cultsizer grunted when Jeff finished.

"Well, I'll be damned. It gives mebbe twenty such places around these parts where the men run, and you had to hit that one."

Jeff leaned forward.

"There's so much in the girl's story that the valleys ought to be warned. Colonel Hunter at Augusta should know. He's the Commandant."

The gunsmith scratched his beard with a gesture much like that of Peter Grube and spoke doubtfully.

"If you was to tell him, he'd laugh. After a bit, he'd turn you over to the sheriff for hanging. Son, that reward caps things. It's way too high. Hell, you couldn't get that much for turning in all three of the Doane robbers."

Jeff frowned and bridled a little.

"Why would Hunter laugh—"

Cultsizer interrupted with a raised hand.

"Happens that I know Hunter. All soldiers is unreasonable, but Hunter is worse. He'd be thinking he was listening to a story told by a man with a price on his head, the killer of his friend, Ribner. The story would have come from a chippy in a Lancaster sporting house, a colored chippy at that. How long would he listen, think you?"

He picked up a heavy ruler and slapped the tabletop with it. "Even was I to go, it'd still be the girl's story. Anyway, I got to be here. Them guns has to be finished. They mean lives." Twisting about in his chair until it creaked, he faced Jeff directly.

"It's that 'Chemung' as makes me believe her. That place is clost to where the rivers come together, and the old hellion of a squaw they call Queen Esther has a town thereabouts. I was to Niagara once. We went up through that place, and along a river of the same name, then another river called Cohocton, and on up to the lake. Them green drest soldiers would be Royal Americans, and they could be marching. Howsomever, it'd take them most of a month for the trip, and you couldn't tell where they'd come down. Mebbe they'd come down the Tiadaghton. Mebbe they'd hit the old Sheshequin Path and come out on the Lycoming. Mebbe they'd follow the North Branch of the Susquehanna, and then they'd hit Wyoming."

"But, Jonas," Jeflf expostulated. "I have to do something. This can't pass. What will I do?"

Cultsizer's answering voice was level, emphatic.

"Just what you planned from the first. You'll not rest till you've spilled the tale to Colonel Hunter in Augusta. You'll say to yourself, let them laugh and be damned. You'll be bullheaded enough to stick your neck into a noose to get that damned wiffet's story off your mind. It ain't advice you want, Jeff. This is jest your way of telling me you'll be traveling."

Jeff looked into the sober, understanding face of his employer and colored a little. Finally, he grinned, and Cultsizer smiled back, showing broad white teeth.

"Anyway, boy, I wouldn't give a damn for you if you didn't. When I was young and full of sap, I'd a gone. But that girl will talk to somebody that'll want that reward. I could keep the officers off your back while you work in the shop, but they'd get you outside. Fifty pounds would be a good fortune to some men,"

He rose and moved about, grumbling aloud to himself.

"Now, who'll I put to looking over them finished guns? Jeff, you are a good man, pretty near too good to hang. Carpenters we could spare in these times, lawyers always, and mebbe a general or two, but smiths—we gotta have them to win us a war."

Monday passed quietly, but in the small hours of Tuesday morning, a thumping at Jeff's door roused him. The visitor was Cultsizer, who entered. Jeff, half-naked, sat on the edge of his cot and listened.

"You got money, son."

Jeff took his buckskin pouch from the pocket of his breeches and up-ended it on the bed while Cultsizer looked at it nodding.

"Behind your back couple of weeks ago, I sent word to Squire Fell that I'd buy your indenture. He sent word there was no chance; thinks they want you out of the road for reasons of their own. There was a feller about town this evening asking questions about a runaway, and I figger you'd best travel. Get your pants on, Jeff. Your legs is as skinny as a Dominick rooster's."

Jeff dressed hurriedly and made up his blanket pack with practiced fingers, putting in his money and the things the Meads had given him. Cultsizer stepped back and reached out the door.

"You ought to have a gun. Couldn't sell this one, so I brought it for you. Obed says it shoots real good."

Jeff took the rifle. His gunsmith's love of a weapon made him forget everything else but this beautiful creation of metal and wood, which he held in his hands. No wonder Cultsizer could not sell such a piece. It was a work of craftsman's art. Shorter than the usual Deckard, it was stocked in curly walnut, not maple. The inserts, little stars and moons, were of silver. The front barrel leycorn sight was a bit of gold likely clipped from a sovereign.

Jeff had completely forgotten his visitor in his admiration of the rifle until Cultsizer threw a small bag on the bed with a thump. "Mold, horn, and worm is in there. The powder is good."

The big hand of the master gunsmith was stretched out. Jeff took it, and for a long moment, the two men gripped hands and looked into each other's eyes. Cultsizer finally grinned ruefully.

"Mebbe, Jeff, if you was to keep away from women, you could get straightened out and come back to help me make muskets." A half-hour later, Jeff was on the road, his few belongings in the blanket pack slung across his shoulder, the new rifle under his arm. He shivered a little in the chill of early morning, but his spirits felt lighter from the fact that he was moving with a purpose. There was surely danger enough ahead: servitude certainly, the rope at worst. But the threat of the tomahawk and the firebrand hung over people who had befriended him as he faced what, for him, was a calculated risk.

He made excellent time. When he neared Harris Ferry, he held hard right and was soon climbing the Kittanning Mountains. He would have been glad now to have had Migun and his unfailing sense of direction with him. Ahead was the vast tangle of mountains, darkly timbered ravines, and wild streams known to woodsmen as St. Anthony's wilderness, a place usually shunned by both white men and Indians.

"Dark country," Migun had described it. "No deer, no bear, just owls and rabbits with fox fire on the old logs in the hollows." Jeff thought of this comment on his first night in this tangle as he sat before his tiny campfire. He traveled fast when morning came, glad to work his way out of such a gloomy place. He had done well so far as direction was concerned. He came out on the river less than a mile from the old McKee post where Squire Fell lived, but it had taken him a whole day to do so.

This time the crabbed old jurist seemed really glad to see his young friend, but he was so cautious that he insisted on closing the shutters while they talked.

"We'll have our words in peace. Open windows and doors have ears about here lately. I've heard good things about you, Jeff. Both Belfort Mead and Jonas Cultsizer speak highly of you. Take a chair and tell me why you came north."

Settled deeply in his own rocker. Fell listened attentively and politely to Jeff's account of his meeting with Melody and her tale of threatening danger. When it was all told, the Squire shook his small head and agreed with Cultsizer.

"God knows Hunter should check that story with scouts, but he won't. The man seems paralyzed by the situation as it is. Now here's a girl in a sporting house that spins a tale of a Tory army on the march. You and I could believe it, but a military man, never. He couldn't send scouts north to Chemung river because it's beyond the Forbidden Way of the Iroquois. No white man crosses that. Besides, the people of Sunbury aren't worried about Wyoming folks. That old fool of a Plunkett tried to drive them out with a little army not long since. Folks on the West Branch are the Fair Play people, mostly, and of no concern to Northumberland country. Hunter wants to vacate the valleys. I would make less work for him. No, Jeff, Hunter won't listen." He talked now of news that would interest his visitor. Things were quiet on the West Branch. Fultz was operating the Ribner post. Like Ribner, he was a confidant of

Colonel Hunter. Abigail Ribner was at the post, but the Squire knew nothing of Fred.

All the other slaves had been sold, and the great farm was neglected. Jeff rose to leave.

"Sir, how would I find this, Colonel Hunter?"

The ghost of admiration showed for a moment in Fell's eyes.

"I suspected you would not listen to reason. Likely you know what would happen to you if you were seen in Sunbury. Here—" He sketched rapidly on a bit of paper and then explained his drawing, pointing out the places with his quill.

"That's where the rivers meet with Shamokin Island in the mouth of the North Branch. Here's Fort Augusta. Colonel Hunter lives on his farm close to the works and on the road that leads down to the river opposite Shamokin Island. Sunbury village is nearly a mile below the fort."

Jeff studied the sketch and memorized it.

"I'm obliged to you, Squire Fell. All I'll do is give the warning to Hunter. The responsibility is his then, not mine."

Fell tossed map and pen on the table.

"Well, it's your neck, son. I guess you've been walking around inside a bear trap so long you're used to it and don't realize how Hunter will act. First, he's likely to listen. Then he'll get it through his head who you are, and I assure you, any trial you get in Sunbury will be a farce. Fultz wants you out of the way, and I can't help you there, till I know what his reason is."

Jeff suddenly grinned at the serious look on the old man's face. "Squire," he said softly, "just worry about Hunter a little. I've no mind to see the inside of his or anybody else's jail." Keeping well back from the river to avoid travelers on the road which followed the east bank of the Susquehanna, Jeff made the final lap of his journey north from Wheterville late in the afternoon following his visit with Squire Fell. He settled himself on the precipitous hill east and north of the small plain on which stood the fort and town. He had no intention of going down before darkness. There was plenty of time now to study the scene.

The panorama was beautiful here, where the two river branches met to form the main, broad Susquehanna. Beyond the deep moving tide was a tremendous headland which ended in a sheer precipice hundreds of feet in height. From this distance, the fort and its bastions looked like toys.

The sun set early, dropping behind the big hill. Jeff shut his eyes to test his memory of the Squire's map. Earlier, he felt he had located Colonel Hunter's home, which seemed to be a stone and log structure with outbuildings set well back from it.

There was no evening ceremony at the fort, no lowering of the limp colors, no sunset gun, just tiny figures moving about inside the works. At dark, a single person emerged from the fort and moved in the direction of the farmhouse. That, very likely, was the Commandant. When he reached the house, he entered, and a moment later, candlelight glowed from a window.

Once he was down from the hill, Jeff reconnoitered the ground thoroughly, having no desire to be cornered here between the river and the hill. He found three boats, each with its oars in place, where the road came down to the river opposite Shamokin Island. The lightest of these, he moved to where it would be easy to shove it out into the river. Then, as a precaution, he hid the oars of the other craft some distance away. With his new rifle hidden in a brush copse close to his boat, Jeff was ready, his retreat fairly secure.

Through the window of the house, he saw that a man, dressed as any local farmer would be, set at a table writing busily. On a clothes rack back of him was a uniform coat, blue with some tan on it. In one corner stood a sword with the belt twisted about the basket hilt of the weapon. This heavily built, ordinary-looking man was Colonel Hunter. A tremendous weight of responsibility rested on his shoulders. In the face of the Indian menace from the north, the safety of the long line of settlers' homes, reaching far back into the wilderness, had to be ensured. Watching, Jeff recalled things he had heard about this man. He had sent his family downriver on what was ostensibly a visit. He had been a friend of Ribner and now of Abner Fultz. Also, he had held his position since the old wars.

Excitement tightened Jeff's throat as he stepped to the outer door. If no one else appeared here at this farmhouse before he finished "his business, he would probably be all right. Putting aside his speculations, he rapped lightly on the whip-sawn door panels. For a moment, he wished for his new rifle, but he touched his pistol's stock with his fingers and felt better. The weapon was thrust into his trouser band for quick action, and it was freshly primed. A heavy voice bade him enter.

"Colonel Hunter, sir?"

The quiet man laid down his pen and took time to study his visitor, from the battered hat to his moccasins, appraising each feature carefully without haste.

"Yes, I'm Colonel Hunter. Can I do something for you?"

"Just listen to a story I heard about a raid by the savages," Jeff told him. "That's all."

"Yes," Hunter said, "heard—" He waited a long moment. "I'll hear it."

Jeff presented the bare essentials of his narrative, and the Commandant's face did not change during the recital. He did not speak until it was finished. Even then, there was what appeared to be a long wait before he spoke, asking a question.

"This Melody woman and Fred were Henry Ribner's slaves?"

Something in the quiet, unemotional tones of the officer was sending out a warning to the young man who faced him. Then it came a bare announcement that was stronger than a threat.

"And you are Jeffry Claus, the bondsman who ran away and then murdered his master."

Jeff did not answer or comment but looked straight into Hunter's eyes, seeing there a slight twitching. The shadow of a sneer was gathering about his mouth. The Colonel continued.

"Almost every hour of the day, I hear stories like the one you have related to curry favor for yourself. We are not blind. Our scouts move up and down the rivers. Now you, a hunted man with a price on your head, tell me a trumped-up tale given you by a slut in a house of ill fame, a story compounded by another slave—"

The sneer was quite open now. Cultsizer and Fell had been right. There was no possible chance of this man heeding the warning. He simply was angry that he had even listened to the gaunt young man who faced him, and Jeff's ire rose to meet that anger. His voice, when he spoke, grated a little.

"Help should be sent up the rivers. I've been up river with Peter Grube. The warriors wait and watch. I've seen Senecas at the Ribner post, and it's below here. They came in there for guns and whiskey."

His anger exploded, and he struck the table until the inkwell jumped and the sandbox overturned.

"If the savages come, Colonel, you'll answer for the scalps taken, you who sent your own family to safety."

The Commandant's eyes blazed. His voice roared.

"You ragged tramp and consorter with slaves and strumpets, you runaway murderer, you dare insult an officer. We'll see what the lash will do for you!"

Jeff's downthrust hand came up with his cocked pistol.

"They told me you were a damned fool. I've had all the lash I'll ever take. I risked my life and liberty coming here to save the settlers. Now all I get is a threat. Get up, you fish-bellied fool, up before I shoot you between the eyes!"

Hunter had led men for many years, and as he read what blazed in Jeff's eyes, he got up with some alacrity. His visitor gestured toward the door. With the pistol pressed sharply between the broad shoulders of this officer who would not listen, Jeff marched the man to the riverside where he had the boat readied. He retrieved his rifle.

"Now, Hunter, I'm going to warn the West Branch country. By God, Colonel or no Colonel, if I find a scalp taken in the household of my friends, I'll come back and nail yours to the gate of your damned fort."

Hunter made a move to run, and Jeff tripped him. While he recovered himself, Jeff gave his boat a mighty shove into the river and leaped in. He was well out in the dark stream rounding the point of Shamokin Island when the first musket flashed. It was followed by a dozen more aimless shots. Jeff leaned on the oars while the unseen marksmen searched the dark water with bullets.

It was unlikely Hunter would start a pursuit in the darkness, so Jeff took his time rowing up river until he came to the mouth of a large creek entering from the east. Up this a hundred yards, he found a hemlock thicket where he camped for the night. Bright morning sunlight wakened him. From a hill, he surveyed beautiful country stretching north and west. Much of it was natural meadowland, and he could see smoke lifting from an occasional cabin chimney. This land was well settled for the frontier. What he saw made him realize this farming area was even richer than the Fair Play country. It was white man's country, safe behind the bulwark of hills to the north, river and hills to the westward.

Fast travel brought him by nightfall past Forth Muncy, which he detoured, and opposite Fort Antes, which lay on the south side of the river. Before he slept that night, he debated crossing the wide stream and warning Colonel Antes or whoever was in charge of the stockade. Finally, he decided that the risk would be too great. Whoever was in charge over there would be a subordinate of Colonel Hunter and bound by military regulations. The thing to do was get word to Peter Grube, who would know how to handle any message that concerned the valley.

That final morning of his trip, Jeff shaved carefully and put his worn and faded clothing in as good shape as possible. He remembered to tie his hair with a piece of black tape instead of the customary eelskin. When he was finally walking up the slope to Travelome, his heart was pounding as though he had been running.

Faith saw him first, and there was no doubt of her welcome as she ran down the porch to meet him, hair flying about her head.

"Jeffry!" she cried, flinging her arms about his neck and kissing him impetuously. "Welcome home."

She was calling to Susan as they walked up to the house arm in arm. It seemed a long time until the girl appeared, wiping her hands on her apron. Before she could protest, Jeff swept her up in a brotherly hug and kissed her. She answered his caress with a brush of fragrant lips on his cheek as he set her down and inspected her from the tips of her small, blunt-toed shoes to the braids on her proudly carried head.

"She's growing up," he told Faith delightedly, and she was smiling.

"Oh, yes, she is doing that indeed, and the young men left in the valley know it and are watching," Faith said banteringly. Susan's face colored.

"Welcome, Jeffry," she said. "Now I must watch the dinner. There will be corn fritters, and they could burn."

"Peter will be here at supper time," Faith told Jeff. "Let's go out on the porch and talk of your travels."

Jeff visited with her telling many of the things which had happened during his absence but withholding the warning he brought until Peter arrived. His welcome, like that of Faith, left nothing to be desired. He swung Jeff from his feet and clapped him on the back.

"Still as gaunt as a good hound, boy. Will you never be putting meat on those ribs? Which reminds me—I'm half starved. I have been patrolling, and when I sit up in the brush, I think about good things to eat until I'm so hungry I could eat a nice tender Indian if somebody else took the feathers off him."

Susan had the table spread with the best white cloth and the silverware, which was Faith's pride. There was a dish of wild grape jelly by Jeff's plate. The girl had remembered how well he liked the spicy preserves. The table groaned with food: venison, beef, potatoes, wild greens, and corn fritters nicely browned. Peter pointed to the meat before he bowed his head to say grace.

"Not quite the fatted calf for the prodigal, Jeff, but then I never figured veal was meat for a man."

Seemingly by polite agreement, no one had questioned Jeff's reason for returning. He had been accepted as a member of the family who would return to Travelome as a matter of course.

However, with the meal finished, Peter pushed back his chair. "Now, Jeff, give us the news like Migun does. Start at the beginning and go on to the end. We're all aching for news."

Jeff smiled and held up his hand. "In a minute, Peter. I'd like to know about the Indians in the valley. Maybe my news will fit in."

Grube rubbed his chin, his own gesture of uncertainty.

"It's hard to say. Our patrols run across little bands of savages here and there. One man was killed up near Sherrod's place on Young Woman's Creek. Farmers have had cattle shot full of arrows. The people are uneasy, just fixing themselves to be real scared. Then they'll stampede, figuring no help will be sent up here."

Jeff leaned back and began his story. Occasionally as he talked, he paused to answer a question. He related in detail his experiences at Mead's ordinary when the soul-seller appeared and finally made it necessary for him to go to Wheterville and Jonas Cultsizer's gun shop. At the tale of the two redemptioners, Peter rumbled in his throat.

"Damned carrion, them soul-sellers. Down in our fine Quaker city, they prate of freeing slaves, yet they let men like Eitler run free with his deviltry."

"Hush, Peter," Faith directed, and Jeff continued. It was embarrassing to explain the trip to Lancaster, but he told it and finally gave Melody's story about the coming raid. Faith and Peter hung on the narrative. Susan appeared either embarrassed or angry at the mention of Melody. Jeff saw that she had lowered her eyes and played with a bit of bread on her plate.

"That's about all. I took the story to Hunter after Cultsizer and Fell said he wouldn't listen, and they were right. I had to come off at the point of a pistol, and they opened on me with muskets later. So I came on up here knowing you'd know what to do, Peter."

Grube waited a long time before commenting, even though Faith looked impatient.

"Hunter's a good man but bothered and scared by the fact that he has almost no equipment and less than fifty soldiers. What he wants is to get all the settlers downriver below Augusta. The Good Book speaks of 'the backside of the wilderness,' well, that's where we are west of the Lycoming. Washington has his hands full. He couldn't send us companies of soldiers, but he did send Covenhoven, Kelly, and Van Campen, which is almost as good." He relapsed into a long silence, during which Faith and Susan removed the dishes and took them to the kitchen. When they were fully occupied, Peter turned to Jeff.

"Migun has been here, Jeff, so we know much of your story, and we're all proud of what you did at Shirleysburg. Now, you risked your neck trying to warn Hunter. It looks to us as if you're forgetting your own troubles in helping other folks, which is mighty healthy. Now about Melody's story. Migun knows Fred is running with the savages, and I wouldn't wonder if they'd come down—hard. The British lost Saratoga. They'll have to redeem themselves with the York State Indians. I'll spread your word about here, Jeff, but God knows what to do about the Connecticut folks. They're bullheaded and might laugh at a warning. Anyway, Jeff, a man's rifle belongs to his home folks first these days."

Faith passed his chair just then. He slipped an arm about her, and she rumpled his hair.

"Don't believe too much of what this husband of mine says, Jeff. He was with one of Plunkett's raids on the Wyoming settlement. He'd be as welcome over there as a Seneca in war paint."

CHAPTER XVII

THE CONFIDENCE Peter Grube had shown in the house the evening before was entirely absent in the morning when he and Jeff were in the shop.

"I've tried to keep the women from worrying too much, Jeff, but things in the valley are pretty bad. What I said about little parties is right. I think they're scouting outfits down here to learn where every man is every hour of the day. Men and boys have been attacked and killed almost everywhere and on a broad front, from the Lycoming Creek to the Sinnamahoning. There's even a story that they really killed Beniel Sherrod, this time somewhere up on Kettle Creek. The little garrison Colonel Antes maintained has been recalled, and there are not over two dozen rifles in all the other little posts, including Fort Muncy."

He shut his lips grimly and made a jerky gesture with a big hand.

"Notice, all the strong places are south of the river: Reed's, Horn's, and Antes' places. We're outside the pale over here, and half of us would lose our hair getting across the river. Folks are most scared of a big war party slipping down the Lycoming and cutting us off. They're talking of leaving more than I expected of them."

Jeff stared at his friend's grim face. If a man like Grube, who had seen war in the old days, was this troubled, the reason for it was good. He was talking again.

"They sent up thirty soldiers from Augusta a couple of weeks past, and I went with them as a sort of guide. Up the river, we had a chance to ambush a party of warriors that looked like Senecas, could have wiped them out, and taught the Iroquois a lesson. That damned fool officer wouldn't let us fire a shot. Said we were outnumbered. Hell, Jeff, soldiers are no good up here in the brush. I'd rather have Van Campen or Haw-kins Boone than a full company in uniform. Another thing, most of our young men are with Washington. Anyway, we'll report your story down at Staier's tavern and see what folks think. Let's start."

On their way down to Staier's place, they left word of an assembly that afternoon. By mid-afternoon, there was a fair and representative gathering at the big tavern. Jeff had spent the waiting time fussing with a pistol Staier had shown him. Finally, he passed it back to the owner.

"The lock's bad. The hammer won't hold. Load it, though, and when you're ready to shoot, hold back the hammer with your thumb. Then let her go."

The tavern keeper took the weapon.

"That's all I want, jest that every shooting iron I have will go off. Things look bad."

Peter walked in just then and surveyed the shelves back of the bar.

"Your stock's pretty low, Staier," he remarked. The innkeeper laid down the pistol and looked at the array of bottles. At the moment, the three were alone in the room.

"Peter, I moved most of what I have into the Nippenose valley and hid it in one of those caves. You've seen them red devils when they're full of whiskey. They're hellish enough without swillin' spirits."

It was plain that Staier was expecting Indian trouble, and he was certainly not the type of man to be easily frightened. This assembly was quite different from the one at which Jeff had been tried. There was no horseplay, and the drinking was limited to one round served with the compliments of the house. No rifles were stacked. As agreed, Peter told the story Jeff had brought from Lancaster.

"Now men," he finished, "there's the story. Jeff risked his neck report-ing it to those damned fools at Augusta. Hunter wouldn't believe a word of it. Jeff and I want to know what you folks think."

Larry Burt, who lived up to the creek named for him, spoke first. Burt had a Delaware wife and was supposed to be an authority on savag-es. Evidently, Fred's position interested him.

"Them red devils does take in black men. I seed six in a party three weeks past. They was all painted, but one of them was nigh as black as my hound, Tobe."

Jim Alexander, who lived pretty far up on the Tiadaghton, spoke emphatically. "The boy's story sounds right. We all know they'll hit somewhere, for they've been pecking at us nigh two years. Likely they know every man and rifle from the Sinnamahoning to Augusta. I say we act jest as if we knowed they was coming. The folks at Wyoming will have to take care of themselves. They never helped us none."

"You mean run for it, Jim?" The questioner was Squire Rude, who had arrived unexpectedly. "Or would you build a fort?"

"No, Squire," Alexander replied. "They'd have to push me and show a lot more feathered topknots before I'd pull out and leave my crops. And I wouldn't build another fort. There's too many of them now for the rifles we got. Mebbe I'd take the cattle where they'd be safe. But I'd wait and give them red hellions a few bullets before they started burning."

Alexander seemed to have voiced the sentiment of the crowd. Clark Francis, who lived just across the river from Fort Antes, summed things up.

"We'll move all critters over the river, through Antes Gap, and hide them in Nippenose and Mosquito valleys. Best keep our horses by us. We start day after tomorrow."

"Jeff, young Henderson, and I will patrol west to Great Island," Peter offered. "You men work the stock."

Brown Henderson was a stout boy of about twenty and one of those interested in Susan. On the morning of the patrol, he reported early and hung about the kitchen while Jeff and Peter prepared to ride. As they went out to where the horses waited, a slight figure came up the slope. It was Migun.

For once, there was nothing courteous or halfway civil about the Delaware. Both his face and clothing showed the marks of hard travel. He refused Peter's invitation to come into the house and eat.

"Cultsizer said Jeff would be here. Now he and I go. You go, Peter, take fat boy."

Jeff repressed a grin knowing Henderson was sensitive about his girth. Indeed now his face reddened, and he took a step toward the Indian when Peter laid a hand on his arm in restraint.

"We go," Migun grunted. Jeff picked up his rifle and followed. They had gone straight north for a full hour before Migun halted and explained the situation.

"Cultsizer was worried. He found Melody, checked over her story, then sent me after you, Jeff. Lord, but you stirred up Colonel Hunter. The man aches to see you lashed to a whipping post and then hanged. Now we go north, try to locate this army in green coats, and see where they go."

They had marched another hour when Migun spoke again.

"I didn't tell Peter, Jeff. Hunter is going to order the West Branch country abandoned. All settlers must go down river. If we find the Iroquois are to strike elsewhere, we'll save the homes from Fort Muncy west. So, we hurry. It's almost life and death." The days that followed were a nightmare of swift travel, always northward, with no regard to hill, valley, or stream. Jeff had never before guessed Migun's capacity to keep going hour after hour at a pace that strained Jeff to the utmost. At sundown of the first day, they flung themselves down beside a tiny stream and ate cold journey cake and dried meat. They allowed themselves a scant half hour before traveling on into the night. Soon they were on a high plateau among the yellow pines and the low laurel bushes that snatched at their moccasins and dragged at their knees. Finally, in complete weariness, they lay down in a thicket and slept as though dead.

In the first gray of the morning, they stirred and looked at each other. Stiff and sore, Migun pulled off his clothes and rubbed his joints with some salve from a wooden box.

"Gokhotit's 'walk salve,' Jeff. If the grease don't help, the rubbing will."

They ate their first cooked meal at noon of that day, two grouse Migun had knocked down with a stick. The meat warmed and cheered them, but both were hungry as they resumed their travel. Twenty-four hours later, on the top of a heavily wooded hill, they stopped just in time. Migun sank slowly to the ground and pulled Jeff down. Not a hundred

yards from them, a long file of painted Indian warriors were moving eastward at a trot. Feathers showed in scalp locks; blankets hung from their
shoulders; tomahawk handles struck against their leggings as they ran.

"Senecas," Migun whispered to his companion.

Twenty minutes later, they had just risen to go on when a second war
party appeared and passed in the same fashion.

"Forty in all," Jeff whispered to Migun, who nodded, then gestured
to the path the savages had used.

"The Forbidden Way. Beyond is all Iroquois country where only a
Long House scalp is safe. Let's move."

Just before nightfall, two utterly weary young men lay on a ridge top
looking down over a wide valley through which a river meandered. It
wasn't the train which interested them. It was the movement down there
as hundreds, perhaps thousands, of men went into camp. Occasionally
the late sun glinted on bayonets or other equipment. Horses moved here
and there. Canoes pulled in to the banks and were drawn up. When
nightfall came, the watchers, pushing their empty bellies against the
ground, watched hundreds of camp fires come alive.

"God," Jeff whispered in a shocked tone. "Nothing on the rivers
could stop that force."

Migun's strong fingers gripped his arm.

"But where will they strike? They could come down the Sheshequin
Path along the Lycoming or down the Chemung and North Branch on
Wyoming."

Gnawing at strips of dried meat, the two friends lay and watched the
fires until many of them winked out. Then they slept to come awake stiff
and sore in the morning.

Again the camp fires flamed up and died down. Fed and rested, the
army got under way. In the center was the long line of darkly uniformed
soldiers, a line that looked endless. Its leading men out of sight before
the last left the camp ground. On either side, spread out on a mile-wide
front, moved the Indian allies.

Migun had made up his mind.

"Brother, we can't scout an army like that. The best we can do is get
back and warn the people in the Fair Play country. No time for Wyoming."

In the next few hours, Jeff learned the truth of Migun's contention. The main force of the British and Indians moved down the river valley. But there were small bands of the savages everywhere. Only Migun's woodcraft kept them from three or four dangerous encounters. Every band of painted and armed warriors was moving eastward. There were no squaws or children, no camp impedimenta in sight. This was a war trail the men of the dark Seneca clan followed.

A little short of noon on the seventh day of their absence, the two gaunt, half-starved, and travel-stained young men entered the cove in which Travelome stood. They walked directly into a scene of confusion. All livestock was gone from the barn, and grain chests stood empty with lids open. Charley and Harriet were just leaving the house carrying bundles.

Migun dropped to a seat on the steps of the front porch, where Jeff joined him. There was no Indian calm about the young Delaware now. The frustration and discouragement of the utterly weary was upon him.

"Too late," he grunted. "Too damned late. They're pulling out."

A quarter of an hour later, Peter Grube found them in the same place. The big man was sarcastic when he greeted them.

"So, the woods runners are back, all ready for a boat ride."

Migun looked at him and noted the expression on the heavy face. He spoke quietly, disregarding the sarcasm that had been aimed at him and Jeff.

"Yes, we went north and saw the army. Fred and the girl were right. Close to fifteen hundred green coats and warriors move east on the upper Chemung."

He stopped, moved by the shocked look on Grube's face.

"God," he said, "nothing could stop a force like that. They'll clean out the river valleys."

He dropped down on the steps beside his friends and told them in monotonous tones that panic had, at last, swept the valley. There had been scattered killings from the Sinnamahoning to the lower waters of the Loyalsock. Two children had been captured, and half dozen cabins burned.

"No big war parties anywhere, but they raised hell. Young Henderson and I found the Jeffry brothers butchered close to Great Island in their corn patch. This time they say Beniel Sherrod is scalped. Well, Hunter sent Covenhoven north to warn us out. Everybody is to move down to Fort Augusta, and we're all going like scared sheep."

He looked out over his fields, shook his heavy head, and struck his big hands together. "I wanted to stand, but there's no one to help, and we have two women." He rose. "Come on down to the boats."

Faith and Susan were there in a loaded flatboat which had been used as a small ferry. Besides this, there were two canoes laden with goods. The women were cheerful and, as their first task, fed the returned scouts while Peter relayed their news.

Everything was in readiness for the departure with frightened-looking Harriet and Charley on the big boat.

"We'll go back and see if we forgot anything," Peter said. The four white people and the Indian trooped back up the hill. Jeff and Migun cleaned up a little while the others looked about. When they were all outside again, Peter turned to Faith.

"Shall I fire the place?"

The slim woman by his side lifted her hand and brushed back a strand of her bright hair. Susan stared at her while the husband and wife looked into each other's eyes.

"No," she answered firmly. "We'll be back."

They moved down the slope slowly. Once Faith turned as if to look back, but Peter laid a heavy arm across her shoulders.

"No, Missy," he said lightly. "Don't look back. Remember Lot's wife."

She walked a little closer to him.

"Just think, Peter, if I did turn to salt, what a price you'd get for me with salt so scarce up here."

At the landing, Grube disposed of his forces: Jeff was to handle the big flatboat, Peter took one of the canoes and would tow the second. Migun looked on while the last-minute preparations were made. As Peter looked at him questioningly, he smiled.

"No," he said. "It may be that an Indian would not be too welcome when the settlers are all together."

Jeff took one of the canoes and ferried the young Delaware across the river. There the two friends talked for a while.

"You're not going down river, Jeff," Migun said. "I think my brother will hide out in this country."

He poked Jeff's chest with his forefinger.

"Nor does my brother think that British force will come into this valley."

Jeff stared. The young Indian seemed to be reading his mind. Now he delivered himself of a proverb before he turned away up the river bank.

"If one will blow on an eagle wing bone whistle when the storm cloud is black, it will scatter."

Faith and Susan made themselves comfortable on a big pile of blankets. Harriet and Charley occupied the stem. As they dropped down river, a strange sight presented itself. All sorts of crafts, from rafts to canoes, were moving. Pigs grunted in their pole pens, and chickens cackled. The children took the whole thing as a lark. To Jeff, the thronged river was reminiscent of Sunday afternoon scenes on English rivers.

Fort Antes and the high fields about it were in a pandemonium during the two days while the settlers waited until their leaders made sure all homes were evacuated and the inhabitants checked. Camp fires by the scores blazed well into the night. Boats of all descriptions were tied up, and children of all ages played and fought everywhere. Jeff noticed at once that the fort was almost dismantled. The swivel guns he had helped place had been dismounted. Even the arsenal doors stood open on emptiness. There was still some grain in the grist mill. On the second morning, a tall, gaunt young lieutenant appeared and made an announcement.

"The colonel orders me to issue free wheat, one bushel to a family. Line up."

It was hard to control the rush for the coveted grain. It was carried away in baskets, bags, and even women's aprons. Many families had brought their coffee mills with them, and these were presently busy grinding the precious grain into unbolted flour for bread.

The morning of the third day was fixed for the exodus, and orders were strict. Jeff saw the scout, Covenhoven, who had brought Hunter's message, walking with Colonel Hepburn, who had come up river to manage affairs. Covenhoven was a big man who chewed on a twig while the officer gave orders.

"Women and children will man the boats. There are fifty-three men here. Thirty-five will march in a skirmish line on the north bank, the others on the south. A canoe will move along each bank to carry messages. You have an hour to man the boats. Start when a shot is fired."

Jeff went down to the Grube flatboat and helped Faith into her place. Colored Charley had recovered himself enough to use the steering oar, and the two canoes were made fast to the big boat's stern. Susan had not yet come down to the river. Jeff went to find her, and she ran up to him.

"I was hunting you, Jeff."

He took her small hand in his big rough one.

"We're all ready, Susan."

She searched his face anxiously with troubled eyes.

"You're coming with us?"

To reassure her, he shook his head.

"No, women man the boats. They're letting me be a man today. I march on the north bank."

She caught his sleeve impulsively and held him while she questioned him. "Jeff, what will they do with you when we get down country? There is that awful reward and the trouble with Colonel Hunter." He smiled at her and tried to evade making an answer.

"Just you take care of Faith, Susan. I'll be all right."

Suddenly she shook him. People were passing, but no one seemed to notice them.

"Jeff!" she cried. "I know it now. You won't be going all the way. You—"

Her arms flashed about his neck, and he caught her close as her fingers rumpled his hair, and her lips met his again and again. She was crying when she released herself and ran down toward the boat. Jeff went to the canoe, which would take him over to his place in the line. His head was in the clouds. Susan loved him. He was sure of that, and nothing else mattered. There had been concern in her eyes and voice, warmth in her lips. At the canoe, he started to step in but missed, and his foot went down into the water. A sardonic voice spoke.

"Thet's all right, big boy. Mebbe you kin walk on the water at that. You 'pear to hev the feet fer it."

The canoe did not pull away immediately. Up on the bluff where a knot of men had gathered, the tall lieutenant appeared and gestured. Then a gray-haired man whom Jeff recognized as Alexander Donaldson stepped forward and raised both hands, turning his face toward the sky. The watchers on the river could not hear his words, but the attitude was enough, and silence spread across the nondescript flotilla. For five minutes, Donaldson held his position. When his hands dropped, the chatter of voices started anew.

Covenhoven, holding a huge silver watch in his palm, was in command. Presently he closed the case with a snap. He had not returned the timepiece to his pocket before the report of a shot echoing against the hills reached them.

"All right, men, spread out. Grube, take the rear guard with two men. I'll be up front."

The company of armed riflemen moved slowly, accommodating their progress to the motion of the boats. Near noon, the messenger canoe moved inshore to set the riflemen dry-shod across the Lycoming. Here more settlers joined the exodus, and the same procedure was followed at the Loyalsock. Beyond the mouth of this deep and wide creek, the river began its slow bend southward to break through the Muncy mountains. Shortly after the Loyalsock crossing, the marching men could see far to the north a single column of smoke lifting toward the sky.

"Injuns," the man next to Jeff grunted. "That's likely a cabin."

That was the only sign of enemy presence. The men marched through a peaceful world, occasionally passing cornfields and wheat already turning the color of ripeness.

Where the river broke through the first range of hills to the south, the flotilla pulled over to the south bank. Canoes crossed to take Covenhoven's men to where the camp would be.

Jeff had left Travelome with his mind only partly made up. It would be impossible to go down to Fort Augusta without losing his freedom. He felt certain the army he and Migun had seen beyond the Forbidden Way would not invade the West Branch valley. It wasn't populous enough, and scalps would be too few. He wanted to go back to Travelome to take his chances with any small bands of raiders. Susan had reasoned that he had not meant to go all the way down river with them. Let him step ashore at Augusta; it would mean the whipping post, the jail, and perhaps the gallows. At Travelome, all he risked was his scalp, and he felt pretty sure of taking care of that. Abruptly he thought of Migun's parting philosophy:

"If one will blow with an eagle bone whistle when the storm cloud is black, it will scatter."

He was smiling when he met Peter.

"Well," he said, "the folks are safe now."

"Yes," Grube agreed, "from Indian hatchets. They're safe as people can be with no homes, no way of making a living. Wonder what'll become of them all."

Jeff fumbled in his pocket. He took out his buckskin moneybag and put it into Peter's hands.

"There's close to eighty pounds there. I earned it at Cultsizer's and some from these folks right here. Likely you have money, but I want to be sure Faith and Susan are comfortable. Once you and your folks are comfortable, spend the rest."

Grube was weighing the bag in his hand and noticed the little catch in Jeff's voice.

"Yes," he interrupted, "spend the rest on folks that needs it."

Jeff scowled, feeling suddenly ill at ease.

"It's just that I don't want to know those poor devils are hungry when my own belly's full of deer meat and roasting ears. It would spoil my appetite."

Peter pocketed the money and took another glance across to the camp.

"I figured right along you were going back, Jeff. Best forget that and work over to Migun's camp. You'd be safe there till we return. You've taken enough risk in that trip north."

They looked into each other's eyes for a moment, each understanding the other. Grube knew even better than Jeff where he would be.

"Jeff, when they come, it'll be in the morning, and they'll ship out of the river mist up the slope. God, I wish I could be with you."

He stopped abruptly and gripped Jeff's hand. Then he stalked off in the direction of the cooking fires.

CHAPTER XVIII

FROM THE TOP of the bold southern ridge, which he had climbed in the gathering dusk, Jeff looked down on the now distant encampment where scattered cooking fires winked feebly against the dark. A faint mingling of the chatter of many voices came up to him like the sound of wild geese going south in the fall. After all that huddle of people, down there by the river was like a bird migration. They were going south, and their only possessions were what they could carry with them. They had left behind their cabins and firesides as the birds had left nesting grounds where their young had been hatched. The birds fled from the onward march of Arctic cold, these settlers from an enemy fully as inexorable.

He slept that night above Antes Gap, through which the cattle had been driven to hiding places in the Nippenose and other mountain valleys. There would be a few cattle guards in there somewhere, but Jeff had no notion of joining them. His mind was settled on what he would do. When morning came, he saw smoke lifting from the place where Fort Antes had stood and several other columns farther up the valley beyond the river. The savages had lost little time with the torch they had been waiting to apply to the homes of the settlers.

Jeff felt a strong excitement as he looked. There was nothing ahead of him to bother about but the red enemy, and he was now sure of Susan's love. He had no right to it. He was a man with a price on his head and servitude stretching ahead of him. But her arms had gone round his neck. Her warm lips had been on his, and he felt strong. The future could take care of itself. Faith had counseled him once to live each day as it came. He would do that now, marking each hour, perhaps each shot at a time. Migun and Uncle Mark had taught him to be at least a fair woodsman. He felt a sureness in himself and an eagerness to play out this dangerous game.

Swimming the river would be the most dangerous part of the journey back to Travelome. That meant wet charges in his rifle and pistol. Also, his head and shoulders would be excellent targets for red marksmen while he was in the water. Luck came to his rescue in the shape of a dead tree uprooted somewhere above on the river and now lodged against the bank. After fastening rifle, pistol, powder horn, and moccasins to the trunk, he waded in and managed to push the unwieldy mass of the tree out into the edge of the current. Keeping his head down and swimming strongly, he guided his makeshift raft diagonally across the stream. When the top grounded, he loosened the knife and hatchet. Then he spent a long quarter of an hour waiting and watching. Birds were singing, and a red squirrel nearby busied himself without chatter. There was no sign of an enemy.

He had crossed a short distance above the Tiadaghton's mouth so the Henderson clearing would be directly in front of him with Travelome farther back in the hills and to the westward. The taint of burned wood was strong in the air. Jeff moved carefully until he was at the edge of the Henderson farm.

As he had expected of cabins close to the river, here were masses of ashes and charred timbers where the house and barn had been. Near the spring lay a dead sheep. It had been too old to take away with the other livestock. Now it lay hacked to horrible pieces in savage wantonness. The drama being enacted just beyond the barn wall made Jeff's fingers tighten on his rifle stock.

Bang was the Henderson dog, a big black hound. He had always been an independent beast with little attention for strangers, but he had accepted Jeff months before as a friend. Likely in the excitement, he had been left behind. Now he stood defiantly with braced legs and raised hackles before a half-squatting Indian who slowly waved a short stick back and forth while he made grunting noises. Jeff's first thought was that the savage wanted the dog to charge so he could split that black skull with his hatchet. Then he saw a second warrior who had been partially hidden by debris. This one was approaching the dog from the rear with a drawn bow. In another second, the arrow would go home.

Jeff knew the thing for him to do was slip away and remain hidden in the cornfield nearby. But Bang was a white man's dog, alone in the valley his masters had deserted. Now he faced the enemy unafraid and ready to use what weapons he possessed. The smooth stock of the rifle came to Jeff's shoulder, and he centered the bright gold bead on the bowman's chest. In anger or in a fight, perhaps Jeff would not have hesitated. Now, at the final moment, he flicked the sight to one side. The bullet struck the red man's shoulder, spinning him around. The arrow was discharged into the air, and the wounded man howled in surprise and pain. Then he ran jerkily for the woods. The squatting warrior leaped up only to be knocked sprawling by a pistol shot. The dog was on him instantly. Jeff reloaded rapidly, but it was all over. The dog had torn the Indian's throat, and it was hard to coax him from his victim.

The red men had two guns, one worthless, the other a big bored rifle which Jeff took together with the two powder horns. These were full of the best British powder. He also retrieved two skin war bags which contained a quantity of dried meat and parched corn. Bang refused the meat offered him. There was Indian smell on it.

The wounded savage would report promptly to others if they were in the vicinity, so Jeff proceeded with even more caution toward the Grube homestead. Most of the savages, he had little doubt, would be following the river and the migration. Since the Grube home stood pretty far back from the stream, it might have escaped the first burnings. In a few minutes, he found that was true. The big house and its outbuildings stood intact and, he discovered later, untouched.

Bang marched along with his rescuer as if glad for company, and he was a help in reconnoitering the farmstead. There was plenty of food in the house: potatoes in the cellar, meat pickled in tubs, even two loaves of stale bread. Bang had no compunction about this food, finishing what was given him and then thumping his thanks on the floor with his tail.

By nightfall, Jeff had completed his preparations for the siege he was sure would come. He had piled heavy furniture against the doors and filled every bucket he could find with spring water. The house loft had loopholes looking in every direction. There was an excellent field of fire.

At first, the dog refused to stay in the house, but after a scolding, settled down meekly enough. During the night, when Jeff woke and listened, he would hear the sound of the animal's toenails on the puncheon floors as he walked about.

Jeff was fully awake and vigilant with the first morning signs. He thought of Peter Grube's remark, "out of the river mist." But there was none of that this morning. However, the usual bird songs and other noises of little forest people were absent. Finally, a rabbit emerged from a brush pile near the barn. He was so close Jeff could see him wrinkle his nose. Then, without warning, the animal darted back to its brush shelter.

Something was about the place, something that had stopped the birds and frightened the rabbit. Jeff descended from the loft with the dog following, but he could see nothing through the shutters. Finally, he stepped outside, keeping in the shelter of the waist-high banister of squared logs about the spring and back porch. Bang pushed past his legs and moved a short distance toward the barn. He barked twice and sat calmly down on his haunches.

"Bang," Jeff hissed, "go get 'em."

The black hound merely turned his head and lolled out his tongue. Across the dog's shoulders, Jeff saw a tattered-looking figure emerge from the brush and come forward. It was Beniel Sherrod, the trader from up-river who had been reported dead. His clothing was in bad shape, but outside of that, there was nothing the matter with him.

"Been trying to git me in here two days past," he grumbled. "There's a little war party above, and I couldn't dodge it without climbing a hell of a high mountain. You're Jeff Claus. Where's Peter?"

Jeff explained what had happened. The woodsman made no comment either on the valley evacuation or the report of the Tory and Indian army up north on the Chemung. He complained that he was hungry.

"Ain't eat too reg'lar. Them red devils chase down every smoke they see, and it spoilt my cookin'."

Jeff prepared a liberal breakfast with bread fried in the grease. This he served with maple syrup. In addition, he boiled a big pot of tea, making the brew as strong as he could.

"My," the tattered woodsman sighed when he leaned back in his chair after dispatching three-fourths of the food and drinking nearly all of the tea. "Tame meat tastes good. I git weary of venison and ain't had much else the last year or so."

He leaned forward in sudden excitement.

"There ain't any potatoes, is there?"

Jeff assured his visitor there were bushels of the tubers in the cellar, and Beniel rose with a rapt look on his face.

"Then, I'm stayin'. Say, since Grube pulled out, how comes you stay behint?"

Jeff frowned at the woodsman's question. He was pretty sure Sherrod had some ideas about him, and he had no notion, for the moment, of talking about his predicaments.

"Beniel," he answered, "this house is worth fighting for. Anyway, I don't think the Indians will be around here in any force." Sherrod nodded soberly.

"Mebbe you're right. I can't see why the folks lit out without a scrap. It ain't like the Donaldsons, the Parrs, and such folks, nor like Peter Grube who fought in them old wars. Anyway, I'm bettin' my hair there ain't a big war party this side of the Sinnamahoning."

Jeff did not comment. He knew the steadily mounting tension under which these valley people had been living, knew its effect on a hardy man like Peter. The final killings had loosed the panic, and Hunter's message had been the last straw. He motioned toward the comer at the guns.

"I've got two rifles, one musket, and a pistol. If I had somebody to load—"

Beniel interrupted.

"You got four rifles; mine's a double barrel. Left tube don't throw too good, so I only use it on Injuns or skunks. That way, I don't strain it none."

Sherrod talked carelessly, but his keen eyes missed nothing. He inspected the weapons and was surprised at their good condition. He looked at the shutters, at the piled furniture, and after that, inspected the barn. Back in the house, he tapped Jeff's chest with a horny forefinger.

"Young feller, likely you stayed behind because you ain't got much to lose. Neither hev I. It's fellers like us with no property or woman ties as kin raise hell with the king's little red brothers." Jeff laughed. He was beginning to like this man with the reckless glint in his gray eyes, the odd mixture of correct and incorrect usage in his speech, and the sure way he handled his heavy short-barreled rifle.

"I thought," Jeff remarked reflectively, "that Peter said you had an Indian wife."

Sherrod hunched his shoulders and belched lightly.

"Oh yes, I've hed mebbe close to a half dozen of 'em. The last I traded to old Quockse on the Moshannon. I jest couldn't break her of the habit of cooking fish whole. I'll bet you never set down to eat a mess of trout and got your mouth full of fish guts."

Jeff threw back his head and howled, not so much at the story as the way the woodsman related it and the casualness with which he dismissed his domestic problem. But both men were soon sober.

"Son, the war party I dodged will be lookin' us up soon as they get a whiff of your cookin'. I figgered they was mebbe two-three hours behint me. Our time's most up. Git the dog into the house." Bang obeyed reluctantly and followed the men to the loft, where they watched for a half hour. Beniel saw them first, five trotting figures coming along the trail from the west, and he summoned Jeff to his loophole. They stopped in a huddle at the edge of the fields. A quarter of an hour passed, and then three of the Indians walked right out in the open, approaching within fifty yards of the house. Their clothing was pretty bedraggled, and their paint had run badly. The only one who carried a gun stepped forward and laid it down. Then all three stretched out right hands, palms up, the gesture of peace. Jeff whispered to Beniel:

"What's up?"

Beniel did not answer for a moment, but his eyes narrowed as he looked first at his priming, then at his companion.

"They know somebody's in here. Empty houses don't fry meat. Now they want to get us in the open and find out how many of us is here. Don't forget they's five of 'em. Watch thet white pine." He gestured toward a big pine, perhaps two feet in thickness, that stood just at the field's edge, a short rifle shot from the front door of the house. The three savages still stood in an impassive row facing the house.

"Injun back of it, Jeff. I seed his feather," Beniel gritted.

"'We'll go down. I'll open the door and palaver whilst you cover me with a rifle."

Jeff demurred. "Not by a damn sight, Beniel; I'll do the showing. You cover."

They descended the stairs, and Sherrod took up his post at the loophole of a shutter which would cover the pine tree. Jeff went to the front door. He couldn't see much reason for appearing before the Indians, but he worked aside the furniture, opened the door, and stepped on the porch. From the corner of his eyes, he saw a brown rifle barrel come into sight at the tree. He pitched himself forward as Migun had taught him when the shot came, the bullet tearing splinters from a post. Almost at the same instant, Beniel's rifle roared behind him. With a jerk of his body, Jeff rolled inside the door.

"Close," Sherrod commented. "I didn't figger they'd be so damned quick."

Out front, one of the three decoys was crawling toward the cover his companions had already reached. Both white men leaped to portholes where they could see the pine. Jeff fired at the flick of a feather, and a figure leaped out and ran. Sherrod's big rifle seemed to hesitate. Then it bellowed. The running figure all but somersaulted and lay still. Beniel held up two fingers.

"One cooked, one half done. I used my Injun bar'l on the first. T'other is much truer," he said callously.

The day passed with no further attack, and time dragged. Dusk brought no lurking shadows. Both men and the dog slept downstairs with the portholes open, so any movement outside would rouse them. It was close to morning but still pitchy dark in the house when the dog growled deep in his throat. Jeff's fingers found the hackles on the animal's neck raised. He got up and peered out the back door cautiously. There was some light outside, but not enough to detect any figures or movement. Beniel tried the front door outlook with no better results.

"Thought I seen something move. Ain't sure, though. Let's git to the loft."

They rebarricaded the doors and had scarcely reached the low room under the roof when there was a light tap on the split shingle roof just above their heads. It was followed immediately by another. Beniel's fingers closed on his companion's arm.

"I smell smoke. Them's fire arrows."

Jeff raced downstairs and returned to the loft with a bucket of water and a gourd. Even in this short a time, a tiny spot of fire showed in the roof. Two gourds of water extinguished it while Beniel crouched where he could look toward the barn. Jeff peered over his shoulder. At first, there was only the darkness. Then a tiny fire torch showed, and back of it, a denser shadow. Beniel's gun cracked, and the report was echoed by a yell of agony. The torch rolled on the ground and winked out.

"Likely he burnt hisself," Beniel grunted.

Three or four shots cracked spitefully from the shelter of the barn, one bullet ripping shingles. Both riflemen crouched, ready to shoot at a flash, but no more came.

"They'll make a day of it," Sherrod grunted. "They'll stick around figgering that white men will always make a mistake and show themselves. Thet's the way Injuns hunt; wait a whole day for a shot."

Full dawn showed an empty farmstead with no signs of attackers. Time dragged on until noon when Sherrod reversed his idea of caution.

"Dammit, Jeff, I jest can't wait till them red sticks is good and ready. Let's carry their war right to 'em. They run me off the Sinnamahoning. It's my time to run them a bit."

There was no arguing with the man. He slipped out the back way after insisting that Jeff and the dog remain in the house. After a good hour, he returned.

"Can't figger it. Nothing bigger than a rabbit in the brush. Birds is singing, and a red squir'l up on a stub wasn't sayin' a damn word." He scratched a stubbly chin. "Only one thing's queer, there's a smell of fresh smoke from over toward the crick. It ain't a campfire this time of day."

Jeff studied a moment.

"Pertman's cabin's down that way. I don't think it was burned when I came here. Beniel, them red devils gave us up and are having a time over there. Come on. I had an idea in the night. We've lots of powder."

Beniel kept a sharp lookout while Jeff worked. He used a big iron cup on which he soldered a lid. After it cooled, he filled it with powder, tamping it down well about a fuse he made from a string rolled in powder. Finally, he corked the hole tightly with a wood plug. What he had fashioned was a crude grenade.

"Damned if I want to play ball with thet," Sherrod said with distrust. "Specially if thet fuse was splutterin'."

About dusk, they fastened the rebellious dog in the house. Jeff carried his rifle and pistol. Over his shoulder was slung the buckshot-charged musket. Beniel had his own double barrel and the Indian gun. The grenade was inside Jeff's shirt, and Beniel had his pipe well-lighted.

"Seven shots we got," the woodsman declared. "Throw away thet damned snowball of yours."

Jeff only laughed.

"They use these in the old country," he declared. "Only they use pieces of pipe."

Beniel did the scouting, leading Jeff through the brush and timber toward the Pertman clearing. Fire still glowed at the end of the partly destroyed house showing the litter of household goods broken and scattered about. A feather bed had been ripped open to add to the disarray. Around a campfire were four Indians, their guns stacked against a tree. Three of them were eating. The fourth was busy roasting a small animal over the fire.

Jeff took out his bomb, pulled Beniel to him, and lighted the fuse from his pipe. Then he unslung the musket and passed it to his friend.

"Give them the buckshot, Beniel. Shoot for the stack of guns when my arm goes up."

Sherrod cocked the musket under the flap of his hunting shirt to prevent any noise and edged away from the now spluttering weapon in Jeff's hand. The white men had approached within fifty feet of the unsuspecting Indians. The fuse was down to a half inch, and Jeff tossed it.

The grenade was much less effective than Jeff had hoped, but it struck in the middle of the fire as it exploded, showering the Indians with burning brands. Beniel's musket shot upset the stack of guns by the tree. Then he threw down the weapon and took a snap shot which must have wounded one of the savages, for he dropped and crawled away. Taking turns with the loading, the two white men searched the brush with bullets.

The Indian guns were in pretty bad shape; Jeff finished them by smashing each piece against a rock. They had certainly disarmed their attackers if this was the party that had besieged Travelome. Beniel found a bag of parched corn which had been left behind and tasted it.

"Good," he declared. "It's fixed with maple sugar."

They went back to Travelome, well satisfied that the Indians had received a good lesson, but Beniel was worried.

"Jeff, the more I see of it, the more I'm sure there are only little bands in this valley. There's big deviltry elsewhere. Couple of months past they was thick as fleas on the river. Cornin' down, I jumped jest the one band."

The woodsman seemed right. The next week they scouted as far west as the bluffs beyond burned Fort Reed and eastward to Larry's Creek without encountering savages. Cabins had been burned, but there were no signs of an enemy. Still maintaining caution, the two men turned to harvesting the wheat now ripe in the Grube field. They gave the last hoeing to the corn, freeing it from the bindweed that threatened to choke the tender plants.

On Monday of the second week, Job Chilloway appeared. He explained the quiet on the West Branch with the horrifying story of the Indian and Tory descent on the Wyoming country. At last, it was certain where that army had gone. It had crossed New York State and followed the rivers until it reached the place where it worked its devilish will on the populace. There had been seven hundred Rangers and over a thousand Senecas. There had been battle, murder, scalpings, torture. A whole section had been devastated with the most savage fury yet loosed in America. According to Job, the British commander had sickened of the awful work and led his force back toward Niagara.

Chilloway finished his story and looked down the slope toward the river.

"So," he said gravely and thoughtfully, "they didn't just destroy the whites in Wyoming. They wiped out forever the power of the Long House. Now an Indian will not be thought of as a man but as a forest beast to be shot as we do wildcats and wolves. A power will rise and move on the Long House, a power that will burn the homes up there and scatter the red people to the four winds."

He ate with them on the front porch and shook hands with them gravely before leaving. Jeff never saw the man again.

CHAPTER XIX

FOR DAYS the shock of Chelloway's message went with the two men as they worked about the farm. The settlements in the Wyoming valley had been much larger and more compact than those on the West Branch. Their complete destruction and devastation seemed almost an impossibility. Yet, Migun and Jeff had seen the army which did it, and Chilloway had described partially the deviltry which had been done. Indignation would sweep the country like wildfire. Job's words were prophetic:

". . . Wiped out forever the power of the Long House."

Ever since America had been settled, the threat and influence of the Iroquois Long House Confederacy had hung in the forests and over the lakes of their own country, ready to be released east, south, north, or west. Other Indian forays had been the work of scattered tribes. Now, here on the North Branch of the Susquehanna, the strength of one family of the Confederacy, the Senecas, had been loosed. Chilloway was sure retaliation would destroy all the Iroquois nations. The massacre had been too awful, even for a complacent Congress.

Beniel was restless for three days before he made up his mind and spoke to Jeff.

"I'm going over there for a look-see. Long time past, I traded in that country. That was before them Yankees got too smart for me."

Jeff saw no point in accompanying the woodsman. He had set his heart on saving Travelome and felt sure he could defend it against small raiding parties. Peter and Faith would have their home again, the house and land they loved. Susan would go about her tasks here, singing. Her picture was with him all the time. Sun-ripened wheat reminded him of her hair. The bending of the grain stalks recalled her gracefulness. Near one of the rear corners of the house, in a place where the ground was a little soft, he found the print of her small, square-toed shoe. Half shame-facedly, even though he knew there was none to watch him excepting the dog. Bang, he covered the track with a piece of bark which he weighted down with stones. Each day he took a look at it, for the print of her shoe made him feel she might be coming around the house most any time.

Sherrod returned at the end of a week, a grim-faced man looking much older than when he left. He had little to say except that Chilloway had only hinted at the extent of the horror which had been visited upon the Connecticut settlers.

"Two hundred twenty-seven scalps they took, so it is said, and half of them was women and kids," he declared grimly.

"Why did they turn back, Beniel? They had army enough to wipe these valleys clean."

Sherrod shook his head.

"I wouldn't know for sure, but I think them Britishers had seen all they could stand and turned back. Even a damned Tory couldn't hev stood seein' more without losing his vittles."

He spat a heavy stream of tobacco juice at a weed.

"When Peter's back, Jeff, I'm going upriver. I've seen the buzzards swing in the sky up there at Wyoming. They was huntin'. I'm going to leave some meat for the upriver buzzards. It'll be red stuff with feathers on it."

Beniel's grim threat bore out Job Chilloway's prophecy that Indians would be hunted like wild beasts.

Migun made another of his appearances, coming from nowhere in particular. He was cheerful, full of news, hungry, and anxious for buckskin to repair his moccasins. He had been down river.

"Colonel Brodhead's at Muncy with troops to protect the settlers coming up to harvest their grain. I offered to scout for him, but he said he wasn't using Indians. The damn fool rides along whistling so loud he don't hear the musket being cocked in the thicket," he said spitefully. Evidently, the Colonel had been less than tactful.

He explained that the Grubes occupied part of a house in Squire Fell's town. They were quite comfortable though there was great distress among the poorer refugees.

"That Susan," he said slyly. "She is like honey to bees, and there were many bees down there: settlers, soldiers, and whatnot."

Jeff concealed a twinge of exasperated jealousy and remembered how Susan said she liked to see people go by when she lived in the city. However, he would not give Migun a chance for further teasing. He had suddenly made up his mind to do a reckless thing. These friends would defend Travelome; he would take the risk of going to Fort Muncy. Peter might have come upriver, or there might be a chance of some action worth entering. At any rate, he was going to take the chance of being arrested. The people at the fort would likely be soldiers rather than settlers who might recognize him.

The half-destroyed stockade looked deserted when he arrived, but there were soldiers about. Jeff was told Brodhead had gone to Penn's Valley, leaving Captain Vernly with a "corporal's guard" at the fort.

"Could I see him?" Jeff inquired from the man who had been talking.

The soldier spat copiously and grinned.

"S'pose you could, stranger, if your time ain't worth much."

Jeff walked into a barnlike building, indicated by the soldier's gesture with his shoulder. His moccasins made no noise on the puncheon floor. A man in a neat buff and blue uniform, looking out of the unglazed window, turned to face the visitor. Small eyes searched Jeff's worn clothes and his carelessly shaven face.

"Sir, I'm from upriver. Can I help as a guide? I'm from Peter Grube's plantation above the Tiadaghton."

The officer walked to the table and riffled through some papers. "We won't need any help you could give. Are you Grube's servant?"

The soldier had cataloged his status from his clothing. Jeff had never thought of what his definite relationship with Peter was.

"No, we saved his house. I know Grube will be glad to know." It was as though Jeff's words had pulled a trigger on the captain's smoldering irritation. His face reddened, and he struck his fist into his palm.

"I've met this loud-mouthed Grube fellow. Now his house stands while all others are burned. So it was at Wyoming, one building untouched; the owner was a bloody Tory."

Rage surged through Jeff as quickly as it had done in the officer he faced. Peter Grube had fought in the old wars, had signed the Pine Creek Declaration of Independence, had spent days of his time patrolling, had been a tower of strength to his fellow settlers.

"You filthy liar!" Jeff roared at him and stepped forward. "Don't ever call a real man names."

The officer moved back, and half drew his small sword. "Names," he snapped in his turn. "Jeffry Claus, I've heard of you in Sunbury. Put up your hands, or I'll run you through."

The blade was out and flicking back and forth in front of Jeff's chest. His first anger had passed, softened by the need to protect himself. He backed away from the narrow blade and bumped his foot against a stool. Not taking his eyes from the enraged attacker, he whipped it up. Vernly had started his lunge and could not stop. His point stuck in the wooden stool, and his weapon was wrenched from his hand.

"Vernly, I ought to beat the hell out of you. I would if you were a real man. I'll find out from Peter why you try to blacken him." None of the loafing soldiers stopped Jeff. He was home by evening after a hard walk, and his first act was to ask Migun about Vernly.

"Don't know him," the Delaware said. "I heard he was a ladies' man, that he tried to be too friendly to Faith one night at a dance. Peter did something unpleasant to him. But I never saw the officer."

Jeff told what had happened at the fort in some detail, emphasizing the officer's threat and recognition of his status.

"Migun, trouble follows me. When peace comes, what chance does a man with a price on his head have?"

"My brother is bitter," the Delaware said softly. "Likely I would be, too, if my back was scarred with a whip."

Migun, his eyes half veiled by their lids, was looking over the long slope to the river, and his voice took on the cadence of the Indian orator.

"All life is in the hands of the great Giver. If a man walks with his face to the sun and hides no misdeeds in his shadow, good will come to him.

Listen. Water flows over rocks, logs, and mud. It turns here and there, but it never really rests until it reaches the sea, for which it started when only a raindrop. So truth may be tangled or twisted, but it obeys a law which says it will sometime have its day. If you do not let bitter thoughts burn away your faith, my brother, truth will make you free."

A catch formed in Jeff's throat as he listened to the rise and fall of the low, vibrant voice. There was hope and quiet confidence in what the Indian said. When he finished, both rose. Migun extended his hand: "Good-by."

Surprised, Jeff met the grasp of the strong brown fingers and protested, "Won't you wait till the folks get back?"

The Delaware smiled and shook his head. "No, the settlers are on their way back, and an Indian won't be too welcome about here for a while. Too many burned cabins."

He poked his friend in the ribs with his thumb.

"Some day, you and I'll go down and make this Abner Fultz talk. A man with a fat belly scares easy when a knife point touches it."

Peter Grube arrived the afternoon of the next day. He had ridden ahead of his people in his eagerness. Jeff heard the clatter of the horse's hoofs and came out of the shop in time to see the big man slide from his saddle and stand staring at the house.

"God," he breathed, almost ignoring Jeff and his outstretched hand. "They hinted it was still here, but I couldn't believe it."

His glance took in the neatly tended corn field and the wheat stubbles. He looked dazed.

"And the crops are in. I'll have to ride back and hurry Faith."

The cavalcade rode up a half hour later, Peter riding ahead with Faith and gesturing expansively at each landmark. There was a string of pack horses all well laden, the two black people and Susan, in a dust coat, riding a dun mare.

Jeff swung Faith from her mount and was kissed soundly on both cheeks.

"Oh, Jeff, how can we ever thank you? I'll never leave the place again."

But he paid little attention to her words. He was hurrying to help Susan. Not as good a horsewoman as Faith, she let herself be unduly clumsy and so he could hold her close, lifting her out of the saddle.

"Not too much help, Jeffry," she whispered. "Not too much—"

But he held her tight before he let her small feet touch the ground. Her eyes were quick to see that Faith and Peter had eyes only for the house. Then she gave him her lips.

Harriet hustled about the kitchen, chirping approval as she found things in good order. She prepared the evening meal following Faith's demand that all they ate must be from Travelome stores. After supper, Peter and Jeff had a few minutes together.

"Fultz is the one who is keeping things hot for you, Jeff. Of course, the sheriff and the prosecutor rankle about the trial. The murder charge won't stick if we can get Colonel Antes to testify, but he's with Washington. Cultsizer had Fell try to buy your indenture with no success though he offered a full hundred pounds for it."

Peter twisted in his chair.

"Jeff, there's something below the surface. From the first, things moved against you: the indenture was lost, then they trapped you into longer service, then the murder. Fultz is wild about the Ribner widow. Jeff, did you—"

He stopped as if unwilling to frame the question. Unwillingly, Jeff's mind went back. He thought of the woman's perfume, the grace of her carriage, her drawling voice saying that he would never forget her. Just an hour or so before, he had held Susan close and knew he loved her. Now he felt disloyal that his mind had dragged up the memory of Abigail Ribner and his hours spent with her. Grube changed the subject.

"It was pretty bad down there. Our people were not too welcome. Of course, our family was all right down in McKee's town, but folks from up here lived in barns, in pigpens, and under lean-to shelters. Food was scarce, Jeff. Your money was a mercy, and I used every shilling of it. Then there were vague threats about the old fines which hangs over us for settling west of the Lycoming."

The big man leaned over and struck the porch railing with his fist.

"Saw a thing down there. They caught a runaway and brought him in before that old devil of a Plunkett. He fastened the fellow, not much more than a boy, to a picket fence and lashed him with leather straps. Then the Justice was going to fine a man they claimed had helped the boy run off a cool hundred pounds. He walked out of the court with a rifle held on the Justice, and nobody wanting to stop him."

Jeff felt the skin on his scarred back crawl. Peter rose to join the others, and Jeff walked out into the gathering darkness to be alone with bitter reminders. He was still a runaway who could be tied to a fence and beaten. These friends who had sheltered him could be beggared with fines for doing it. What good was his love of Susan? He had no right to claim her. Even with the murder charge dismissed, years of bond service stretched ahead.

With Brodhead in the valley, the settlers were returning, but not in a mass as they had gone out. They came in by families or small groups of families, and their coming was not the glad arrival of the Grubes, who had found their home intact. They were disillusioned, knowing that, with a little help, they could have held the valley and saved their homes and crops.

In so many cases, a family would return carrying all their meager belongings on their backs. They faced the blackened ashes and logs of their home. For a day or so, they would camp under a brush shelter. Then the axes would begin cutting the logs for a new home in the wilderness. Few stopped to be thankful that the terrible red force from the north had spent itself in the Wyoming valley. These people were concerned with their own immediate problems, and their troubles seemed worse because they had been brought on unnecessarily. They saw clearly now that they could have defended their homes more or less easily with just the minimum of help. The valley slogan had become:

"That damned Hunter sold us out."

There were two bright spots for these people. Most of the wheat could be harvested without loss, and the corn, excepting for weeds, was in fine shape.

In a week or so, stories began to be passed along. The returned settlers were both reckless and ruthless in respect to Indians. One yarn ran that an old Delaware and his wife had been camped well up Larry's Creek. No one knew the perpetrators, but the couple were found neatly hanged on the limb of a butternut tree, their few belongings a charred mass under the bodies. Up beyond Great Island, four painted warriors had been surprised, killed, and scalped. The scalps were nailed to nearby trees to indicate that white men set no value on this sort of trophy dear to Indian pride.

Jeff heard the stories and knew both Migun and Job Chilloway had understood thoroughly what the situation would be like. He had another thing to worry about. Peter Grube's home had come through unscathed, and his neighbors were secretly envious. Several times when he and Peter had taken horses to settler's clearings to help with the house-raisings, their offer had been rejected. Jeff remembered Captain Vernly's remark, and he knew that Peter was hurt, although he did not speak about it. Certainly, the Fair Play country had lost much of its friendliness because of the exodus and return.

Then came news that broke many of the tensions along the river. Colonel Thomas Hartley was in the valley with headquarters at Fort Muncy, which he was rebuilding. The rumor ran that he was about to move north and punish the invaders of the Wyoming country. Three days after the story reached Travelome, a rider dressed in a mixture of military uniform and buckskin cantered into the barnyard. He slid from his horse and advanced toward Peter, holding out a big hand.

"I'm from Colonel Hartley, sir. You are Peter Grube."

Peter took the proffered hand and nodded. The man went on explaining.

"I'm Sergeant Westover of Hartley's Dragoons. The Colonel has heard there is a good gunsmith in your home, and he'd like very much to borrow the man."

Peter called Jeff, who was nearby, and introduced him.

"This is Jeffry Claus, Sergeant Westover. There is a little trouble with the Northumberland courts about this young man even though Colonel Antes has vouched for him. Also, Jeff recently had a bit of trouble with a Captain Vernly at Muncy. Perhaps—" Westover brushed some dust from his nondescript clothing and grinned.

"The colonel knows something of all this, sir. He wants a smith and directed me to say that Claus will not be molested by anyone, civilian or military officers included. The need is great."

"I'll go," Jeff said. "Wait until I get my tools."

Sergeant Westover and Peter went to the front porch to wait while Jeff entered the shop and selected some tools he felt he would need. He was just ready to emerge when Susan appeared at the back kitchen door and beckoned to him. She led the way to the house corner and pointed to the weighted piece of bark which covered her footprint. Bending gravely, she removed it and set her small shoe in the track. Jeff looked into her eyes and then gathered her close in his arms. Standing on tiptoe, she raised her lips for his kiss.

"Be careful, Jeff. Oh, be careful. There are such evil men."

She gave him her lips once more before hurrying into the house, and he stood for a moment with his head in a whirl. Hearing Peter and his guest coming, he hurried out to meet them.

"Almost forgot something," he explained. From the way Peter looked at him, he knew his ears were red.

"Yes," Grube commented, "you forgot to saddle the horse."

The sergeant proved to be a discreet young man, able to keep the conversation on pleasant lines as they rode side by side. He admired the countryside, the corn crop, and the streams. He said he was an enthusiastic fisherman. Finally, he spoke of Colonel Hartley.

"Colonel Antes told Hartley you set up his swivel guns when he built his fort."

Jeff was pleased that Antes had remembered him that well.

"I helped a little. Colonel Antes was kind, the sort of man you like to do your best for. Perhaps I was worth more at the guns than with the ax."

Westover changed the subject by taking out a rifled pistol and passing it to his companion, who examined it as they rode.

"The damned thing shoots pretty hard but never twice in the same place. What's wrong with it?"

Jeff passed the weapon back.

"Bring it into the shop. The front sight is bent, and the bore should be freshened. That's not much of a job on a pistol."

The owner put the weapon back in its holster.

"You know, friend, I took that from a Hessian officer at Trenton who was too drunk to know which end of it to point. Folks in this valley think we're getting licked in this war. I wish they could have been with us at

Trenton and Princeton. Our militia can fight when they've a mind to it. I've seen them match British regulars in battle and shoot a damned sight better. Then I wish the folks could see some of 'Tony' Wayne's Pennsylvania regiments. They can handle a bayonet with any troops, though that sticker always makes me feel a little sick in the belly." Westover wasted no time in reporting when they arrived at the now rejuvenated Fort Muncy, thronged with soldiers. He took Jeff to the shop and showed him the tools and his room over the place as it had been at Ribner's.

"Make yourself at home. You mess with us sergeants."

He left his pistol with Jeff and took his leave.

There was enough work already stacked up to have kept Cultsizer's shop busy for a while. Muskets and rifles stood in the corners. Pistols, swords, and bayonets were piled on the workbenches. His first job was to recondition Westover's pistol. When the officer returned and opened the door, Jeff saw a sentry outside. He pointed to him.

"Does that mean I'm under arrest?"

The Sergeant's grin showed excellent teeth.

"That's the Colonel's guarantee that you won't be disturbed. Come on and eat. I'll have you a helper in the morning."

Henry Josslyn, a middle-aged man who proved to be an excellent general smith, was the helper. Working together, Jeff and he classified the jobs ahead, and work moved smoothly and swiftly. Occasionally an officer would drop by to check weapons belonging to his men. Westover was delighted with his pistol. One day, he brought in a pair of blunt, businesslike weapons.

"The colonel's, Jeff. He saw mine and wants his fixed up."

In his third week at the Fort, Jeff was working alone one evening by candlelight on the broken stock of a rifle that belonged to a member of the sergeant's mess. He did not notice for several minutes that he had a visitor. Though he had not yet seen Colonel Hartley, he recognized the uniform and insignia.

"Sir," he said in embarrassment, "I did not see you come in." Hartley stepped forward with a most unmilitary walk. His short figure was well-filled out, and his big face was round and thoughtful. He was smiling.

"Claus, you've been a godsend to us. Weapons are scarce, and we're a long way from armorers. We count ourselves lucky to have found you."

Jeff, embarrassed at the hearty commendation, took down the pistols Westover had brought him.

"Your pistols are ready, sir. I lightened the trigger pulls and took a liberty."

He held one barrel close to the light.

"I crowned this, sir, because that way, it's easier to load." Hartley took the weapon and examined it casually.

"I'm sure you did right though I'm not much of a gun man. I did not come about the pistols, Claus, but to keep my word with a friend of yours and mine, Christian Fell. Let's go to your room." Colonel Thomas Hartley had a way of ridding a man of his hesitancy. He did it now with Jeff, who led him to his narrow room. The officer seated himself on a stool and leaned forward.

"I have not come to pry, but I would like your full story. Fell told me much of it, and I dislike seeing a useful man wasted." Jeff remembered how he had thought of consulting a lawyer in Lancaster but had been afraid to do so. Now he had the opportunity of telling his story to a man who was known as an excellent counselor before he entered the army. It was a satisfaction to have Hartley listen as closely as he did. When Jeff spoke of the will written on the indenture paper, the colonel stopped him.

"You could sue Fultz to produce the indenture, but all that would accomplish would be to make him go to Philadelphia for the copy in the hands of the mayor. Only—"

His eyes twinkled.

"The mayor might make him prove that he is the legal heir of his uncle, Mark Fultz. From what I hear, such proof was passed over pretty lightly up here in the sovereign county of Northumberland. Go on, young man, finish the story."

Jeff related the whole sordid tale with the exception of his relations with Abigail Ribner. He spoke of Melody, the muskets, the liquor to savages, then of the beating and his rescue followed by the accusation of murder. He finished with the account of the Fair Play trial and his vindication. Abruptly, Hartley shook his heavy head.

"You've left some out. You didn't seem to play along with Squire Fell to any great extent. Doing it might have curbed the Indian trade."

Jeff colored, and his face set in stubborn lines. He had talked freely so far and would say no more. Hartley frowned.

"You're a young man, Claus. I think that woman down there, the one who now leads Fultz by the nose, has led you a little." He stood up and tucked the pistols into a capacious pocket. "The murder charge won't stand up. The reward is offered so they can get their hands on you. Your chances at freedom would be pretty slim in any court unless we can turn up something else. The woman, my boy, she's the key. Perhaps it was on her account that Ribner hated you, as Fultz does now."

He hunched up his heavy shoulders and thrust out his lower lip.

"When I finish this campaign, I go back to the practice of law. I'll look into this, partly because of my friend, Christian Fell, but more to help a stubborn, dark-visaged young man who has been very useful to our cause." He grinned and added a sentence. "But who seems to have a way with women, even though he does get trapped for it."

With something like a wink on his broad face, he turned and descended the ladder to the lower floor.

CHAPTER XX

THROUGH SUCCEEDING DAYS, while he worked away in the shop, Jeff thought of the conversation with Colonel Hartley. It seemed to him the officer did have some hope of getting him released though he had not said so definitely.

"The woman, my boy, she is the key," was Hartley's conclusion. That could well be, for Abigail Ribner had dominated her husband, and Fultz would be putty in her hands. Jeff was sure some large plan engrossed her, something which had moved her to come up here on the Susquehanna with a husband she certainly did not love. Jeff had been her plaything for a time, perhaps merely to break the boredom she had felt.

Another talk with the soldier-lawyer was out of the question. Hartley's days were crowded with duties and frustrations. In the sergeants' mess, Jeff heard a great deal of what had brought the colonel upriver. His was an expedition against the wasp nest of Iroquois, half-breeds, and Tories at Chemung. It would be a desperate venture, a march of a hundred miles through rough-timbered country, then a quick stroke and return. The major problem was to keep the plan from the enemy. If warned, almost any of the Iroquois nations, with the exception of the Tuscaroras, could put enough warriors in the field to destroy Hartley's small army.

"Colonel's getting touchy," Westover commented one evening. "That Garvey man he didn't trust disappeared. He was always snooping around. Of course, the red sticks may have caught him in the brush, like they did three or four others, but he might have gone north."

Fred Stewart, youngest of the noncoms, waved his pipe. "There's no hiding this thing. There were Tories at Wyoming, and likely we've got them about here. When we start for Chemung, I'm going to tie my hat down tight over my hair. I want to bring it back."

Stewart's comment was typical of the feelings of these battle-hardened men. The venture afoot was a desperate one, but they would carry it through.

In the first week of September, Jeff visited Travelome. Beniel Sherrod had just returned from hunting ginseng, and Peter was happily busy on the farm. When Jeff had a chance to talk to him alone, he was very much interested in Hartley's comments and offer.

"He's a good lawyer, Jeff. Sometimes I feel we could risk a trial for you in Sunbury. You'd certainly be cleared of the murder, and the treatment you received might bring you freedom. Of course, to stand trial, you'd risk everything, maybe your life, if we couldn't get Colonel Antes' testimony."

He touched Jeff's arm.

"You know why Faith and I are double anxious. Susan will be free before snow flies, and I'll not have her break her heart about anything, not even you, Jeff."

There was exact justice in what Grube was saying. It amounted to a statement that Jeff must clear himself before he had any right to hope for Susan. He loved her enough to know that he would give her up rather than have her tied to a man who was a fugitive with a price on his head. Later, he was alone with her for a while.

"I've been worrying," she told him. "There must be a lot of Northumberland people down there at Muncy, and that fifty pounds must look big to many."

He reassured her by telling of the sentry at the shop and of Colonel Hartley's visit and tentative promise.

"Susan, he and Peter think the murder charge will have to be dropped. A court might set me free because had I returned to the Ribner post, it would have been at the risk of my life."

Her eyes were troubled, and she made a little gesture with her hand.

"But, Ribner's dead. Fultz and that—"

She paused, and it was as though a shadow had passed over her eyes. Jeff leaned forward and took her hand.

"Susan, shall I risk the trial?"

This time she was silent so long, with her head lowered, that he bent to peer into her face. She was crying. Contritely, he put his hands on her shoulders and shook her gently.

"That was cowardly of me, Susan. A man must stand on his own feet, take his own risks. Only, you know how much I want you, and I will not have you unless I'm free."

They rose, and she held him by the thrums on his new buckskin hunting shirt while she spoke softly.

"Jeffry, the time is long. You will have to make up your mind how much risk you will take and what it is worth."

Before they retired, Jeff talked with Peter.

"I've been a fool all along in one way or another. I—"

Grube was tapping out his pipe.

"Perhaps admitting it is the beginning of wisdom," he said dryly. Jeff looked at him sharply, the lines of his dark face deeper than usual.

"When Hartley comes back, I'll give myself up and stand trial. I've been afraid too long. Maybe it was the whip scars that made me so. Were you ever touched with a whip, Peter?"

Grube did not answer, but as they walked into the house, the big man laid his hand gently on the younger one's shoulder.

Jeff got back to Fort Muncy just in time for a general muster of soldiers, militia, and all civilians. Colonel Hartley faced the assembly with a stern face and bitter tongue.

"Men and women," he announced, "all of you know that we march north against the savages. Our force is small. Many of the soldiers I expected could not be sent, but I march with what we have. If word of our purpose goes to the savages, all of us will die under Iroquois hatchets. We are putting our heads into the lion's mouth, but I want to destroy some of the hell holes of Indian towns with their drying scalps and torture posts."

He paused as a growl went through the ranks of the militia. "We think someone has already carried word north about how few we are. Now listen to me. If you suspect anyone of being a Tory lover, bring him to me, and I'll hang him higher than Haman. If you see somebody slipping away north, shoot him. He'd be putting a hatchet to our heads. Dismissed!"

That evening Colonel Hartley summoned Jeff.

"Claus, I called you here to tell you I'd like to take you with us in the morning, but I cannot."

Jeff looked at him with disappointment written all over his face, for he had been sure of going. Hartley continued:

"My orders are to take no Indians, indentured servants, or men from the Fair Play country. I'll try to see that you are paid some wages for your fine service here at Fort Muncy. Perhaps you are lucky. Our hair may all be drying in Indian lodges next month at this time. When I return, I shall look into your case. It seems to me you have paid enough to live in this America we call free." The expedition moved out in the morning without waiting for the reinforcements Hartley expected. If news had been carried north by Tory sympathizers or spies, delaying the start of the expedition would only give the enemy time to mass forces. Nevertheless, the three hundred men marching in columns of four made an impressive sight, filing through the main gate of the log stockade and moving out on the old Sheshequin Path toward the north.

The dozen mounted troopers in their leather caps and high polished boots, led the procession with sabers swinging and carbines balanced across their saddles. The rank and file of the soldiers were well and strongly dressed, though not in any regulation uniforms. Jeff noted that their equipment was in good shape. Weapons were polished, footgear was in especially good condition, and the baggage animals were well-groomed and fat. With a man like Hartley leading, this small army could be an effective striking force.

Four or five incapacitated soldiers had been left behind to guard the fort and whatever stores remained. Directly after the army had left, the civilians, including the colored laborers, made their exodus. There was no longer anything to hold Jeff, so he packed up his own tools and went to the barns in the hope of renting or borrowing a horse for the trip back to Travelome.

Susan and Peter had warned him of his possible arrest at Fort Muncy, but having a sentry stationed at the shop for so long had made Jeff careless. Now, of course, the sentry was gone. He walked over the parade ground to the barns, which were almost empty. He was looking into one of the stables when a heavy blow on the head dropped him to his knees. Men piled on him before he could rise. A grain sack was drawn over his head, and leather straps fastened his arms and legs. He was carried and dumped into what he knew was a boat.

Minutes later, when the rocking told him they were out on the river, the sack was jerked from his head. Tom Dilson, the man he had beaten at Staier's, leered down into his face.

"So, my skinny friend, we have you, at last,"

Bending, he twisted Jeff's ear savagely between his thumb and forefinger.

"Don't worry. Our friend Abner Fultz wants his goods in nice shape. Fifty pounds, he'll pay. Hell, I'd pay a pound myself just to even things. Look at this arm."

The arm was crooked where it had been broken in the fight. The look of hate on the dirty, unshaven face was sickening. Jeff's body was propped against a thwart. He could see that Dilson had two companions, both as unsavory looking as the bully himself.

They made good time, going ashore at noon to eat. Jeff was not given any food, and Dilson managed to kick him on several occasions. In the boat, he walked roughly across Jeff's body as he changed positions with the man who was steering. Near nightfall, they sighted the joining of the rivers. It was all but dusk when they drifted past Fort Augusta, the boat keeping close to the west shore.

"After Fultz pays," Dilson told his prisoner, "you'll go over there. Old Plunkett's whipping fence is ready. So's the tree they use for hangings."

A little distance below Sunbury village, the boat pulled in. Rough hands jerked Jeff to his feet and through the water to the land. They're one of the men loosened the strap about his ankles. His legs were almost too numb to support him. His captors drove him with kicks and savage blows until they came to a dark cabin set a little way off the road. When candles were lighted, he recognized the place. It was the old Ebner cabin, long deserted and not much more than a half dozen miles from the Ribner post.

The men made their prisoner secure in a corner and sat about and ate. When he finished, Dilson faced Jeff.

"Now, sonny. I'll be reporting to the man that loves you fifty pounds' worth. If the fat boy welches, we'll take you to Sunbury, and they'll put the screws to him till he hands over. You'll have a nice wait here. Just be comfortable."

With the flat of his hand, he slapped Jeff twice across the face. Then with growled instructions to his companions as to what they should do in his absence, he stalked out into the cold rain, which was already seeping down from breaks in the roof.

The two men left behind took turns sleeping. Jeff kept working his hands and feet to get the circulation going but without success. Rain dripped on him, but his bonds would not let him avoid it. The hours dragged on miserably. In sheer weariness, he slept a little, only to be roused by the tramping of horses. The guard on duty stirred his companion, who sat up. The candle still burned on the decrepit mantel, but it was down to a stub.

Neither man had time to pick up a weapon before the door swung open, revealing a tall, cloaked figure with a hat pulled low over his face. As Jeff's two guards stared in surprise, the visitor's arm swept out, and a heavy pistol covered the two.

"Cut him loose!"

The command cracked, but the two men stood still as if paralyzed by surprise. The next instant, the cloaked intruder stepped forward and knocked one guard down with his heavy pistol barrel. Then he kicked the other savagely until he scrambled to release Jeff. Five minutes later, the two men were tied together with the bonds taken from their prisoner. Jeff followed his rescuer outside, where three horses and a mounted figure waited in the rain.

"All right?"

A woman's voice asked the question, and the man answered briefly: "Yes, let's ride; this rain is cold."

His rescuer seemed to realize that Jeff was almost helpless. He virtually lifted him into the saddle. Then he swung up on his own horse, and they were moving southward, one on either side of Jeff. He realized now, with a sense of shock, that the woman was Abigail Ribner. There was no mistaking her voice. He was sure, too, he had heard the man who had rescued him speak before. From the tone of his command and his quick, decisive actions, he must be a soldier.

After half an hour of hard riding, they trotted into the familiar grounds of the Ribner post and up to the back door. Light showed through the back windows. Jeff eased himself down from the saddle. In the semi-darkness, he saw the cloaked man lift the woman from her mount and noticed that he held her close for a moment.

"Thanks," she said in a low tone, "it won't be long now."

The kitchen door opened, and a serving woman stood there holding a candle. Jeff had just one glance at the man, enough to see the strong hawklike face clearly, before he turned away.

"I must ride," he said in a deep voice. "I'll turn your horses into the barn."

"Come, Jeff." Abigail Ribner's voice was gentle. "We'll go into the house."

After she had bathed his face and arms with warm water, the serving woman gave Jeff wine and food. Abigail Ribner walked impatiently up and down the room in manlike strides. When his meal was finished, she signed to the woman to leave.

"You're wet," Jeff told her. "Better get on dry things."

She smiled.

"Help me, Jeffry. Once you knew how."

His fingers fumbled, but he loosened her coat and flung it across a chair. She was still smiling as she bade him open her dress and let it drop to the floor. Sudden, stirring excitement moved him powerfully. His arms locked around her as the familiar perfume lifted to his nostrils. For a moment, she rested in his embrace, her hands lifting to loosen her cloud of brown hair. Then she drew away.

"No, Jeffry, perhaps that is all past. Get my robe. It will soon be morning, and I want to talk."

He found the garment and draped it over her smooth bare shoulders. She sat down, motioning him to sit, facing her.

"Believe me, I am grateful—"

"Yes," she said, interrupting him, "you should be. Fultz was away when his trained ape came with the news. It was good that I had a friend here. Now listen to me. I would let you wait and choke the truth from Abner Fultz, but it is not yet time."

"Fultz wants you," Jeff said. She smiled and then suddenly sobered.

"Listen carefully, Jeffry. Once there were three of us, Henry Ribner, Abner Fultz, and I. Now there are two. Fultz overreaches himself, tries to follow the lines Henry Ribner did, and he will someday bring disaster to himself. He has been plotting as my husband once did. Colonel Hartley has gone north. You do not know of it, but the Congress plans a great march on the Iroquois. This army, moving into the forests, will be supplied up this river. Fultz is getting together weapons. He is laying plans to break those supply lines and is being paid."

She rose and whirled about the room, her robe loosening and her hair flying. Then, all but breathless, she dropped into her chair.

"It's been so long, Jeffry. I came here for a purpose, and the end is in sight. Once there were three, now two. Perhaps there will be only one. And the money, the gold, is now in the countinghouses of Lancaster and Philadelphia—"

She leaned forward and clutched Jeff's shoulder so hard he winced.

"I will not tell you why Ribner and Fultz trapped you. If I were a strong, black devil like you, I would have long since choked the answers out of Fultz. He is a man afraid of his shadow. Listen, you are a bondsman. Come with me. Someday you might be free."

Her lips were parted a little, and her breath was coming faster. He tried to answer but could not shape the words. She laughed.

"No, he thinks of the little yellow bird upriver whose name is Susan. This yellow bird and the black crow of a Jeffry will be happy together. Only sometimes—"

She did not finish. The first morning light was showing through the blinds when she rose.

"When Hartley returns, bring men and come here. Find the slave, Fred. Fultz fears him greatly. Bring Squire Fell to whom I have talked. Then, methinks, you will know everything. But go now. I do not want Fultz to get you or to know I helped you until my plans are ripe."

She accompanied him to the door, and her perfume was in his nostrils. Hunger he could not deny surged in him. She was warm and yielding when his arms went around her roughly. Her lips brushed his.

"Jeffry, Jeffry."

It seemed as though there was pleading in her whisper, but she released herself and gently pushed him through the door she opened. The early morning air was chill.

All through the following two days of fast marching toward Travelome, Jeff debated about what he would tell the Grubes and Susan of his experience with Abigail Ribner. It would be hard to look into the girl's eyes and remember his weakness when the other woman was near. He did not love the dead Ribner's wife, nor she him, but that would be beyond his power to explain to a girl as strong-minded as Susan.

He went by the way of Muncy, where he got his bag of tools. He was less than a half mile from Travelome, passing through a belt of timber when a voice little louder than a whisper hailed him:

"Jeff."

He stepped behind a tree. Then Beniel Sherrod appeared. The grizzled woodsman shook hands gravely.

"Mebbe you should have stayed home, Jeff. I been watching fer you come two days now, you or most anybody. There's been Injuns."

Beniel did not need to explain. Jeff followed his fast lead. When they were in the open, he saw it. The barns and outbuildings of Travelome were masses of ashes and charred logs. The side of the house was badly scorched. Jeff gripped Beniel's shoulder.

"The folks," he demanded. "Susan, Faith, Peter?"

Sherrod shook his head and explained.

"Three or four days I was up river. I dodged a little war party of mebbe six or eight warriors. I followed them down but got here too late."

Jeff tried to interrupt, but Beniel pointed to the barn.

"They was two burnt bodies in there. Could hev been anybody. I buried them right aways. None of 'em would have wanted to have folks see them thet way."

Jeff's mouth was opening and closing, but he wasn't saying anything. There had been two bodies. Which one had escaped? Where were the black people? Indians seldom bothered them. It had been a surprise attack. Peter probably had been careless, engrossed in his work.

"Beniel," he said sharply, "get down country and look for Susan. I'll-"

He finished his statement by a gesture in the direction the raiding savages would have taken if they followed old paths. Sherrod spoke ruefully:

"I figgered you'd be doing that. I'm getting kind of short of friends."

Jeff dumped his tools into the house, which did not look disturbed. Less than an hour later, he crossed Tiadaghton, holding his rifle high to keep the priming dry. Murder and desperation were in his heart, and the driving hunger to see an Indian, any Indian at all. He understood now what moved men like Pentz and Sherrod to their killings. It was no time to waste, though, on the desperate nature of his own business. Had there been a possibility of return, Beniel Sherrod would have marched with him.

CHAPTER XXI

DRIVEN BY A TORMENT of mixed anger, grief, and anxiety, Jeff followed the old trail for hours. He crossed the big creek and traveled on until sheer weariness made him stop for a while. Sitting there on a log, he admitted to himself the futility of what he was doing. The Indian trail would now be two days old. Jeff knew he was no tracker like Migun or Beniel. He was a smith, and following tracks was not his business. In these two days, the raiders could be well across the Forbidden Way in the dark homeland of the Iroquois. Doggedly though, he got up and started forward, unwilling to acknowledge by turning back that the fate of Susan and the Grubes was hopeless.

Just before nightfall, he entered a narrow hollow through which a brook coursed. Here he lay down to drink. When his face neared the water, he saw a track of mud in it. When he had his fill, he looked about. A yard from where he had knelt was the print of a moccasin on the damp, moss-covered ground. To Jeff's eyes, it was fresh; Migun would have read a great deal from the track, but the main thing was that it had been made not long before. It looked as though the heel had caused an abnormally deep imprint. It was Migun's contention that an Indian foot touched the ground with even pressure.

Night overtook him in tangled country, and he made his bed in a clump of brush. Weary though he was, it was impossible to shut out the pictures and thoughts that flooded through his brain, keeping him awake. There was the picture of Susan's track at the corner of Travelome, the one he had covered, and she later found. Then there were Faith's words that she would never leave Travelome again and Peter, who loved his acres of corn and wheat and hay to the point where he must have grown careless. Yet it scarcely seemed possible that a man of his experience would be trapped and burned in a building.

The little noises of the night in the sparse timber and brush came close to Jeff. There were vague, light stirrings, sleepy bird chirps, and the soft sounds of crickets. Tiny puffs of wind moved in the trees, whispering in the pine needles and rustling the chestnut leaves. By and by, he slept.

He awakened to an ominously silent morning. There were no bird songs in the bushes, no squirrel chatter, and even the crickets were still. Half drugged by heavy sleep, he raised his head and understood the quieting of forest sounds. An Indian was sitting directly in front of him on a large stone. The savage was naked but for his breechclout and high moccasins. The paint on his face had run a little, revealing a scarred cheek. The gray feather back of the man's ear was battered, but it had once belonged to a goshawk. While the man was motionless, his musket barrel was trained exactly on Jeff's middle. The piece was, most likely, loaded with slugs. At this distance, it would tear a man almost in two.

Jeff, turning a bit, slowly raised himself on one elbow to see better. There were three other Indians and a white man with a tired face who wore the green coat of a British Ranger. Jeff remembered the long column of such men he and Migun had seen on the Chemung. Probably the man would say he was a Royal American. On the turned-back brown reefers of his coat were insignia indicating he was a noncommissioned officer. Then Jeff saw something else that brought him almost to his feet. One of the band, though painted and dressed like one, was not an Indian but a black man. It was Fred!

Jeff stood up. His chagrin at being captured this way before he had struck a blow left a bitter taste in his mouth. At his movement, the seated savage calmly raised the gun muzzle. Jeff saw a sight that sent an unreasoning and reckless fury through every nerve of his body. About the Indian's greasy middle, twisted and tied like a British officer's scarf, was a woman's red dress. Jeff recognized it as one of Susan's. Without any hesitation, he leaped like a cat at the Indian's face and throat.

The cocked musket exploded harmlessly into the air, and the warrior went down with Jeff's iron-hard fingers digging into his greasy throat.

"Where is she? Where is she?" Jeff was screaming.

The savage gagged and twisted in an agonized fight for breath. His companions went into action, striking brutally with musket butts and the flat of tomahawks until they were able to drag the half-stunned Jeff away. The snarling warrior who had been choked gained his feet. With one hand at his injured throat, he jerked out his war ax with the other. So far, the white man had taken no part in the melee. Now he snapped one word in the Indian tongue. With savage reluctance, the warrior slid the tomahawk handle back into its loop. The white man turned to Jeff.

"Keep your hands off them and shut up if you know what's good for you."

"Where is she?" Jeff snarled. "What did you do with her?"

The Ranger lifted a black-nailed forefinger and pointed at the prisoner.

"Likely, you're one of Hartley's scouts and a prisoner. Don't be snapping at Corporal McNight, one of His Majesty's officers. You're naught but a damned dirty rebel at best."

He gestured to the Indian who held Jeff. They jerked back his elbows and pinioned them brutally with rawhide thongs. Then a longer strap with a noose in it was slipped about his neck, and the free end tossed to the warrior whom Jeff had attacked. At the corporal's order, the party with its prisoner filed out on the trail.

Keeping up with an Indian raiding party was grim business at best, and Corporal McNight was setting an unusually fast pace. When Jeff stumbled, the noose shut off his breath. The thongs at his elbows and wrists grew painful inside a half hour. The hardest thing, though, was to be dragged behind this big, greasy savage with Susan's dress about his filthy painted body and to wonder how much she was suffering at this moment if she, too, was a captive.

At noon the party stopped long enough to eat black-looking corn-bread and dried meat, but none was offered the prisoner. They spread out the things taken from his pocket and gravely divided the few coins, the tobacco, clasp knife, and neckerchief. This last was slit through the middle; the better to share it. In twenty minutes, they marched again.

The sun climbed higher, and its rays became stronger as the steady northward march was maintained. Jeff's mouth felt as though it was filled with cotton from the heat and the repeated choking from the leash. In mid-afternoon, the party stopped where a small sand spring lifted its bubbles, becoming the source of a tiny rivulet. After McNight had satisfied his own thirst and had wiped his mustache on a greasy sleeve, the others drank, swooshing up the cold water in noisy gulps. For a moment, the warrior who held the leash dropped it, and Jeff pitched himself forward to reach the life-giving water. Before he could take a drop, the man saw him and, snatching the leash, jerked his captive back.

Both men were now on their feet, and there was as much savagery on Jeff's face as on his painted captor's. The Indian was shortening the thong. Plainly he was about to thrash his prisoner. He was coming closer, intent on the pleasure he would get from causing pain. But he had forgotten that Jeff's feet were free. The red arm went back over the naked shoulder, ready for the blow. Jeff's eyes were on Susan's dress as he lashed out and upward with his foot. With a howl of agony, the warrior went over backward, clutching at his groin as he fell. Jeff wasted no time but dropped to the water and sucked up great mouthfuls.

Thirst satisfied, he came up to his knees as his victim struggled up, murder in every line of the painted face. His lips drew back from the yellow teeth. Death was coming now from the small bright ax already out of its loop. For the moment, Jeff did not care. The ax would be better than the torture stake. Susan and his friends were gone. Death could not mean too much. His arms and wrists ached, and his neck was raw from the chafing of the noose.

But again, McNight saved him. Pitching down his musket, he shoved back his sleeves and, with a quick movement, snatched away the hatchet.

"You damned red scut," he roared. "You'd kill a prisoner before the major sees him. You're welcome to him after that, but not before."

The Indian must have made some threatening movement hidden by the officer's big body. McNight's fist snapped forward and stretched the big red man flat on his back.

"Macoga," he snarled, "I'm boss here. Reach for a knife again, and I'll spill your guts on a laurel bush. Fred!"

McNight tossed the thong to the pleased colored man when he came forward.

"You handle him. Now let's move."

Fred was almost too obviously delighted as they filed out on the trail, the chastened Macoga ahead, the corporal next, and the others in single file. The colored man had a new idea, an elaboration of Indian cruelty to captives on the march. Jeff was placed ahead of him, and Fred carried a long pointed stick with which he goaded his prisoner forward. McNight came back during the next momentary stop, seeming to feel he should explain his lapse into mercy.

"Don't get any fool ideas. When the major's done with you, the red devils are welcome to you, and they'll make it hot."

Jeff stared back at him as threateningly as he could. As they walked forward, in spite of the Negro's almost constant use of his goad, he watched the savages filing ahead. There was some consolation in the fact that none of them carried a scalp. Only that bedraggled and pitiful dress about Macoga's greasy middle indicated this band had been at Travelome. Jeff's lips closed tightly. The only hope in his heart was that he might be able to kill the devil he had twice attacked. An Iroquois fire would not be too dreadful if he could first avenge his friends. Sweat softened the rawhide on his wrists, and he worked his hands as he walked. His fingers must be kept supple for the red throat up front.

The party turned westward toward a mountain gap. When they entered it, they broke file and bunched together, Macoga gestured toward the captive, and McNight nodded impatiently. Jeff had the idea that the Indians and their white leader were uneasy about something. They stood so close together he could smell the sweetish, sickening Indian odor as it worked through the paint.

Two sharp turnings of the narrow path followed. Then the defile opened into what frontier people call a "kettle hole." What startled Jeff was that on the flat floor of this hill-hemmed mountain valley, a small army was encamped. To the right were rows of tents set in the orderliness of British military camps. Everything was spaced exactly. Pack horses were tethered in line, and tent ropes were stretched just so. There were a few bought shelters. Under these soldiers, uniformed like McNight, loafed. Armed sentries paced back and forth before stacked muskets, and cooking fires smoldered.

It was quite a different story on the other side of the path which divided the valley. Here were the Indians, several hundreds of them. Their belongings were piled at random, according to the individuality of the owner. Where a savage dropped his gear was his camping place. There his lodge would be raised if one was set up at all.

Presently a sentry stopped McNight's squad. After the corporal had grunted some communication to him, another soldier was called to escort them to the commander.

As they passed through the camp following the guide, Jeff used his eyes. He noted, to his dismay, that this was a force able to annihilate or capture the one led by Colonel Hartley. Undoubtedly it was here to ambush the colonel, awaiting the chance to leap out and destroy.

Three officers in green sat about a small table. One who wore a major's insignia glanced up and acknowledged McNight's salute. He had a heavy face, red from either the weather or drinking, and his eyebrows grew down over small, piercing eyes. The soldier who had brought the band in from the sentry saluted as the officer rose. "Major Pritchett, Corporal McNight and his squad."

Jeff had been right in his surmise. The corporal and his men were uneasy, evidently not fancying this interview with their commander. The line of Pritchett's mouth went straight.

"So," he said, "two days late, one man short. Of course. Corporal, we can afford to await your pleasure."

"We have a prisoner, sir," McNight offered, "one of Hartley's men. He'll have more news than I could pick up."

Abruptly the big major shouldered the party apart, so he stood before Macoga. With a huge forefinger, he poked the red dress, now sadly soiled with sweat and dirt. Then the same hand snapped up and gripped the warrior's hair and hawk feather.

"Raiding again, Macoga. That's a white woman's dress."

With a savage sweep of his arm, he hurled the Indian aside so roughly he all but fell. Then he turned his fury on McNight.

"I sent you to scout to keep out of sight and bring back news. You, like a damned fool, let these filthy brutes raid a house somewhere, and the news will get to Hartley. Rangers and Indians seen raiding after Wyoming. Good God, you may have mecked our whole enterprise."

His hand rose as if he would strike the noncom, but he dropped it and paced back and forth, fighting to control his temper. His tongue dripped venom when he spoke again.

"Yes, my dear Corporal, you disobeyed orders and took a prisoner. Was he, my dear fellow, wearing the dress your stinking Macoga wears about his middle? Sergeant!"

The snapped order brought another noncommissioned officer at the double.

"Put this squad under guard. Leave their prisoner with me for ten minutes, then come for him."

Jeff now faced the three officers, the second of whom wore the same uniform as did the major. While the third man wore a green coat, his breeches were of buckskin, and his soft linen shirt was open at the throat. In a moment, Jeff recognized the narrow, crafty face. This man had been at the Ribner post. His name was Jedediah Minnich, a local Tory who had fled to the British. "Your name," Pritchett snapped.

"Jeffry Claus."

"How many men has Hartley? How many horses?"

Jeff looked back into the flinty eyes searching his and shook his head. Pritchett spoke softly as he leaned forward, "Friend, the boys over there could make you talk—plenty." Minnich started, and half rose.

"Major," he cried, "I know this man. He's Jeffry Claus, Henry Ribner's bondservant. He killed Ribner, and Fultz, the partner at the post, offers fifty pounds' reward for him."

Pritchett leaned back until his camp chair creaked.

"Fifty pounds. God, we've sent the man enough money lately so he could pay it. Fifty pounds, and he's as scrawny as a starved deer. Claus, I don't need your information, for I know every man, horse, and musket

Hartley has, even down to the last keg of spruce beer his woods lice are drinking. When we wipe him and his silly army out, we'll clean this river till every settler runs for Lancaster county with his tail between his legs."

His eyes searched his prisoner sharply to see if he had made an impression. Evidently, he felt he had not, for he shot another question savagely.

"Why are you up here, Claus?"

Jeff scowled and twisted his hands behind him.

"Ask the damned red apes you lead. They butchered my friends, burned their buildings. Give me ten, no five minutes with that Macoga who wears her dress about his stinking middle."

Pritchett shook his head, then smiled in satisfaction. He had roused the prisoner.

"They brought no scalps. Yes, what you say might be interesting, but I'll have to keep our red brothers in good humor till we finish your lawyer-colonel. Fifty pounds. What a pity to waste it in a Seneca fire."

The sergeant who had taken McNight and his men away returned and stood waiting.

"Bernst, take the prisoner to the colored man, Fred. Let him guard him."

The Negro was delighted. He placed his charge with his back to a sapling. Then he changed his mind and tethered Jeff like one would a horse, using the noosed leash as a hitching strap. This way, the prisoner could stand or sit, but his cramped hands were still bound together. Fred sat down, pulled out some meat and cornbread from a pouch, and started eating. Jeff was ravenously hungry, having eaten nothing now for days. He could not keep his eyes from the food. When the colored man finished, he tossed the remains of his meal on the ground close to the sapling.

"Help yourself, white folks. Don't mind me if you have to crawl for it."

The odor of the meat was strong in Jeff's nostrils. Finally, he sat down, rolled on his side, and began gnawing at the piece of meat, which proved to be beef. Without his hands to help, he could not get much of a hold. The meat was almost eaten when Minnich and several other men sauntered up.

"Well, well, Fred, nice cheap dog you've got."

Jeff resumed his seated position as Minnich stepped closer. Suddenly the Tory's foot lashed out in a savage kick that sent the prisoner sprawling.

"Always liked to kick dogs," Minnich boasted, "and—"

He got no further. Jeff launched himself forward and upward, knocking the taunting Tory flat on his back. Then he was upon him, striking with his knees until Minnich's flailing hand went across his mouth. Jeff bit the man so savagely that Minnich howled in pain.

Pritchett must have been passing and observed what had occurred, for he was there when Minnich gained his feet, blood dripping from his hand.

"Minnich," he snapped, "there will be no whites tormenting whites in my camp. That's an Indian privilege, and we can't have the red devils getting ideas."

After testing the thongs on Jeff's wrists, he ordered Fred to loosen them and tie them in front so it would be possible to sit down comfortably.

"Fifty pounds," Pritchett said softly again, looking at Jeff and Fred. "You, my colored boy, might bring another fifty."

In the night, sometime, the sound of low voices roused the prisoner, and he lay motionless. Fred and Minnich were talking.

"Yessir, Mr. Minnich, wuz we to turn him over to Abner Fultz, he'd pay cash money, and mebbe he wouldn't care too much ef we turned him over dead. But how kin we git him down there?" Minnich did not answer for a moment. There was a rustle as he changed positions.

"Don't know. Looks like I can't get off till we finish Hartley."

"I could slip him off alone," Fred offered.

Minnich swore. "Hell, I wouldn't trust you around the corner."

There was no further conversation. Minnich must have walked away. When morning came, a company cook approached carrying a slab tray on which were meat, bread, and a mug of strong tea. He started to untie and rub Jeff's wrists when Fred protested. The cook scowled at him.

"Shut up, you. The major sent me to feed and rub him like I'm doing."

Jeff ate ravenously until every scrap was gone. His wrists felt better for the massage even with the bonds replaced, this time more loosely than before.

"Much obliged," he said, and the soldier grinned.

"That's all right. I been in trouble too. If this damned little gray ape don't treat you right, sing out. The major seems kinda touchy about you."

The long day passed slowly. Whenever he dozed off, Fred roused him with a poke of his stick. Toward evening Jeff spoke sharply.

"Freddie, someday I'll get my hands on you again. You killed Ribner. Fultz paid you to do it. Now get to hell up there and find me some supper."

The Negro's eyes widened, and his face turned grayer. Jeff felt his random shot had gone home. Fred had almost admitted the crime. He brought back food but made his prisoner eat with tied hands.

At dusk, Pritchett approached with a soldier who carried a bayonet fixed on his musket.

"Stand guard over the prisoner, Felty. Don't stand for any queer stuff. The man's worth fifty pounds. Relief comes at twelve."

Jeff wanted to laugh as he looked at Fred's dismayed face and remembered the conversation of the night before. He wondered if the major might have overheard it. Anyway, for the first time, he appreciated having a price on his head. It just might save him from an Indian fire.

CHAPTER XXII

EACH TIME the sentry was changed during the night, Jeff awoke. But he dropped off to sleep again, for his body seemed drugged with weariness as if his worries had changed themselves into physical strain. His thinking told him his position was hopeless. The only ray of light so far was Pritchett's remark: "they brought no scalps." Peter might have fought it out from the barn, or he could have died with Faith and Susan in the flames. It was some consolation that there were no fresh scalps dangling from the thong belts of any Indians he had seen here at the camp, and the commander had raged when he learned his men had been raiding the settlements.

Jeff kept one thing clutched close in his mind: the wish to kill. Death was sure for him, but he didn't want it to come until he took at least one of this unholy crew with him. He had tried twice for Macoga. His fingers would not loosen again if he held that red throat.

Unlike the previous day, the camp was astir before dawn. Fires flamed up, and the smell of cooking food was in the air. The soldier cook who had fed Jeff before came up with tea, meat, and bread. When he was leaving, and Jeff thanked him, he clapped the prisoner between the shoulders.

"Chin up, buddy; you ain't half dead yet."

Immediately after breakfast, camp was broken. All tents were pulled down, and all gear neatly packed away in the panniers of the pack train. At full light, several Indians who seemed to be chiefs or head men met

Pritchett in an open place between the two encampments, close enough to Jeff for him to hear.

"Not a shot nor a sound until the whistle blows. Do my brothers understand?"

He held up the now familiar whistle of the Rangers, the instrument which had signaled the bloody attack at Wyoming and in a hundred other places when the British loosed the wolves on settlers. Jeff had never heard it in action, and it stirred in him a feeling of frightening urgency. Time was short. This would be the attack on Hartley, and there was no one to give warning. It would be an ambuscade, Indian and white lurking, ready to send a shower of British lead into an unsuspecting column.

Fred jerked on the leash, which he had made a full yard longer. Rising, Jeff saw that McNight's scouting party had come up. The prisoner was their property, and they would guard him for their own purposes.

The motley crew of Indians moved out of camp first. Many wore their tribal garments. An equal number wore bits of white men's costumes like hats into which feathers were thrust, watch coats, even though the day promised to be warm, and dirty linen shirts with the tails outside their belts. One warrior passing close to Jeff sported white cavalry gloves and nothing else but breechclout and moccasins. Macoga still had Susan's dress tied sashlike about his middle.

Jeff's hands tightened. Perhaps he had better take his chance now in the confusion of starting the march. He found that he could slip his hands free. Fred's knot was not secure. The place was all movement, with the Rangers bringing up the rear. There was a tingling sensation between his shoulder blades. He could slip his hands free, snatch a hatchet, and sink it into Macoga's skull. But if his captors took him all the way to the ambuscade, he might be able to warn Hartley by some diversion.

Once out of the gap, Pritchett moved his men south and east through the timber in the direction where the Sheshequin Path must lie. From the top of the first low ridge they crossed, a winding stream could be seen far to the eastward. Doubtless, this would be the Lycoming, along which the old path would run for many miles. An hour of hard marching in that direction brought the column to the top of a second and lower ridge. Below them, the big creek broke through low hills. It flowed through a small valley covered almost entirely with natural meadowland where the grasses were now brown. Below where they had crossed was a mountain bench which looked as though it had slipped away from the parent ridge down the slope to crowd both the stream and the valley floor. It was covered with sparse timber and heavy brush through which protruded the tops of good-sized boulders.

Few men better understood the making of an ambuscade than these Tory Rangers and their Indian companions. White officers and red chiefs moved about placing the men. Riflemen were stationed close to where the stream broke into the valley. The Indians were well down front all along the line because of their ability to conceal themselves in scanty cover. In a half hour, the little valley was a pleasant open place with no hint of danger, which a mountain defile might suggest. Yet it was a death trap. When Pritchett's force struck, there could be no retreat past the posted riflemen. Dispersed, Hartley's men could be dealt with piecemeal.

Pritchett made a final round of the ambuscade. He was accompanied by a sharp-eyed chief who wore a red neckerchief, turbanlike about his shaven head. The major missed nothing. McNight's squad was close to the riflemen commanding the entrance, and the officer spoke to Fred as he pointed to Jeff.

"Gag that prisoner. Don't let him yell a warning."

Fred obeyed promptly, using a dirty piece of rawhide for the purpose. Then Jeff's heart sank. He had missed his chance. The colored man tightened the wrist lashings so that Jeff could no longer free his hands. As a final precaution, the little gray man tied the lead thong to his belt. The other end was still loosely looped about the prisoner's neck. Fred looked over his captive carefully. His face twisted in hate.

"I'll be helpin' build a fire on your belly when this is over, white folks."

Then he spat full into Jeff's face.

Pritchett and his red companion dropped clear down to the creek for their inspection until satisfied. Then they rejoined their comrades lurking along the deadly bench.

More than an hour of inaction followed. The Indians kept down with all the patience of mountain cats stalking game, but a green coat showed occasionally for a moment. While the wait was on, Jeff saw something else. Far up the valley, close to the defile, stood a bough lodge. Even at this distance, he saw a squaw seated before the lean-to doing something with her hands. A second figure lounged against the shelter. That bough house would catch the eye of any scout and make him less careful about the hillside where the enemy lay.

While McNight's squad was close to the riflemen commanding the valley entrance, he was no longer with his men. Evidently, he was in disgrace. Fred, with his sharpened stick, compelled Jeff to crouch exactly where he wanted him and where he was sure to be uncomfortable. He did not untie the leash from his belt.

An hour past noon brought the first notice of the approach of Hartley's little army. Three buckskin-clad scouts came through the defile along the stream. Two of these men were on the side of the ambuscade; the third was a little to the front and across the creek. When directly opposite from where Jeff crouched, the scout over the water signaled to the others, pointing upstream to the bough lodge. A full minute passed until all three men passed on, moving slowly. Jeff could see the strained look of eagerness even on the painted features of the Indians. Fred, licking his lips nervously, had his cocked musket thrust out before him. Off to the right, an officer whispered to his men.

"Steady. Wait for the whistle. Easy, easy."

Six more scouts followed the stream and advanced a hundred yards into the valley. Then they stopped, and one of them trotted back out of sight. A rifleman swung the barrel of his rifle, and a sergeant cursed him.

"Easy, you damned fool. Pritchett will buck you if you fire." Jeff twisted his wrists frantically, and his heart pounded. The rawhide leash hung slack and loose. Fred's attention, with that of all the others, was riveted on the scouts down there beside the peaceful creek. Only minutes were left now. Jeff tried to bite through the rawhide gag, but it merely choked him. The ambuscade would be successful. The scouts had seen nothing unusual but the bough house and its occupants. None of them had more than glanced at the deadly hillside.

Jeff pushed his chin down on his chest to keep from watching, and the loop of the leash ran open. Fred had seen to it that the thong slipped easily so he could snap it tight with a light jerk. Suddenly Jeff had an idea. He worked his head and neck cautiously until he widened the noose so that his chin passed through it, and the loop of leather rested across the gag in his mouth. He tested it carefully. It would be possible to leap against it without choking. The scouts had moved on, but now Jeff had a plan!

Faintly but growing louder each instant came the rhythmic sound of many men marching and talking together. In the beginning, the noise was indistinguishable, but coming closer, one could pick out the tramp of horses, the jingling of equipment, and men's voices. Colonel Hartley had his force moving on both sides of the stream. A few uniforms showed, and those only on the cavalry. One squad, probably from Hartley's own regiment, marched steadily and in cadence. About Jeff, the breathing was so loud it seemed it must reveal their position.

Jeff tested the loop once more and found it lay smoothly against the leather gag. He could swing his weight into it now and not get choked. His toes in the broken moccasins found a purchase. In a moment or so, he would die. The clock of his personal fortunes had run down, but his mind and body were set on giving a warning before Pritchett's whistle shrilled. Oddly, he had no thoughts of Susan. His mind was past all regrets as it despaired of hope for himself or his friends. What he did think of were the tiny corn flour pancakes Uncle Mark Fultz used to make.

He took a deep breath while all the nerves of his body tingled. Then he was up, leaping powerfully. The leash, fast to Fred's belt, jerked the colored man forward like a hooked fish. The cocked musket exploded, and a scream followed its discharge from an Indian below their line. Jeff was bounding down the slope, Fred dragging like a sack behind him. He had not thought of the Indian line until he was in it. Below, Hartley's men were swinging into formation. For weeks they had been drilled for just such an emergency. They were taking cover even while their rifle shots searched the hillside. Jeff was in the savages' line where warriors fired point-blank at him. Gunfire from below swept up. Then a hammer blow on the side of his head pitched Jeff forward into blackness.

Hartley's men were charging the hill. The horsemen, sabers swinging, hit the Indian line viciously, breaking and scattering it among Pritchett's

Rangers. The explosion of Fred's musket and Jeff's running figure had startled every man in the ambuscade. Before they could recover, Hartley's men were among them. Rifles were blazing, and hatchets were swinging. Most of the attacking militia had lost relatives and friends at the hands of men like these they now attacked. There was no mercy shown. Vengeance fell on Indian man and green-coated Tory alike.

It was very quiet and still in the tent when Jeff opened his eyes. Some light showed through the partially open door flap. His head ached abominably, and his body was stiff and sore. Presently he was aware that a man sat in the heavy shadow. When he saw the patient was conscious, he approached the cot and bent over. Close to a minute passed. Then Jeff said:

"Migun, you always come."

The Delaware drew up a stool and seated himself.

"My brother has had a long sleep. A bullet sings a good lullaby."

"How long?" Jeff demanded and moved his body impatiently. Migun chuckled as he laid a hand across the patient's lips.

"My brother will keep still while Migun talks. He has been here a little more than two days. A bullet creased his thick head, and he has several small flesh wounds. But he saved Hartley's army with his daring, and the army smashed the ambushers."

"Fred?" Jeff grunted his question, and Migun chuckled again. "The little colored man with the gray face was hit by many bullets. Before he died, he wanted to go to the white man's heaven and so talked to Colonel Hartley and others. He killed Ribner, using your knife, for Fultz's pay. Then he ran off himself, fearing Fultz would have him killed. He told how he spied on you and carried news to Ribner."

With a strong palm, Migun pressed the impatient wounded man back on the cot when he started to rise.

"Colonel Hartley has gone on, and when you're able, we are going down to Muncy to wait for him. He told his officers he would have you cleared."

Jeff closed his eyes tightly, fighting back tears. Freedom was coming too late, far too much so for what he had planned and hoped. He felt old and tired, no better than a smudge of strong powder after it was burned. Migun continued talking, but Jeff paid no attention until suddenly, part of a sentence registered: "So, Peter sent me to . . ."

"Peter!" Jeff yelled, sitting upright. His head whirled, and the Indian's face was a blur. "Peter!"

"Yes," Migun continued calmly, "he wasn't hurt much, but he couldn't travel. Beniel hunted me up, and I came to find you."

Jeff snatched at Migun's sleeve.

"Tell me everything, quick."

Migun looked at him, apparently puzzled, then he understood.

"I'm sorry, I forgot that you left before Beniel returned. It was this way. Word came that you were arrested. Peter, Faith, and Susan started for Augusta. Then we learned that raiders were in the valley, and Peter returned to Travelome with some men he picked up. Poor Charley and his wife had hidden in the barn, and it was burned. The raiders grabbed a few things, the clothes on the lines, and some tools from your shop when Peter struck. They lost one man and got away, but Peter was hit in the leg. Beniel overtook the Grubes in Muncy and told them you had started north."

Jeff eased himself back with a long sigh. Susan was safe. He was sorry for poor Charley and his wife, dead in the barn. But Peter, Faith, and Susan were safe—safe and waiting.

In two more days, they traveled, sending the escort Hartley had left with them to join their fellows up north. The two friends moved slowly while Migun enlivened the trip by references to the old days with Uncle Mark's pack train.

Near Muncy, they stopped, and Jeff shaved with the tackle Migun had brought. When he finished, he looked at his friend for a comment.

"Well, Jeff, my friend, you look better but still not good."

At Muncy, they learned that the Grubes had gone upriver to Fort Antes. Word of Jeff's exploit had gone ahead of him. The soldiers at the fort insisted on furnishing the two men with horses, so the last leg of the trip did not take long. They crossed the Susquehanna below Long Island and climbed to the flat land on the bluff.

The little fort had been rebuilt, as well as some of the cabins. A man, sitting on a porch, saw the horsemen and called to somebody indoors.

She came running, her corn silk hair loose about her small head, sunlight glinting on the buckles of her flying shoes. Then she was in Jeff's arms. Migun looked at the pair a moment, shrugged his shoulders, and walked over to the man on the porch.

"He is a damned fool, Peter," he said almost reverently. "Only such a man could have saved Hartley's army."

CHAPTER XXIII

COLONEL THOMAS HARTLEY finished his dangerous mission against the savages and returned to Fort Muncy the first week of October. He and his little army had made a circuit of over three hundred miles, beating the enemy in several pitched engagements. They burned Queen Esther's town and turned back from Chemung only because Hartley's scouts brought him word that an overwhelming force of more than five hundred Tories and Indians were gathered there. He brought back fifty cattle stolen from settlers in savage raids, twenty-eight canoes, and other valuables. He had lost less than a dozen men, killed and wounded. In the dark northern forest, he had found and destroyed some of the little houses in which the savages smoked scalps. It had heartened the frontiersmen immeasurably to have a chance to strike back hard against the force that had cost them so much in blood and material loss.

Promptly on his return. Colonel Hartley expressed himself as deeply proud of the men whom he had led into the dangerous wilderness. They had marched and endured with him the hazards, discomforts, and hardships. His records showed that they had forded the Lycoming Creek twenty times, following the old Sheshequin Path most of the way northward.

Jeff at Fort Antes was extremely anxious to meet the Colonel as news of his return was brought up river. What he had been told of Fred's confession buoyed his hopes. Susan was as eager as he and more hopeful.

"Things will be all right," she assured him. "I feel it in my bones."

He laughed.

"That's the way an old lady talks, Susan, and what they feel is just rheumatism," he told her, and she turned up her nose at him.

Peter had his horses and was well enough now to ride. So he and Jeff went down to Fort Muncy and found the little post thronged with soldiers and people from the countryside. To avoid the crowd, they tied their animals outside the stockade and walked through the gate where a knot of soldiers stood about a man Jeff recognized as Sergeant Westover. He looked up, jerked off his hat, and yelled:

"Here's Claus, men, here's Claus."

To Jeff's surprise and chagrin, more soldiers who had marched with Hartley rushed up. They hoisted him on their broad shoulders and made a circuit of the parade ground before they set him down in front of Hartley's cabin headquarters. The sentry there passed him in with a friendly grin. The colonel was working at a table. He rose and gave Jeff a warm handclasp.

"First, we march and fight," he declared. "Then we write and write reports, details. I'm delighted to see you, Jeffry. Every man of us is in your debt."

Jeff tried to say something but got it all mixed up. Hartley motioned him to a seat.

"Migun has probably told you the news about Fred. He also has explained how and why you got into Pritchett's hands. The murder charge will be dismissed. Fell writes me that he suspects this Fultz is doing some treasonable work. My duties will hold me here a week. You be at Squire Fell's place a week from today. Then we'll set to work."

He scratched his head back of his ear with a pen for a moment, and his voice was apologetic when he spoke.

"Jeffry, I must crawl a little. You should be mentioned in my dispatches as saving the army from defeat, perhaps destruction. But I only obtained consent for my expedition after much argument. Even His Excellency objected at first. If it is shown how near disaster we did come—"

He frowned and ruffled the papers in front of him before he looked straight into Jeff's steady eyes.

"You will keep your counsel, for what I tell you is a military secret though I am afraid the generals talk about it too freely. A great force is to move against the Iroquois to lay waste their whole country. Many high officers oppose it. If they could show how close our venture came to failure, they might have the project abandoned, and again this area would be threatened with Indian forays. So, my friend, your name will only be mentioned along with others who did good service, no more."

Jeff grinned.

"I would not have it any other way, sir. After all, I had the choice of the torture pole or running. Any man in my place would have done as much and perhaps quicker."

Hartley was examining his pen critically, and Jeff could not refrain from adding: "Besides, sir, I am a bondsman, and my name would not look right on an army report."

Hartley's face reddened. Jeff thought he had said too much, but the officer's voice remained kindly though his jaw was set.

"That I propose to rectify. Fultz was a murderer, and I think he cheated you. Be at Fell's a week from today."

Jeff walked out, grinning to himself. It was the first time and probably the last that a colonel, and a popular hero, had apologized to him, Jeffry Claus, a bondsman. After all, he did not figure that he had done much. He had been about to die anyway, and Fred's carelessness about that noose had given him a choice as to how he would lose his life.

The Grubes, Susan, and Jeff used the waiting time to go back to Travelome. Peter limped about the burned barn making plans for rebuilding. Luckily the livestock had been pasturing when the raid was on, but the stored wheat and hay were gone. None of them talked about poor Charley and his wife. Doubtless, when they saw the Indians, they had hidden themselves in the loose hay and so died.

Jeff and Susan walked down to the Tiadaghton one day, taking a picnic lunch and some fishing tackle. Susan found the place where a small stream entered the big creek, and there was a stretch of level land. From it, one looked north toward the jumbled mountains covered with the deep green of pines and hemlocks. It was not far from the rough road the settlers used in passing up and down river.

"This, Jeff," she said, "would be a place. There's enough land for a garden and—"

"Water to run my rifling machine," he interrupted.

They grew silent as they looked about the prospect. They walked hand in hand, noting things: timber for building, stone for a fireplace and forge.

As the time to leave Travelome drew nearer, Jeff became more and more uneasy. Things had slipped for him too often. He was not worried about the murder charge; that was settled. But he was still a bondsman, and nothing would bring him freedom but finding that indenture paper on which Uncle Mark had laboriously written his will. It could be that Abner Fultz had destroyed it, a very likely procedure if he had found it. There was a reason, too, why Ribner and Fultz hated him, but he could not fathom it. Of course, later, Fred might have told the trader of Jeff's visits to his wife, but the hating had come before that.

The Grubes and Susan elected to go to Sunbury on horseback, but Jeff decided that he would go down to Squire Fell's place by canoe. In spite of Hartley's promises, he did not feel like entering the town where posters might still proclaim him a murderer and a runaway. There was plenty of time to think during the long quiet hours in the canoe. His mind was no easier when he landed at the old McKee town and climbed the hill to Squire Fell's home.

Before he entered, he stood on the porch a while, thinking of Abigail Ribner, whom he would soon see. She had rescued him from Fultz's thugs, had spoken of her partner's possible treasonable acts, and had urged Jeff to choke the truth out of the man. But she had spoken cryptically, merely hinting at things: "Who knows," she had said. "Some day, you might be free."

From here, he could see the distant tip of the Ribner roof. She was there, perhaps holding the key to the whole situation. There was a challenge about this woman that shook a man's reason and weakened his resolutions. Once, she had all but put a knife into his hands and made him a murderer. He shook himself like a dog emerging from the water and rapped on the door.

Fell was a very excited, very happy little old man. He beamed at the sight of Jeff and rubbed his hands.

"We are coming into our own this day, Jeff. All of us are proud of you. You will have Hartley's complete help. He, the prosecutor, and the sheriff are coming down. Let's get over."

The day was lovely, with a warm sun above and the first signs of autumn showing. Gum trees were already scarlet against the soberer green tones of chestnuts and oaks. Jeff did not paddle fast, and the squire was not impatient, for he was busy with a huge packet of papers. They were late when they reached the road and found the Sunbury people on hand. There were four of them: Colonel Hartley, Baxter, Sheriff Safert, and a deputy who had driven down in a cart.

Baxter and Safert greeted the newcomers with sour looks. Hartley took charge of things, directing the deputy to remain with the horses while they walked to the post.

"Safert," he said, "have your warrant for Fultz ready. The crime, murder. I shall do the talking."

In spite of the fact that the fields of the big farm lay fallow, the Ribner post was still a beautiful place with well-kept lawns and buildings. None of these last, with the exception of the house and horse stables, showed much sign of use. On the driveway was a laden cart. The heavy draft horse hitched to it was tethered to a post.

Safert, at Hartley's nod, sounded the knocker on the wide front door, and there was a wait of several minutes. The sheriff was about to knock again and had just raised his hand when there was a quick step inside. The wide door swung open, framing Abigail Ribner.

She wore what was obviously a riding costume of some rich fabric which had a touch of red in it. Her heavy brown hair was coiled low on her head. The collar of the dress was slightly open at her throat, where rested a tiny medallion held in place by a thin gold chain. Jeff felt a catch in his throat at the sight of her. She was curtsying, the tip of a black kid shoe and a silver buckle appearing for an instant.

"Gentlemen, I am honored by this visit even though I was about to leave."

She gestured toward the cart and smiled.

"But come in. You are very welcome, and I was rather expecting you."

Hartley bowed and presented each man, finishing with Jeff.

". . . And Jeffry Claus, whom you know, Mistress Ribner."

She had bent her head a little as each name was given. At the mention of Jeff's, she smiled, speaking partly to him and partly to the others.

"Welcome back, Jeffry. You have been gone so long, and Abner Fultz will be glad. By all means, gentlemen, come in. Bring our Jeffry with you."

The big living room was partly dismantled, with furniture and pictures covered by dust cloths. Their hostess explained.

"I am leaving the post. My cousin, Captain Moore, waits down the road to take me to the city and to my friends. However, there is rum. Mr. Fultz is lost without it."

She took a bottle and glasses from a cabinet.

"Help me, Jeffry."

Her warm fingers touched his as he took the bottle. Their backs were to the company as they filled the glasses. Her whisper was scarcely audible.

"So you came, Jeffry. I had hoped it would be sooner, now—"

She broke off. When the men had their glasses, they toasted her formally. Then Hartley spoke.

"Thank you, Mistress Ribner. We will not keep you long, for our business is with Mr. Fultz. Will you have him called?"

She took Hartley's empty glass, smilingly.

"Of course. He works the post, you know. We were partners, my husband, who is dead, Fultz, and myself. But I have lost interest since my husband's death. The frontier is no place for a weak woman."

Fultz must have been waiting just outside, for she had only left the room a moment when a heavy tread sounded, and he entered.

The man had changed greatly since Jeff had seen him last. While his clothing was still foppish, his face had become looser, heavier, and there were pouches under his eyes.

"Abner," the woman said quietly, "these gentlemen have business with you. I have explained that I am leaving. Our Jeffry is back. I'm sure you are glad."

Fultz bowed to the company, most of whom he must have known. As his eyes flicked across Jeff, there was a wicked glint in them. He lifted his pudgy hand to his throat in a nervous gesture.

"Abner Fultz," Hartley wasted no time in preliminaries, and his voice was hard as metal. "The Negro, Fred, is dead. Before he died, in the presence of witnesses, he told how you paid him to kill your partner so you could gain possession of his property. Further, you have been selling arms and liquor to the enemy." Abigail Ribner was a superb actress. She stared at Fultz with wide eyes.

"Why, Abner, you said—you thought Jeffry—"

"He was seventy miles from here when the crime was committed, Mistress Ribner," Hartley explained, then swung his attention back to Fultz.

"We have a search warrant. There is war material in the post now."

The accused man had not moved. His eyes swung back and forth across the group, finally stopping at the woman whose features registered shock and horror.

"Oh no," she cried. "Surely this is not true."

Something drained out of Fultz as he listened. He stood as if supported by only a lath framework. His clothing hung loosely like that of a scarecrow. Lifting a shaking forefinger, he pointed it at Abigail and mumbled through set teeth.

"She—she planned—"

Safert, with a warrant in his hand, was stepping forward. He was not quick enough. Fultz, with surprising swiftness, took two backward steps and snatched up a pistol from where he had evidently placed it on entering. Jeff recognized the weapon from which he had copied his mistress' small one.

"Don't move," Fultz threatened. "I shoot rather well."

He backed to the rear door, jerked it open, and leaped outside. Then he must have pushed some heavy object against the door, for Safert, with the others helping, spent precious minutes getting the panels open. The running figure had just entered the barn. Probably the horse had been bridled and saddled for Mistress Ribner's departure. Fultz was in the building only a moment before he came out mounted. Safert tried to get in his way, but the desperate man's pistol roared. The shock of the bullet in his shoulder spun the sheriff half-around and dropped him to his knees. From that position, he fired his own weapon at the escaping man; Fultz pitched his arms wide and fell from the horse, which cantered away, stirrups striking its sides.

Safert, hand pressed to his shoulder, walked forward.

"Is he dead?" he demanded from the others who had approached the body.

Fultz was gasping. Blood was welling out over his ruffled shirt. His wild eyes went from one to another and settled on Jeff.

"That paper—Ribner—"

Whatever he had wanted to say was beyond him. Abner Fultz was dead.

Abigail Ribner had come to the doorway and, from there, watched the confusion. The deputy brought up his cart, and the dead man was loaded into it. Then the sheriff was helped up to the seat beside the driver. He was hurried to a doctor to care for his wound. A serving man appeared and caught the frightened horse.

"Come in," Mrs. Ribner said to the group. The four men followed her into the living room, where they took their former places.

"Gentlemen," she said when they were all quiet. "We must finish this ghastly business. A few days past, I prepared a written story and gave it to Squire Fell. He thought, however, that I should tell it to you, and now the death of Fultz settles everything."

She had been standing. The men had seated themselves at her gesture. Now she took a seat between Fell and Jeff.

"I must hurry. My friend waits and may have been alarmed at the shooting. Many things have been said of me, and I care little. I came to your river with a purpose. I hated my husband in my heart for a reason I shall not tell you, nor did he suspect it. However, he used some of my money and sank it in his schemes. His death meant no more to me than that of Fultz, who had hounded me for favors over the months. The three of us were full partners. If any of us died, the property went to the survivors or survivor.

"I was the treasurer. This agreement is in writing and deposited in the countinghouses of Lancaster and Philadelphia. I cared little how the money was made, but there was a great deal, and it is now my property."

No one challenged her claim. They looked at her sympathetically as her slim fingers twisted in her lap. Jeff noted the rise and fall of the small medallion at her throat.

"Fultz came into Ribner's power years ago; how I am not sure. There was something about gambling, probably more, and there may have been a woman. I won't trouble you by telling everything. My husband rented this place from Mark Fultz. He developed the farm and probably was a British agent when the war opened. Anyway, they brought him money. Well, when Mark Fultz died, Ribner forced Abner to turn over all papers to him. This included deeds to Thread Hollow and this place. It was given out that Abner Fultz's uncle had died intestate."

She paused again and touched her lips with a fine handkerchief. "Ribner kept the papers to add to his hold over Fultz, who feared the law and feared exposure, for he felt sure men like Fell suspected him. One day the papers disappeared. Ribner blamed Fultz and threatened him. There were bitter words, and Fultz was afraid. Then it was that he must have hired Fred to do his murder. Afterward, he took over the things of the man who had dominated him for years. He had ambitions even to take over Henry Ribner's wife."

She lifted her head a little and noted the shock in the eyes of the listeners.

"Gentlemen, I took the papers, for I sensed I must have some hold over these men if I needed it. A woman must use the weapons she finds at hand."

She made a signal to Squire Fell, who unwrapped a packet. Jeff half came to his feet as he recognized a big leather wallet worn from much handling. He had seen it often in the hands of his old friend and master, Mark Fultz. Fell opened it and laid out the papers.

"Gentlemen," he wheezed, "I can tell you now why Henry Ribner bought and tricked Jeffry Claus. He had to hold him or kill him, and that he almost did."

He slapped a paper on his knee.

"Here is the indenture of Jeffry Claus, and on it, witnessed by the Indian, Migun, is the statement that, in event of Mark Fultz's death, this same Claus was to be set free with a hundred pounds and tools in lieu of freedom dues."

He placed the paper in Jeff's trembling fingers and picked up another sheet, this one badly wrinkled and stained.

"This also is a will. It is not witnessed, but I am sure the courts will honor it. By its provisions, and it was made less than a month before the old trader was killed, all his property, real and personal, beyond the bequest mentioned for Jeffry Claus, is to go, share and share alike, to . . ."

He looked from face to face challengingly before he finished. ". . . to Christian Fell, Jeffry Claus, and Migun."

In the dead silence that followed, Abigail Ribner moved closer to Jeff. Her perfume was in his nostrils, and her face was sober. Her fingers turned round and round the riding hat she had taken from a table.

"They robbed Jeff and us," Fell said musingly. "But from Jeff, they stole more; freedom, hope—"

He might have continued, but the men were standing as Mistress Ribner donned her tiny hat. She had a last word to say.

"I kept the indenture for a number of reasons. And perhaps I—wanted to own this Jeffry Claus."

She raised herself on the tips of her kid shoes and touched Jeff's forehead with her lips.

No one spoke as she left them. Through the window, they saw the serving man holding the horse. She placed a small, silver-buckled shoe in the stirrup, and there was a flash of silken ankles as she went up into the saddle. The lumbering cart, laden with trunks and boxes, got underway, slowly following the swift pace of the mounted horse. At the first turn, a man rode out of a clump of woods and joined the woman. They rode on side by side.

EPILOGUE

JEFF HAD WORKED most of the morning. He was uneasy about something he had caught Peter Grube showing Susan the other day. Finally, he tossed down his file and walked to the wide door of the smithy. All the buildings stood as he and Susan had planned them long before they were married. They were stout structures of hewn logs and stone. The big creek skirted the narrow fields, and the garden was now green and bright after the light shower. From the north, the timbered hills looked down over a pleasant land. Inside the house, Susan was singing as she often did.

Jeff walked to the garden. His wife had complained about the depredations of that rabbit. He was a lone warrior with an appetite that played havoc among the cabbages Susan had planted with such care. She had protested to Peter Grube, and he had shown her how to make a snare with a piece of string and a bent shoot of wild plum. As Jeff approached, he saw the trapping venture had succeeded. The rabbit hung by his noosed hind leg, his eyes wide with fright and helplessness.

The singing in the house continued. Jeff glanced that way and felt he was unobserved. He took out his clasp knife and tested the blade on his thumb. The snared rabbit turned round and round, the long ears dangling. Jeff drew his keen blade across the cord, and the little animal dropped to the ground. It remained motionless for a moment before darting away toward the woods while Jeff returned to the shop.

Inside the house, Susan continued to sing, but she had watched from the kitchen window and observed the whole performance. She had been angry at first. Then a sober look came to her face, even though the song she sang was a gay and lilting one.

THE END